ANNA O

MATTHEW BLAKE is the author of the international bestseller *Anna O*, which is published in 41 territories and being developed for the screen by Warner Bros/Netflix. The book hit bestseller lists across the world and was called 'the most talked about thriller of 2024' by NBC's TODAY show. In addition to his writing, Matthew worked for ten years in Westminster as a political advisor and media strategist. As a screenwriter, he currently has multiple feature film and TV projects in development with production companies on both sides of the Atlantic. He lives in London.

www.matthew-blake.com
 @matthewblakewriter
𝕏 @Matthew__Blake

ANNA O

Matthew Blake

HarperCollins*Publishers*

HarperCollins*Publishers* Ltd
1 London Bridge Street
London SE1 9GF

www.harpercollins.co.uk

HarperCollins*Publishers*
Macken House,
39/40 Mayor Street Upper,
Dublin 1
D01 C9W8
Ireland

First published by HarperCollins*Publishers* Ltd 2024

This edition published 2025

1

Copyright © MJB Media Ltd 2024

Lines from *Elm* by Sylvia Plath, from *Collected Poems* by Sylvia Plath,
reproduced by permission from Faber and Faber Ltd
Excerpt from 'The Trauma of Facing Deportation', Rachel Aviv, *The New Yorker* (2017)
Excerpt from 'Man who killed his wife while sleepwalking goes
free', Anthony Stone, *The Independent* (2009)
Excerpts from *Medea and Other Plays*, Euripides and translator Philip Vellacott (Penguin, 2002)
Excerpt from 'While You Were Sleepwalking', Shreeya Popat and William Winsdale, *Neuroethics* (2015)
Excerpt from *In Cold Blood*, Truman Capote, first published by Random House, 1966

Matthew Blake asserts the moral right to
be identified as the author of this work.

A catalogue record for this book is available from the British Library.

ISBN: 978-0-00-860783-8 (Paperback)

Typeset in Sabon LT Std by Palimpsest Book Production Ltd, Falkirk, Stirlingshire

Printed and bound in the UK using 100% Renewable Electricity by CPI Group (UK) Ltd

MIX
Paper | Supporting
responsible forestry
FSC
www.fsc.org
FSC™ C007454

This book contains FSC™ certified paper and other controlled
sources to ensure responsible forest management.

For more information visit: www.harpercollins.co.uk/green

I am terrified by this dark thing
That sleeps in me.

Sylvia Plath

1

BEN

'The average human spends thirty-three years of their life asleep.'
She leans closer, enough for me to catch a gust of expensive perfume. This is usually the moment when I know. 'And that's what you do?'

'Yes.'

'A sleep doctor?'

'I study people who commit crimes when they sleep.' I have 'Dr' before my name on business cards. Dr Benedict Prince, The Abbey, Harley Street. I am an expert in sleep. Nowhere do I claim to be a medical doctor.

She sees that I'm serious. 'How's that even possible?'

'Don't you ever wonder what you might have done when you were asleep?'

Most people get uncomfortable right around here. The majority of crimes have a distancing factor. We revel in stories about people just like us; but who are also not like us. But sleep doesn't allow that qualification.

Sleep is the one universal, the night as constant as the day.

'What kind of crimes?'

She hasn't changed the topic. I still have her attention. 'All the worst ones.'

'Surely people would wake up?'

'Not if they're sleepwalking. I've known patients who lock their doors and drive their cars while still asleep. Some people even kill.'

'Surely you'd remember?'

'From the lines around your eyes, I'm guessing you slept five and a half hours last night.'

She frowns. 'It's that obvious?'

'Do you have any memory of what happened during those five and a half hours?'

She pauses, cupping her chin in her right hand. 'I dreamt something.'

'Like what?'

'I can't remember.'

'My point is proved.'

Her eyes suddenly change now. She looks at me differently. Her voice is louder, the body language animated. 'Wait, there was that case. What was it called—'

This is the final point. Few dates ever reach this far. I bore them with my job description. I scare them away with stories about crimes committed during sleep. If that doesn't work, then this last thing always gets me.

No one stays once they realise.

No one.

'Anna O,' I say. I take a final sip of my wine – an expensive Merlot, more's the pity – and then reach for my jacket.

'You're the guy. In the photo. The psychologist.'

I smile dimly. I check my watch. 'Yes,' I say. 'I was.'

It was the photo on the front of every major daily newspaper after it happened – that brutal, blood-soaked finale. The fateful moment after which nothing could be the same. Before the exile and the fall. I am the bespectacled figure with mussed hair and the slightly donnish dress sense. I have remade myself since. The beard has aged me; the hair is greyer at the tips. My glasses are chunkier and less like a reject from the Harry Potter props department. But I can't change my eyes or my face.

2

I am a different person. I am the same person.

I wait for the question because it is the question I am always asked. It is the one mystery that, despite everything, still lingers. It divides families, spouses, even friends.

'Was she guilty?' my date asks, or the woman who was formerly my date. I am nothing but a ghoul to her now, an anecdote for Christmastime or New Year. 'When she stabbed those two people. Did she really get away with murder?'

PART ONE

One year earlier

2

BEN

London

The mobile rings.

That's what I always remember.

The first thing, the beginning.

It's late, the darkness already heavy, inked in. I am half-asleep, nesting in an armchair with a tray of lukewarm curry and a half-empty glass of cheap wine. A black-and-white movie continues to play, flickering in the corner of the room. It's *Strangers on a Train* tonight, my favourite. Everyone else picks *Psycho* or *Vertigo* as their ultimate Hitchcock piece. But they're wrong. *Strangers on a Train* has the tennis scene.

The mobile's vibration snaps me back to the room. My eyelids droop. I wipe grease from my hands and glance at the caller ID: 'BLOOM, PROF (The Abbey)'. I slide the button across, brace myself, choking down a messy yawn.

'Hello?'

'Ben, sorry for the unholy hour. I'm afraid this one couldn't wait.'

She sounds serious. And, in the blur of night, it startles me. Professor Virginia Bloom is usually the first one with a joke or aside. She is often found marching down Oxford Street in a kaftan and heels or at her corner table in the Langham with a decanter of whisky and a pocket of stimulants.

I hear the distant clatter of feet and voices on the line. It sounds like Bloom is still at the Abbey. I check the clock. It's nearly midnight.

'Is something wrong?'

'You could say that.' Bloom clears her throat with that grumbly, smoky sound. 'It's one for you, I'm afraid. A new request that's just come in. It's somewhat on the sensitive side.'

I am a forensic psychologist. I have consulted for most major crime agencies. The NCA, FBI and Interpol all have this number. But this sounds even more secretive than usual. 'Does this request have a name?'

There's further background clatter down the phoneline. Bloom seems distracted. 'Come round to the Abbey, will you. I've been told not to discuss anything on an open line.'

I'm officially on a week's leave. My latest journal article is on a deadline. I have three patient files to write up. I was planning to work from home tomorrow and tackle the mountain of paperwork. Even so, there are only a few sleep-related cases that are too sensitive for an open line. I am blackmailed by the mystery of it, just as Bloom intends.

'You have to give me something.'

I hear a suck of air on the other end of the line. Bloom is silent and then she sighs loudly. 'You might not thank me for it.'

It's arctic outside, a filthy sky full of September drizzle. I am already dreading the journey from Pimlico to Harley Street. I can stay in the stew of the front room with my Hitchcock film and another glass of wine. But that isn't how I'm wired.

It's why I answer. Why I always answer.

'It's the Anna O case,' Bloom says, at last. 'There's something they want us to see.'

3

BEN

The Abbey Sleep Clinic occupies a small corner of Harley Street, part of an old mews house with shapely Edwardian bricks and an air of complete discretion. Visitors often remark on the churchy hush of the place, an oasis tucked behind Oxford Street and between the clatter of Regent's Park and Cavendish Square. Parts of the building look like they've been carved from Portland stone. The Abbey has a regal aspect to it, fit for bewigged marquesses and second-rank royalty. It feels like a sanctuary.

The night – or possibly the day, I'm not sure, given it's now gone midnight – is still grey and ugly as the cab slices through puddles and deposits me on the empty street corner. I duck out of the rain and shake the moisture off my faulty black umbrella. The cab pulls away too quickly, spritzing the back of my trouser leg with rain. I curse Bloom again for the summons.

I walk up the single flight of stairs and type in my passcode, the rain already making each digit buttery and hazardous. The old house stands on four floors now, long since converted into office space, with just a small silver plaque outside denoting 'The Abbey Sleep Clinic'. There is a telephone number but no email address. The Abbey's website is conspicuously bland, listing staff qualifications without revealing any photos. The image is deliberate, as everything here is. We are attendants hovering in the wings, useful to swell a scene or two. It is the golden rule for all mind doctors: we are heard but never seen.

Nothing happens. I wipe down the buttons with my sleeve and retype the security code. Finally, there is a tell-tale metallic cluck as the door shifts. I wonder if Bloom has called any of the others in, my fellow sleep specialists and esteemed colleagues. But the reception and waiting areas are still largely unlit and deserted. It's like turning up for school and being the only pupil in the assembly hall. There is something strange about seeing a workplace stripped of its usual bustle.

'Professor?'

I call out, but the sound echoes and dies. I flick a ceiling light on. It illuminates an array of neutral and soothing colours. New carpet has just been laid, still squashing pleasingly underfoot. The air feels unusually pure, pumped out through special filters built into the walls. Usually there is music too. The sound envelops visitors until the bill snaps them back to reality. The Abbey has a womb-like oblivion to it, away from the squall of the outside world. Sleep is primal, after all.

'Professor?'

Still nothing. I stow the umbrella near the coat stand and wriggle out of my own soaked jacket. There is a bank of security monitors by the reception desk showing camera feeds from the back and front of the building. Our clientele requires it. Celebrities before a wedding, politicians battling for their careers, footballers in a rough patch of form, royalty facing scandal – all of them troop through the tasteful entrance with their pouchy, sleep-deprived faces. Sleep, like food or water, is one thing no human being can do without. The Abbey is a modern-day temple where psychic demons are soothed. People pay silly money just to sink into their beds.

I jiggle the security monitors to life. The front and back entrances flicker dully. I leave the monitors on and wait patiently by the lift, too tired to take the stairs. There is a scatter of magazines on the finger-marked coffee table by the lift doors and I reach for a copy of the *New Scientist*, skimming it as I wait. We are mentioned again, a small news-in-brief section. The Abbey has a useful sideline consulting on criminal cases across the world, maintaining lucrative contracts with the Metropolitan Police and other law enforcement agencies. All of it is ultimately shepherded by Professor Bloom, once dubbed 'Britain's top sleep guru' in *The Times*. The article is still framed on her office wall.

The lift chugs up. I realise I know every inch of this building. I try to calculate how many nights have been lost to one of Bloom's whims. Too many, I decide. But the Anna O case is different. Bloom wouldn't tease me with that. Anna O is the holy grail for all sleep experts. Ever since it happened, over four years ago now, she has been the one mystery to beat them all.

No, Bloom isn't that cruel. At least not with me.

I reach the top floor. This is the so-called executive wing. Really it is more of a broom cupboard. This is staff-only, which explains the Alcatraz-themed interior. There are seven of us who work full-time here, alongside another ten auxiliary staff – neurologists, psychiatrists, psychologists, psychotherapists and myofunctional therapists – running the full gamut of sleep-related treatments. My office is at the end of the hallway, one of the few with a functioning lock. Bloom's office is the first and largest, newer than any of the others and bedecked with gilt-framed art and a hidden drinking fridge.

Bloom is waiting for me in her office doorway with a vexed, knotted look. Her mane of grey hair is tamed into submission, her hair clip moving in time with her yawns. She is mid-sixties, scattily dressed, an operatic thickness hidden by colourful layers, swaddled in canary-yellow and strawberry-pinks, her eyes framed beneath Hank Marvin glasses. Despite rock and roll appetites, she rarely betrays tiredness or any need to sleep. Bloom boasts hollow legs for drink, a bottomless capacity for food. She is the last of her generation: the two-bottle lunches, the occasional afternoon nap, a permanent middle finger for all things HR. She commits the unspoken sin of her sex by being stridently un-maternal. A gourmand, raconteur and wit. She thinks her way through life. Her gift and curse.

Behind her I see another figure. He, by contrast, looks ferrety with a pinched, lawyerly demeanour. A stranger. I'm intrigued.

'Quite the welcome party,' I say, feeling my right trouser clinch damply to my leg. 'Mind telling me what's going on?'

I walk into Bloom's office. The ferrety man stands up. Up close he looks more imposing. His hair is stiff, precisely combed. He is fifty-ish, at a guess, with a beaky nose and widow's peak. A folder on the table beside his chair has a crest on it: 'Ministry of Justice'. My palms begin to sweat. Bloom was serious, then. Above law enforcement, even above the National Crime Agency. The MoJ is ministerial level.

'I'm sorry,' says Bloom, 'but this really couldn't wait. Dr Benedict Prince, meet Stephen Donnelly, Deputy Legal Director at the Ministry of Justice.'

Donnelly stretches out a hand and shakes mine limply. He holds my gaze and says softly, 'Before we begin, Dr Prince, I'm afraid there's a few house rules to go through.'

I tuck my surprise away. 'Oh yes?'

He talks through a head cold, sniffs punctuating each sentence. 'Yes. There'll be a few forms to sign at the end if you don't mind.'

'Saying what?'

'First, this meeting tonight never happened. Second, you've never met me. Third, what you're about to learn will never leave this building or, indeed, this room. If anyone asks, you came to the office to collect some patient files before returning home. Is that clear?'

I want to smile, but I see that he's not joking. 'What is this?'

'Is that a yes to the terms?'

'Do I have a choice?'

'Not really.' Donnelly indicates the vacant chair. 'Please, take a seat.'

4

BEN

Bloom shuts the door and doesn't lubricate things with refreshments either. This is strictly business. Instead, she eases herself down into the plump leather desk chair. Then, finally, she nods at Donnelly to begin.

He has an executioner's smile. 'I won't insult your intelligence, Dr Prince. I know you're already familiar with the Anna O case and the two murders back in Oxfordshire in August 2019, yes? That's why I asked to see you.'

I stare at Donnelly, wondering how high his authorisation goes. Above him is the Legal Director, his boss, then the Permanent Secretary at the MoJ, then the Justice Secretary, and finally the Prime Minister. Why would someone this senior really want to meet me after midnight at the Abbey with instructions not to brief out details on an open line? What could possibly be so important?

Few people alive are unaware of the Anna O case. There have been podcast series, Netflix options, countless op-eds, as well as bestselling books and articles in obscure academic journals, several of them written by me.

'Of course.'

Donnelly nods. 'A paper of yours has recently come to the

attention of some, well . . . let's just say some very important people.' He reaches for his small leather attaché case and removes a slim manila file. He reads from the title page. '"Resignation Syndrome and the Criminal Mind: In Search of a New Diagnostic Model". *The Modern Journal of Forensic Psychology*. This is your latest work on the subject, am I correct?'

I glance at Bloom. But she just gives me a wintry smile. 'Yes.'

'You look surprised?'

'I am. That article hasn't been peer-reviewed yet. It certainly hasn't been published. I only submitted it to the editor three weeks ago.'

Donnelly looks at me pityingly, as if unused to such naivety. 'Contacts of ours help out by occasionally flagging items of potential interest. I can assure you that your work on psychosomatic disorders has already attracted quite the following in Whitehall.'

I feel sullied and fascinated in the same breath. I see the message from my Gmail account disappearing with a whoosh. The article was attached as a Word document. Does the editor forward it on, I wonder, or do these people keep a constant watch? Do I even want to know?

Donnelly glances down at his manila file again. 'Your article majors fairly heavily on the Anna O case, just like your last book. Though the article proposes a potential cure whereas the book doesn't. Do you mind if I ask why her case specifically?'

I sit back, flicking another angry glance at Bloom. This is a stitch-up. There's been no warning, no time to prepare. I wonder how much to reveal. 'That was largely the editor's idea,' I say. 'She thought it would get the piece some attention. Possibly even some broadsheet coverage. The book was a bestseller. She hoped the academic journal might enjoy similar success. I went along with it.'

'You've studied the Anna O case in detail then?'

There is no way to avoid the truth. I say, 'My wife was the first police officer on the scene back in 2019. She was working for the Thames Valley Serious and Organised Crime Unit. This was her first case as SIO. Though I imagine you already knew that.'

Donnelly just says, 'I see.'

'Anna O has been part of my family's life almost as long as our own daughter.' I add the disclaimer, as I always have to. 'Not, to be clear, that my wife ever betrayed any privileged information. I combined what is open source with other less controversial examples of resignation syndrome from around the world. That's how I wrote the book and the article.'

'Mainly the outbreak of cases in Sweden, I recall.'

'Alongside another cluster of cases in Kazakhstan. Two small former Soviet mining and farming towns called—'

'Krasnogorsk and Kalachi. Yes, yes, we're well acquainted with those.'

Impatience gathers in me now. I am tired of this faceless man and his gnomic answers. 'I don't mean to be rude, but why would a pop-psychology book and an obscure academic journal article be of interest to the Ministry of Justice?'

Donnelly smiles again, as cruelly and quickly as before. 'In your article, you claim to have developed a new diagnostic method to help patients wake up from resignation syndrome. Is that correct?'

He's clearly read the article or a summary of it. He knows that isn't right. Which means he's testing me. 'No.'

Donnelly feigns surprise. 'No?'

'My article sets out a new framework for understanding psychosomatic conditions, especially those involved in sleep-related acts, including the phenomenon of sleep crimes. I'm interested in whether or not sleepwalkers are technically conscious of their actions when they commit a crime. Like a murder, say. The same applies to patients suffering from resignation syndrome. Are any of us aware of what we do while sleeping? Can we be held criminally responsible? When does sleep take over and consciousness end?'

'A controversial subject.'

That answers my next question. He's already seen the blogs and social media accounts attacking me. Of course he has. Ever since my book hit stores, I've been a target for trolls from all corners of the globe.

'Some people are still stuck in prehistoric divisions between neurological disease and so-called "functional" disease,' I say. 'They think because something happens in the psyche, then it isn't real. My work attempts to alter that perception. Some people take issue with that.'

'Does that mean you can help patients with resignation syndrome to wake up?'

I am struck by the bluntness of the question. 'Well, that depends.'

Donnelly looks steadily at me, those beady eyes staring into my soul. 'On what exactly?'

I shuffle, fuss, compose myself. I long for some water.

'How long the patient's been asleep mainly,' I say. 'What external factors may have caused the illness in the first place. My book was the mass market pop-psych write-up. My paper does the heavy academic lifting, setting out new theories and looking at the current data. But it's not a cure-all.'

'For Anna O, as an example.'

'Four years is at the extreme end of resignation syndrome. My data was largely focused on those within one to two years.'

'So it's still purely theoretical?'

'For the moment, yes.'

'How long would it take to test your new theories? In the real world, I mean?'

I laugh. 'How long is a piece of string?'

'Surely you have an estimate.'

'At a guess, three months,' I say. 'That would be a minimum.'

Donnelly looks at his watch. He seems newly impatient now. He tidies the file and slides it neatly into his attaché case, as if he's heading back for another post-midnight shift at the office. Donnelly looks at Bloom and nods briskly.

I turn to Bloom, my anger still simmering. 'What am I doing here?'

Bloom takes over now. She shifts her bulk on the chair, with the balletic ease of the truly corpulent. She is briskly matter-of-fact, speaking to me like a prisoner being read their rights. 'The Secretary of State for Justice and the Attorney General for England and Wales have just authorised the temporary release of Patient RSH493 from the Coral Ward at Rampton Hospital into the secure custody of the Abbey under my direct supervision. The MoJ order is protected under the Official Secrets Act and anyone who leaks the information, in this building or elsewhere, will face prosecution. Do you understand?'

Prisoner RSH493. I know that number. Every newspaper reader does too.

Rampton Secure Hospital, the last high-security medical facility to admit women. Patient number 493.

Ms A. Ogilvy.

Donnelly and Bloom stand now. Automatically, I stand with them. Dryness crawls all over my mouth.

'No,' I say. 'I'm sorry, but I don't understand. What is this?'

Bloom glances at Donnelly again, then says, 'Amnesty International is about to appeal to the European Court of Human Rights in a bid to get Anna Ogilvy released on the grounds of inhumane treatment. Before that happens, the Crown Prosecution Service and the Ministry of Justice need to put her on trial for murder or risk losing her case entirely.'

I digest the new information. 'Which means Anna Ogilvy must be fit to stand trial. To be fit, she must—'

'Do something she hasn't done in four years and wake up. Yes.'

And there it is, the real explanation. For a moment I think of all those horror stories from school history lessons: the half-starved teenage conscripts in WWI plucked from the trenches, patched together then marched towards execution, shellshock mistaken for cowardice. This feels eerily similar. I'm a psychologist, not a prison officer.

'I treat people,' I say. 'I don't condemn them. There must be other sleep experts you can call on.'

It's Donnelly again, weary of this now. 'We already have. We've spent years flying in world-class consultants from America, Europe, Asia and beyond. The best of the best. But the field is still under-resourced, and their methods proved sadly unsuccessful. Your paper, Dr Prince, is the last credible chance we have.'

'Why bring her here?'

'If you turn up at Rampton Hospital every day, the news will leak. The Abbey's also the only sleep clinic in London that can accommodate a case of this nature. You can cope with the strict confidentiality requirements. We have no other choice. She will be transferred tonight, escorted by police liaison and registered under a different name. As far as you're concerned, you treat her like any other patient.'

'She'll be recognised.'

'Four years ago, maybe. Not now. Nearly half a decade asleep does things to a person.'

'What about other staff?'

Donnelly says, 'A nurse from Rampton will accompany the prisoner and work here under the alias of an agency worker. You will be her day-to-day point of contact, while Professor Bloom co-ordinates your efforts with our side. Ms Ogilvy won't leave her room. You won't tell anyone that she's here. Only family members, who you may also liaise with, know otherwise. The Secretary of State has vowed to personally go after anyone who ignores the terms of her temporary relocation.'

I feel dizzy with the audacity of it, angry too. 'This is absurd. You can't seriously believe Anna Ogilvy is a danger to the public. Or is it just the headlines you're worried about?'

Donnelly doesn't rise to it. 'Try telling that to the victims' families. Anna Ogilvy can't be released, and she can't be indefinitely held. This saga has to end. Sign the OSA and walk away or put your theories to the test in the real world. It's entirely your call, Dr Prince.'

'And what if I can't wake her?' I say. 'What if my theory doesn't work?'

Donnelly finishes buttoning his coat. He sighs, hollowed out by the day's events. He stares at me with those cold, grey-green eyes.

'Then, sooner or later,' he says dryly, 'Anna Ogilvy will be free to kill again.'

5

BEN

The bare facts of the Anna O case are relatively straight-forward. That's, I think, why everyone remembers the case. There's something shocking about the raw simplicity of it.

At 3.10 a.m. on the morning of August 30th, 2019, Anna Ogilvy, the twenty-five-year-old daughter of a senior shadow government minister and founding editor of the magazine *Elementary*, was found asleep in her cabin at a farmhouse retreat in Oxfordshire with a twenty-centimetre kitchen knife. In the neighbouring cabin were the bodies of her best friends: Douglas Bute, twenty-six, and Indira Sharma, twenty-five.

The post-mortems later found ten stab wounds on both bodies. Anna's fingerprints were the only dabs on the knife and there were bloodstains on her clothing. Forensic analysis subsequently made a positive match between the clothing and both victims. Digital forensics, meanwhile, found a WhatsApp message on Anna's phone containing a partial confession sent before the deep sleep took hold.

From the level of rigor mortis, the estimated time of death was several hours prior. Both victims were beyond saving, their wounds fatal. DI Clara Fennel from the Thames Valley Serious and Organised Crime Unit was the first officer to reach the Farm and attend the crime scene. She discovered Miss Ogilvy still dressed in the bloodstained items of clothing. Despite numerous attempts to rouse the suspect, Miss Ogilvy remained asleep and unresponsive and was later transferred by ambulance to the John Radcliffe Hospital on Headley Way.

All tests proved normal. She was alive. Her body was functioning. The mystery illness causing her deep sleep was impossible to identify.

But she never opened her eyes again.

The public fallout was brutally swift. Anna's mother, Baroness Emily Ogilvy, resigned her position as Shadow Home Office Minister with immediate effect and stood down from the House of Lords. Richard Ogilvy, Anna's father and a global fund manager, abandoned plans to open a new office in Manhattan. The nickname itself came from Anna's social media handle: @AnnaO. Most murder suspects are low-IQ males with cauliflower ears and grim histories of domestic violence. Anna O was young, female, highly educated and already a public name as a magazine journalist and writer. The story was every tabloid's dream.

The press soon dug up everything else about Anna too: the childhood in a Hampstead townhouse; the rumours of teenage drug use; the rent-a-quote boyfriends from Oxford; even the other staff and interns at *Elementary*, the magazine which Anna founded alongside Indira and Douglas. If I've learned anything as a psychologist, it's that all high-profile murders are about timing. August was the perfect month, right in the middle of silly season. A few months later, and it might never have caught fire.

Luckily for me, Anna Ogilvy chose her moment well.

Soon, of course, even the tabloid names became a dividing line. Believers in Anna's innocence called her 'Anna O'. Believers in her guilt dubbed her 'Sleeping Beauty'. No one, however, could take their eyes off the story.

Truthfully, neither could I.

6

BEN

The four floors of the Abbey are not equal. The ground floor is the reception room, an ode to good taste and professional interior design. The basement houses the kitchens and other domestic services. The first floor is for drop-ins, as we call them, the fly-by-night patients who want help with some sleep-related problem but without committing to the full immersion, all tinted Mercedes and private flights from London City.

Floors two and three, meanwhile, are for the truly committed, those whose sleep problems are life-denying. The residents. Each residential patient at the Abbey gets their own private room and en suite. The ambience is similar to a private hospital or a boutique townhouse hotel. There are menus for room service and books, newspapers and magazines on demand. The only exception is anything digital: no mobiles, no laptops and no iPads. There is no Wi-Fi on floors two and three. We are gloriously analogue here, relics from a distant past.

The top floor is staff-only. The sea-blue walls become scabbier. Minimalism is replaced by public-sector scruff. Offices gargle up papers and files. And, tonight, I stand by the window of Bloom's office and watch Donnelly disappearing inside a sleek government Jaguar down below before being swallowed by the lamplit darkness.

Cold leaks through the old windows. Every room on the top floor is draughty. I think now of that email sitting in my inbox. It was a job offer of sorts from the Pro Vice-Chancellor at the University College of the Cayman Islands. He dangled the prospect of a Visiting Fellowship and a chance to lead their new graduate course on the psychology of sleep. Stupidly I declined, choosing rainy British streets instead of glorious Caribbean beaches. The offer remains a sun-soaked what-if, haunting these damp, squally London nights.

Bloom and I decant to the staff cafeteria at the end of the hall. I wash a brace of coffee cups and excavate some out-of-date cheesecake from the small portable fridge. We eat it off paper plates and cool our cups of Nescafé instant. Bloom, as usual, consumes the lion's share. I make do with the crumbs.

Then Bloom says, 'I imagine you have some questions.'

I always have questions. It's been like that from the very beginning.

Bloom removes another slim manila file, much like Donnelly's, and slides it across the crumb-filled tabletop.

I take it reluctantly. 'Another mystery document. Am I meant to guess this one too?'

She smiles. 'If you like.'

I turn my attention to the file. I note the Ministry of Justice crest again and the high-security classification. RESTRICTED glowers from the cover in blood-red capitals. I open it and see a large photo on the first page with a white, tubular hospital background. It shows a robed patient in some kind of medical bed.

The patient is female, age indeterminate. Her eyes are closed despite her hair being newly combed and washed. The hair appears freshly cut, too, though with the faintest pinprick of white at the root. The face, meanwhile, looks peaceful but no longer young. Despite everything, it still takes me a moment to compute.

Anna Ogilvy.

Bloom watches closely. 'I had the same reaction.'

'So Donnelly wasn't kidding. She seems—'

There is some mistake, I'm sure. Back in 2019, Anna Ogilvy was peaking. She had a twenty-something swagger, life still brimful of possibilities. Her photo was featured on countless newspaper supplements and online profiles, with that punkish grin and pixyish hair. The figure in this new photo, by contrast, is a stranger. There's a deadness to her, overwhelming all the other features. Her hair looks wig-like. There's an alabaster quality to her entire body, a figurine from Madame Tussauds.

I swallow my surprise. 'She looks like a ghost.'

'The woman's been asleep for four years. She practically is a ghost.'

'What about brain activity?'

'Apparently it's remained the same. EEGs, the lot. All the monitors suggest she's simply in a deep sleep. It's just the sleep in question has lasted for nearly one thousand five hundred days.'

'There's been no change at all?'

'Flick to page five,' says Bloom.

I reach the page. It consists of a series of graphs. They show Anna's brain function and physiological response. People stagger into sleep; most usually snap out of it. The EEG results are normal, as they always have been. But the physical response levels tilt up just a fraction near the end.

'When was this?'

'Four weeks ago, apparently. The only event of its kind. The monitors showed her becoming more stimulated by external events.'

'It could be a fluke, of course.'

Bloom sniffs, unconvinced, then says, 'Try the next page.'

I turn. I still feel used but can't help myself. The mystery of it hooks me in. The next page shows the anomalous results in greater detail. I check the days, then the weeks. For some reason, Anna almost woke up four weeks ago. The graphs can be read in no other way. Something happened.

24

'Was there any explanation?'

'No,' says Bloom. 'Or at least none that the medical team could find.'

'A mystery then.'

'Another one to add to the pile.'

The silence is broken by Bloom's mobile vibrating. She answers, listens, then mutters a few affirmatives and ends the call. It is odd seeing Bloom as the employee for once, bowing and scraping to a higher authority.

'They've arrived?'

'ETA five minutes.' Bloom gets up. 'Read the rest of the file when you have a moment. It contains the details of the alias we'll be using for her. Plus, there's some emergency contacts in case things get sticky outside the Abbey.'

I feel the first cramp in my stomach. 'How sticky?'

Bloom dismisses the concern, her usual palm-waving flick. 'Someone waiting at your flat. Following you on the Tube. Reporters, that sort of thing. All the same old precautions.'

I see myself in the snug of my flat with nothing more than vinegary booze and a classic movie to worry me. Dull, yes, but safe. 'What do we say to the other staff?'

'The usual drill.' Bloom gathers up a manila file and then leaves, heading towards the lifts. I trail behind her, stepping inside the lift doors. She presses for the ground level. Despite doctor's orders to take the stairs, she is always resolutely lift-bound. Exercise, like diets, is for mere mortals. 'An A-list client with a medical insurance clause in her acting contracts who can't let it be known that she has a sleep problem without triggering all kinds of legal hell. Top dollar for added privacy and total anonymity.'

There's a special part of floor two with added security for those choosing the 'VIP package' at the Abbey. Hollywood stars, CEOs of listed companies – anyone for whom the admission of a sleep-related problem could move markets or put multi-million-insurance claims into doubt. London is a favourite venue for international clients, dressing up their treatment as a week-long sightseeing holiday. We have specially designed back exits, signal-jammers located around the VIP section to ensure no footage of their presence here can be leaked. There are even separate eating and exercise areas to ensure the VIPs are seen by staff only. The Abbey has been in business for two decades and employs the best privacy lawyers on retainer. Never once has there been a leak.

'Donnelly mentioned police liaison. Is it anyone I know?'

Bloom doesn't look at me. The lift bumps downwards until we reach the ground floor. Silence is always her get-out clause.

'Who?' I say, stepping out into the plush foyer, surrounded by hotel brightness.

She turns fractionally now, the tell-tale tension in her jaw. 'Given your presence on the case, it was decided that the Met liaison should be someone already inside the circle of trust. I'm sorry, Ben. It's been her case from the beginning. I had no say in the matter.'

We reach the front door. Already I can hear the cars stopping outside.

'Please say you're kidding me.'

'I wish I was.'

Even then, I know there's only one person it can be.

7

BEN

It's the scenario we've both tried to avoid.

'Ben.'

'Clara.'

'You look good.'

'Thank you.'

'Though slightly weightier around the midriff. All those nights on the sofa with a ready-cooked lasagne. Back on the biscuits, are we?'

'Good to see you, as always. If you'll just follow me.'

The secure VIP treatment room is accessed through a labyrinth of scanners on the second floor. We walk in silence and wait for the lift.

'Weight jokes. Really?'

Clara – or DCI Fennel, now, since her last promotion – doesn't glance at me. 'We're professional, Ben. That's what we agreed. I'm not enjoying this any more than you are.'

'Could have fooled me.'

'You've been ignoring my calls.'

Despite everything, I miss her. That's what I can't say. I miss our old house in Oxford. I miss our daughter Kitty sprinting down the hallway when she hears my key scraping the lock.

27

I miss the lazy Sundays in bed with the papers and those golden snatches of freedom from a ringing mobile and a new shift. I miss the family we used to be.

Ever since our divorce, the Child Arrangement Order means Clara has residency and I have access, mainly because Clara kept the house before she moved to London. My push for joint residency is undermined by the lack of a second bedroom at the Pimlico flat.

I can't afford a bigger flat; Clara won't budge on joint residency until I do.

Neither of us want to take things to court.

We reach the entrance for the VIP section of floor two, accessed by a different entrance from the main stairs. The team from His Majesty's Prison Service have already done the heavy lifting, securely moving the prisoner/patient to her designated room. The nurse is getting her bearings. The SCO19 officer, well disguised in agency civvies, is acquainting himself with the CCTV system. That just leaves the two of us.

I type in the passcode for the VIP section and wait for the light to throb green. Everything is more clinical here with its splashy whiteness, like a conference centre mixed with old echoes of the asylum. I see the VIP room up ahead.

'Just remember what you're dealing with here,' says Clara.

'A patient who needs my help?'

'No, a prisoner who stabbed both of her victims ten times each. Don't make this a lab study for your mind theories. Wake her up then let us do our jobs.'

'If you and the MoJ will let me do mine.'

Clara wears that old disdain, as if we're still duelling it out over the dishwasher. She is a senior detective; I am a footloose consultant. She graduated with the Baton of Honour from Hendon and has a master's in Applied Criminology from Oxford. I am a sleep expert with an Open University degree and a decade of night classes. Somehow those small differences became larger over time, a scratch turning into a wound.

'And, technically, she isn't a murderer.'

'Stabbing two people doesn't count as murder for you?'

'Or, as yet, for a jury of twelve men and women and a judge recognised in any court in the land.'

'A technicality.'

'No, a fact.'

'For God's sake, she sent a message to her own family admitting she did it.'

Those seven words from that family WhatsApp message have become infamous, quoted thousands upon thousands of times. Almost all Anna O documentaries start the same way. *I'm sorry. I think I've killed them.*

Most think she must have been conscious to send that. Which means she must have been conscious when committing the crime. Guilty. But they haven't studied sleep like I have. People have done far more complex things than sending WhatsApp messages while still technically asleep.

'Innocent until proven guilty. The court of public opinion doesn't count.'

'You weren't there that night, Ben. You didn't see what I saw.'

I've heard the stories. I can only imagine the horror of it. For Clara, the family, for Anna herself. If she had snapped awake after the act, then the sight of those bodies would have been enough to tip her into a deeper, everlasting sleep. The body shutting down. A mental overload.

I can feel that ancient ache now, the sort that feels like love and hate at the same time. There is so much I want to tell Clara, so many things I regret. But our relationship curdled long ago. It's hard to find a beginning.

'By the way, it really was a genuine mistake,' I say. 'Last week, I mean. Missing your calls and the school pick-up last time round. It shouldn't have happened. I'm sorry.'

Clara pauses, stroking a strand of hair from her face. 'Just calm her down this weekend, yeah,' she says, kindness leaking back into her voice. 'She hasn't been right since seeing those photos. She responds to you in a way she never does with me.'

'That's not true.'

Clara smiles sadly, then checks the time. 'It's nearly two in the morning and I have the school run to do in just under six hours. Let's get on with it, shall we. It's time to meet your new point of contact.'

8

BEN

Harriet Roberts, the senior nurse seconded from Rampton Secure Hospital, continues patrolling the treatment room.

'We try to give her some routine.'

'Such as?'

There is a sharpness to her voice, like some of the gym teachers I remember from school. She is thin and elfin, with oak-coloured hair tickling her shoulders. The kindness in her face is at odds with the parade-ground firmness, a disciplinarian forged by decades on the ward. Rampton, like Broadmoor, has shades of the prison house. Innocence doesn't survive first contact. Gentleness is erased; substituted by self-protection.

'Curtains open no later than eight in the morning. Lights out at ten sharp. First part of the day is muscle work. Second part of the day is for mental stimulation.'

'What about the monitors?'

'Plump the pillows, keep the blood flowing, give her some chat. Those are my instructions from the medical side.'

'I see.'

I've offended her somehow, perhaps just by asking her these questions. That's the problem with being a psychologist. The neurologists look down on you. The psychiatrists lecture you.

And the nurses enjoy belittling you. The medical reference isn't accidental. Then again, it's hardly an enviable life. Nurses train to guide people back to health, not massage the legs of murder suspects. I wonder how she ended up at Rampton rather than a normal hospital. What compelled her to treat society's outcasts, spend her life shadowing the violent and insane.

I decide to ask the question, regardless of her coldness. 'And you've been with the patient ever since she was admitted, is that right?'

Harriet nods. 'More than four years now. I've been the constant point of care. Hard to believe that much time has gone.'

I sense a certain pride in her response. People sometimes think this is just a job. Few ever appreciate how much more it can be. Despite her outward lack of sentiment, Bloom was the one who taught me what true investment means. Not words, but actions. 'Above and beyond the call of duty. Four years is impressive.'

Harriet smiles. I see some residual emotion now, carefully buried. 'This has never been a normal job for me. It's a vocation. The fact she can't talk back probably helps.'

'So you were with Anna four weeks ago when those anomalies in the monitors came through?'

She glances at me, newly interested. She sighs. 'Apparently it was just a technical blip. The doctors checked everything.'

I sense the hesitation in her voice. 'Did you have another theory?'

Harriet looks mildly embarrassed. 'Sounds daft, I know, but I thought it might be some kind of external stimuli. But that's probably just a nurse talking. None of the docs took it seriously.'

'Such as?'

'Look, it sounds silly.'

'Try me.'

'One of the new cleaners was listening to Spotify on her phone with the shuffle off when she cleaned. The same track over and over. That was the only thing that was different then versus the last four years.'

'What was the track?'

'"Yesterday", the McCartney song.'

'You're sure?'

'The doctors were having none of it, mind. Told me it was a load of psychobabble. I guess they know what they're on about.'

'Neurologists, right?'

Harriet nods, coy about talking out of class. 'Uh-huh.'

'Were there any other signs you noticed physically?'

'Her eyes. Usually they're still. But there was a flicker when the music played, in her right hand too. The docs said it was just muscles spasming, completely unrelated. But I noticed it several times.'

I nod. 'I can take it from here.'

Harriet finishes her work, then moves away from the bed. 'Fine. I'll check back shortly. You have my number if you need anything.'

'Of course.'

The door closes. The heavy lock snaps into place. It feels so odd being alone in the room like this. Over the years I've read all the articles about the case. Even now, there's still regular commentary-about-the-commentary in the *Guardian* and *London Review of Books* damning the entire 'Anna O' phenomenon. A symptom of the male gaze. A media creation. The fallen woman. Eve reborn. There's even a course at Goldsmiths now on misogyny, myth and the media in which Anna's case features prominently.

For many, the myth of 'Anna O' is really an inversion. She is not the villain here, but the victim. I try to imagine Clara's reaction and decide never to mention it. I am as guilty as all the rest. My main listing on Amazon is for 'Prince, Benedict. *Anna O and Other Mysteries of the Mind* (Viking, 2021)'. It is technically a bestseller, but only in Belgium.

I approach the bed now. Monitors flash. Wires curl. Tubes whorl into each other, until the entire thing looks like a giant bowl of spaghetti.

I cough nervously into my mask. The first thing to notice is how small Anna looks in person. The photographs recycled by every media outlet don't do her justice, or not any longer. This is a different creature from the rebellious politician's daughter. She is vulnerable here, stripped of all her armour, looking so much older than someone in their late twenties has any right to.

'Anna O', I realise, is a figure of tabloid legend. Anna Ogilvy, however, is five foot six and used to weigh just under nine stone. According to her medical file, she had tonsilitis as a child, glandular fever as a teenager and broke her right leg playing hockey in the lower sixth at school. At the time of the murders, she was twenty-five, moderately – if not overly – fit, with a reasonable body-fat ratio and slightly advanced metabolism.

She is, in short, a perfect fit for her chosen method of murder. Stabbing requires persistence rather than brute strength. The weapon used for both attacks was a soft-grip stainless steel carving knife with a twenty-centimetre blade. At the time of the murder it was available from John Lewis for just under twenty pounds. The knife slices through vital organs like a chef chopping meat. Only the number of stabs requires physical effort, suggesting frenzy of some kind.

There is a stool nearby. I sit down by the bed. I watch the monitors flicker and the tubes ripple with activity. I check the cameras and then take out my phone. I scroll through to Spotify and 'Yesterday', already downloaded, my gloved forefinger sticky against the glass screen. It's an appropriate song choice. My diagnostic theory – still entirely embryonic and unproved – is based on using cultural stimuli to rouse a patient through memories of a happier time in their lives. I've seen other patients respond to similar cues from their past: music their mother played, old church songs, the jangle of a favourite TV theme tune. The acoustic guitar thrums from the speakers now. I hold the phone near to Anna and keep watch, flicking between the monitor and Anna's face. Then the vocals start.

There is nothing to begin with. The lines on the monitor refuse to move. Anna's face remains immobile on the pillow, not even a twitch. I'm about to give up and turn off the music and ascribe it to fluke. Perhaps the neurologists were right after all. Just before I press the pause button, however, I see Anna's left eye flicker. It is so brief that I almost miss it, convinced my eyes are tricking me. But there it is again, just as the nurse described. There is the faintest kick of recognition, as small as it is surprising.

I glance at the monitor and see the line jag faintly. It is the same blink-and-you-miss-it result as in the file from four weeks ago. I play the song twice over but there is no further reaction. I tuck away the disappointment.

The nurse enters again soon after. I pocket my phone. Strictly speaking, no electronic items other than medical equipment are allowed into residents' rooms. I wonder, for a moment, if the Ministry of Justice maintains a constant watch, someone in Whitehall monitoring my every action. My skin pimples at the mere idea.

'We need to feed her now,' says Harriet, still talking in that clipped, dismissive way. 'Was it helpful?'

'Yes,' I say, deciding not to tell her about my musical experiment. I need more time to think about what I saw. Or think I saw. 'Thank you. Very helpful.'

I leave the room and walk down to the ground floor. Clara is getting ready to leave. She sees me approach and says, 'Benedict Prince. Psychologist and miracle worker?'

I smile. 'Even I'm not that good, or that fast. She's still sleeping.'

'You weren't tempted to grab a quick selfie for the collection?'

It is one of those remarks that reminds me of the murkiest parts of our marriage. The six months after Kitty was born, say, or finding those texts to another man on Clara's phone. I think of those shocking news stories about serving Met officers taking selfies with dead bodies, or the odious WhatsApp chats fantasising about murder and rape, and I shudder. I wonder what Clara brings back to the house each night. It is one of the reasons I want to get joint residency rather than just the occasional weekends. I am determined KitKat won't become another victim of the job.

'Tell me,' Clara says. 'All the doctors say her condition isn't neurological. Every test they run – EEGs, CAT, blood tests, lumbar punctures, you name it – turns up nothing. So how can a healthy brain send someone to sleep for this long? Why has no one been able to break the spell?'

I gather my thoughts, debating whether to tell her about the musical theory. These questions have haunted us for so long. On that fateful night four years ago, Clara was driving back from a late shift at Abingdon Police Station, seeking a quick shower and costume change, when the alert came over police radio about an incident just outside Burford. She was the nearest to the scene and the first on-call. She made a detour, reached the Farm and took charge of the investigation before anyone else could. It was her debut as SIO. For the sake of a late-night drive, her police career – and our lives as a family – were never the same again.

'Because it isn't her brain that's doing it,' I say. 'It's her mind. An altogether more complex phenomenon. Then again, I would say that.'

'Next you'll tell me it all goes back to her childhood trauma.'

'There's an idea.'

We reach the front door and become formal again.

She says, 'I thought today was a day off?'

I stifle another yawn. 'It was.'

'I meant what I said. Make sure Kitty has a good weekend. School's been a bit rough lately. She needs a boost. And talk to her about the nightmares she's been having.'

I feel that gut-punch again. I've been so wrapped up in my own mess – the separation, the temporary flat – that I haven't noticed my daughter's troubles. So that's why she doesn't talk about her new school. Once upon a time I knew every small detail of her life. Now it's just the brushstrokes.

'I'll pick her up at three thirty tomorrow.' I look at my watch. 'I mean today.'

Clara nods. 'Don't be late. Not again.'

I manage a smile. 'Don't worry, I won't be.'

9

BEN

Being late is a familiar sensation. It is the one constant theme that unites my schooldays, university, those first nursery steps in the working world. But this time it feels different. As I run from the Tube station and the sweaty dampness circles my neck, I can already see the judge in the family court flashing their disapproval at me like the final act of a Greek tragedy. I don't lose my bid for joint residency because of substance abuse or criminal behaviour, but shoddy timekeeping.

It's not the judge I ultimately fear, though, or at least not yet. There is a certain way Kitty looks at me. Call it emotional intimidation, even blackmail. I am the one with the power, the wallet, the authority. And yet a single look can reduce me to feelings of inadequacy unmatched by any headteacher, ex-girlfriend, work colleague or critic. People warned me, of course, that it was not a job for the emotionally vulnerable. But only now do I fully believe them.

Being a parent really is a mug's game.

I can see Kitty – or KitKat, as I always call her, much to Clara's chagrin – standing forlornly at the school gates. Her gym kit and over-heavy schoolbag languish around her ankles. Her violin case is balanced uneasily against a nearby wall. One of the teachers

– Mrs Raymond, if memory serves, a severe biology teacher with an aquiline nose and slightly hawkish aspect – is waiting with Kitty, glancing disapprovingly at her watch. I arrive outside the gates with my shirt loose and my left shoelace trailing along the pavement. Both details seem to make my lateness worse.

I fell asleep in my office. I closed my eyes for a power nap and woke up three hours later. The sleep doctor taking an afternoon nap. The irony isn't lost on me.

Time check: 4.01 p.m.

KitKat doesn't acknowledge me. She reaches, instead, for the violin case and readjusts her rucksack. Mrs Raymond sees my dishevelment, then sucks the air, as if deciding I'm already well beyond saving. There is a momentary volley about the rules, Mr Prince, and why all pupils need to be officially registered for the after-school club. I concoct some outlandish story about being called in by the Met Commissioner personally to interview a high-profile murder suspect currently being held in custody and watch as Mrs Raymond's eyes bulge with alarm. I'm about to sprinkle the odd detail – anything mortuary-related usually does the trick – but the ploy has already worked. Mrs Raymond hastily departs. I am left alone with KitKat.

'Sweetheart, I'm so sorry. Daddy got caught at work.'

She doesn't answer, now or for the rest of the journey. We take the bus back to Pimlico as she's still scared of the underground. She is very much my daughter in moments like that. Clara has a briskly procedural take on things. I am the parent with the fears and superstitions, habitually attuned to the mind's irrational terrors. Before she was born, I often prayed that KitKat would inherit Clara's fearlessness and my sense of humour. Fate didn't smile that day.

Everything changed then, anyway. I spent so long planning for the expected hiccups – unequal distribution of childcare duties, the slog of sleepless nights, the commas and colons of dividing up household chores – that I missed the unexpected ones. The hiccups the parenting books didn't mention. What to do if your wife suffers from terrifying postnatal depression. What to do if you find text messages between your wife and a male doctor friend. That single hinge moment when the end became inevitable. She never told me his name. But I could tell from the messages that it was someone from her past. I went through every school and university friend I could think of who had a medical degree and wondered which of them was responsible for ruining my marriage. No, after KitKat was born, nothing was ever quite the same again.

The new flat in Pimlico is still in its beta phase. The whole place has a scrappy, lived-in air. What was once minimalist and edgy is now drab and uniformly grey. I've tried to revive it with swatches of colour. But it still can't escape its origins. More recently Clara has started referring to it as 'HMP Pimlico'.

I cook supper. We watch a forgettable kids' movie on Disney+ while eating off trays, a rare concession on my part. I feel in a charitable mood. Fuelled by more than one glass of wine, I allow KitKat an extra half hour of screen time before bed. Then, as usual, I feel faintly compromised and guilty.

She's getting ready for bed when I decide to broach it, as naturally as talking about tomorrow's swimming lesson or problems with maths homework. I've debated how to word my questions ever since Clara bearded me at the Abbey.

'KitKat.'

She murmurs unintelligibly. I usually interpret it as a yes.

'You know the other day when you saw some of Mummy's work things . . .'

There is a glassy look of unease on her face.

'Mummy told me about the nightmares you've been having. And the files from Mummy's police work. And how you haven't been sleeping.'

She nods sheepishly now, and pulls the duvet closer to her chin, like a flimsy form of protection to ward off evil spirits.

'You know you shouldn't go in Mummy's home office, KitKat, don't you? That the study is only for grown-ups.'

She does her apology face now, an overemphasised dip of the head and pendulous, droopy upper lip, like a Labrador begging for forgiveness. 'But I didn't go in. They were just there.'

I stroke her hair and continue tucking her in. 'I know, sweetheart. Mummy was very silly in leaving the door open. Silly Mummy.'

'She didn't leave the door open. They were in her bag.'

As a psychologist, it always amazes me that humans are the only animal with the ability to create fiction. Language allows us to imagine things other than they are; imagination lets us lie; lying gets us out of trouble. I am impressed by Kitty's development, even if the lie lacks plausibility. I decide not to get sidetracked.

'But those photos you saw—'

'The dead people.'

'Yes, sweetheart, the dead people. Well . . . it's time we had a little talk.'

I stop. I realise how immune I've become to it all. Clara and I are both professionals. To us the tools of our trade – crime scene photos, forensic reports – are dry objects to be analysed and dissected. It takes a child's perspective to see the truth.

Ironically, of course, here comes my own lie. It's a white lie, but a lie all the same. It is forgivable, I tell myself. A necessary fiction. 'You know they were only pretending, don't you?'

Her face scrunches in confusion now. 'Why?'

'You know at school when you did the nativity play and you pretended to be Mary and you walked around the stable and the manger. And that other boy, Aidan, was Joseph. And Miss Hardcastle played the piano when you did the songs.'

She nods. It is her proudest scholastic achievement. The performance was filmed. Clips were shared on various family WhatsApp groups. Clara's parents flew back early from their beach house in Florida to witness the spectacle in person. I was an expert witness that day in court and unable to make it. None of the family forgave me. I still haven't quite forgiven myself.

'You weren't there.'

That bluntness, again. Clara dents my fragile ego with a well-chosen word. Bloom chips away at my pretensions. Even some of my students at the Birkbeck night classes like to strut their stuff, trying to expose some gap in my knowledge. But none of them wound me like KitKat can.

I smile at her, in danger of losing the room. 'You know that Mummy catches nasty people.'

She nods again, this time less vigorously.

'Well, this time it was the other way round. The people you saw in the photos were actually helping Mummy. They were pretending to be injured so Mummy could help train other people how to catch the nasty people. It's called a training exercise.'

It sounds even less convincing when said out loud. I wait. There is a small crinkle on her brow. She seems to be buying it.

'Why?'

'Do you remember when you and Mummy went to that event with the St John Ambulance people? At school with the sirens and the people in paramedic uniform, the green ones?'

She nods at the word green. She can remember the green people. This is encouraging.

'You remember that one of the teachers had to pretend to be a patient – pretending like you did when playing Mary – so that the paramedics could demonstrate how to help someone if they collapsed? Mr—'

Damn. The man's name has entirely disappeared in my memory. He is lean and gangly with caramel tufts of hair and a large, slightly jowly grin.

'Sidebottom.'

Kitty looks at me with impish relish. She can't restrain her giggle. I remember a time when saying the word 'bottom' was backbreakingly funny. I feel sorry for Mr Sidebottom and the endless carousel of sniggering schoolkids in assembly, year after painful year. It's the sort of name to change by deed poll, or to turn anyone off a teaching career. If Clara were here, she would impart some stern parental lesson about empathy and good manners. But she isn't. And I can't resist the look of pure, unalloyed joy on my daughter's face, the endless delight in a silly name.

'Yes, KitKat, the famous Mr Sidebottom.'

There's another guffaw from Kitty, stifled by her hand reaching for her mouth, covered in flecks of spit.

'Well, the people in those photos were like Mr Sidebottom. They were part of a training exercise which Mummy was leading.'

She is more serious now, her face cowled with suspicion. 'Why were they bleeding?'

I steady myself again. It pains me to think what the grim adult world can do to a child's undeveloped mind. As a psychologist, I should know better than most. I think of Clara just after Kitty was born and those terrible few months. The rages, the anger, the withdrawal, the thoughts – how totally postnatal depression consumed her. Clara became someone different. She didn't sleep, eat or talk. One in ten women experience it. And yet, at times, it felt like we were the only couple in the world. That is the power of the human mind. The only sin is to underestimate it.

'Mummy trains other detectives in what to look for at a crime scene. No one was really hurt. They were all just pretending. See?'

There is silence. She squirms under the bedclothes, fidgeting as usual. She breathes heavily, almost like a sigh, and then seems to make up her mind. 'Daddy . . .'

The tension is almost unbearable. Has it worked? Or is my daughter psychologically scarred for life?

'Yes, KitKat?'

She smiles at me now. 'Next time, can I pretend?'

10

EMILY

'And you're sure you're okay to lock up?'

Emily Ogilvy looks at him with a death stare. If there is one downside to retraining later in life, this is it. 'I think I can just about manage,' she says.

'Remember. The key needs—'

'A bit of a shove and wait for the click. Got it.'

The curate smiles, in a way that only men in their mid-twenties can, as if still waiting for the world to appreciate the full immensity of them. Emily manages a flat smile in return, counting down the seconds until the office door closes. She gratefully escapes into the little kitchenette at the side of the church office and brews herself a strong mug of English breakfast tea, adding an illicit spoonful of sugar. She even searches for a chocolate digestive.

They warned her, of course. She can still see the puzzled looks from friends and family when she relayed the news. Few directly contradicted her. But the reservations were expressed in curious pouts and arched eyebrows. But once she'd resigned from the big job, there weren't many other options. And so, to general astonishment, Baroness Ogilvy of Kensington remade herself as Emily Shepherd, ordinand and priest-in-waiting at St Margaret's Church, Westminster.

There is nothing but oat milk in the fridge – the twenty-something man syndrome again, bludgeoning them all with his health act – and she begrudgingly stirs it into the tea, wincing slightly at the flavour. It is a rare thing to be left in charge here, even if only for half an hour.

The tourists, of course, always head towards Westminster Abbey. St Margaret's is the church of the politicians, home to the annual parliamentary carol service. That is the one event she is dreading. It will be like returning to an old school and seeing former friends ogling you in a new uniform. Then Emily stops herself. She's in her mid-fifties. And yet, somehow, life never really changes. People remain stubbornly familiar.

Emily is about to head back towards the main body of the church when her mobile buzzes. It's funny to remember a time when she always carried multiple devices. In her government and shadow ministerial days she had a personal phone, a parliamentary iPad, her ministerial secure phone and then the variety of inboxes monitored by an army of staff. Getting a message to her was often a five-stage process. Now she has one small iPhone, a truly ancient model, with a Gmail account and WhatsApp. This latest missive has come via email. She glances at it once, then again, feeling that all-too-familiar hole in the centre of her stomach.

It's been four years. But there's barely a day when it doesn't come up. This isn't the usual message, though; the trolls with their bile and hate and threats.

No, this is different.

FROM: benedict.prince@theabbeyclinic.com
TO: ordinand2@stmargaretschurch.org
SUBJECT: Anna Ogilvy meeting

Dear Ms Shepherd

Please forgive this email out of the blue. My name is Dr Benedict Prince and I'm a partner at the Abbey Sleep Clinic in

Harley Street. As you will be aware, your daughter was recently transferred to us for treatment by the Ministry of Justice.

I have received authorisation from Stephen Donnelly, Deputy Legal Director at the MoJ, to approach family members of Ms Ogilvy as part of a new treatment plan I am working on that aims to establish a diagnostic model for resignation syndrome.

To that end, I would very much like to speak with you at your earliest convenience. I am very near St Margaret's, if you are able to suggest a time and date that suits. Please also find attached my CV and list of professional qualifications and publications.

I look forward to hearing from you.

Yours sincerely
Ben

Dr Benedict Prince
Senior Partner
The Abbey

When she looks up, Emily notices that tea is seeping across the office carpet from her mug. It's just as well no one's around. She finds the supply cupboard and mops the spillage as best she can. A quick power-shower of Dettol and a bristly scrub usually gets the worst of the stain out before it settles. She does her best, then leaves it, hoping none of the others notice.

Almost reluctantly, she steps out into the main body of the church and sits at a pew near the front. She reads the email for a third time, then checks the attached PDF. There is a small passport-sized photograph showing a handsome man in his late thirties or early forties with a cowlick of hair curling across a smooth forehead, framing emerald eyes and the suggestion of day-old stubble. Dr Benedict Prince. There was a time when every medical professional looked like a younger version of Spock from *Star Trek*. She has heard of the Abbey, some kind of celeb bolthole like the Priory. Perhaps every B-list celeb really wants an appointment with Dr Dishy. She doesn't entirely blame them.

Emily puts down the phone. She breathes rhythmically. She has done her best here. She's buckled down to the relatively menial tasks of a new ordinand as a distraction from those other thoughts. But now, deep into the evening, her defences are fragile. She feels the familiar nightmares creep back in. She sees it playing out like a reel from a movie: the sounds, the stink of mud, the knife slick with blood – the full horror of that night at the Farm.

The worst moment was the split second in between, the old world morphing into something else. She still half-expects Anna to jump up and declare the entire thing a hoax, or for Theo to pull back the curtain and reveal the last four years never really happened.

But she can still feel it, as vivid as any feeling in her life, the exact moment when hope fell away. She and Richard stood there in silent, ghostly vigil. Knowing the police would soon arrive. Anna would be arrested. Emily would have to resign. The family, the marriage, the future – all would falter, then break. But those seconds were precious. They stood there at the Farm and saw their old existence shatter. Those final, silent seconds were an elegy for the past.

The visitor door of St Margaret's creaks open. The sudden noise startles her. Emily gets up from the pew, still feeling jumpy, and snaps back to the present. A stooped, elderly lady enters with her grandson, clearly familiar with the place. Emily smiles and nods, then occupies herself by tidying some hymn books in the choirstalls at the other end of the church.

No one else ever understood, of course. There was only

Richard and Theo, the secrets corroding everything, until the marriage and family fell apart. No one else ever really knew what happened that night, the terrible choices that had to be made.

Emily finishes fussing with the hymn books and steps out towards the altar. She stands there, transfixed by the polished gold, still awed by the majesty of it. She checks behind her and sees that the two visitors are still otherwise engaged.

Emily represses a shudder. She kneels and closes her eyes. She bows her head and begins to pray.

God can forgive her. Even if no one else can.

11

BEN

I am in the kitchen now, desperately trying to eke out the last drop of wine. At heart I have always been the romantic type, though hidden in that very English way. I never longed for the rock-star, groupie, alpha male fantasy. My dream was always more contained: a happy marriage, contented children, a small unit of domestic bliss that compensated for the turbulence of the outside world. A tribe.

Loneliness is my new normal. I've allowed my life to shrivel to work, chores, routine, telescoped further since the separation. I cling, instead, to these precious moments with KitKat. I want them to be perfect and for our time together to somehow heal the wounds of the split. But I know that's stupid. The damage is done. The symptoms may not present for years, but the disease is already planted.

Broken families. Parental squabbles. No one escapes without scars.

I should have worked less, listened more. Not assumed that domestic bliss was attained with a ring and a vow at the altar. Spent more time with Clara and KitKat rather than lavishing attention on strangers at the clinic. Increasingly, now, my future seems bleakly inevitable: fewer visits from KitKat, more time at work, doomed to the life of the single man in all its loveless squalor.

This isn't what I dreamed of. I want to fall asleep to the rhythm of someone else's heartbeat, to feel the radiator warmth of their hand in mine, to wake to a yawn and a smile from the other side of the bed. I want a family home bursting with tussles and laughter. A hallway cluttered with photos of holidays and graduations and special events.

It sometimes feels as if I'm living someone else's life.

This isn't what I signed up for. I want a refund.

The cupboards are barer than they should be. The flat is colourless, stark even. I'll have to get up early and nip to the local Tesco to ensure Kitty doesn't go home complaining of Nutella sandwiches and Diet Coke for breakfast. At least not again. It feels like everything is slowly spiralling, gravity pulling me into pre-arranged patterns. I can't bear the thought of being estranged from KitKat, gradually shoved to the margins of her life, demoted from the lead to the understudy.

I take the wine across to the sofa and begin flicking through various apps. Netflix, iPlayer, Prime, until I circle round and return to my Apple TV library. It's a different Hitchcock film tonight, I've decided. Another of the lesser-known gems – *The Wrong Man* with Henry Fonda, a black-and-white masterclass dripping with Catholic guilt, a riot of innocence and sin. I check my work emails and see the inbox bulging with unread messages. The subject lines are all addressed to me.

#STOPYOURMINDCONTROL
#FREETHEPATIENTS
#WE'REWATCHINGYOUDRPRINCE

I stop, read them again, feel a sickly sensation in my throat.

No one knows that Anna is at the Abbey. Surely the news can't have leaked so quickly. None of the messages mention her name. The Abbey has been featured in the news recently, the higher profile leading to more threats and anonymous messages. My profile is on the Abbey website. My name is known because of my books. Yet, still, the three messages unsettle me. They are threatening, violent even. Someone watching me is only one step from someone promising to hurt me, or a person close to me. The thought is terrifying in its black-and-white simplicity.

I read the messages again. The flat is still, but I react to every twitch and rustle. I think of KitKat asleep upstairs. Sleep makes us vulnerable.

I get up and glance outside. The background flicker of the Hitchcock film speckles the walls. Solitude smothers me. I am tired of crime, of sleep, of night terrors, the circus act of human psychology and all its horrors. I want to slip under warm, fresh sheets and feel the heat of Clara's body beside me and the safety of hearth and home and her.

I stop curtain-twitching and go upstairs and check on KitKat. I open the door and stand there, trying not to wake her. I left her in perfect symmetry with the duvet tucked and cornered. Now she sprawls across the bed in bohemian disarray. Hair glued, snowman arms, legs cancanning across the sheets. Love sneaks up on me, so overwhelming and intense. I can't bear the thought of her growing up. I will be relegated to fidgety coffees, then biannual lunches at uni, before the last-minute presents become WhatsApp updates and complex summitry just to meet my own grandchildren.

There is nothing I wouldn't do to protect her. And yet the cracks are appearing. Clara hears first-hand about school and swimming lessons and homework problems and nasty kids in class. I sound like a stranger, always playing catch-up. I want to be a good dad. But I don't know how anymore.

I close the door. Stop being selfish. For a horrible moment I wonder if there was something unusual about her reaction to the photos. Whether Clara has misdiagnosed the nightmares after all. Perhaps Kitty isn't scared of the dark but intrigued by it, wrestling with this newfound knowledge. Children are like sponges at her age, after all, especially for the darker side of the human mind.

But, no, I'm being ridiculous. I've watched too many movies, read too many of those sensationalist American profiler accounts, binged a glut of Netflix true crime shows and even appeared on a few myself. This is not the final episode of *My Child the Psychopath*.

I shake the thought away. I head downstairs and take a screenshot of the threatening emails and send it to the Abbey's security team and continue watching the movie. I can't go to bed, not yet.

#WE'REWATCHINGYOUDRPRINCE

I am about to get up and search through the cupboards again when my work mobile beeps. The security team, possibly, working late. I reach for the device, take another aimless sip of wine, and feel the weight of the last twenty-four hours sit at the centre of my skull, crushing every original thought.

Then I read the message again. I place the wine down, sit up straighter, feel my heartbeat quicken.

I'm needed back at the Abbey.

12

BEN

I breathe in the cold, tangy air and glance around the small square of garden. The sounds of Harley Street echo in the near distance. Kitty is inside by the reception desk with an iPad to watch. Clara will slaughter me, but there are no other options. Babysitters aren't on tap.

Bloom is ahead of me.

I continue walking. 'And what did you say?'

She seems unusually tense. There is a sarcastic edge to her answers, an angular stiffness to her posture. The pressure is mounting, I realise. There are signs of sleeplessness orbiting her eyes. 'What could I say,' she says. 'It was just after ten thirty when I got the call.'

'You're sure it's not a fishing expedition?'

Bloom sighs tetchily. She reaches the end of her third circuit round the garden and spies her usual bench ahead. 'They say vigorous exercise never killed anyone. But I say why take the chance.'

It's a shop-soiled line, as most of Bloom's are now. She heaves herself onto the wooden bench and exhales in a cloud of flint-grey, still bristling at the chill despite being wrapped in industrial layers of wool and fake fur. She reaches into her giant coat pocket and takes out a Liquorice Allsort. The sweet tug of addiction.

My mind is still fixed on Kitty's words about the photos. And the fact she is currently sitting bleary-eyed at the Abbey swaddled by a dressing gown. I feel guilty for hauling her out of bed this late. Yes, I would lay down my life for her. But that's not where the true acts of love occur. It is the smaller, everyday things. I should have told Bloom to wait until morning. That's what a good father would do. I failed just by answering the phone.

I force myself to concentrate on the present. There is a new crisis. One that could doom everything. My hopes of waking Anna O may already be up in smoke.

'What was the name again?'

I turn to Bloom and see the matter-of-fact glare. 'The medical correspondent at the *Mail*,' she says. 'Isabelle something-or-other.'

'What did she say specifically?'

Bloom exhales loudly for a second time, shivering with unease. 'That she had a source claiming the Abbey had been approached by the Ministry of Justice to provide consultancy services on the Anna O case ahead of a possible trial and seeking to confirm if that was indeed correct.'

'You saw the screenshot of those email threats I received? Saying they were watching me?'

'Yes, security passed them on. None of them specifically mentioned Anna.'

'Does that make it better?'

'No, but it makes it different. For now, Anna is our only concern.'

I absorb Bloom's words, the clinical indifference to my safety or KitKat's. I want to get up and leave, collect my daughter from reception and tell Bloom to stop treating me like her personal gofer. Instead, I say, 'Harriet, the nurse from Rampton Hospital, she was convinced that Anna responded when played

54

a certain song. The neurologists ignored her. There's a strong chance Harriet mentioned that fact to a boyfriend, sibling, parent or someone else and the rumour was simply passed on. It's been known before.'

'That still doesn't necessarily give a journalist the connection to me. You heard what Donnelly said. One whisper about this and the arrangement's off.'

'Perhaps it was a lucky guess on the reporter's part. How many sleep clinics are there on Harley Street? They hear the rumour then work the phones until someone gives the game away.'

'A charitable interpretation.' Bloom removes her leather gloves and flexes her right hand, wincing at the bony crack of each joint. 'But if you sup with Whitehall, then sup with a very long spoon indeed. Look what happened to Britton. Get this case wrong, Ben, and we could soon be heading in the same direction. A leak to the press might even be a blessing.'

I know the reference well enough. Paul Britton was one of the pioneers of forensic psychology, at the cutting edge of behavioural science during the eighties and nineties. His most infamous case was the murder of Rachel Nickell. He was part of setting up a long entrapment operation which ended with the imprisonment of an entirely innocent man, condemned on flawed psychological theories. Forensic psychology took decades to recover. Britton's career never did.

'Have you mentioned this latest development to Donnelly?'

'Yes,' she says. 'It was one of the conditions of hiring us. Non-negotiable. Full transparency all the way.'

'How did he take it?'

'He was overjoyed. Naturally.'

'I'm worried they'll start trying to drag Clara back into this. Resurrect all those absurd leads about police involvement. Target Kitty at school. You know how bad it got last time. None of us can go through that again.'

Bloom looks at me now, like a tribal elder despairing at the next generation. 'You're right. And I'm sorry. But Clara knows more about the Anna O case than anyone else in the force. She has institutional knowledge we can't ignore.'

'And if the press starts digging up those laughable Oxford stories or targets my daughter on social media?'

'Then it's the price we pay, Ben,' says Bloom. 'It always has been.'

13

BEN

We are walking again now. The air is sharper on the skin. I hear the cold certainty of Bloom's response. I feel that old annoyance with her too. She's getting old and indulgent, detached from the rest of us. She might be willing to sacrifice everything for a last chance at glory. But that doesn't mean I am too.

I breathe deeply, burying the resentment.

Eventually, I say, 'Are the lawyers on this?'

Bloom nods solemnly. 'Our lawyers. The MoJ lawyers. If there's a sniff of anything we'll slap an injunction on them faster than they can say the name Anna O. That doesn't mean it won't leak out somewhere else online. It's bound to eventually.'

'Surely that's the MoJ's problem, not ours.'

'If only life were that simple. One of the perils, I suppose, of taking on the highest-profile murder case in Britain.'

'Meaning?'

She smiles. 'You have a young family to support. My career is almost done. A bit of mudslinging from the press can't do much damage to me. Not at this stage. I'm offering you an exit route, Ben. Say the word and it will become my problem and mine alone.'

I don't respond immediately. My income is carefully sliced in two parts: the part-time lecturing on forensic psychology at Birkbeck; then my work here at the Abbey, consulting for the Metropolitan Police, Interpol, FBI and the National Crime Agency on sleep-related crimes and evaluations. My career is flatlining. This case could bring it roaring back to life. I want to show Clara I can still make something of myself; to give KitKat a dad she can be proud of. Stepping away from the biggest case of my life isn't quite that straightforward.

I know Bloom is testing me. 'Psychology is a practical discipline or it's nothing,' I say.

'One of my better lines.'

'No practitioner worth their PhD would turn down the opportunity to work on the Anna O case. I'm no exception.'

'The OSA forbids any monetary gain from your activities, mind. No book deals, no TV documentaries, no podcasts on BBC Sounds or golden handshakes with Spotify. If you're still dreaming of pound signs, then forget it.'

'I'm presuming academic journals are the exception.'

'You presume correctly.' Bloom turns now, beginning the short walk back across the gardens to the Abbey. 'Your paper was strong on general claims but light on specifics. I presume you do actually have a plan for treating her?'

The last day has been frantic. I have been preoccupied with seeing Clara again, KitKat's fears of those crime scene photos, the circus of having Anna O here in the Abbey building. But I am not an observer. My job is to play miracle worker, coaxing the dead back to life.

'I do.'

'Which is?'

'Simple,' I say, as we reach the door and the promise of well-lit warmth inside. 'I need to give her back some hope.'

14

LOLA

It's the story that time didn't forget. Which is odd, considering every other headline – murder, scandal, you name it – is here today and forgotten by the afternoon. People trend on social media for hours, then drop from the face of the earth. Sometimes Lola calculates how many murders have occurred in the four years since that night on the Farm. Hundreds, thousands even, all round the world. But none get front pages like she did.

No, there has always been something unique about Anna O.

It's morbid, really. Lola is the first to admit it. First it was Facebook groups, then more serious, encrypted channels when the public groups got gatecrashed. Now there are communities in every time zone: @Justice4SleepingBeauty, @ImWithAnnaO, @WakeUpAnna, @TheFarmTheTruth. Lola likes to anonymously dip in and out of all of them. But too much is bad for the brain.

Today, however, may well be a landmark, her biggest post yet. That's the thing which gives her most enjoyment. She can finish her shift, wash off the detritus of another boring day, and then get started on her real passion. Lola clicks on YouTube and the Birkbeck channel and finishes watching the latest lecture: 'Psychology and Sleep: An Introduction – Dr Benedict Prince, Visiting Fellow at Birkbeck, University of London'.

She turns up the volume and listens closely:

'The average human being spends thirty-three years of their life asleep. The ancients thought of sleep as a kind of death. Poets have eulogised about sleep as a second life. There is a whole world of sleep which our present society barely references. But what really happens when we sleep? And, more importantly, why can't we remember what happened when we wake . . .?'

He is good. She must give him that. He reminds her of Robin Williams in *Dead Poets Society*. Dr Prince is trim with a brush of ash-blond hair fashionably shaved at the sides. He favours open-necked blue shirts, dark chinos and the stylish variety of loafers, as if auditioning for a slot on BBC2's latest pop-science documentary. He is handsome, she supposes, in that endearingly foxy librarian way, with a symmetrical smile and pleasing tilt to his cheekbones. He must have more than his fair share of admirers in class.

She continues listening. There are jokes about Freud, more jokes about Freud. He interacts with students over how much people sleep, who among them sleeps too little or too much, who might even be sleeping together. It ends with a final joke about Freud – naturally – then she clicks off. Lola returns to the wording for her new post.

Yes, this will be the one. She is sure of it. She even posed as a health reporter from the *Mail* earlier to goad the Abbey, a little red herring to confuse them. There's no way anyone is stopping her now.

Lola goes through her usual pre-publication routine. She makes a cup of green tea, treats herself to a chocolate biscuit, and returns to the laptop for the very final read-through. Other people's posts are sprayed with grammatical errors. It's always been a point of pride that every post from @Suspect8 is flawlessly presented. English was never her choice subject at school, always more of a science girl at heart, but she has no tolerance for sloppiness. She is not one of the blogosphere's conspiracy nuts or hardcore Anna O true crime junkies. This might be her audience, but everyone knows she is a cut above.

She goes slowly, combing each line for clarity and errors:

NEW POST: HANDSOME PRINCE IS
CALLED TO SLEEPING BEAUTY

Hey all, a quick update for you. Whispers reach me @Suspect8 that a startling new development has occurred recently on the case of our beloved Anna O. I can report that Anna's case is being looked at by a new UK-based sleep expert called – irony of ironies – Dr Benedict Prince. Here's a link to one of his lectures on the theory of sleep and its link to criminal behaviour. The timing also can't be a coincidence. We know the legal case will conclude soon. It looks like the establishment is trying to jolt our beloved Anna back to life just so they can condemn her from the dock. Is that sick or what? Dr Prince has written about the power of music and culture to help patients with resignation syndrome wake up. It seems like it's the establishment's final shot. There's a shadow hanging over Anna and we must do whatever we can to help save her.

Previous experience has taught Lola to leave it brief. Mystery is best. The diehards in the group will bombard her with questions. Then the post will emerge on other platforms. She can always add further detail later. It's best to leave them hungry.

It's why she chose that handle, after all. Lola has what none of the others do. All official histories of the Anna O case show there were eight named suspects at the Farm on the night of the murder: Anna Ogilvy (prime suspect), Emily Ogilvy (mother), Richard Ogilvy (father), Theo Ogilvy (brother), Melanie Fox (managing director of the Farm), Owen Lane (groundskeeper), Danny Hudson (intern) and Lola Ridgeway (health and safety consultant). All were interviewed at the time of the murders. All were eliminated from police inquiries.

But not all of them left empty-handed. Lola picks up the notebook again and flicks through to the end. This is her treasure trove. The holy grail for all devotees of the case, plucked from the Blue Cabin before the police arrived. The source for every teasing detail and clue she has planted over the last four years. She glances at the last entry and the sloping hand, the beautiful cursive in jet-black ink, almost an exact match for what comes before. Fountain pen not rollerball or biro. The writerly flourish stretching elegantly across each tightly written line. She inhales the smell of the pages. This notebook belongs to her now.

Lola puts the notebook down and reluctantly finishes checking her post. Then she presses 'SUBMIT'. She waits while the encrypted system does its thing and sees her new post go live. She turns back to the notebook, as she always does, ready to disappear into its pages again. Not just any notebook.

But Anna's notebook.

There'll be no point sleeping tonight. Someone is always awake somewhere in the world. And little do they know who is really among them. Not just another blogger, no. Not a sad act bedroom-dweller with a Sherlockian fantasy life.

She is quite different. She is special. The clue is in her handle. @Suspect8.

Because Lola was there on the Farm that night.

And she knows who's guilty.

ANNA'S NOTEBOOK

2019

August 30

It is dark outside. It is morning, not evening. This place is silent.

I am sleeping, surely, but I can't wake up.

Blood sticks to my clothes. It spits round my neck, blobs wetly on my chin. Even now, as I write this, the page cloys with it.

And that single memory won't go.

I am standing in the doorway of the cabin. I look ahead and see them both sleeping deadly in their beds.

There is a voice beside me. It is a woman's voice. Serpentine, lustful. But her instructions won't leave me.

This is my final act of revenge.

I see the figures and the woman and the cold handle of the knife; and those words intoned almost prayerfully.

There can be no turning back now.

Four words that signal my new beginning.

For they must die.

PART TWO

15

BEN

The email from Stephen Donnelly at the Ministry of Justice comes through the next morning just after 11 a.m. marked 'SENSITIVE'. Various meeting locations are suggested and then dismissed. The Abbey in daytime is too risky. The Ministry of Justice itself, located at Petty France near St James's Park, is too public. Eventually, we settle on a more mundane solution. Few journalists ever trouble the top-floor café of John Lewis on Oxford Street with its jam-smeared tabletops and freshly baked scones. It is the perfect hiding place.

The café is self-service. Stephen Donnelly takes his second latte of the day and two packets of biscuits. I browse the selection of teas. We find a table tucked round the corner. I brief Donnelly on my proposals while he ignores the pings on his official MoJ phone, more weekend interruptions. I have my pitch down to a brisk five minutes. He hears me out with a bland, dutiful expression.

Finally, he says, 'Hope?' He looks down at the first biscuit packet, as if disappointed to find it empty.

'Yes.'

'You're not just winding me up?'

'No.' I am stuck on green tea, the healthy option, and stir it unenthusiastically. 'Anna is still in there somewhere. According to the literature, such as it is, hope is the only thing that has worked across multiple decades and regions.'

'Your article seemed more, well . . . technical.'

'It was. But it all boils down to the same thing. Happiness is the greatest medicine mankind has ever known. Hope is right up there too.'

Donnelly doesn't speak, quietly assessing his options. He's a lawyer, a civil servant, fluent in the language of rules, regulations, minimum standards and legalese. 'Is there another technical term perhaps?'

I have prepared for this. 'Resignation syndrome is a functional neurological disorder. What we refer to as an FND.'

Donnelly perks up slightly. The civil service gorge on acronyms. He can use this. 'I remember that term from your article.'

'FNDs in the past have been called psychosomatic. Or, historically, they loosely map onto what Freud termed hysteria. It's not an organic disease of the brain, as such, but of the psyche itself. The common feature across all continents and timelines is that patients suffer from resignation syndrome when confronted with the total absence and removal of hope.'

'Like the children in Sweden?'

I nod. The best-known case of resignation syndrome is still from the refugee communities in Sweden. Children emerging from hell in Syria and the Middle East slept for months and sometimes years, waiting as their asylum claims went through multiple appeals.

I continue, 'For the children who got better, it was usually because they regained hope of some kind. They were no longer at risk of being deported and forced back into the abyss of their old lives. A similar pattern recurs in the examples from Kazakhstan. The two towns in question were wealthy former Soviet mining and farming centres. When the Cold War ended, their old life disappeared. Hope was extinguished. The sleeping sickness started.'

Donnelly takes another sip of coffee. 'If this is similar to Freudian hysteria then presumably the day-to-day treatment is a talking cure?'

'No,' I say. 'Or not exclusively.'

'You don't believe in talking cures?'

'I'm a psychologist. We all believe in talking cures. I also have an annotated copy of *Oedipus Rex* on my bedside table.'

'I presume that's a joke.'

'The same mistake my father made.' I smile. 'Fatally, as it turned out.'

Donnelly smiles back. 'I'm a lawyer, not a professional psychologist, Dr Prince. I read your paper and understood about half of it. What's wrong with Freud?'

'Freud thought all hysteria or psychosomatic behaviour was caused by some unexplained trauma in the patient's past. Modern FND theory, by contrast, has a far more holistic view. The days of therapists endlessly searching for childhood abuse are long gone. Freud is still useful in some contexts. But he sent psychology down a sex-obsessed blind alley from which it's taken almost a century to emerge.'

'I see.' Donnelly wipes a foamy moustache from his lip. 'That was our mistake, presumably?'

I am careful not to overstep the mark. Irritating the MoJ isn't in my job description.

'Some of your world-leading experts, mostly in their sixties or seventies, might be the last unreconstructed Freudians. They have too much to lose by moving on from that paradigm. They may have searched for some moment of abuse in Anna Ogilvy's past, yes.'

Donnelly flinches. 'Another blind alley?'

'It's not how we're ever going to cure the patient. At least not how I propose to cure her. And, after all, you were the one who came to me.'

Donnelly looks tense and impatient now, fidgeting with his watch. 'How then?'

16

BEN

I finish my green tea. Donnelly continues sipping his latte. He gazes at the empty packet of shortbread again, the slightest tremor in his hand. I almost feel like hiding it just to calm his mood.

This is the tricky bit requiring a deft political touch. I am in danger of losing him. 'The only way I can help Anna is by discovering more about her past.'

Donnelly has given in now. He unwraps the second biscuit packet with a lover's delicacy. 'I thought you didn't believe in hunting around patients' pasts?'

'I don't believe in searching for sexual explanations as the root cause of all human behaviour. That doesn't mean I'm not fascinated by a person's backstory. The only way I can restore hope for Anna is by finding out why that hope was extinguished. What led up to her killing those two people that night. Why did her mind react the way it did. Without a knowledge of her history, we have no knowledge of her present.'

'I take it Bloom filled you in on the *Mail* reporter?'

'Yes.'

'There's a blog too, apparently. Possibly related, possibly not. The *Mail* didn't seem to have an on-the-record source to give

70

the story legs. But one loose source and the entire exercise could come crashing down around us. We've slapped a DSMA-Notice on Fleet Street for the time being, though the blog is rather outside our control.'

I've read the blog. @Suspect8. It unnerves me. DSMA-Notices work for the printed press, not the digital wilderness. I can see why Bloom was so worried before. I half-feared that Donnelly would use our meeting to cancel the project. 'I understand.'

'Good.'

There is no alternative but to ask, no matter how unlikely. 'I also need access to the Met case files. Memories alone aren't enough.'

Donnelly taps his spoon against the edge of his coffee cup. The stress is grooved into his forehead. 'Tell me. How much do you remember about the original investigation?'

'I read the papers and watched the news. I went back over archived pieces for my book and the journal article. I remember most of it.'

'Everyone remembers the killer and the other suspects. No one remembers the two victims. Make of that sad fact what you will.'

'Douglas Bute and Indira Sharma. Both were found in their cabin with ten stab wounds each from the same kitchen knife later recovered from Anna Ogilvy. Her fingerprints were the only ones on the handle. She sent the WhatsApp message to her family saying she thought she'd killed them.'

Donnelly looks impressed.

'There were eight people at the Farm on the night of the murder, including the Ogilvy family and the two victims.'

'Not forgetting your wife, of course?'

'Ex-wife,' I correct him. 'And she was on-site for the aftermath. Not when the crime was committed.'

I can see the Ogilvy family now, helpless against vultures heading for a feed. Every corner of their private lives was excavated. The New Labour politician mother, the financier father, the drop-out wannabe TV presenter brother and the crowd of artsy and occasionally scandalous friends, including Douglas Bute and Indira Sharma.

'Well?'

Donnelly's voice is hoarse, fractious even. 'I can speak to the Met. As a registered BIA, you shouldn't have too many problems gaining clearance for the case files.'

'Do I have your blessing for the interviews?' I've already sent the emails with the interview requests. But I need political cover.

Donnelly hesitates. 'The statements from the case files really won't be enough?'

'Anna had no criminal record. No history of public violence. No history of mental illness or murderous intent. There has to be something more. I'm sure of it.'

Donnelly toys with another biscuit. 'There's really no other option?'

'Not if you want results within weeks. Give me a year and it's a different answer.'

Donnelly's mobile begins vibrating. 'Fine. You have my blessing. But this is strictly off-the-books.' His eyes look bleary. 'If anyone asks, this didn't come from me.'

17

BEN

I return to the Abbey by late afternoon, still mulling on the meeting with Donnelly. He doesn't want a psychologist. He wants a shaman, a miracle worker.

Somehow, I must summon the dead back to life.

I go through my diary for the next few weeks then brew litres of black coffee, snaffle a doughnut from the staffroom and head to the second floor.

Harriet finishes up and joins me outside. I offer her a spare doughnut and coffee. We sit on swivel chairs watching Anna's room on the monitors. I tell Harriet about the meeting with Donnelly and the police files. She updates me on today's progress, or the lack of it.

At last, she says, 'So what now?'

She usually wears a neutral expression. It is a nurse's face, allergic to any kind of false hope. But slowly, away from patients, warmth creeps in. There's a pureness about her smile.

'I believe you,' I say. 'About the Beatles song.'

'At least that's one doctor on my side.'

'Not a medical doctor.'

'Neurologists are overrated.'

'Try telling them that.'

We both continue looking at the monitors. It is still strange seeing Anna here. I think of Lazarus, the patron saint of resurrections, and the way in which sleep is a harbinger of death. I also think of Clara's view about Anna being a cold-blooded killer. I am within touching distance of a murderer. The thought is disturbing in every possible sense. Evil, in some people's eyes, is literally sleeping in the next room.

Harriet shakes her head. 'How does anyone really stay asleep for four years?'

I think of Clara asking the same question. I have the same answer. 'Honestly? No one really knows.'

'And dishonestly?'

'Primo Levi had a term for fellow inmates in the concentration camps. They were known as *Muselmänner*. Translated quite literally as people who lost the will to live. They endured something worse than death. A living death.'

'That's what Anna's suffering from?'

'Possibly. Blame dualism too. The idea of the rational mind being somehow separate from the physical body. It set the tone for centuries of discussion about the psyche.'

'You don't think human beings are rational?'

'I think we're animals,' I say. 'Primates with bigger brains than anything seen during the five billion years of the earth's existence.'

'But?'

'We're still animals. Trying to probe the mysteries of the mind is like trying to discover the genetic structure of love or the exact properties of beauty. There is the rational side of homo sapiens and the animal side. People think the animal side is the body and the rational side is the brain. But it's often the other way round.'

'What class do you teach?'

I try to gauge whether she's genuinely interested or joking with me. 'Introduction to Forensic Psychology,' I say. 'Night classes at Birkbeck. You should come along sometime. You might enjoy it.'

'I thought you were a sleep expert?'

'I'm a forensic psychologist who specialises in sleep-related crime.'

'How do the neurologists at the Abbey feel about forensic psychologists?'

'One rung down from nutritionists and spiritualists. Though, arguably, that's being slightly harsh to nutritionists.'

She smiles again. The door leading through to the rest of floor two is thick and soundproof. The glass is clouded, like a giant bathroom mirror. There is silence.

We are the only ones here. Harriet's personal mobile pings with a new WhatsApp message. She checks it and types out a quick response. She notices my stare.

'My partner,' she explains. 'Well, occasional guest seems to be their preferred description.'

I'm intrigued. 'Married?'

'No. They've just got divorced. Kid too. I'll spare you the gory details. Let's just say it's complicated.'

'Join the club.' I look back at Anna in the treatment room. She lurks there, present in every conversation. The sleeping killer behind the glass. There is an energy to her, even at rest, that makes all conversations feel dangerous. 'Do you ever think she's in pain?'

Harriet pauses, as if wary of betraying a confidence. She looks over at Anna too, both frightened and intrigued. Sensing the forbidden. 'Can I tell you a secret?'

'Of course.'

She reaches down into the pocket of her uniform. She pulls out a little container. It looks medical, a vial of some sort. 'I have a sixth sense sometimes for when she's in distress. There's no physical signs, but I know. It's almost intuitive. When that happens, I give her a little sip of this. Apparently, it used to be her favourite. Jack Daniel's Black Label.'

It's my turn to smile now. 'Mankind's original cure. Happiness in a bottle.'

Harriet nods, suddenly sheepish. She tucks the container away. 'A nurse's little remedy. One of my early mentors swore by it.'

'Don't worry,' I say. 'Your secret's safe with me.'

18

BEN

The police files arrive just before 10 p.m. with all the expected ceremony.

Alongside the two Murder Squad detectives, there's a studious official from the Cabinet Office – beanpole thin with a rumpled mackintosh and rimless glasses – who waits impatiently while I read through every term and condition. Then, once my signature is done, the official and the two cars disappear in a haze of rain, gliding back to Whitehall like something illusory and deniable.

I always like the Abbey after dusk. Most of the staff have fled for children, home and their better halves. I brew unhealthy quantities of Yorkshire Gold and think of Harriet again and the warmness of her smile, that friendlier private self hidden beneath the surface.

The box of case files is heavy, like a small item of furniture. I find a pair of scissors and prise open the masking tape, seeing another ream of red-letter instructions regarding how the files must be handled.

I select several randomly and start picking through the debris of the investigation: witness statements, summaries of CCTV, a list of all house-to-house inquiries, made more difficult by the sheer remoteness of the Farm's location. There are ANPR updates, the pathologist's reports on both victims, a comprehensive forensic overview and written submissions from knife experts on the geometry of the wounds.

One file contains more background on the victims and attendees at the Farm, culled from the witness statements, cell site data and forensic trail, like a narrative synthesis after the crush of archival material. Glancing through, I realise how distant the world of 2019 now seems.

I take another sip of Yorkshire Gold. I nibble on a digestive. There is an excerpt from Melanie Fox's witness statement. She was the one who ran the Farm, owned it even. Melanie Fox was the impresario who lost it all. She was the one who hired Lola Ridgeway; she talked to the press and had her fifteen minutes of fame and then went quietly into oblivion.

I turn to her statement.

The thin paper prickles against the skin. I sit back in the office chair, listen to the whir of central London behind me.

I focus on the page and begin.

19

LOLA

Rearranging the evidence is one of her favourite hobbies. There is something mentally stimulating about having different pieces on the wall. The investigator can inhale the entire thing at once.

Because that's what Lola is. Not a blogger or influencer or any other pejorative term. She has Anna's original notebook. She is a truth-seeker. She is as much a detective as any of those pen-pushers with a warrant card. Her job is to follow evidence, investigate symptoms right down to the root cause. She is a surgeon too, every cut perfectly timed.

Lola refreshes the browser. She sees another 326 people have viewed her latest post in the last few minutes. Virality is like love or happiness, almost impossible to actively achieve. It is usually fluked and then reverse-engineered into a formula. But this post truly has gone viral. Nearly a million page views, six-figure likes, four-figure comments. It's by far her most successful post yet.

Lola closes her laptop. She checks her phone but there are no more messages today. They used to message constantly, back in those heady youthful days. Now it's once daily if she's lucky. But their bond was forged in blood. Nothing can break them apart. After all they've been through, nothing ever will.

She puts the laptop and mobile in a drawer and heads back to the boards lining the walls. She isn't stupid. Many would say this is an obsession. Perhaps they're right. But one person's obsession is another's cure. The boards are her lifeline. And, after what happened that night, something has to be.

Lola finishes cutting out the headshot of Dr Benedict Prince and then walks across to the second board. The key suspects go on Board 1. The investigators and other official parties go on Board 2. Boards 3, 4, 5 and 6 are for timeline, forensics, location and then hypotheses.

Lola reaches up and jabs the drawing pin into the top of the photo, feeling the corkboard give way and the pointy nose of the pin sink deep. She stands back and looks at the organogram she's created. At the top is the original SIO on the Anna O case: DI Clara Fennel from the Thames Valley Serious and Organised Crime Unit, once working narcotics and since moved to the Met's famous Murder Squad; the drive home that turned into a career-breaking detour. There is a list of Deputy SIOs, then other positions like Exhibits Officer, Family Liaison Officer, Crime Scene Manager and the key uniform in charge of door-to-door. The other photo is already there: Harriet Roberts, staff nurse at Rampton Secure Hospital, seconded to the Abbey for the duration of Anna Ogilvy's stay. Yes, the perky nurse and the handsome psychologist. The new double act on this case.

It's taken years to get all this information. But almost anything is discoverable with enough time. She's had to brush up on the police, too. Her bookshelves bulge with fat, glossy tomes: *Blackstone's Senior Investigating Officers' Handbook*, *Introduction to Criminology: New Perspectives* and, the latest purchase, *Dead of Sleep: An Introduction to the Forensic Study of Sleep Disorders and Dream Analysis* by Dr Benedict Prince himself. His first book before *Anna O and Other Mysteries of the Mind*.

She also has every edition of *Elementary*, the magazine Anna founded with Indira Sharma and Douglas Bute, and has read each issue a minimum of eight times.

Harriet Roberts is easier, of course, a nobody with a quiet private life and a yawn-worthy Facebook account. The latest update shows photos of a countryside walk and the usual ephemera of overpriced pub lunches and flasks of lukewarm coffee. No husband, no kids. Dr Prince plays the part of poster-boy thinker. Nurse Roberts plays the gamesy, no-nonsense, classic English nurse. They both play their parts so well.

Lola takes a final look at Dr Prince and Nurse Roberts – their showy competence, their put-on smiles – on Board 2. Then she sidesteps to her right and looks at Board 3. It is the board she always comes back to, crawling with Post-It notes and spidery felt-tip pen. The board where the case truly comes alive. The information has been painstakingly compiled from her own memory, media reports and the occasional police statement. It aims to be a definitive chronology of August 30th, 2019. The night it happened. The hours that changed everything.

She reads it again, almost mouthing the words as she goes:

AUGUST 30, 2019
LOCATION: THE FARM, OXFORDSHIRE
PERSONNEL:

ANNA OGILVY (25)
EMILY OGILVY (51)
RICHARD OGILVY (52)
THEO OGILVY (30)
INDIRA SHARMA (25)
DOUGLAS BUTE (26)
MELANIE FOX (39)
OWEN LANE (48)
DANNY HUDSON (22)
DI CLARA FENNEL (35)

That last name is contentious, if technically accurate. DI Fennel broke protocol and raced to the scene before anyone else could take the case, not waiting to be pushed aside for someone more senior. CCTV at the entrance of the Farm proved it, as did an examination of the police vehicle – a Volvo S90 T8 plug-in hybrid.

Lola doesn't include herself, of course. She only goes on the official records.

She looks through the rest of the timeline now and goes back to the previous day, the 29th, and lingers over another entry: '4PM–12AM: the Forest'. Not only is it the longest entry in terms of duration, but it is also – in Lola's mind at least – the most consequential. It is the reason why people visited the Farm, after all. It made the Farm notorious, or even infamous, a favoured off-site destination for bankers, corporates, hen parties, stag dos, and family weekend outings.

It was how she got her invite. A cut-price health and safety gig, one no reputable firm would touch. A website, a business card, and bingo. She was in.

The guests arriving on the twenty-ninth. The stink of mud and booze. The party dividing into two teams – one playing Hunters, the other Survivors. Then the game itself, stretching for eight tortuous hours. The Forest was an adjunct to the Farm, a patch of scrubland crowded with trees and a crepuscular sense of menace. It was like a cross between Go Ape, Center Parcs and paintballing, gussied up with ladders and ropes. The Hunters could move more freely. The Survivors could make a narrow escape.

Owen Lane, the groundskeeper, put the frighteners on guests when they arrived. But that was the point of the Farm. This was the place where that CEO was found weeping into his rations, where those two corporate high-flyers found love while hiding on the forest floor, where reputations were made and broken, deals sealed, and animal spirits emerged in all their ugly glory. Or, at least, that was the marketing strategy.

Except something had gone wrong that day. Lola still remembers it with such clarity. The Forest was stripped of ornament, largely thanks to the deluge of rain, and Melanie Fox's insistence that the event go ahead. The Ogilvys had booked the 'Family Package' for six guests, three in both teams, including all equipment, accommodation (such as there was) and food.

Lola glances at the list again. You can only understand what came after by what came before. The mud still fills her nostrils. The boggy grass slurping her boots. Her record of the Forest on August 29th:

SURVIVORS
Richard Ogilvy
Emily Ogilvy
Theo Ogilvy

HUNTERS
Anna Ogilvy
Indira Sharma
Douglas Bute

It's the mystery no one has ever solved. What could possibly have occurred in the Forest during those eight hours to persuade a twenty-five-year-old woman with no history of violence to stab her two teammates to death a total of twenty times?

But, then again, that's the problem with amateur hypotheses. All those columnists, pundits and supermarket sleuths weren't there that night. They didn't see all the evidence.

They didn't have the notebook. They weren't in the Blue Cabin just after it happened. They saw through the glass darkly.

None of them knew the secret behind it all.

20

BEN

The first reply to my interview request comes several days later.

Emily Ogilvy is clearly a night owl like me. The email drops into my inbox just after 1.30 a.m. I open it and, as I read, I think back to the Ogilvy family photo used just after the murders and those buoyant smiles. They are slim, healthy, fit, tanned, finessed with their pearly-white, symmetrical grins, coiffed hair, expensive clothing. Luck envelops them: where they were born, the education they received, the careers chosen. Less than twenty-four hours later, one of them would be arrested for murder; a year later, the two parents would file for divorce; six months after that, Theo Ogilvy had a near-fatal overdose and fled to permanent exile in South America. Hubris punished by the gods.

The email is a polite but cursory message informing me of a cancellation in her diary and offering to meet at St Margaret's Church later that morning. She signs off with her full name, almost like a formal letter.

I can't face schlepping back to Pimlico so grab some sleep in my office, instead, and shower in the on-site facilities. I email the reception team to say I'll be working from home today and then head down to St Margaret's Church.

Parliament Square and the entrance to the Supreme Court are largely deserted when I arrive. I look up at Big Ben and the Palace of Westminster. St Margaret's sits like a squatter, clinging to the coattails of Westminster Abbey.

St Margaret's is sparsely attended this morning. Inside the church there are a few politicos praying for absolution and a handful of robed clergy mingling near the front. I never quite know whether to sign or bow or show some other token of respect. In the end, I scan the pews. I see the back of a woman's head near the altar. Even from behind I can tell how much Emily has changed. From her old photos online – in ermine during her swearing in to the House of Lords, manning the phonelines at party headquarters, in her New Labour heyday as minister – she always seemed to be a middle-aged woman trapped inside a younger woman's body. Now, finally, the exterior matches the interior.

The back of her head is peppery. She leans forward in prayer, both hands clasped devoutly. It is hard to believe this was the woman who could reduce other peers to tears with a single line. Or who pioneered mental health services as Health Minister during the late nineties and early noughties. Emily Ogilvy was once a zealot for politics. Now tragedy has made her a zealot for God. I wonder if she has found true meaning in either.

I sit down in the same pew. Emily, for all her newfound unworldliness, still has some of the old political tradecraft. The pew is nicely distanced from the others, tucked behind a corner with the sightline obscured. No one will catch us here. She has made sure of that, a lifelong antenna for a camera flash.

'What's he saying?'

Emily doesn't flinch. She sits back, slowly opening her eyes, looking unsurprised to see the pew occupied. 'I'm sorry?'

'God, I mean.'

'That's not really how it works.'

I settle into the pew, feeling as if I'm at school again, sliding my hands rebelliously into my pockets. I find myself unable to resist. 'Poor bloke must have a postbag the size of Mars. Worse than most politicians.'

Emily smiles, indulging my casual blasphemy. 'The only difference in that analogy is that politicians, even former Ministers, don't have the power of God.'

'That would be news to most of them.'

'I don't doubt it would.'

She is more amiable in person. On TV Emily always seemed brittle, a 'piranha in pearls' as one of the red-tops claimed with memorable misogyny. But that veneer has largely gone. There is a teacherly glint to her eyes. The world of Westminster reacted with astonishment to the news that she was to retrain for the priesthood, replacing the Baroness with Reverend.

Though, technically, even the surname is different now. Since her divorce from Richard Ogilvy, she has reverted to her maiden name. She has an air of parish-council respectability. I compare her with Anna in the treatment room and see a fleeting resemblance.

'I was confused when I got your message,' she says, the warmth frosting over now. 'I said everything during the original investigation. There have been so many experts with wonderful theories. All of them have come to nothing. Excuse my cynicism. But it sounds like more of the same.'

'Perhaps,' I say. 'But perhaps not. The benefit of the doubt is all I'm asking for.'

Emily doesn't sound enthused. 'And you hope to achieve what exactly? Another impressive case for your CV?'

'No,' I say. 'I hope to bring your daughter back to life again.'

21

BEN

The church itself seems too stifling. We leave in search of caffeine.

Starbucks is crowded so we order and take the drinks outside and start walking back down Victoria Street. The faceless office buildings give way to gothic splendour. A helicopter hovers near Downing Street for an aerial shot of the Prime Minister's motorcade.

I am struck by how much Anna has missed since she fell asleep. Downing Street was home to a different occupant. Building sites have become new office blocks. The world has altered in the last four years.

Emily breaks her silence. 'What, may I ask, do you have that the others didn't?'

The question is forensic, the sort of gotcha line flung out on parliamentary committees.

'Well, for one thing, I believe the mind is more powerful than the brain. Most other clinicians would believe the opposite.'

'That sounds like a grand but ultimately meaningless statement.'

'Not at all. The ancients knew it, so did the pre-moderns. Blame the Enlightenment. Only in the last few centuries have we ignored the idea of the mind and concentrated so narrowly on fixing the brain. Anna, like most patients with resignation syndrome, has been stuck in a medical setting with no stimuli. My method is to overwhelm her senses – sounds, smells, voices, touch – that evoke safe memories of her past. I want her body to kickstart her mind into thinking it is safe to emerge again.'

Emily looks solemn, reaching for something. 'The mind is its own place, and in itself can make a heaven of hell, a hell of heaven.'

'Milton wasn't wrong.'

'He wasn't always entirely right either. I studied *Paradise Lost* at university. It seems like another world now.' Emily finishes inspecting me, as if finally accepting my bona fides. 'What is it you want to know? Did we deprive Anna of sweeties when she was little? Did my husband tap her on the bottom when she put her fingers in sockets? Are early bedtimes the cause of Anna's sleeping problems?'

I decide against giving my usual speech on hope. 'I've seen the case files. That's not what I'm worried about. I know about the site map, the Forest, the Hunters versus the Survivors, the WhatsApp message, the forensics on the knife. What none of the files tell me is *why.*'

'Who says I will?'

'If you can't, then no one can.'

'You have a rather naïve view of mother–daughter relations.'

'At the age of twenty-five your parents still know you best. For a child, it's their entire lifespan. For a parent, it's one season among many. I think you know more than you let on.'

'Your ex-wife was the first officer at the Farm that night, am I right?'

'Yes,' I say.

Emily looks mournful suddenly, weighed down. 'I'm sorry for her, really. Getting dragged into all this. I read all that stuff in the tabloids, the gutter comments online. Conspiracy theories about police involvement and her colluding with Anna just because they both went to Oxford. I know what it's like better than most.'

I remember the rows Clara and I had about my book, the way in which publishers and agents wanted me to put the Anna O case front and centre. I am rewriting history, though. Our marriage was already in freefall by then. I'd become more distant. Clara had found solace elsewhere.

'I want to know what Clara and her team didn't find out,' I say. 'The deeper, emotional truth. It's been four years since it happened. Enough water under the bridge.'

We reach Parliament Square and stop by the Supreme Court building. The Palace of Westminster shadows the entire scene. We sip our coffees.

'The media focused on Anna's success,' I say. 'The clean-sweep GCSEs, the three A stars at A level, the congratulatory first at Oxford. Then the start-up success with Indira and Douglas, a media entrepreneur in the making. But resignation syndrome doesn't happen because of success. It happens because of failure. A lack, an absence.'

'Is this on the record?'

'I'm a psychologist, not a police officer. There is no record.'

Emily sighs, as if building up to something. 'The first thing you must know is that Anna always was a girl of extremes. If you understand that, you have a hope of understanding the rest. Not many do. But it's ironic, I suppose, given what's happened.'

'Ironic how?'

'As an adult her eyes are never open,' says Emily. 'As a child they were never shut. That's how the nightmare began.'

22

BEN

The day is overcast, fizzy with the promise of rain. We drift towards Whitehall. The scenery becomes different here, nineties minimalism morphing into baroque splendour. Nelson's Column looms in the foreground. The fountains of Trafalgar Square. The hoot of the Strand. This ancient capital stirring from sleep into life.

'When was the first time it happened?' I ask. 'She's a sleep-walker, I presume.'

Emily nods. She seems hesitant, even fearful. 'As far as we know, it was on a family holiday to Cornwall.'

'How young was Anna?'

'Nine. We decamped in an ancient travel-van with the kids and the dog and found a small cottage for a week. The first two nights were fine. On the third night we watched a film together in the cottage. Richard and Theo wanted one of the Bond films, but I thought Anna was too young. Anyway, they won. It was the second Timothy Dalton one, I forget the name. All guns and death and violence.'

'*Licence to Kill*,' I say. I remember watching an illicit VHS version, trying to replicate the brutal suaveness of Dalton without much success. 'What happened?'

'Nothing. Well, nothing as we watched the film. Anna swore she wasn't scared. Theo and Richard did their whole little boys routine. Even Buttons, the dog, enjoyed it. We went to sleep like any other evening. Really it happened quite out of the blue during the night.'

I wait. Emily won't be hurried. 'Anna?'

She nods, distracted now. Her eyes mist over slightly. She is no longer seeing Parliament or the statues but a small cottage in a remote part of Cornwall and a darkened room which haunts her two decades on.

'I remember waking to a sound from the kitchen. I thought a door might still be open. It was an animal sound, the dog perhaps. It was just after two a.m. when I walked into the kitchen.'

'What did you see exactly?'

'Buttons, our dog, was lying on the floor in a pool of his own blood. One of the carving knives from the kitchen had been stuck in his side. Anna was just standing there.'

'Like the Bond movie?'

'Yes. Well, sort of.' Emily glances at me. Her eyes glitter with relief, the knowledge that someone else understands. 'Buttons had mistakenly bitten Anna the year before. She had to get stitches and go to A&E. At one point we thought we might lose the dog. She was fine around him, but never close. Buttons was part of the boys' club. Their pet rather than hers.'

'What was Anna doing exactly that night?'

'Just watching. There were specks of blood on her pyjamas. It was clear from the angle that she was the one who'd plunged the knife in.'

'Did you speak to her?'

'Yes.'

'Did she respond?'

'Yes, but it was like talking to a different person. Her voice was different.'

'What then?'

Emily doesn't grope for detail. She knows this story well enough; every cadence is automatic. 'I was too shocked to do anything. I checked Buttons but he was clearly gone. I led Anna away from the scene and back towards her bedroom. And then, well . . .'

Emily drifts off. The punchline that has been building. The truth that haunts everything.

I say, 'That's when Anna finally woke up.'

23

BEN

I hear the rest without quite taking it in. In her confusion, Emily didn't wake the rest of the family. She cleaned up the kitchen and carried Buttons out into the garden and towards a stream that ran by the end of the cottage. She dug a small grave and left him there without a collar or identification. The next morning, she broke the news that Buttons had escaped in the night. Theo and Richard launched a search party. They roped in some of the fellow holidaymakers. But it was useless. Emily had dug the grave deep enough to bury the evidence.

'The next morning,' I say, 'did Anna remember anything?'

'No. She tried to find Buttons as vigorously as the others. It reminded me of when people talk about exorcisms. It was as if my nine-year-old daughter had been purged of something.'

'How long was it until you got a diagnosis?'

Emily pauses again. 'You're going to think I'm a terrible mother.'

'Try me.'

'I was still a Minister then. The whiff of scandal – even one about the death of a family dog – would see me fired in the next reshuffle. My daughter was young. I'd let her watch a violent film. She'd copied elements of it. I chalked it up to an honest parental mistake.'

'How long before it happened again? Or that you knew of?'

'That's not entirely the same thing.'

'No. It isn't.'

Emily finds a bin and chucks away her half-empty coffee cup. She draws her coat tighter. 'Anna was a teenager. Fourteen, or thereabouts. I got a call from her boarding school. Items had been stolen from the housemistress's flat. The housemistress raised other concerns too.'

'Such as?'

Emily is hesitant again. She seems caught between telling the truth and protecting her daughter. 'Anna was always a slightly strange child. Obsessive, really. She became fixated on murder and true crime for some reason. One book above all. *In Cold Blood*.'

I know the book. There is a dog-eared copy in my Pimlico flat. The full title is *In Cold Blood: A True Account of a Multiple Murder and Its Consequences*. Truman Capote's masterpiece transformed the genre by using novelistic techniques to recount a factual story. It's a way to ease my Birkbeck students into the forensic psychology course, an icebreaker for the first term.

'I used to joke that Anna was always the sort of person who would kill for her fifteen minutes of fame,' says Emily. 'She needed to see her name in lights. She wanted to win World Cups or become President. When it came to writing, my daughter didn't want to be a good writer. She wanted to be a great one.'

'I sympathise.'

'She was even working on some true crime piece for the magazine just before that night at the Farm. Her own attempt to rival Capote. She became similarly obsessed with Broadmoor and that ghastly Sally Turner case from the late nineties. The Stockwell Monster.' Emily looks embarrassed, then bashful. 'I urged her to focus on happy things. Joyful things. But that advice fell on deaf ears.'

The Sally Turner reference intrigues me. Britain's most infamous female killer. The mother who murdered her own stepchildren in the quest for the 'perfect family'. Bloom has often regaled me with stories from her time at Broadmoor. It is the first thread of connection. Anna and the Stockwell Monster. It is not what I expected. 'Do you know if Anna ever wrote the piece?'

Emily shakes her head. 'Just about to, I think. Before, well, everything . . .'

'What happened with the school incident?'

Emily sighs. 'The housemistress had a security camera installed in her flat. Anna was caught stealing. Her eyes were clearly open even though she claimed to have no memory of doing it. She was expelled. I managed to keep the scandal out of the papers thanks to a very expensive defamation lawyer. Anna still denied it.'

I can't quite tell if Emily is just sad or something more. There is a flicker of guilt. Then I realise it's not that, or not really. It's something worse.

Shame.

'Treatment would have required explaining the school incident,' I say. 'That, in turn, might have leaked to the papers and jeopardised your political career. So you hushed it up again and did nothing. Politics over parenting.'

Emily doesn't protest. 'Yes. It sounds unforgivable in the cold light of day. But to jeopardise all that work – all I'd put the entire family through – for the sake of a teenage misdemeanour seemed crazy.'

'Did you connect the school incident with the holiday incident?'

'I'm a politician, not a doctor. I thought Anna was troubled in a general sense. Theo and Anna were brought up by a succession of Norland nannies and ad hoc babysitters. She was a child of the internet age. I wondered if that contributed to it.'

'What made you change your mind?'

There is another pause, a long intake of breath.

Emily looks pained, as if this memory is even worse than the others. 'Everything changed,' she says, 'the time Anna tried to attack me.'

ANNA'S NOTEBOOK

2019

January 1

Another tepid New Year party at the flat. The family, of course, have their own shenanigans. Theo drinking too much as usual. Mum busy with House of Lords business. Dad counting his money and tied to his phone. I plump for Indira and Doug and their giggly friends and the wagon wheel of disappointment at the fireworks by the Embankment. I watch the spray of too-bright colours by the London Eye. Doug is stoned. Indy is sympathetic. I am bored and fidgety.

2018 is dead. Long live 2019!

We troop home to the rented flat in Camden. We drink on into the morning. A new year that feels curiously like the one before.

The others are asleep as I write this. This notebook was a Christmas present from Mum, probably purchased by one of her little minions at the Palace of Westminster gift shop. Age is stealing up on me. I have nothing in my own name to show for it. Keats died at twenty-five. Jane Austen wrote *Pride and Prejudice* at twenty-one. Raphael was already considered a genius by this stage. Even those unknowns from uni are now columnists on proper papers. I edit a tiny magazine with too few readers and too many pretensions and no bylines.

I don't have the stamina for novels. I don't have the soul for poetry. This will have to do. At the start of every week, Pepys-like, I will record my thoughts here. I will finally be a writer who actually writes something. Indira mocks me when I say things like that out loud. Douglas is the pretentious one, the adman prima donna with his peacocky stylings and ambitions. I am the workhorse, the dark horse. I play the role too well.

No, this year can't be another twelve months on the hamster wheel. It's time to live. To breathe. To die and be reborn.

I am going to write something this year.

Carpe diem and all that crap.

January 7

The flat is our office. The office is our flat. Like all good start-ups, we live and breathe the magazine. Beer o'clock. Siesta time. But, more often, toil and trouble.

The three amigos in our Camden flat. Indy is serenity incarnate. Doug is as Dougie-tastic as ever: smart, flamboyant, seethingly ambitious, intermittently kind. That poster-boy coolness. 'No man is a hero to his valet.' It must be updated: no man is a hero to those with whom they share a bathroom in a small flat.

But life, surely, is more than twenty-something marketing bros with faultless hair and too much moisturiser. The next birthday is the last acceptable one to celebrate. After that is an abyss of rising numbers and plummeting metabolism. It is wrinkles, belly fat and the slow gravitational slide into well-earned mediocrity.

I sit here and pick up my copy of *In Cold Blood* and

read it for the zillionth time. I can write something like this. I can be as waspish and austere as Truman Capote with his tilted fedora and camp, piggy eyes. Apparently, Capote was inspired by a 300-word article in the *New York Times*. So I must hunt for inspiration too.

I must write something.

I need a decent murder.

24

BEN

Harley Street feels even quieter after the bustle of Whitehall. I return to the Abbey through the back entrance, wary of any freelance journalists sniffing for a story.

Bloom is in her office finishing a call. My own office has been cleaned since last night and thoroughly aerated. I sit at my desk and try to process what Emily told me about the final incident. It was a summer trip to Greece to celebrate Anna's graduation. Emily woke up in the middle of the night. Anna was screaming in her room. Emily opened the door and tried to help. Anna lashed out and attacked her. Anna's eyes were open. But, like before, she was no longer Emily's daughter. She'd become someone else.

I check my emails then debrief Bloom on the first part of the interview. She looks at me in that owlish way of hers, like a sage quietly troubled by her pupil.

Finally, she says, 'And you're sure about the sleepwalking diagnosis?'

'It's all there in that WhatsApp message. "I'm sorry. I think I've killed them." Anna woke up to find the two bodies and the knife in her hand. Classic sleepwalking. Or she was still sleepwalking when she sent the message.'

'Or she was never sleepwalking and has simply used sleep as a way to get away with murder.'

'Yes,' I say. It is the most common conspiracy theory, the key argument for the Sleeping Beauty brigade. 'Or that.'

'What about further back?'

'There were three specific incidents we know of. The family holiday when Anna was nine years old, the school incident when she was a teenager, and the time Anna attacked Emily when she'd just turned twenty-one.'

'With a common trigger?'

'Yes. Change or trauma of some kind. Holiday, boarding school, leaving Oxford. Emily worried the stories would leak if they sought treatment, so she hushed it up.'

Bloom nods, sighs. She laces the fingers of one hand into another. There are even more vintage rings than usual. 'I suppose it explains why the sleepwalking theory was never raised seriously in the press.'

'It also explains why it wasn't anywhere in her medical notes. Emily did try raising it during the police interview, apparently, but it was written off as special pleading.'

Bloom adjusts her feet on the small footrest. I look at her now and wonder what she returns to each night. She lives alone. Her long-term partner died six years ago. Their two-bed house in Islington is filled with books, all of them nicotine-yellow at the page tips. I imagine Bloom padding around the empty space and contemplating retirement. Perhaps that's why she clings on here. She needs an audience. Old age doesn't suit her.

'There was nothing else?'

'Incidental trivia. Your old beat, actually. Anna was working on some true crime piece for *Elementary* magazine before the attack. She was looking into Broadmoor and the Sally Turner case.'

There is silence. Pure, uncomfortable. Bloom seems distracted, then says, 'Sally Turner?'

'Yes.'

'You're absolutely sure? The Stockwell Monster?' Bloom's voice is different now.

'Why?'

Bloom is still staring into the middle distance. I wonder why the name Sally Turner provokes such a strong reaction. Beyond the obvious, of course. Sally Turner is like Harold Shipman or Myra Hindley – a name etched into the national consciousness. She joins Eve and Medea as shorthand for evil femininity, the wicked stepmother.

I go on. 'At the end Emily also gave me something else. A personal item from Anna's bedroom.' I take the small black paperback out of my rucksack and hold it up. '*Medea* by Euripides. Apparently, Anna started reading it obsessively before the incident at the Farm. It became her second favourite book after *In Cold Blood*. There are some pencil annotations inside. Emily thought it might help me understand Anna's state of mind in the lead-up to the attack.'

Now the unease on Bloom's face worsens. She doesn't speak.

I'm unnerved by Bloom's reaction. I wonder if I've missed something. I track back through what I've said. The Medea reference. Sally Turner. The Stockwell Monster.

'What is it? Why do those names bother you?'

Bloom's voice is snappy, irritated, as if I've interrupted a train of thought. 'Do we have a second source on the rest or just the mother's word?'

'Not yet. There's a chance we might still be able to recover the CCTV footage from Anna's school.'

Bloom shakes her head. 'The school will have scrubbed the footage immediately to bury the scandal.'

She rearranges her face quickly now. She is the master of that. There is a performative aspect to her: the clothes, the epigrammatic wit, the self-styled detachment from sentimentalism. She is back on full form. The anxiety has been carefully wiped. The vulnerability gone.

'Medea,' she says, her voice musing and abstract. 'A woman

who enters history as the archetype of evil. A mother who kills her own children. One step up from a woman who slays her two best friends.'

'What is it?' The unease grips me tighter, the mystery deepening.

She continues, as if I'm not even there. 'Can two wrongs ever make a right? Is evil something that must be exterminated from the body, a psychological cancer, rebuilding the patient from scratch? Or is it inherited, biological? What does evil even mean?'

There is a disturbing intensity to Bloom now. She stares at the bookshelves, lost to the present. I have rarely heard her talk like this. I feel the dog-eared corners of the paperback in my palms. I look down at the cover of the Penguin Classics edition of *Medea and Other Plays*. It shows two figures in burned orange, a mother and a child. The child reaches out a hand. The mother presses down on the child's head.

The silence is broken by Bloom. She huffs and puffs her way out of the chair, gravity working against her. 'I'm sorry, Ben. But there's something I've got to attend to. I'm not feeling all that well.'

I have known Bloom for over twenty years. Never once has she asked me to leave.

'Is there anything I can do to help?'

She stares at me and looks defeated. 'No,' she says, 'you've done quite enough.'

Then she hurries me out of the door.

25

BLOOM

It's almost 8.15 p.m. by the time Bloom decides to leave the Abbey. But, even then, she can't quite make it to the door.

She stops pacing and reluctantly takes her seat again. She is panicking, which is the very thing she tells others not to do. Panic induces a fight-or-flight response. The body tenses, the mind fogs, all instinct is forgotten. No, she is getting too old for this. She hardly sleeps at all now. There are too many memories, too much past.

All she can hear is that snippet from Ben's interview with Emily. Anna's last piece for *Elementary* magazine.

Broadmoor. Sally Turner.

And that one word. If only he hadn't mentioned that single godforsaken word.

Medea.

It can't be. And yet . . .

Bloom takes a key from her cardigan pocket and unlocks the bottom drawer of her desk. Her palm is moist, licking the key with sweat. The drawer opens and she reaches inside, removing a weathered patient file with tea-stained pages and a blue cardboard cover.

All medical notes, of course, are meant to be properly declared.

Nowadays this sort of extra-curricular scribbling would be a sackable offence. And yet this patient file is her form of protection. She needs a record of the past: dates, times, session notes, all of it decipherable only to her.

She scrolls back until she finds the entries: 'July 2nd, 1999. Cranfield Ward, Broadmoor Hospital'. The sessions are still so vivid. Usually, she only has hazy memories of patients. But not this one. It was among her first cases at Broadmoor. That ghoulish, benighted place with its asylum smell and towering Victorian walls. All these years later, she can pick out the individual moments. This patient was always singular, even as a child.

Her hands shake. She is full of arthritic tics and twitches. It is fear. She turns the page, feeling the edge dampen with her touch. She thinks of Anna lying nearby, muffled by sleep. The case has become so marbled by rumour that it is difficult to separate fact from fiction. Now, after what Ben has told her, the danger has returned.

Bloom reads the final page of the patient file. She gets up and ignores her coat. Instead, the bare facts of the case repeat themselves: the Farm, the knife, the two bodies, the Ogilvy family, the police arriving.

August 30th, 1999.

August 30th, 2019.

The twentieth anniversary.

It is possible. That's what frightens her most. It is possible that this case is not what anyone thinks at all. That returning Anna to the Abbey isn't coincidence or luck but something far more sinister indeed.

She looks at the next line and the name at the top: 'Patient X'. The alias was given by the Home Office. It was designed to ensure the name couldn't leak, avoid a repeat of similar cases earlier in the decade.

Bloom locks her office door. She takes the lift down to the ground floor and barely registers the nods from the reception team. Yes, she is convinced. She can feel it in her water, in the deepest and darkest depths of her soul.

Something is wrong here.

Something is very wrong indeed.

ANNA'S NOTEBOOK
2019

January 14

The kitchen is squalid. Crusty pans, foamy glasses, cutlery scabbed with blood-rust Bolognese. It is there that I discover Douglas's iPhone, still running a timer from last night's dinner. His passcode is easy: 100194. His birthday.

Douglas is not an original man.

I snoop, as I like to sometimes. It is the wannabe investigative journalist in me. I applied for all the starry grad schemes: *Times*, *Telegraph*, *FT*. Reader, I failed. It's why I started *Elementary*, hiding conventional career failure under the gloss of a start-up, like all good media entrepreneurs.

I continue scrolling through Doug's phone. There is a surprising absence of scandal. Few flirty exchanges, no questionable viewing activities. I imagined more dirt. But there is one new WhatsApp group that wasn't there the last time I pried.

'Takeover Talk'.

There is only one other user. I recognise Indy's number. It's almost as familiar as my own.

I scroll and read and mull. I know what this is about. Deep down. I have seen the looks between them. The furtive discussions that end whenever I enter the room. I have sensed the distance growing between us.

Indira: Meet set up with GVM biz affairs. 2pm.

Douglas: Coffee with accountant. Next week?

Indira: Best on private email. I've set up joint account to discuss RO etc. xx

The chat clearly migrates to an encrypted email channel. I wonder if they suspect I might pry. I must snoop further and find the private email.

A website for GV Media comes up on Google. It is a new media brand based in Seattle with a mix of ad-supported digital platforms and subscription titles specialising in late millennial and Gen Z consumers. The predator. *Elementary* being the prey. Indira and Douglas are the so-called commercial brains of the operation. I am relegated to idiot savant, the artist in her draughty garret. Tied to a laptop like some sweatshop grunt and tapping out copy until I die. I search for 'RO' too. Alongside mildly obscene slang usage, it is apparently a financial acronym for 'roll-over' which means: 'the reinvestment of funds, as from one stock or bond into another'.

Typical Indy with her MBA pretensions and City girl acronyms. A woman who eats coins for a living. Those messages stir up thoughts. Much like the thoughts I used to have. Back then. BC rather than AD. I feel the rumblings start and take a long walk.

I must sleep tonight.

Yes, it will all be better in the morning.

January 21

I have fantasies sometimes. I think Freud would call them daydreams. *Studies in Hysteria* is the only one of his I like. I keep seeing those prim Viennese women trundling towards Berggasse 19 with their immaculate frock coats and oh-so-refined repression.

I turn towards the first chapter. Written by Breuer, rather than Freud, a widespread misconception. It concerns the first-ever patient of psychoanalysis. My namesake. I read:

> Fraulein Anna O. fell ill at the age of twenty-one (1880) . . .
> Of considerable intelligence, remarkably acute powers of reasoning, and a clear-sighted intuitive sense, her powerful mind could have digested, needed even, more substantial intellectual nourishment, but failed to receive it once she had left school. Her rich poetic and imaginative gifts were controlled by a very sharp and critical common sense . . .
> Her will was energetic, tenacious and persistent.

I wonder if there is a single word that doesn't apply to me. I imagine 'Anna' in 1880 – almost 140 years ago now – but who still seems so vivid on the page. That's what fascinates me about writing. Perhaps it's why I do it. Anna O is as alive to us today as she was to original readers in 1895.

The right words in the right order can confer immortality. They turn flesh-and-blood people into literary Olympians. Words are an elixir.

Sleep is a struggle now. I am too frightened to close my eyes. I can feel the past returning. The ghosts of my own histories let loose. I see those old illusions, the ones that felt so real, and I stay awake.

I wish I could be normal.

Most of the time.

January 28

The flat. The living room. The sofa with a Pret salad and Aldi wine. Indira and Douglas are out seeing an advertiser at the Ned apparently. I know they are really sipping margaritas at Scarfes Bar in Holborn with one of the GVM business affairs team. I see them finishing the meeting and sneaking off to a room. But, no, I am back to daydreams again. I am editorial. They are sales. They are doing what salespeople do.

Man United lost with a disappointingly apathetic display tonight. I miss those old TV sessions with Dad. It is the one thing we used to do together. Sometimes I imagine Dad watching the game in a hotel room on his travels and I message him to trade tactics about which striker is useless and why we need a new right back. Sometimes he even replies. Money interests him more than people or offspring.

I am tired. It's ragged, bone-aching, mind-fuzzing tiredness. Matchstick eyes. I try and calculate how long it's been since my last episode. I pick up my iPad and Google 'sleepwalking cures' again.

I imagine Indy and Doug at the bar. Then lying on the ground, blood pooling round them both. The thought is sticky, lingering, troubling. I get up, turn off the TV, make a strong black coffee with three ladles of Nescafé. I retreat to my room and lock the door and place a chair against it.

I check the windows are locked. I do my breathing. I long for the light of the morning.

I want the night to end.

26

BEN

It is already dark. I stand by my office window and watch Bloom leave. I track her unmistakable stride towards Great Portland Street for the lonely Tube journey home. Her reaction this afternoon won't leave me. I can hear the violence of the words, that flash of certainty about rebuilding a patient from scratch.

I am the last senior figure here. The other nurses and agency staff bustle around floor two. We have six patients in residential care tonight, including Anna. The others are: an insurance broker, an investment banker, a Swiss divorcee, a former Cabinet Minister and an international rugby player. They are wealthy, but not paparazzi famous. All five can live without fear of being hounded. None of them know that, nearby, lies the most famous murder suspect in the world.

Anna O, Sleeping Beauty, a figure of myth and reality.

I enter the passcode for the VIP wing. I realise for the first time that I'm looking forward to seeing Harriet again. I feel a mild thrill, so unusual these days. It catches me off guard.

I stand by the door and spend a moment watching Harriet with Anna. There is a familiar rhythm between them, despite Anna's condition. They operate more like siblings than patient

111

and carer. Harriet is tender with Anna, wiping her face delicately, always treating her as a person rather than a fleshy, bed-bound body.

I stay there and lose track of how long I've been watching. Eventually, Harriet spots me. I catch a small smile. She turns and begins packing up for the day now. She looks smaller in her coat, hair loose.

'Mind if I drop in?'

'It's your gaff, doc. Not mine.'

That is technically true. But it's a golden rule to never annoy the nurses. 'I've met a lot of nurses who would disagree.'

'Do you think I'm one of them?'

'I think you know more than most neurologists and psychiatrists. Certainly more than most psychologists.'

'You do yourself and your profession down. You shouldn't.'

Her honesty stops me. I realise that humour has become a defence mechanism, a way to cover for professional insecurities. There is something gentle but firm in her voice.

'You're right. I don't know why I keep saying it.'

'If you say it enough times a myth can become reality.'

'Now you sound exactly like a psychologist.'

She smiles, even squints comically at me. 'What did I just tell you?'

'Sorry, sorry. No more picking on lowly psychologists.'

'Glad to hear it.'

I miss this sort of camaraderie. The downside of having A-list clients is the lack of bedside chat. Everything is expensive, which means everything is rather po-faced too. I like Harriet. She is fresh and new, something this place badly needs. 'Anything I should know?'

We click into professional mode now. Harriet updates me on today's activities: exercising Anna's legs and core muscles; hydration; the usual prompts of old TV shows. There is a small adjacent washroom. I scrub my hands thoroughly and then put on a mask and gloves. Harriet zips her jacket but stays as I finish my preparations. We exist in studious silence as I finish the last part, the final prop from the dressing-up box, and wave her a gloved hand goodbye. With another warmer, freckly smile, she is gone.

The treatment room is like the holy of holies. The gloves, the mask, the blinking monitors and tubes – all of it is theatre. I sit down on the small stool placed to the right of the bed. I see the camera above me, the levels of voyeurism multiplying. Me watching Anna. The camera watching me. Harriet sometimes watching us both.

There is a line from *The Tempest* that I used as the title of my first book on sleep disorders and dream analysis: 'We were dead of sleep.' It seems apt now. I look at Anna's thin, peaceful face. I think of the stories Emily told me: the kitchen knife plunged into the dog's flesh, the pretend hunt the following day; the calculation with which Anna stole the items from the house-mistress's flat at boarding school; the terrifying attack in the Athens hotel room, bludgeoning her own mother with demonic fury.

I imagine living a second life without knowing how or why. Human beings can endure so much pain but no more. At some point the body and the mind hibernate, protecting themselves. It is called resignation syndrome for a reason.

My phone pings. I disobey the rules and take it out of my trouser pocket. There is an email from Richard Ogilvy, eventually replying to my earlier message. He has copied in his PA who has already followed up with a suggested time for a meeting. I ignore it for now. Instead, I open the email Emily Ogilvy sent me after our interview. It contains a list of songs Anna listened to as a child: 'Yesterday' by the Beatles, 'Imagine' by John Lennon, 'Tiny Dancer' by Elton John and 'Songbird' by Eva Cassidy. It is all part of my therapeutic model. As is the Penguin Classics edition of *Medea and Other Plays*. I reach into my bag and take it out. I look at the figure in the bed and the annotations on the page.

Past and present meeting.

'Imagine' is already downloaded on my Spotify. The familiar piano chords start. I watch the monitors and Anna's reaction. If my sensation theory is correct – if my entire diagnosis is at all accurate – this sound will continue to stir something. Soothing the unconscious with memories of the past: safety, hope, security. Anna has been denied stimulus for over four years. It's time to correct that.

John Lennon's mournful voice penetrates the silence. It's like an echo from another universe. I look for the faintest uptick on the monitor, a ripple on Anna's face. But, before I have a chance to see anything, the volume of the Spotify track fades.

My phone starts buzzing.

I want to dismiss it.

Then I see Bloom's name on the caller ID.

27

X

Professor Bloom is old. That is the first advantage. The younger Bloom wouldn't have been so careless. No, that Bloom would always have been one step ahead: aware of the phoneline at the Abbey being bugged; the cameras nestled in her office; each movement monitored and analysed for exactly this moment.

But real people are so messy, so disappointing.

Old age does that, even to the very best.

Take the security precautions, for example. The house locks are standard, as is the security system. The replica key works. The door clicks open. The entrance is noiseless, barely audible through the mottled glass of the inside door. The code for the alarm is personal, memorable. The date of a deceased partner's birthday. The light blinks and the security system relaxes.

It is so familiar inside, like returning home. There is the retro seventies décor in the hallway and those old, kitschy countryside paintings on the walls. Dust smears the furniture tops. The entire place is fogged with a funereal, light-starved gloom. The professor's voice rings through the small house, broken only by occasional pauses and the rattle of movement. She is on the phone to someone.

There is a mention of Anna Ogilvy, then a pause.

Shoes off here, socked feet on the carpet. There is a task to perform, a mission to complete. The gloved hands will leave no dabs on the door handles; the knife will ensure the job is quick, and nearly painless. Bloom deserves that much at least. Chaotic murders are for amateurs. This is calculated down to the very last detail.

Bloom's voice falls silent. There is a fuzz of movement, as if she suspects something. Slowly now. The study – a typically cramped space piled high with old newspapers – is directly ahead, the door minutely ajar. It is another sign of Bloom's forgetful state. But the study is too obvious. No, this needs to take place elsewhere. The victim must be drawn out towards the main room.

The memories threaten here. Other thoughts, too. They can wait. This must be tended to first. Bloom has made the connection. She must be dealt with, just like the other victims. It is basic logic, primal self-preservation.

The study door opens further. The grey hair with its disorderly plume, the tent-like ripple of her clothes.

Yes, this must happen now.

There is no time for mercy.

28

BEN

Everything moves quickly after the call.

Already I can feel the gravity of this situation. The mystery of her instructions to me. The fear in Bloom's voice.

No, not fear.

Terror.

Yes, it is more than fright. Much, much more.

I imagine my movements being analysed in the days to come by detectives. It's not enough to be innocent.

No, I must act innocently too. From this point onwards.

One mistake will undo me.

I debate how to reach Bloom's house. Uber is playing up. The Tube will take too long. I look at the time, calculate how empty the roads will be. There's no time to leave instructions for the other staff.

I grab my phone and jacket and head onto Harley Street, praying for the caramel glow of an empty cab. I find one near Oxford Street and give the address for Bloom's home in Islington. Then I leave a voice message for the senior nurse on duty at the Abbey explaining I've been called away.

I check the time and see it's already late. I try calling Bloom's number again, but there is no answer. I debate whether to call the police. But Bloom was insistent. This must be dealt with privately. Only me. Her instructions were clear.

I can't start doubting her now.

The cab slices through the rainy streets of central London and heads north. The view is soaked with lamplight and the ghostly embers of shops still ablaze but deserted. I replay the conversation but can make no more sense of it. All I can hear is the sound of unease behind every syllable. Bloom is the bravest person I know. Terror doesn't come easily. But her voice was laced with panic.

Listen carefully, Ben. There's something I need you to do.

It feels like an eternity until we reach the approach for Islington. I can see the garish signs for overnight roadworks. There is a spectral menace to the whole thing: the traffic lights, the growl of engines, the echo of Bloom's voice on the phone.

The cabbie parps his horn at a car dawdling in front of us. My entire upper body is damp. We are nearly there, I know, a minute from the signature front gate of Virginia Bloom's long-time North London bolthole.

But too much time has already gone. I can't wait any longer. 'Just drop me here.'

I pay. I check the time again. I hear Bloom's voice.

I get out of the cab. I see the tail of vehicles behind us and the emptiness ahead as the builders pause to let vehicles through.

The cab speeds off. My muscles feel like iron. I know the way, or think I do, and finally escape the industrial fury of cars and builders. I am racing down a snicket, emerging onto a tree-lined street of shabbier housing. I am nearly there.

I replay Bloom's instructions.

The file. You must find the file.

I see the house ahead of me. The oak door and the dull, quiet normality of it all.

The dread, even a premonition, of something terrible waiting for me inside.

Even before I reach the front door, I know it doesn't feel right.

I ring the buzzer of Bloom's home. But there is no answer. I can smell the unease, the danger. My mind fills with possibilities: blood trickling across the carpet, butchery behind the humdrum facade, the worst catalogue of human crimes.

What if this is how it ends. One foolhardy act and a knife between the ribs by a killer trying to make their escape. My throat slit. Dying here as nothing more than collateral, an afterthought to another murder. So dramatic and yet so mundane. In this mothy house on a quiet street. Dumb bad luck. Nothing meaningful or noble, but the wrong place at the wrong time.

I ring the bell one more time.

I try her phone again. Nothing.

My hand is shaking. Courage leaves me. I'm afraid. More than that. Bloom's terror is contagious. Every part of me wants to survive this. It is instinct, basic biology.

When there's still no sound inside, I search under the flowerpot for the spare key.

I must not walk away. Despite everything, I must do what I came here to do.

All I can hear is that tone of animal alarm. That childish pitch and strain in her voice on the phone.

Ben, what if Anna Ogilvy coming to the Abbey isn't just chance or coincidence? What if it's something more?

The key works. I wish it didn't. I am through. The musty smell, the dated carpet, the shrine to elaborate 1970s design. I call out here, confusion building, part of me still hoping for an innocent explanation. For the panic to lift, calm to restore.

There is still no reply.

I pass through the kitchen and enter the living room. As I open the door, those horrible premonitions grip me again. Sickly, cloying almost. I have attended crime scenes, witnessed death in the raw. Once done, it can't be undone. Mortality clings like a smell.

I hear a sound elsewhere in the house. A thud, a footfall. My senses conjure all sorts of fears. In this heightened state, I can almost taste the hot breath of the attacker, feel the coolness of the blade.

But I can't think like that now.

I focus on the present. I hear another sound. Waiting for me. Someone or something. I am the next victim, stupid enough to be here alone. More sounds. An old house twitching in the wind. An open window, a half-shut door.

Or a killer waiting patiently for its prey.

I breathe. Concentrate.

The call, the drive, the key under the mat. I have been here before. I have tasted an atmosphere like this. I turn back to the living room and walk further inside.

And then I see it before I'm ready.

Professor Bloom's body lying there in front of me.

Sleeping like the dead.

ANNA'S NOTEBOOK

2019

February 4

Home, again. Or the parental chateau. Schloss Ogilvy. The Hampstead House of Horrors. Both parental figures are absent, as ever. Or as good as. Mum is politicking in her study. She barely raises an eyebrow at my arrival. Dad is printing money in New York City and probably romancing some Eiffel Tower blonde with impeccable lashes and a degree from Wharton.

Theo is my only company. The freelance TV presenter life involves lots of resting. This is a temporary rest after the last temporary rest. I pretend to believe him. He pretends to pretend that I am not pretending. I almost tell him about the takeover. But siblings can't show weakness to one another.

It is an Ogilvy family rule.

Eventually, Mum emerges from her lair and pours a large glass of wine. Theo disappears with friends to some flea-bitten club in Mayfair. Dad FaceTimes from Manhattan.

I boot up the BBC Sounds app on my iPhone and look at the My Sounds section and see the show I have saved, daring myself to listen. BBC Radio 4. *Mysteries of Sleep*.

The presenter is a neurologist and sleep expert called Dr Guy Leschziner. There are three episodes: 'Sleepwalking', 'Dreaming' and 'Sleep Deprivation and Insomnia'. The last two don't interest me. I long for insomnia. I have night terrors rather than dreams.

No, the thing I fear is sleep.

I order a Deliveroo and retreat to my old family bedroom and lie on the bedcover. I feel the pressure in my head, the slight tightness around my jaw, like a harbinger of another episode, a return of the sickness. The looming inevitability.

I will stay for tonight. It is safer here. The bedroom is pre-equipped, after all. Sturdier locks on the door. Firmer chairs to barricade me in. More furniture to trip over and bruise me back to life. Indy messages asking where I am. I think of telling her about their Proton email account, all the messages I've seen, the snooping I've done.

But I don't. Lying is so much simpler.

I reread the blurb for the podcast, willing myself to confront my demons.

Finally, I press play.

February 11

I have listened to the first episode of *Mysteries of Sleep* six times. In the shower, on the bus, while writing.

I listen to the story of 'Jackie' who has been a sleepwalker all her life. She gets up, leaves the house and rides her motorbike with her eyes open. But her brain is still asleep.

'James' has night terrors which are so violent and shocking that his marriage has been driven to the point of collapse.

'Alex' is convinced that he must save people from floods and is found by his flatmates trying to stop invisible people drowning.

Then, most disturbingly of all, there is 'Tom': he was

convicted of raping his ex-partner. Once out of prison, he was diagnosed with a condition called sexsomnia. His version of sleepwalking involves sex acts. His eyes are open. He appears fully conscious. But tests show his brain is stuck in a non-REM parasomnia.

It is a few days later. I can't stop thinking about this. I am on the 'Sleepwalking' page on Wikipedia. I am transfixed by the bottom section:

> As sleepwalking behaviours occur without volition, sleep-walking can be used as a legal defense. An individual can be accused of non-insane or insane automatism. The first is used as a defense for temporary insanity or involuntary conduct, resulting in acquittal. The latter results in a "special verdict of not guilty by reason of insanity." This verdict of insanity can result in a court order to attend a mental institution.

There is a quote from Lord Morris, a former judge and Law Lord, from 1963 in the case of Bratty vs A-G for Northern Ireland. Lord M said that if a person committed a violent crime while unconscious 'then such a person would not be criminally liable for that act'. Thus precedent was set.

Beneath is a list of homicide cases involving sleepwalking. I have memorised them. The names of those acquitted blur: 'The Boston Tragedy' (1846), Sergeant Willis Boshears (1961), Steven Steinberg of Scottsdale, Arizona (1981), R vs Burgess (1991), the defendant found not guilty by reason of 'insane automatism', R vs Parks (1992), heard at the Canadian Supreme Court.

Then the list of those not acquitted: Pennsylvania vs Ricksgers (1994), Arizona vs Falater (1999) and California vs Reitz (2001). In the last instance, the defendant's parents testified about their son's lifelong sleepwalking. He was still convicted of first-degree murder.

Finally, the hospitalisation cases. In 2001, Antonio Nieto killed his wife and mother-in-law and attempted to murder his son and daughter before waking. He was interned in a psychiatric hospital. In 2003 Jules Lowe killed his father but claimed he didn't remember the murder and used the legal defence of automatism. He was acquitted by reason of insanity and detained in a secure hospital.

I have been too afraid before. I shut it off and hoped it wasn't real. But there is so much to explore. From the comic ('Sleepwalker mows lawn naked') to the disturbing ('Sleepwalking woman had sex with strangers', *New Scientist*, 2004) to a case I distantly remember on the news. It is an article from the *Independent*.

MAN WHO KILLED HIS WIFE
WHILE SLEEPING GOES FREE

A man who strangled his wife during a nightmare in the belief he was attacking an intruder walked free from court yesterday after the case against him was withdrawn. Brian Thomas, 59, of Neath, South Wales, killed his wife Christine, 57, while they were holidaying in West Wales in July 2008 . . . The prosecution told the jury that it was no longer seeking a verdict of not guilty by reason of insanity.

I read the whole article. I do more research on the other cases. There is one entry on the Wikipedia page, however, which lassoes my attention. I was too young to remember it. But every student of true crime knows the name. It was the original tabloid crime. A byword for evil.

I look at the final paragraph and the brief commentary. It is the most notable sleep-related British homicide of them all:

1999, R vs Turner: Sally Turner was accused of murdering her two stepchildren in Stockwell with a kitchen knife in January 1999. She claimed to have no memory of the attack and used the legal defence of insane automatism or sleepwalking. Despite a public outcry and rival expert psychological opinion regarding the diagnosis, Turner was found not guilty by reason of insanity and sentenced indefinitely to Broadmoor Hospital in Berkshire. Turner was found dead in her room on August 30th, 1999. The coroner ruled it as suicide.

Sally Turner. Aka the Stockwell Monster.

I click on the dedicated Sally Turner Wikipedia page. I read the section about her suicide. A sharpened plastic knife was found in her room. No one knows how it got there. Eight years later, all female patients were moved out of Broadmoor. Some went to Rampton Secure Hospital; others were housed in The Orchard, a medium-secure unit in West London.

I see the true crime documentary already. And the germ of my long-form piece. Truman Capote had the *New York Times*. I have Wikipedia.

My inspiration. The spark.

A twentieth anniversary retrospective. Women, madness, murder, morals. With a newsy hook.

Did Sally Turner kill herself or was the Stockwell Monster murdered?

I finally have my story.

PART THREE

29

BEN

She is lying in the small dining room.

Even without checking Bloom's pulse, I'm aware in abstract that she is dead. The blood, the wounds, the knife by the body. Shock stuns me. But I need the physical proof. I am crouching now, trying to understand this. The knife looks so plain and insubstantial, the weight of it. I pick it up instinctively. The shine of the blade. The smooth heat of the handle. The angle to the body. Yes, the physical proof is the only thing that makes it real.

Bloom's eyes are glazed in a way which can't be faked, as if the soul has evaporated clean from the body. I replay her call in my mind, still sweaty after the rush from the Abbey. I hear the fevered tone. Those final instructions.

I see the knife still clasped in my hand and, suddenly, sense returns.

I place it back.

I finally understand what Anna Ogilvy must have felt that night on the Farm. Anna standing in the doorway of the Red Cabin. Her two best friends lying there before her, their bodies punctured with knife wounds. I imagine the overwhelming, obliterating psychological shock. The full scale of what she had done. The infamous nature of the crime she committed. Twenty stab wounds in all. Again and again and again.

I look around now, suddenly calculating every movement. Bloom's words were clear. I walk into the adjoining kitchen and see a box of Kleenex tissues by the sink. I take several and wipe my palms, careful not to let my fingers graze the box side, already aware of leaving any dabs which can't be explained later.

It is madness, even now. The knife. The handle in my palm. I should call it in immediately. I know that. But Bloom was adamant on the phone.

There is one task to complete first.

I know the house almost like my own. Bloom's study is a former bedroom converted into a home office, complete with a dusty TV set and acres of mouldy newsprint. Old magazines jostle for space with hardbacks and paperbacks in regimental order. I reach the study now, careful not to let my fingerprints smudge on the door handle, already unsure how I can explain this later.

There's a document I need you to find.

Bloom's safe is hidden beneath a cabinet door to the right of the desk. I crouch down and use the tissue to shield my fingers. I type in the passcode: 1895. It is her signature, the publication date for Freud and Breuer's *Studies in Hysteria*, the start of modern psychology. The moment that changed medicine.

The safe light is green. I ease the silver door open. In typical Bloomian fashion, the safe is heaving with files of various colours and ages.

The blue file. Beneath all the others. The cardboard file.

I sift through the files, noting the titles. I am sweating. I must avoid leaving a drip-trail of clues. Bloom chose me to do this because she knew I had the necessary expertise. I was her last contact. Other than Clara, I was her last true friend.

I remove the blue file. I see Bloom's scrawl in red biro on the front with the case reference number. My usual teaching bag is with me, a scuffed and trusty old Gladstone. I place the file inside and belt the lanyards shut, before closing the safe door and checking there are no signs of my presence here.

Once I am sure, I pocket the tissue and leave the study.

I resume my position in the small dining room and take out my phone.

For whatever reason, Bloom didn't want the world to know her secret. The last few minutes never happened. The names on the phone screen flicker. This next call could determine everything.

I look at Bloom's body again and make my decision.

Only one person can help me now.

30

BEN

Thirty minutes later I watch Clara turn into the road and stop her car outside Bloom's house. The vehicle she's using is police issue but unmarked. After the trauma of the last few hours, I feel a whole-body relief.

She takes a breath and switches into professional mode: safe, resilient, calm. I was always the brooder, consumed by events. Only once in all our time together did those roles reverse. Sometimes I still hear the plates and glasses smashing on the kitchen floor, the residue of those overwhelming rages, begging her to eat but being met with silence, before slowly the shadow and depression passed. She became Clara again. Our roles switched back. They have remained so ever since.

I sit on the front step, shivering in the cold. She beeps the car locked and glances at the house and the door still slightly ajar.

'Ben?'

I strengthen now, recovering some dignity. I stand up. She looks behind me and sees fresh vomit on the grass.

'You said it was an emergency.'

'It is. Clara . . . it's Bloom.'

And then I tell her: the call, the cab ride, the house, the dining room, the body.

I watch as she absorbs the news. There is pain, then detachment. It is why Clara is such a good detective, sacrificing part of herself in a way I can't. She can distance herself from events, separate personal emotion from professional evidence.

She heads into the crime scene alone. I wait outside on her orders and run through everything again. I think of the file and the lie I just told Clara and wonder what other mistakes I've already made, like picking up the knife. Then, quicker than I expected, she is outside again. She calls it in and moves into fluent police-speak. I spot the shake of her hand, the mirror-shine of tears. The small human frailties poking through the mask.

The Met cavalry descend within the hour. Police cordons are erected. Forensic vans line the street. Clara is locked in earnest conversation with her colleagues. I'm guided to an unmarked car and given tea.

I sit and sip and watch the circus around me. Any moment now the pain will start. Bloom was more than just a friend. For both Clara and me, she was like family. I can't imagine the world without her. Or perhaps I just don't want to.

At last, Clara finishes issuing instructions. She is in a full forensic suit now, lowering her mask just enough to be audible.

She comes up beside me, looking enviously at my cup of tea. 'They'll need your clothes shortly for elimination.'

I nod. This is Clara at her best. The forensic intelligence, quiet competence, warm bedside manner. Marrying her was my greatest achievement; separation was my greatest mistake. I miss her more than I ever thought possible.

'Of course.'

'We'll have to take you down to the station and get you to sign your statement. Given the potential conflict of interest, another SIO will take over from here.'

'I understand.'

The formalities over, Clara stands and takes a moment. She chokes down the raw emotion. 'Christ, Ben, I'm sorry. I just can't believe this has happened.'

The shock is so fresh. I'm consumed with Bloom's call, the panic in her voice, the order to retrieve the file. Something in it triggered Bloom's moment of revelation. Something which also sheds new light on the mystery of Anna Ogilvy.

The noise from the house jolts me back to the present. There is something jarring about the forensic teams against Bloom's decaying home. I imagine it as a salon, like those cafés in Vienna before the war or Paris in the twenties. I see Bloom holding court, circled by poets, artists, psychologists, musicians and writers. So much life has been extinguished tonight. An entire epoch fallen.

'I assume cause of death is fairly straightforward?'

Clara nods to some fellow techs. The pain on her face lessens now. 'The pathologist will be here shortly. But it looks like the stab wounds sliced right through her. She never stood a chance.'

Memories pierce the stillness. I see the kitchen knife lying there on the floor and the sprinkle of blood. In the haze of it all, the shock pulsing through me – yes, the memory is clear, horribly so, in fact – I am stooping down, disorientated, hungry for answers.

The thought overwhelms me. I can't suppress it. Fear pinches at me until the pain is overwhelming.

The truth, the anxiety.

'There's something else,' I say, looking to Clara and feeling sick. I think about getting Bloom's call, the sense of having to account for my actions. I can't break now. 'It's about the knife.'

ANNA'S NOTEBOOK
2019

February 18

A night alone with Indira. Wine, food, more bad telly. Up close, Indira is sickeningly symmetrical. She has that gazelle-like, wafty presence. My mum loves her, Dad too. They wish I was more Indy and less me.

Like all creatives, I do fireball intensity, a Jekyll-and-Hyde act that blows loud and mute, depending on how the mood takes me. Indira belongs on Mount Rushmore or among the statues in Parliament Square. Economics degree, Finance master's, Bloomberg grad scheme. Master of the Media Universe.

I have seen the latest emails on the takeover. I glimpsed Douglas's Proton account when he was too stoned to notice. Lawyers. Accountants. The CFO at GV Media. The big boys and girls. Figures mooted. Dates referenced. Terms and conditions scrutinised.

Indira asks how I'm feeling. She notes my symptoms: red-eyed, sleeping pills, GP appointment, specialist referral. She has no idea about the locks, the chair, the ritual of night-time. She doesn't know about the past or what I am capable of.

I lie and say everything is okay. I am a decent liar.

I beg off early and go to my room.

In bed, the sleep research continues. I type and click and scroll. I get deeper into the theme of sleeping sickness. I discover an article in the *New Yorker* from 2017 on refugee children in Sweden who fall into a permanent sleep as they face deportation. In particular, the heartbreaking tale of a Russian refugee called Georgi:

> All he wanted to do was close his eyes. Even swallowing required an effort that he didn't feel he could muster . . . He hadn't eaten for four days and had not spoken a full sentence in a week . . . The next day, a doctor inserted a feeding tube through Georgi's nostril . . . Georgi was given a diagnosis of *uppgivenhetssyndrom*, or resignation syndrome.

I type 'resignation syndrome' into Google. Even more stories come up:

'Resignation syndrome: Sweden's mystery illness'
(BBC News, October 26, 2017)
'Resignation syndrome in refugee children – a new hypothesis'
(Centre for Research Ethics & Bioethics, February 22, 2016)
'Resignation syndrome: Catatonia? Culture-bound?'
(*Frontiers in Behavioral Neuroscience*, January 26, 2016)

I click on the links and continue reading.

I forget about Indira and the takeover.

There is no chance of sleep tonight.

February 22

Westminster. The Old Palace. Another parental pistols-at-dawn moment. It is the time-honoured tale. Dad has a thing with one of his co-workers in the office. Mum finds out. The Other Woman. Or Yet Another Other Woman. Mum worries rumours will spread among her political enemies.

She needs me as a prop again.

So here we are. We sit in the middle of the Peers' Dining Room with our stodgy puddings and prattle on about nothing. Politics is perception. We play happy families, like we always do when one of Dad's indiscretions flares.

I mentally list all the Other Women there have been. I want to find her name this time. The latest threat to our nuclear family unit.

I almost tell Mum about the fear, the recurrence. How scared I am. How helpless I feel. But she, too, is consumed by the Other Woman.

So I stay silent and say nothing at all.

February 25

The perfect murder is a postmodern enterprise. Discuss.

I am knee-deep now. Sleep and murder. The sickness of sleeping. Sleep as death. Or death as sleeping. I will purge my own sleepwalking demons with an exploration of someone else's.

This is my long-read for the magazine. I will write the definitive case history of the Stockwell Monster with all its contemporary resonances: sleep crime, automatism, the fallen woman, the blended family, insanity and femininity, the terrors of dreams, contested facts and multiple truths.

And I already have my first lead.

The expert witness at Court 1 of the Old Bailey. The sleep expert who testified that Sally Turner was sleepwalking when she killed her two stepsons. An expert in non-REM parasomnia.

I review the woman's CV again. She's worked as a consultant clinical psychologist at Broadmoor; Professor of

137

Clinical Psychology at King's College, London; Managing Partner at the Abbey Sleep Clinic in Harley Street.

She was on the staff at Broadmoor when Sally Turner was sent there.

Witness and therapist, saviour and supervisor.

I make a note of her name.

Professor V. Bloom.

She is my way into this case.

31

BEN

Clara doesn't flinch. She is in work mode, immune to normal human concerns. 'What are you talking about?'

The shock is thinning now. Facts return. Sensations, smells, the memory. 'I went into the room and saw the body and then it was just lying there. I couldn't understand it, or not at first. I think I bent down and picked up the knife.'

'You think?'

'I was hardly thinking at all. It was just . . . instinct.'

Clara sighs deeply. 'Did you try and wipe it?'

'No.' This is the truth. Well, almost the truth. 'I panicked. I held the knife then placed it back when I realised.'

She doesn't speak. I know the look on her face. She is in survival mode, computing possibilities. This is what drew me in and pushed me away. She can be almost superhuman and stone-cold in the same moment, insulating herself at all costs.

I fill the silence. 'Say something. Please.'

Clara checks no one else is in earshot. 'You know what I'll say.'

I do. It is Clara's Golden Rule. *The truth will set you free.* That moral lesson has been drummed into Kitty from birth. Sometimes Clara's drive for the truth terrifies me. She rides roughshod over red tape to secure justice for victims; disobeys rules so loopholes don't allow rapists and murderers to walk free; ignores the protocols of defence lawyers, lazy judges and bureaucrats. Clara flirts with disciplinary action, even suspension. There is a puritanical side to her, born from the best intentions. The truth is all that matters. Pettifogging rules be damned.

'Is that my ex-wife talking or a friendly copper?'

'Both.' Clara glances at the house, uncomfortable at her dual position.

'I don't want to land you with another disciplinary charge.'

'I solve cases rather than just sit on them. They'll find a way to kick me out sooner or later. Why were you here anyway?'

'I told you. Bloom called me.'

'Why did she call you at this time of the night?'

I could lay out the facts: Bloom told me about a file hidden in her private safe relating to the Anna O case. That the past was the only way to explain the present. She sounded more frightened than I'd ever heard her before.

But I say nothing. I made that decision when I took the file. I tampered with a crime scene, wiped my prints from handles and surfaces. I removed potential evidence. I am already guilty. I can't drag Clara into that too.

'She was worried about something. She didn't say what.'

Clara nods. 'The team will have to take you to the station and get the statement signed. After that I'd head home and get some rest.'

'Sure.'

'Only you can make the call on this one, Ben.' Clara looks at me differently, the final residue of love. 'But I'm always here if you need anything.'

It's so long since we've spoken like this. We have almost forgotten how. 'Is KitKat okay?'

Clara flinches at the nickname. 'She's at a sleepover.'

I nod. We have reverted to being young again, full of awkward pauses and shuffling evasions.

I watch her give final instructions to the team. Then she gets back in her car. I imagine KitKat at her sleepover and the game to stay up all night. I turn back to the house. Soon the body will be carried out of the property and placed in the mortuary van. I know the gruesome details of what follows: the bleached smell, the bloodstained metallic table, the gowned figures carving through flesh. I catch myself already thinking about Bloom in such corporeal terms. I wonder what I've become.

I'm almost relieved when two of Clara's colleagues emerge, peeling off their masks and paper suits. They are firm but pleasant. I am not arrested, or cautioned, but my presence is needed at the station. I am ushered into a nearby police car.

My head is clear. I am focused.

It's how I will survive this. All of this. Everything I have done tonight.

My Gladstone bag is still beside me.

Before her death, Bloom gave me one instruction.

I intend to honour it.

32

BEN

At Islington Police Station my clothes are removed and placed in evidence bags. My prints are taken. I'm usually the behavioural investigative adviser hovering in a small anteroom with weak coffee and stale biscuits. Now I'm on the other side. A witness, possibly a suspect, not an investigator.

It takes another three hours to give my full statement to two DCs and then sign the typed-up version before I stumble out onto Tolpuddle Street. I walk for five minutes before finding a cab. I give the address for the flat in Pimlico.

The cab pulls away from the kerb. I check my Gladstone bag.

The file is still safe.

When I enter the front door of my flat it feels like the first time in months. It's then that the emotions finally catch up with me, a spurt gathering into an eruption. I slide down the wall in the hallway and slump onto the wooden floorboards. Tears on my cheeks, leaking through my hands, the shock of everything that has happened momentarily destroying me.

The tears don't stop. These are childhood tears: copious, unapologetic, a wail of anguish at the harshness and unfairness of the world. I sit there for hours. My sleeves are damp. Bloom was more of a parent, in some ways. I saw her most working days of my adult life.

I don't feel hungry or want to get up. I want to close my eyes and wake up to a world where Bloom is resurrected. She was a barrier to my own mortality. While Bloom lived, death was a distant prospect. Now she's gone I realise just how vulnerable I am. Clara, too. Bloom talked of old age as sniper's alley. I look around the small flat and the acute sense of loneliness hits me. Life is so short and, thus far, I have made such a mess of it. There is no one else to blame for my mistakes.

It is sometime later that I eventually get up off the floor. I dry my eyes, shower, change my clothes. I cope in the way I always have done. I am like Anthony Hopkins in *The Remains of the Day* without the immaculate tailoring. I find refuge in the austere comforts of the stiff upper lip, emotional repression and unhealthy resolve to mask deep fears through petty house-hold chores.

Clara always used to joke that my method for coping with trauma was to load the dishwasher or start hoovering. I assess the state of the flat and then seek solace in dusting and ordering. My emotions may be messy. But my flat can be controlled. Going-through-the-motions is my therapy, my Freudian couch. As a psychologist, I think I should trademark it. Not the talking cure but the tidying cure. Move over Marie Kondo.

The place needs a thorough clean, reeking of too many takeaways and unwashed mugs. I mop the floor, hoover the bedroom carpet, change the sheets, work furiously at the sudsy stains around the shower and tenderly get the bathroom mirror to shine. As I clean, I think of that night in the Abbey garden with Bloom and my hopes of using this case to revive my career and impress Clara and KitKat. That seems laughably naïve now. Bloom is dead. Clara is rescuing me, not the other way round.

I eventually finish cleaning and replace all the equipment. At a loss, I glance at the ceiling, as if my own flat could be bugged.

The paranoia is still with me. Bloom's voice looms through the stillness – the urgency, the terror. Whatever Bloom discovered is dangerous, fatally so. I can't believe that I am alive and Professor Bloom is gone.

I desperately need another distraction. I check the time and then wait until after seven thirty. I might just catch KitKat before she heads to school. I speed-dial the number on my mobile and wait as it rings.

There is nothing for several seconds. Then, like a gift, the rings stop and a small, hesitant voice answers.

'Hello. Kitty speaking.'

I smile. The last few hours fade. The shock and grief are temporarily stilled, numbed even. I taught her to say that. It reminds me of when she learned to say goodbye and inflicted it on every adult she saw from then onwards. Sometimes I long for those days so much I can hardly face the mornings. The tears loom at me again, needling my eyes. I didn't realise love could be this painful, this debilitating and all-consuming. I never had proper worries before becoming a parent. My old life now seems almost ludicrously flimsy, debating jobs and exams and bad dates. As if any of that mattered.

'Sweetheart, it's Daddy.'

The formal tone perks up. 'Hello, Daddy.'

'Hello, KitKat. All ready for school?'

'Yes.'

'Is Mummy there with you?'

'She's upstairs.'

This is the pain of separation. It's why I hate speaking on the phone. Children need a face, a hug, something physical to connect with. A voice on a phone is too abstract. Their brains haven't developed enough to fully understand what's going on. I hear feet on the staircase, the sound of Clara telling KitKat it's time to go.

'Mummy says I have to go now, Daddy.'

There are so many more questions I want to ask. What lessons

144

she's going to have. If it's a PE or music lesson day. Which classes she's most looking forward to. What she had for supper last night. The daily trivia.

'Okay, darling. Daddy wishes you a very happy day. Love you lots.'

'Bye bye, Daddy.'

I can hear Clara's voice nearby. The line stays open. She will be annoyed with me for calling and unsettling KitKat before she goes to school. I am only usually permitted to phone in the evenings, if at all. There is a sigh. Clara is about to take over, but I hang up before the rebuke arrives. It is cowardly, I know. Clara has just saved me. But I'm too tired to fight. I dock the phone, make extra-strong coffee, and then wearily troop into my small home office and sit down at the desk. The inevitable can't be put off much longer.

The file.

I sigh and look up at the framed poster above my desk. It's the original poster for *Psycho* with its gaudy array of yellows and blues. Janet Leigh sits disrobed and suspicious; John Gavin is shirtless and six-packed with jet-black chest hair; Anthony Perkins, meanwhile, peers from the side, a peeping tom and a mummy's boy with matinee idol looks and sociopathic appetites. It was a gift from Clara after we married, a joke about my work as a forensic psychologist. Despite the subject matter, it reminds me of the glory days.

I return to the grim task at hand. I ease the file from the Gladstone bag. It is precious, delicate. There is something specific about this file – a thin, tired, handful of pages – that triggered Bloom's moment of realisation. The fear in her voice.

Somehow, I must figure out why.

I look at the file reference number: 'X389043BMH'. There is a scrawl in Bloom's trademark red ink on the first page: 'Patient X'. Ever since Freud and Breuer published their case studies, it has been a tradition for psychologists to christen their patients with an alias. Freud's patients are iconic even now: the

Rat Man, the Wolf Man, Dora, Elizabeth von R and, of course, the original Fraulein Anna O.

Opening the file feels transgressive. Bloom was always severe about medical confidentiality. The Abbey's reputation rests on secrets. All new patients fill in a questionnaire about their personal lives: sex, childhood, bowel habits, peccadilloes. Many are a gossip columnist's dream and therefore each is strictly anonymised. No name, no age, no profession and always gender-neutral pronouns.

I see the pages bleached with whisky and smell the fug of tobacco. Bloom was always suspicious of technology. She wrote in longhand. Dull paragraphs became makeshift coasters. I feel like a scholar finding Shakespeare's lost letters or Byron's missing memoir. There is something sacred about touching a primary text.

I stare at the top of the first page and those final three initials in the file reference number.

BMH.

I know what they stand for. A hidden part of Bloom's past even more secret than her work at the Abbey. A place infamous in Western psychological treatment.

Once an asylum for the criminally insane. Then an institution. Today a secure medical facility.

This file can only be from one place.

Broadmoor Hospital.

CASE NOTE 1

PATIENT X, REF: X389043BMH, DR V. BLOOM

JULY 2, 1999
Cranfield Ward, Broadmoor Hospital

Our first session today. We get the child-friendly meeting room with its plastic toys and colouring books. It is embarrassingly pre-school for a teenager. X is early, brought in by a nurse. I immediately see a difference in them. Most teenagers have a slightly droopy gait, like new machines in need of oiling. Their over-long arms flail, the back curves. They are still children acclimatising to their ever-changing bodies.

But X isn't like that. Or not quite. There is a composure to them that almost takes the breath away. They are still childlike, of course. But the events of the recent past have clearly accelerated the ageing process. X looks older than their years. More than that, X's brain is clearly developed in a way that's uncommon at their age. I have decades on X, but it feels almost like meeting an equal.

X sits down. They stare around my office, then say, 'So you're the mind doctor.'

I wait, deciding on the best tone. 'I'm a clinical psychologist,' I reply. 'I specialise in sleep-related disorders. Insomnia, sleep-walking, night terrors, dream analysis, that sort of thing. Does the mind interest you?'

I already have a good idea that it does. But I don't spoon-feed my patients. Some want empathy. Others demand parental sternness. The third category – the rarest – seem to want nothing from me at all. They have a hunger to know how their brains are wired. They are also by far the most dangerous.

X frowns now. 'There's a line I read once. "The mind is its own place and can make a heaven of hell and a hell of heaven." Milton, I think. Smartarse.'

My face betrays me. I look impressed. X notices the expression like a small victory. The eyes judge me.

'You like Milton?'

'Like is an overused term. Milton is Milton. Whether I like him or not has nothing to do with it.'

The Oxbridge erudition seems at odds with the accent. I feel ashamed for even thinking that. But it's the first thought that occurs. I have the patient notes. I know about the mother, the home life, the stepdad, the stepsons. I know about the suicide attempts, the bullying at school, the hell of childhood. And, now, the hell of adolescence. But I need to find out for myself. 'Did you study *Paradise Lost* in school?'

'I found it at the library. School is boring. No one ever learns anything there.'

'Do you often go to the library?'

'My friend takes me.'

'Who's your friend?'

'That's very existential. Or should it be ontological? I'm still on the poetry section. I haven't read the philosophy section yet. My friend is my friend is my friend.'

A compulsion to show off? A defence mechanism? 'How long has this friend of yours been taking you?'

'Since it happened.'

I play along. I'm not sure whether this friend is real or part of a rich and disturbing fantasy life, an escape from trauma. I suspect the latter. The reports all note X's loner status and antisocial behaviour. And we both know what the 'it' is. That night, when X found themselves in a house of horrors, steeped in blood. I imagine X in a quiet corner of the library with a gnarled, billowy copy of *Paradise Lost* and an imaginary companion. Seeing the visions of the book translated into real life.

'Did your mum ever take you to the library?'

X smiles. 'My mum drinks. The library doesn't serve alcohol. The two don't exactly fit.'

'How much did your mum used to drink?'

'Why don't you ask her?'

'I'm asking you.'

'Enough to make her crazy, if that's what you mean.'

I am silent. Later, of course, I will regret it. I should stamp my authority here, provide boundaries. But X intrigues me. Most teenagers fake worldliness. X doesn't need to fake anything. They seem to be two steps ahead, anticipating my next question.

'What does the word "crazy" mean for you?'

X smiles again, as if the question is amusing. 'The same thing crazy means for most people.'

'Can you give me an example?'

'When Mum drinks she starts sleepwalking. The more she drinks, the more she sleepwalks. That makes her crazy, psycho, nuts, mad, bonkers. Take your pick.'

'Has she always been a sleepwalker?'

'Yes.'

'What's it like when your mum sleepwalks?'

'She looks normal but she isn't there. It's someone different. Like I told you, she becomes crazy. She doesn't respond to stuff.'

'So you've seen her sleepwalking?'

'Yes.'

'How many times?'

'Enough.'

Usually, the first session is all warm-up. But I'm not going to get more out of X that way. Specifics are needed. 'Is that what you saw on the night of the murders?'

'Why?'

'I'm curious.'

'Yes.'

'You're certain?'

'She didn't know who I was. The lights were on but no one was home.'

'Where did you find her?'

'In the bedroom.'

'What did you do?'

X sighs. 'I tried to get the knife. Then the bitch turned on me. I fled and called him. And we all lived happily ever after.'

'Did your mum come looking for you?'

'No. She stayed put.'

'She didn't recognise you at any point during this episode?'

'No.'

'Did you witness your mum stab either of the twins in the bedroom?'

'Not specifically.'

'How can you be sure she did?'

'She had the weapon. She was covered in tomato ketchup. Didn't have to be Einstein to make the connection.'

I nod. 'I suppose not.'

My brief is simple. I'm to provide a psychological evaluation of Child X which will be used by social services in determining the next stage of care. Is the child irreversibly damaged by what they witnessed that night. Are they suffering from years of mental or physical abuse. Do they require urgent psychological or psychiatric care. Are they fit to be fostered, reintroduced to the education system, resilient enough to cope with a new identity and foster family. To put their old self behind them.

I look at X and know how much power I hold. One note here, a signature there, and their future will be different. It is one of the few times in my professional life when I can't summon the distance needed. I wonder what it must be like for any child to have gone through so much. To have a ring-side seat to such events. I would invent an imaginary friend too. We all would.

'What do you think sleep does to your mum?' I ask. 'What was she usually like?'

X continues to look at the walls. 'Drunk. Angry. Embarrassing. IQ of an orc. She can't think things through like I can.'

I don't respond immediately. X is tantalising me, suggesting an answer then withdrawing it. 'Do you consider that a weakness?'

'Don't you?'

After a beat I say, 'What about when your mum was sleep-walking? What were the changes you noticed?'

X mimics my pause, unsettling me further. 'She was like an animal, I guess. An animal moving in for the kill. Like a nightmare.'

There is total silence. I am too absorbed to notice anything peripheral: the time, whether it is light or dark outside, the nature of my next appointment. There is just X. This thin, strange teenager with eyes that haunt me.

This is the most important question. The one I must answer. A diagnosis that will either liberate X or haunt them until their dying day.

'So,' I say. 'Why don't you tell me about your nightmares?'

CASE NOTE 2

PATIENT X, REF: X389043BMH, DR V. BLOOM

JULY 7, 1999

Our second session starts more easily. We dispense with introductions. X takes a seat with their usual caution. I let the first
thirty seconds hover silently.

I begin with my usual question. 'How are you feeling today?'

'Tip-top, guv.'

'Have you been sleeping?'

'Like a log.'

'Does it scare you being in a hospital like this?'

'No,' says X. No longer mocking me. Or not as obviously.

'Have you seen your friend recently?'

'Yes.'

'Does your friend have a name?'

'Yes.'

I have been thinking about X's imaginary friend. A devil on
their shoulder, a psychological cushion. I debate whether to
include it in my report. The imaginary friend could be both help
and hindrance. I am being badgered by social services for a verdict.
X's mother may be in the dock. X is not. Our consultations might
take place in Broadmoor, given my need to be on-call for an emergency. But, unlike the others, X is here voluntarily. They can leave.

'Last time you mentioned the nightmares or bad dreams you sometimes have,' I say. 'Let's explore that a little more.'

If anything, X has grown cannier since our first meeting. Then I was struck by the contrast between the cub-like appearance and the voice, as if they were literate in all things adult. Today X defuses things with silence. They are adapting to the environment. Finding a way to beat me.

'Doesn't everyone have bad thoughts from time to time?'

I nod. 'Every person experiences them differently. How do you experience them?'

'Sometimes I dream of hurting people.'

'General people or specific people?'

'Depends,' says X. The voice still contains too much wisdom for the rest of the face. 'Most of the time it's specific. I want to get back at the people who hurt me. I want them to know how it feels. Tit for tat. Like for like. Medicine tasting.'

I write a note. It gives me a natural moment to formulate the next question. We are getting somewhere.

'Who are the people who hurt you?'

X shrugs. 'Other kids at school. Teachers. Adults generally. The world's full of bastards.'

'How do teachers hurt you?'

'They don't like the fact that I'm cleverer than them.'

'Do they pick on you?'

'Yes.'

I decide not to probe too obviously. X will recoil. 'What do the other kids do?'

'They don't like that I'm cleverer than them either.'

'Is it verbal or physical?'

X doesn't respond. Then they roll up the sleeve on their left arm. I lean forward and see the burn marks. I try not to react too clearly.

'How did you get those?'

'One of them holds me down. The others put out cigarettes on me. Stupid wankers. They find it funny. The teachers don't stop it.'

'What goes through your mind when they do this?'

X, true to form, also pauses here. They play for time. 'You're trying to determine whether or not I'm a psycho, aren't you?'

I am used to bluntness from patients. But the voice is so calm that it tilts my balance. 'What makes you say that?'

'It's what you do.'

'Is it?'

'The police and the courts and the justice people want you to tell them that I pose no danger to anyone. That I'm not going to go nuts like my mum.'

'That sounds like you have doubts yourself.'

'I'm half her. Perhaps she passed it on. Deadbeat mum, deadbeat kid.'

I don't answer right away. X is sparring with me. I do what the manuals suggest. I feign ignorance, play dumb. 'Do you think sleepwalking or mental illness is genetically transmitted?'

X smiles. 'You're the doctor.'

'Your file says you read psychology books from the library. I want to hear what you think. Does your friend help you choose those too?'

'I think madness is like greatness. Some people are born mad. Some people achieve madness. And others have madness thrust upon them.'

'Which category does your mum belong to?'

X waits. I hear my stomach tighten. 'Everyone says she's evil. Must have popped out like that. A wrong 'un from the start.'

'What goes through your mind when those other kids at school bully you?'

X doesn't smile or laugh. 'Revenge.'

'What type of revenge?'

'I want them to feel powerless and helpless. I want them to feel pain.'

I don't make another note. This is what terrifies the box-tickers with their bureaucratic checklists. They put a sentiment like that together with X's home background and decide safe is better than sorry. That is how teenagers end up in this place for constant treatment. Nature over nurture.

'Do you ever try to turn those thoughts into reality?'

'No,' X says. Then they startle me. 'Pain is good. It makes my brain work quicker. If people felt more pain, perhaps they wouldn't be so dumb.'

It is said with almost biblical authority. I wonder again how much pain this child has known. What other secrets lie in that household. There are certain questions the authorities want me to ask. Only then will the lawyerly, clerkish types be satisfied that no blame can trickle back to them.

I am careful here. I am not a therapist who is interested in unpicking the wounds of the past. I believe in looking forward. The past is fertile ground for novelists, historians and poets. But not for people trying to move on with their lives.

'What do you think triggers those bad thoughts? Those dreams of hurting people?'

X looks dismissive. 'I don't like people having power over me.'

'Is that the same with the teachers too?'

'Possibly.'

'What about at home?'

Memories are dangerous things. With enough alcohol, drugs or sleep-related fugues, memories turn into actions. The veteran who hears a car backfire and responds like they're in a warzone. The child who witnesses a tragedy and, one day, repeats the same motions, violence birthing more violence.

'Sometimes.'

'Was that power verbal or physical?'

'Verbal. I was older than the twins. They were good talkers but weak.'

'Did you resent your stepdad having power over you and your mum?'

'Yes.'

'Did you ever have bad dreams about your stepdad or the twins?'

155

'Yes.'

'Why?'

'Tom liked to be the big man of the house. He liked to show his power.'

'Did you ever think about hurting Tom?'

A look of irritation. 'No.'

'Did your mum ever talk about hurting Tom?'

'Yes.'

'What about the twins?'

X recovers. That flash of annoyance goes. They are poised, ready for anything. 'Depends if she'd been on the bottle.'

I see the hint of a smile on X's face. I remember how young they are. That the eyes are deceptive. The soul is a metaphysical concept, not a medical one. Yet I can't deny it: X's soul disturbs me. It is like nothing I have encountered before.

One final question for today. A question I must ask.

I clear my throat and prepare myself.

Then I say, 'Do you ever dream of killing someone?'

CASE NOTE 3

PATIENT X, REF: X389043BMH, DR V. BLOOM

JULY 12, 1999

It is our third and final session. I have reviewed the file overnight. Depending on my decision, X will either be detained within a secure hospital for further monitoring or admitted into the protected persons scheme. They will get a new name, new passport, new documents, a new location and new foster parents. All traces of their old identity will be wiped. Their old self will disappear.

A DA-Notice was issued to the press at the time of the arrest stopping any media from reporting on the age, name or gender of the prisoner's biological child. X is treated separately, an innocent not to be confused with the lifers sentenced to the Broadmoor corridors. Apart from senior figures within the Met and criminal justice system, I am the only person to have the complete file.

I have my list of questions. My decision must be made by the end of the week. An entire person's existence hangs on my diagnosis and signature. I imagine X with a new name, free from the past. I see them serving others, doing some good in the world. Redemption, rehabilitation, revival. I believe that is possible. Cycles of violence can end. That's why I do this job.

'I want to talk about something different today,' I say. 'I'm going to ask some questions about your future. Quick-fire. Just say whatever comes into your head.'

X pauses. 'Fine.'

I can never tell whether X is being sarcastic or genuine. Sometimes I think X isn't sure themselves. 'If you won the lottery, what would you spend it on?'

'Leaving the country. Buying a house. Putting a Ferrari in the drive.'

'What do you think of when I say the word "love"?'

'Love-hate. Love is blind. Cupid. Love is all you need. Arrows. Hugs. Kisses. Sex. Weddings. My friend.'

I stop. 'Do you love this friend of yours?'

'Yes.'

'Does this friend love you?'

'Yes.'

I want to probe more. But I am not X's counsellor. An imaginary friend is often bad. Love is often good. Perhaps they cancel each other out. 'What do you want to be when you grow up?'

'I want to be where you're sitting.'

'The person with the power?'

'Overlord of Planet Earth.'

'Why?'

'My friend says it's fun. Having power over other people like that. Being medical or legal or a mind doctor.'

'Is your friend medical or legal?'

'Maybe.'

I've built up to this last question. I keep my eyes firmly on X. 'Do you recognise what your mum did was wrong?'

This is the last obstacle. They must accept what happened. They must demonstrate an ability to make their own moral choices. They must show that history doesn't always rhyme.

X hesitates, lost somewhere in their own mind. 'Why?'

'Please just answer the question.'

The trial is over. The verdict of not guilty by reason of insane

158

automatism has been delivered. That is why X's mother is here. Why X is also here.

But I want to know. The mystery of it tortures me.

'Do you believe your mum was sleepwalking when she carried out the killings?' I say. 'Do you think she intended to kill her two victims?'

X looks at me. The answer stays with me, that night and far beyond, poised between sarcasm and sincerity.

'Maybe.'

33

BEN

I return to my office at the Abbey and read the case notes a second time. Skim first, analyse second. When I finish I look up to find the pages are damp in my hand. Bloom was the last person to touch them. I think of her body lying on the floor. I imagine her fingers on these pages and almost feel the heat echo through time. The sheer fact of her death hits me again. All she has left me is this signpost to something. But to what, I am not sure.

Anna O. Medea. Sally Turner. Patient X.

The case notes cover a very short period during July 1999. They were written at the Cranfield Ward of Broadmoor Hospital. They concern a patient Bloom was treating known only as 'X'. Given the date, location and veiled references within the document, it seems to be the teenage biological child of Sally Turner, aka the Stockwell Monster, who died in August 1999. The link with Anna's investigation for *Elementary* is the obvious cross-reference. There are several mentions of 'sleepwalking'.

Beyond that, I am in the dark.

Bloom has given me a road sign without a destination.

I get up, pace the office. I brew coffee to keep me awake. Then I walk through the rest of the Abbey, seeing other patients docile and dead-looking in their rooms. Eventually I am through to the VIP wing and the secluded hush of the treatment room. The door is soundproofed. It is the calm of the dead. I scrub myself, put on gloves and a mask, then cross the divide like a pilgrim preparing to enter a holy place.

Being alone with Anna always feels different than with any other patient. There is a sense of ceremony. I am standing only metres away from one of the few people in the Western world who doesn't know about the Anna O murders: the woman herself.

I pick up the stool from the corner of the room. I place it within touching distance of Anna's bed. I sit and watch her, the soft pulse of her breathing. I have read more about Anna than any other patient. I feel like I know her. The bond is a noiseless spool of thread linking us both.

I pick up the patient file at the end of the bed. Harriet's neat handwriting is inscribed on each page. It is a dry document setting out the treatment that Anna has received so far. Most of it falls under basic housekeeping: the nasogastric tube providing nutrition; the regimen for exercising Anna's joints to stop them becoming tight; the twice-daily washing of her skin to prevent bedsores and other itches, allowing the skin to be hydrated and moisturised; the constant effort to avoid ulcers by moving the patient and maintaining the illusion of physical action; taking care of essentials through a catheter; then, lastly, maintaining basic dignity with teeth-cleaning and mouth-washing, ensuring Anna's teeth and gums are in box-fresh condition when, or if, she ever wakes.

I flip a page to the next stage of treatments. This is where things become looser, subjective even. There are so few examples of patients with long-term sleeping sickness that the best clinical practice is based on comatose patients or those in a 'minimally conscious state' or MCS.

My methods build on that foundation. As I tell my students at Birkbeck, no treatment is ever entirely revolutionary. Galen, a physician, was debating the unconscious nearly two millennia before Freud. Aristotle discussed the meaning of dreams. So does the *Epic of Gilgamesh*. In Genesis, Joseph is both dreamer and dream interpreter, insisting that analysis of dreams is so divine that 'interpretations belong to God'.

Even in the Bible dreams and sleep can be dangerous things.

The main thrust of Anna's treatment is sensory stimulation, something she has been denied ever since being detained at the Farm that night. Her senses are barren, empty, malformed and stumpy. I need to reawaken them.

I must stir memories of August 2019. Of what really happened with Indira and Douglas. Of how Anna ended up here, some memory that will clarify her actions in the Red Cabin all those years ago. Provide hope, possibly even salvation.

With Bloom gone, I feel somehow closer to Anna now. We are bound together in death as much as in life. I can carry out Bloom's final wishes, help wake Anna and solve the mystery of her illness. That is my motivation.

I need to know what really happened at the Farm that night.

34

LOLA

The lies come for her now.

That is the problem with sleep and dreams. The conscious she can handle. It is the unconscious that causes problems. Her mind at sleep jumbles so many events, adding a lethal coherence to each one, until she wakes to clammy bedsheets and a soaked-through top and a breathless lungful of stale, midnight air.

Perhaps it is a guilty conscience.

Lola repeats the same dream night after night.

The Farm. Late August 2019.

Melanie Fox, the trustafarian aristo, flaunting the family jewels one moment and pleading poverty the next. Her idea for the Farm has taken off and now she lusts after pound signs, profit margins, cash in the bank. She prefers creased notes to electronic bank transfers, deniable calls to emails. That's how Lola gets her access. Melanie Fox needs a health and safety consultant but without paying the big bucks. A business card, a brown envelope, a hush-hush understanding – it is seamless, just as Lola intends.

The Farm itself is almost medieval. Lola imagines the peasantry tilling the land, the new money patrolling the Ruins, the Forest with its ghouls and punishments. And tonight, yes tonight, there will be more of both. She almost laughs as the Ogilvy family decamp from their cars, paying to sample Mother Earth before zipping back to the glassy, air-conditioned delights of London.

Melanie Fox looks mildly high. Owen, the groundskeeper, keeps things ticking. Lola checks the paintball guns and runs through checklists. Then, at last, the hour arrives. The centrepiece of the Farm experience. The crown jewel.

Hunters versus Survivors.

The two teams are supposedly chosen at random. But no one quite believes that. The Farm is reality TV without the cameras, each plot point and row scripted by the devilish producers. Melanie Fox devises each survival game for maximum tension. Anna versus her own family is box-office.

Lola subtly suggests the rest. It is vital for what happens later that the Forest takes on a mythology of its own. Something for the bloggers and trolls and rent-a-quotes to soliloquise about. No, it is vital that Anna, Indira and Douglas are on the same team. And vital that everything else happens after the Forest.

The Survivors get a running start. As health and safety consultant, Lola takes up her sentinel position in a small watching post with a vantage on the game below. She has binoculars and can follow each participant, catching glimpses of them through the gaps. The game can only be stopped if there is a risk of serious injury. Lola has a horn which alerts Owen and the intern. They will then enter the Forest and locate the participants. But the protocol has never been invoked. The point of the Farm and the Forest is that guests are plunged back into the wild. It is red in tooth and claw, survival of the fittest, a Darwinian bloodletting.

Lola keeps a constant scan through her night-vision lens, seeing small greenish figures darting out between trees. Each participant is also issued with a heat tracker, allowing Lola and the team to monitor the location of each guest via a small laptop screen. The first sign of trouble comes several hours in. Colours on the heat map start mixing. To the north of the Forest a

Hunter and Survivor are aligned. At first it looks like a classic tactical manoeuvre: the Hunter creeping towards the Survivor, watching and waiting, then marking the Survivor suddenly in the darkness, the whiplash of the paint bullet.

The two dots overlap. They stay like that for seconds, minutes. No escape, no parting. Lola watches as a third dot approaches too. Another Hunter. The third dot hangs back from the first two, watching stealthily. And the three dots stay like that. Lola tries to find the spot through her night-vision binoculars. But the Forest is too vast. They must be canopied by trees. She waits. The laptop screen reloads. The dots remain.

It is minutes before the third dot leaves. Ten minutes before the two main dots depart. And still no shots fired. This is not how the game is played. Three participants, half of the entire haul, are straying outside the rules. Lola keeps her binoculars trained on the north of the Forest, trying to make out any shapes. She eventually sees one green figure, the third Hunter dot, fleeing along the Forest floor. Female, young. Either Anna or Indira, then. Both will have leading roles later. There can't be any complications now.

Lola is more watchful after that. The chronology of the next part is too tight for errors. The meal in the Ruins with its pauses and silences. Then each party retreating to their cabins, the clockwork sequence. Not a second can be wasted. Because that's what none of them realise. Not Anna, Emily, Richard, Theo, Indira or Douglas.

They have no idea what tonight really is.

The game is about to turn hideously real.

And then it's over. Lola wakes now. She sits up. Her skin is dewy. She breathes, recovering, adjusting to the city darkness and the skein of lamplight through the curtains. It was so vivid tonight. The Forest, the Farm, the heat map, the guests, the anticipation of what came next.

She rises and goes downstairs and sits in front of her boards and contemplates the symmetry of it all. She picks up Anna's notebook and remembers seeing it for the first time in the Blue Cabin, those electric moments after it happened.

None of them understand they are pawns in a game; or that each move was scripted for them that night before they all arrived.

The first part went beautifully.

Now it's time for the final reckoning.

ANNA'S NOTEBOOK
2019

March 3

The London Library. Old books, chipped desks, mediocre coffee. When Indira and Doug get too much, I retreat to my happy place in St James's Square. All those blue plaques on the walls. I see carriages and frock-coated statesmen arriving for lavish dinners in full Edwardian splendour. I imagine myself wandering through history.

This is my salon, my atelier, my studio. I sit in one of the reading rooms and celeb-spot in the stacks. I burrow further back into the past. February 1999. Two decades ago. I have all the newspaper clippings culled from the archives at the British Library. I have read the articles from Professor V. Bloom in worthy academic journals like *The British Journal of Psychiatry*, *The Lancet Psychiatry*, *Psychotherapy and Psychosomatics*, *World Psychiatry* and *Psychological Medicine*.

I must concentrate on the Stockwell Monster case. Yes, that is the task in hand. But, like most writers, I'm easily sidetracked.

I am gradually becoming an expert on my own condition. There is a piece from *Neuroethics* magazine that grabs my attention despite the clumsy title: 'While You Were Sleepwalking: Science and Neurobiology of Sleep Disorders & the Enigma of Legal Responsibility of Violence During Parasomnia'. It concerns the case of Kenneth Parks in 1987. Mr Parks drove fourteen miles to the home of his parents-in-law and then killed his mother-in-law and tried to kill his father-in-law. Afterwards, Parks told police 'he "thought"' he might have 'killed someone'. His lawyers claimed he'd been sleepwalking. The jury believed him. Parks was acquitted of murder and attempted murder.

The authors discuss the difference between *actus reus* (the crime itself) and *mens rea* (criminal intent). Both are needed to convict someone. The lack of *mens rea* is the most common reason for acquitting a suspect who uses the defence of sleepwalking.

There is one section further on in the piece which gives me a lead for the next part of my investigation. The authors mention the relationship between a sleepwalking suspect and their victim:

This leads us to another troubling exception . . . These individuals are obviously in proximity to the sleepwalker. However, there can be some suspicion of an underlying motive because the sleepwalker typically knows them quite well. In these situations, the relationship between the sleepwalker and the victim should be thoroughly investigated.

Like Sally Turner and her two stepsons.
This will be my flagship piece.
Two fingers to Doug and Indira and the takeover betrayal.
It is time to find out more about the Stockwell Monster.

March 11

The Pugin Room in the Palace of Westminster. Mum is in one of her fouler moods. She thinks she's going to get bumped from the Shadow Cabinet at the next reshuffle. She does a good servant-of-the-people act. But I know the seedier truth. She wants Number 10, Downing Street, World King status. Opposition is for losers.

She has summoned me – official, as ever, via one of her pustular PAs – for a catch-up. She insists on the Palace for two reasons. First, her less-than-subtle political grooming campaign, persuading me to ditch journalism and become a paid-up politico and party mouthpiece. Second, so she can show me off, position herself as matriarch for a future political dynasty. It helps soften her image. The doting mother. No more piranhas in pearls.

I want to tell her about the GVM takeover betrayal and my investigation into the Stockwell Monster case. But, like some politicians, Mum sees the world as an extension of herself. I'm a prop for Christmas cards and campaign events.

She doesn't ask. I don't tell. That's not why I'm here.

Families are strange things. Sally Turner was a trained nurse in Stockwell with a secret alcohol addiction and a teenage child of her own from a previous relationship. She met Tom Cornwell, a local businessman, in the spring of 1998. By the autumn, they were living together as a blended family. There was Sally and her biological child and then Tom and his two sons. Tom was a shady character with previous stints inside for fraud.

Neither stepson liked Sally and were trying to drive the couple apart. Sally was from a broken home herself and had, according to subsequent court reporting, an 'obsessive desire for the "perfect" family'. That perfect family, however, didn't involve the stepsons. Fearing Tom would leave and choose his sons over her, Sally carried out a calculated and chilling attack, waiting until Tom left for a business trip before stabbing both stepsons to death in bed and then claiming she was sleepwalking and had no memory of the crime.

According to the defence, it was a very different story: Sally Turner soon realised her dream relationship was her worst nightmare. Tom Cornwell wasn't a legitimate businessman but a drug dealer. He performed a 'cuckoo' operation – using her council house as a clean location to carry out his business dealings. Witness testimony suggested Tom even used his two sons as couriers. The sons relentlessly bullied Sally, both verbally and physically. Tom failed to intervene. She was already slipping off the wagon. High alcohol consumption increases episodes of parasomnia. On the night of the attack, Sally believed she was being brutally assaulted by the stepsons. She claimed self-defence while in the middle of a bad sleepwalking episode.

It makes the Ogilvy clan seem almost harmonious.

We manage twenty minutes this time before Mum is whisked away to the Lords on official business. Journalists have spotted us together. I sprinkled some youthful stardust in Mum's direction. Now my work here is done. Mum pecks me on the cheek and fluffs her goodbye lines. I have a family security pass and find my own way out.

Afterwards, I tour Hatchards on Piccadilly and continue my article research. I find another connection to the Abbey Sleep Clinic. The book is called *Dead of Sleep: An Introduction to the Forensic Study of Sleep Disorders and Dream Analysis* by Dr Benedict Prince, published by Cambridge University Press.

I read the author biography on the flap:

Dr Prince is a Senior Partner and Psychologist at the world-renowned Abbey Sleep Clinic in Harley Street where he leads on the clinic's forensic work. Following a brief spell working as an orderly in various secure psychiatric hospitals, Dr Prince retrained at the Open University as a forensic psychologist specialising in sleep disorders and dream analysis. He's lectured around the world and currently teaches at Birkbeck College, London. This is his first book.

I recognise the Shakespearean quote in the title. But it is something else that draws my attention. Secure psychiatric hospitals. The same background as Professor Bloom. The common cause with the Stockwell Monster. Though Prince would have been an orderly. Not on the medical team. Perhaps not even at Broadmoor.

An afternoon of reading later, I am strangely fascinated by Dr Prince. I make further investigations. The scruffy handsomeness, his preoccupation with the darker recesses of the human mind. His talks, lectures, books and podcasts. I download his podcast appearances and listen to his voice on repeat.

Back at the flat, I feel the afterburn of the meeting with Mum. I remember how the episodes started before. Slowly, cautiously, then the explosion.

My body craves sleep. My mind fears it.

Sleep is the witching hour. The benighted shadows. The realm of the id, the animal, the unconscious. My own mind scares me.

Dead of sleep.

I wish for it.

35

BEN

Eyes, ears, nose. Sight, sound, smell.

If my theory is correct, then aural treatments alone won't be enough. Visual stimuli are impossible given that Anna's eyes remain shut. But her nose and sense of smell should still be operational.

Today, as I enter the treatment room, I have two items to test. Both have been recommended by Emily Ogilvy in another email follow-up, in the same spirit as the childhood music. I have a white cardboard box with the Chanel logo on the side and the iced violet flower arrangement from Blue Florist in Kensington. Both are echoes of Anna's childhood. I arrange the flowers in a vase and position them close to Anna's bed. Then I lean over the bed and squirt two sprays of the Chanel bottle on either side of Anna's neck. Her mother's perfume. Occasionally her own.

The smell is strong. I see Clara getting ready for a night out, the heady, seductive promise of the small perfume bottle. The standard regimen for comatose patients is to experiment with sensory stimuli. But I think that's too gradual. My method relies on the concept of sensory overload, a blitzkrieg on the senses, shocking each one back to life and breaking through the sleepiness. I want to jolt Anna's senses, like kickstarting an engine.

Next I take a pair of Beats headphones from my rucksack. I have a list of Anna's favourite music from her early teenage years and decide to try a more intense experience. I sync the Beats with my iPhone, open Spotify and then scroll down to the medley of bubble-gum, late-noughties pop, the hinge between childhood and adolescence.

I place the headphones on Anna's ears, adjusting them for comfort. I can still smell the Chanel. The flowers – white LA lily, purple freesia, blue veronica, purple lisianthus, eucalyptus and pistache – also perfume the room now.

Music, smell.

Now for the final sense, the last sensation.

I hear the twangy guitar of a Taylor Swift song through the headphones. I move the stool forward. I use my left hand to unpeel the glove from my right hand. I have scrubbed it clean, sheared every pointy fingernail. Apart from Harriet's nursing, Anna has spent four years without any proper touch. The feel of skin-on-skin. That most elemental human need. The one thing that no primate can do without.

I take a breath. I silence the cowardly voice in my head. I reach out my right hand and take hold of Anna's left hand. I'm expecting a chill. But the hand is warmer than I anticipate, alive in a way I still can't quite explain. She is in there. Her brain is active. Her body is too. Only the link between her brain and her body, her mind and the rest of her, is faulty. A living death is so much worse than an actual death.

I keep hold of her hand. I move my fingers so they stroke the skin, gliding along Anna's palm, her fingers, in the gaps between her fingers. My touch is soft then firmer. There is nothing romantic or predatory. Instead, it feels almost primal. It is the sort of scene in a nature documentary where two primates pick fleas from each other, a basic ritual of shared humanity, a vindication of the other primate's existence.

I hold her hand for another few minutes. Then I reach for my last flourish, the most theatrical. I can hear the laughs, the scoffing, the naysaying. But the average human touches their face twenty-three times an hour. That's three hundred and sixty-eight times a day. I have a selection of feathers and begin touching Anna's face with them. Lightly, at first, then with a ticklish, playful swipe. Then harder, itchier, around her eyes and cheeks, an irritant she needs to wake up and swat away. I wonder when Anna's face was last touched in a way that wasn't functional or medical.

I sit there waiting to see if Anna reacts. The illness is both psychological and physical. The treatment must be too. I think of Freud's early breakthroughs in his small consulting room at Berggasse 19 as he laid the palm of his hand on the forehead of patients and began developing the talking cure. Mind and matter, head and heart, brain and body.

At last, it is time for the boldest move of all. So simple, so odd. Touch, sound, smell. Now for speech. I must talk to Anna as if she is awake, as if this is the most normal thing in the world. I rehearse the guidelines for MCS patients again.

First, announce who you are.

Second, talk about your day.

Third, be aware that the patient could be hearing everything.

Fourth, and most importantly, show them love and support.

And so I begin. For Anna to become fully human again I must stop treating her like a patient. She must be more than that to me.

I feel that flutter of connection again, as if Anna and I are the only ones who can continue Bloom's quest. A team united against the world. These methods our little secret. I think of those case notes that Bloom left behind and the carnage at her house and how that file can possibly relate to the woman asleep in front of me.

Anna is my only hope of solving this mystery. She is my golden source.

The Prince and Sleeping Beauty.

I clear my throat and say, 'Hello Anna, my name is Dr Benedict Prince.'

36

CLARA

They set off late. The drive over to Ben's flat is a nightmare. Five minutes into the journey Kitty realises she's left behind her favourite toy which means a further delay as they circle back and start again. The recent all-nighters are playing havoc with Clara's body clock. She narrowly avoids colliding with a large man on an e-scooter with a tenuous grasp of the Highway Code. She is about to scream blue murder at the windscreen, then remembers Kitty sitting beside her and makes do with a muttered curse instead.

The final insult is trying to find a parking spot in Pimlico. Comparing Ben's new place to a prison is admittedly unfair. Prisons have far easier parking systems than Cumberland Street. After circling round three times, Clara finds a tiny space within five minutes' walk of Ben's flat. She checks her mobile and sees three missed calls from him and several emails from her team about the conference arrangements. She longs for the distant days of eight hours' sleep. Once upon a time she even had lie-ins.

Clara bundles Kitty out of the car and checks she has everything. Ben's flat is on the top floor of a stuccoed building not far from Churchill Gardens, currently being rented from a friend. The lift is broken. The foyer smells of damp. The flat itself is small and undistinguished, largely filled with chipped IKEA furniture. Kitty is always too excited to complain about the décor. But there's a divorced dad feel to this place which Clara detests. It reeks of middle-aged men with empty evenings.

They reach the top floor. Today is a rare break in the custody arrangements. Usually, Ben only has Kitty at weekends. But Clara is away at a conference for the next two days. Ben is cheaper than a childminder. And more fun too. She can hear them already, the usual effortless patter.

'Hello, Daddy.'

'Hello, KitKat.'

'What's for tea?'

'It's a surprise.'

'What type of surprise?'

'If I told you that it wouldn't be a surprise.'

'Are there chips?'

'There might be.'

'I like chips.'

'I know you do.'

There is the sound of Kitty running away, her mind entirely occupied with the parental promise of fat-fried potato. Clara finishes hauling the overnight bag up the stairs and dumps it gratefully inside the hallway.

'Why did I hear the word chips shouted in a loud, high-pitched voice?'

Ben takes the overnight bag and stows it in the kitchen. 'One of the neighbours downstairs. I think it's his mantra. Cuppa?'

Ben sounds like he's trying too hard to be normal. His voice is louder than usual, his mannerisms exaggerated. Clara notices his hand shaking as he prepares the tea. His face is pale, drawn even. She wonders whether to say anything, but holds back. She's not his wife, at least not anymore. They haven't been emotionally honest in so long. It's too difficult to start again now.

The kettle finishes boiling, the low grumble filling the kitchen.

Two mugs are already out, pre-loaded with bags of Yorkshire Gold. Clara sees Ben brew both and pull out a chair at the rickety kitchen table.

She looks at her watch. 'I should really get back.'

'Five minutes. Don't stay for me. Stay for the complimentary Hobnob.'

She smiles, then catches herself. It takes her back to that very first date. Ben was clever, awkward and shy; he always used to say that happiness looked so good on her. She sometimes wonders if their marriage would have been different without the events of that night, the baggage of the Anna O case. It all changed then. The pressure of being SIO, the move to the Met's fabled Murder Squad, the lack of time for anything other than work and childcare.

Clara takes a seat and exhales for the first time all day.

She decides to stay.

37

BEN

I brew two cups of Yorkshire Gold in the kitchen, pour milk in both cups and stir shakily. My body jitters and fidgets. I struggle to stay still. Intrusive thoughts of blood and Bloom and Anna flicker darkly when I least expect them.

Breathe. In. Hold for four. Out. Hold for four. Box breathing, they call it. Apparently, it's what Navy SEALs do before battle. My heart rate slows.

Forget the past. Manage the present.

This stay has been in the offing for months. It is one of the rare times I get KitKat to myself for part of the week. Clara has a conference in Brighton – lots of po-faced seminars on community engagement and gang-related violence – and I get to play the parent-in-charge. The flat has been cleaned. The fridge is restocked. Soothing music plays on my Apple HomePod. I know Clara hates this flat. I don't blame her. But I must put in a good performance. Every little detail counts.

I remove the packet of Hobnobs – chocolate-covered, no less – and offer Clara one. She takes two, then grabs the cup of tea. I know her tea routine by heart: handle with the left hand, testing the temperature of the mug with the right, two long cooling blows, then the first tongue-scorching sip, like a dare.

There is a poem by Carol Ann Duffy about the intimacy of sharing tea like this and thinking of a lover's cupped hand as they sip. Clara read it to me once from her phone. I still remember each line.

I nod towards the sound of KitKat playing in the living room. 'Anything I should be aware of during madam's stay?'

Clara glances at the door. 'She's still waking up in the middle of the night. Plus, her schoolwork's suffering.'

'I'll have another chat.'

'Because the last one went so well? Why did you tell her the people in the photos were pretending?'

'It's all I could think of.' I see Clara raise her eyebrows, then take another bite of the Hobnob. 'Any news on the post-mortem yet?'

There is silence. I feel grief tighten inside me. Usually, she would tell me to mind my own business. But Clara looks almost relieved to move on to professional matters. She stares at me, though, and I wonder how I appear to her now. My damn hand won't stop shaking. I'm done in by recent events. Each movement seems alien, like I'm re-learning basic human intercourse.

'Nothing major,' says Clara. 'We got confirmation about the ten stab wounds. The blade marks and wound profile are consistent with the others.'

She doesn't say it, so I do. 'A replica of the murders at the Farm then.' I stop, consider the word choice. 'Bloom killed in the same way as Indira Sharma and Douglas Bute.'

Clara clearly doesn't want to reveal anything more. She says, 'I'm told you rocked the hell out of those grey PJs at the station.'

The humour is dark; it always has been. That was the rhythm of our marriage. 'Does this mean I get my actual clothes back?'

'Not a chance. They'll be kept in storage somewhere.'

'Memo to self. Don't wear your best shirt to a potential crime scene.'

'As long as you don't abscond to the Caribbean, you should be fine.'

I smile. It is another marital in-joke. Clara has always teased me about that tantalising offer of a Visiting Fellowship from UCCI, the University College of the Cayman Islands, and teaching sleep psychology in the Caribbean. Since then, the prospect has become my default fantasy life. I move to the Cayman Islands and do my own *Grand Designs* project on the prettiest part of the Seven Mile Beach. The house is on five floors, self-sufficient and remarkably cost-effective. I make my own rum. Clara does some consulting work for the Cayman Islands police. KitKat runs wild and free on the beach from dawn till dusk. I teach part-time and write my books.

We grow old there, help our grandchildren take their first steps into the sea, build sandcastles and see out our final days. I build a small makeshift cricket pitch next to the house. It is an impossible fantasy now, but not yet fully abandoned. It symbolises so many things. The Grand Cayman idyll is one of the reasons I still have hope.

'Did Bloom ever say anything about her work at Broadmoor to you?' I ask, moving the conversation on. There is a small catch in my voice. Those old memories of happy families on the Seven Mile Beach gnaw at me sometimes. The separation feels so much like failure.

'Broadmoor? No, why?'

'I'm just clearing out some of her old papers. Never mind.' I rearrange my face. I am getting too old to lie convincingly.

'Have you woken her up yet?'

My mind is so focused on Bloom's file that it takes me a moment to realise she is talking about Anna. I ignore the mocking tone. 'If my theory's right, then exposure to memories and sensations from her past will bring her back. Books, movies, music, scents, touch. But it doesn't happen instantly. I told Donnelly it would be months.'

Clara starts on the second Hobnob. 'You do realise your job is to wake her, not to save her. It's bad enough with all those pervy male columnists going on about Sleeping Beauty. She doesn't need a Dr Prince in shining armour to give her the kiss of life.'

'The Prince would be struck off nowadays. Probably put on some sort of register.'

'I'm serious.'

'So am I. He's a danger to princesses throughout the land. Good riddance to him. Dirty bastard.'

'Sometimes just doing the day job is enough, Ben.'

She is right. I know she is. And yet the mystery has its claws in me.

'Focus on the living, forget about the dead.' Clara finishes her biscuit, then gets up from the kitchen table.

'What about someone who's both alive and dead at the same time?'

Clara places a supportive hand on my shoulder. 'Remember your daughter. And ta for the Hobnobs.'

I see Clara leave. I watch TV with KitKat before she gets restless and starts demanding chips. Together we go for a guilty trip to Five Guys and share a burger, fries and banana milkshake. Then the customary negotiations begin over bedtime. It is only later that night, once KitKat has gone to bed at the third time of asking, that I resume my position in front of the TV, lowering the sound so it doesn't drift through to the spare bedroom.

Tonight's film is *Shadow of a Doubt*, a lesser-known film from the war years but Hitchcock's own personal favourite. The story revolves around Teresa Wright's character being visited by her charismatic uncle played by Joseph Cotten. There is a serial killer on the loose and Teresa gradually realises that Joseph is a monster.

The film doesn't calm me. It reminds me too much of Bloom's murder. A killer on the loose, hiding among us. Someone broke into Bloom's home and knifed her to death. Someone with a link back to the patient in Bloom's file and the psychological wilderness of Broadmoor in the late nineties.

I should have watched something more uplifting.

I don't sleep, imagining footsteps approaching KitKat's room, blood flecking the kitchen floor. When I do doze off, my dreams are full of sinister threats lurking in plain sight. I see bodies falling onto train tracks and secrets being hushed up.

I wake just past three thirty. I hear a noise outside. I can't tell if it's a person or the wind. My eyes adjust. Shadows spread across walls. I am permanently disturbed now. The shake in my hand isn't better. I should take something for it. I get up and tiptoe across the flat, careful not to step on the wonkier floorboards. I reach the door to KitKat's room.

This is becoming a habit. Seeking comfort when the nightmares get too scary.

Those flashbacks again: Bloom's house, the front door, the immediate sense of something, then the body on the floor and the halo of blood. My mind suddenly conflates that door with KitKat's door and, without quite being aware of the division between then and now, I push into my daughter's bedroom with animal panic, breathless, searching for signs of danger.

Nothing.

I become fully present again. Blink, rub, reset.

She is asleep. I see her little nose quiver with an intake of breath. She kicks a leg involuntarily under the covers. My daughter is alive and oblivious to me. She is peaceful. I stay and watch for a moment and then quietly leave, careful not to wake her.

I feel ridiculous and out of control. Selfish and ashamed again too. I distract myself, as usual, with routine. I yawn, make some strong coffee, wipe down the kitchen counter again, brush crumbs from the floor, resist the urge to take out the hoover. I sit at the small breakfast table and keep the door open so I have direct sight of KitKat's bedroom.

I maintain my vigil all night.

I realise, now, how much this case has got to me. Played with my head.

I open a cupboard and remove the packet of chocolate

Hobnobs. I sip more coffee. Poor sleep means I need another energy source. Or that's what I tell myself. Caffeine, sugar. I wait for the dawn to rise. I flinch at every noise, pounce on each sound. This is what fear feels like.

Madness, too.

Most of all, I watch the bedroom door. I think of Bloom's house and the killer invading her sanctuary. No matter who is out there, and what danger they pose, nothing will stop me doing this. I have one solemn responsibility. The only thing I would willingly die for.

They can come for me. But me alone. No one else.

Whatever happens, I must protect my daughter.

38

BEN

Another day, another session.

It is early. KitKat's visit is over. I am alone with Anna, instead. She is now almost part of my daily ritual.

'Good morning, Anna,' I begin. I have become used to this, the embarrassment lessening each time. I keep my voice loud, clear, authoritative. 'You are currently lying in a room in central London. It's a beautiful morning. Damp, frostbitten, the sort that demands a cup of milky tea and a slice of warmly buttered toast.'

I am by one of the windows looking out across Harley Street. There is a voile to protect our privacy. Anna looks so waif-like, so dead. And yet that is exactly what I cannot think. I must speak to her like a person. A living, breathing, sentient person denied human interaction. Someone trapped by their mind; protected by their body.

'I've had KitKat, my daughter, staying with me,' I say, aware again of speaking to a silent room. 'I took her for a burger, fries and milkshake the other day. She had a massive sugar-rush. In years to come, when she's scarred by nutritional abnormalities, no doubt the root cause will end up being me.'

It is still odd talking and hearing no response. But it's why I want to be here on my own. Why I increasingly come here first thing in the morning or last thing at night and just sit by her bedside and talk. A third party changes the atmosphere. In here, with Anna, I'm no longer the senior staff member, the grieving colleague, the wounded husband, or the flustered father. I can finally be myself. And yet the sense of being watched never fully leaves me. I imagine Harriet tracking me from behind the glass, silently observing my secrets with voyeuristic stillness. It excites and unnerves me in equal measure.

'As you know, we've been trying some basic sensory stimulation techniques. The TV, the music, increasing the sense of touch, trying to conjure up some scents from your past which might help unlock things.'

I return to the bed. In the early days of psychoanalysis, the analyst would sit out of sight. The best analysts would say very little. The patients did most of the talking. It feels like we've swapped seats: I am free-associating, spilling my thoughts in the safety of the treatment room. Anna is my silent analyst.

I shuffle the stool nearer. I try not to speak like a therapist. 'I want to be honest with you, Anna, and outline other treatment options. I believe you can hear me and can consent to treatments. I want to give you the chance to do so.'

I hear the chorus of doubters. This is psychology, they say. A therapist talking to a sleeping woman as if he expects a response. But for them a patient is always a patient. They are a fleshy abstraction on the operating table. For a psychologist, a patient is granular and specific. The little personal quirks are everything.

'We will continue the sensory stimulation exercises and talking therapy. We can also look at combining that treatment with medication. The literature is not very helpful, given how few resignation syndrome cases there are globally. But it's an option.'

I feel uneasy. I should be honest with her. Honesty means talking about Stephen Donnelly, the Ministry of Justice, the petition by Amnesty and the drive from Whitehall to put Anna on trial for the murder of her two best friends. The Amnesty motion before the ECHR looms ever closer. The MoJ are demanding results before then.

I look at my watch. I have another five minutes until Harriet arrives. I pick up the book that Emily gave me and look at the black cover of *Medea and Other Plays* by Euripides. I think of Bloom's reaction when I mentioned it and her behaviour thereafter.

There is something about this book.

I turn to the introduction and see the passage which Anna has underlined in faded pencil. I want a passage that she might remember. One that has meaning for her. This seems as good as any.

I glance at the words:

> Marathon and Salamis had made the Athenians vividly conscious that the establishment and growth of civilized values in a barbarous world lay with them alone as the leaders of Hellenic culture.

Marathon is the only word circled. That strikes me as odd. Random, in fact. The text is referring to the Battle of Marathon. Athens vs Persia. 490 BC. Ten years before Euripides was even born.

I look at the text and look at Anna and all the old doubts re-emerge. I wonder if I'm clutching at straws, whether the Sleeping Beauty faction are right. I see Anna opening her eyes and looking at the blood-soaked bodies of her two best friends and then seeing the murder weapon tight in her palm. Whether she meant to or not, Anna killed them both. No context – sleepwalking, drugs, intoxication – can remove the crime. Those soft, tiny hands may look innocent; but they are a killer's hands.

A sound breaks through the silence. My work phone buzzes with a calendar reminder. I check the screen and see the details for my second appointment of the morning.

It's time to meet Anna's father.

ANNA'S NOTEBOOK

2019

March 18

Cold. Black. Empty.

I wake up. Not just outside the flat. But outside the building.

Street paving. Uneven, flecked with rubbish. I am wearing only pyjamas and it is March. The weather is inclement.

I am dreaming, surely. But I know I am not.

The old sleep-fuddled sensation takes over again. I blink, I swallow, I cough, I blink again. I was tired. I was thinking about Indira, Doug, GVM, the takeover, Mum, Dad, the Stockwell Monster, Broadmoor, Dr Prince, Professor V. Bloom.

The street and no key. This is the nightmare. Family holidays, school dormitories, the same chill and shiver. There can be no denying it. I am locked out of the building. With no mobile. No flatmates. And sub-zero conditions.

I have been sleepwalking.

Survival is all that matters now. There are flats below and above mine. I consider buzzing and asking to be let back in. But the flat will be locked too. I see newspaper headlines. BARONESS'S DAUGHTER FOUND HALF-NAKED ON LONDON STREET. Mum fuming. Theo laughing. Indira and Doug using it as an excuse to capsize me from the magazine and finalise the GVM buyout.

There's a small 24/7 café two streets away. It does a roaring trade with early-morning shift workers. I retreat there. I lie about the circumstances and get a free coffee out of it. I hunker by the window feeling thoroughly ridiculous and ignore leers at my skimpy nightwear. I use the café phone to ring an emergency locksmith and promise payment once I get back into the flat.

By eight thirty, I've forked out three hundred quid for the locksmith. The downstairs neighbour spots me but doesn't comment. I retreat to my bedroom and hear those porcelain princesses at boarding school mocking me again. The poor unfortunate whose demonic tendencies only surface at night. I was on my way to being someone else. A full reinvention.

Now I am back to that old me.

The Werewolf. The Walker.

Howling my rage into the night.

March 25

The London Library. A week gone. Yet no Google News Alerts. No Twitter or Insta mentions. No sidebar of shame. No grainy camera-phone image of yours truly in Marks and Sparks nightwear with a crowd drooling into their full English.

I pause my Sally Turner/Stockwell Monster research. Today the sleuthing is personal rather than professional. I go back into student mode and consult the stacks. I find an armful of books on sleepwalking and a smart copy of *Studies in Hysteria*. It is like going back to an old friend.

That line from Freud and Breuer's preface always stays with me:

. . . we have for a number of years been searching among the most diverse forms and symptoms of hysteria for their precipitating cause – the event which, often many years earlier, first gave rise to the phenomenon in question.

I skip onwards, scanning the pages until I reach my other favourite line. It is from Freud later in the book. He talks about 'the intimate relationship between the story of the patient's suffering and the symptoms of their illness, a relationship that we still seek in vain in the biographies of other psychoses'.

The biography of psychoses. That is how I must approach my own condition. Going back to that first-ever episode. And the precipitating cause. The shaky moment as a child when I woke up in a different place than I went to sleep. Mum telling me not to be naughty. Dad refusing to believe me. Rhetoric and experience failing to match.

I feel sorry for that little girl in those sweat-soaked pyjamas. I want to reach through time and tell her it will be all right. That she really did close her eyes in bed and open them downstairs with no memory of how she got there.

That she is trapped with a mind she can't control.

But it is two decades later. The episodes have returned.

I am scared about who I become at night and what I might do.

I am scared by the dark thoughts that sleep inside me.

39

BEN

The houses in this part of Belgravia look identical. One so easily blends into another. I continue down Chester Square and find the right house number. All the expected elements are here: the alabaster-white front, the showy columns, the small flight of stairs up to a black door with a winking silver knocker and the bristling patch of garden, as if the whole thing is wrapped in clingfilm and never risks being used.

There is a housekeeper who speaks with a Spanish accent. She shows me through to a drawing room pulsing with interior design. It is a room to be admired rather than lived in, with its look-at-me furniture and impractical curtains. The floor is carpeted. There's a coffee table in the middle with a scattering of hardbacks; from one of those smart Mayfair bookshops, probably, who moonlight as library designers.

I spot one book on Picasso, another on the sights of New York, a further one on Verbier. I can see the harried bookseller getting the client brief and extracting relevant information. No doubt Richard Ogilvy spends a lot of time in New York, holidays in Verbier and once owned – or still possesses – an original Picasso. Or, then again, maybe these books add glamour to a more humdrum reality. I stay standing and turn only when the door creaks open.

Despite being a financier not a politician, Richard Ogilvy is more performative than his ex-wife. She looks like a mother haunted by tragedy. Richard, by contrast, has a chameleon face. There is something of the actor about the teasing length of snow-grey hair and the teaky, skin-smothered tan. The shirt is tailored, the shoes moccasins. I should be taking style tips.

'Richard Ogilvy,' he says, shaking my hand. 'You must be the sleep doctor. Good of you to come. Please, please, take a pew.'

'Thank you.'

'Emily mentioned you visited her and made some rather unfortunate comment about God? I'm rather surprised you made it out alive.'

I sit down on a creamy-gold sofa. He sits opposite. 'I think God's big enough to cope with my comments, don't you?'

Richard smiles at this. 'It's one of the shocks of a long marriage,' he says. 'You wake up twenty, even thirty, years later and realise your other half is a stranger. If you'd told me Emily would end up wearing a dog collar and attending morning prayers, well . . . it's that Sherlock Holmes line, I suppose.'

'Yes.' It's one of my favourites too. 'When you have eliminated the impossible, whatever remains, however improbable, must be the truth.'

He smiles, nods. There is a boyish gleam in his eyes. He doesn't look like he's spent four years mourning his daughter. His tigerishness unsettles me.

'When I first met Emily, she smoked thirty a day, drank like a fish, had zero interest in politics and thought Germaine Greer was almost puritanical. It was the eighties, after all. Mind you, I thought capitalism should be dismantled and the Red Army could occupy Buckingham Palace. Three years later, I became a merchant banker. Marry in haste and repent at leisure. Are you married, Doctor . . .?'

'Prince,' I say. 'Benedict Prince. And no. My wife and I are divorced.'

'You'll know what I mean then.'

It's a statement, not a question. Already, I'm aware of Richard playing me. This is very much his meeting, not mine. I suspect he's accustomed to dominating other people – clients, colleagues, children. He has a winner's grin.

'Anyway,' Richard continues, 'Emily told me all about the new technique you're trying. Something about overloading her senses. You're from that Harley Street clinic where all those celebrities go. Remind me.'

'The Abbey.'

'Indeed. And this new-fangled method?'

'The method is based on a paper I've written for the *Journal of Forensic Psychology* on treating functional neurological disorders. FNDs, in the jargon.'

Richard nods, still looking bluffly unimpressed. 'Yes, I've read your stuff. Psychosomatic, then. You think it's all in her head?'

I flinch. 'The truth is resignation syndrome is a mystery to us. Much in the same way as multiple sclerosis, Alzheimer's and motor neurone disease, even Parkinson's. Neurologists don't really know the cause of any of them. They can't be fully explained or cured. Resignation syndrome is no different.'

'What are the chances it will work? Bear in mind I like percentages. Give me some data to play with.'

'I believe your daughter won't wake up until hope is restored in her life,' I say. My tone is steady, unapologetic. If I sound weak then the argument will be weaker. 'To help Anna wake up again, I must give her a reason to live. Getting her to the Abbey is one positive step. Reintroducing elements of her old life – music, films, touch, smells, conversation – is another. Your ex-wife has already told me about Anna's sleepwalking. But I want to know more about her mood, her behaviour. I'm afraid percentages are anyone's guess. The treatment has been going for several weeks. I'm confident we might start seeing results soon. Possibly very soon.'

'My ex-wife thinks sleepwalking explains the lot.'

'Sleepwalking might explain the murders. It doesn't necessarily explain the resignation syndrome. Unless, on some level, Anna was conscious of what she'd done.'

Richard eyes me with a new look of respect. 'Ah, yes. The catch-22. If she wasn't conscious, why did she fall asleep. If she was conscious, then she couldn't have been asleep when she killed them. Either answer damns her.'

'It does.' He talks about his own child like an object. The more I treat Anna, the more protective I feel towards her. The world has savaged her reputation. Her family are still reeling from the fallout. Harriet and I are the only two people she has left. I am a gatekeeper between Anna and the world. I'm the prince from the fairy tale, sworn to protect and liberate her, however odious that notion is to modern sensibilities.

'How well did you know Douglas Bute and Indira Sharma?' I ask.

Richard grimaces here. His body language tightens. 'Possibly saw them around the house now and then, I suppose. Why?'

'What did you think of them?'

'Douglas seemed a nice enough chap. No idea about Indira, I'm afraid. Can't say we ever shared more than a few words.'

He seems touchy talking about Anna's friends, particularly Indira. Perhaps he fears a legal trap. I wonder how she offended him. I take out my phone and find the right video. This is a risk, but a necessary one. It's the only way to explain my theory.

'One of the nurses noticed Anna responded when played the song "Yesterday". Your ex-wife confirmed she used to play it on the piano when Anna was young. Despite the mournful lyrics, I believe that song carries a subliminal meaning in Anna's mind. It confers safety and optimism. Hope, in other words. We are putting Anna through a programme of extreme sensory stimulus. The collective force should gradually bring her to the surface again. But it will likely be one small event – a trigger – that will finally tip her over the edge.' I hand over the phone. The video whirs to life: the song, the monitors, the flicker of activity in Anna's face.

194

I wait a beat, then say, 'Everyone has focused on the Farm on the night of the murders or the preceding hours in the Forest. But I believe it's more deep-seated. Something happened in the months leading up to the Farm that triggered a severe episode of sleepwalking and, combined with the events of that night, a lapse into a prolonged bout of resignation syndrome. Something extinguished all her hope. Unless I can find that cause, your daughter will likely never wake up.'

Richard's face is expressionless now, digesting what he's just seen. He hands the iPhone back to me. The video of Anna has punctured his air of self-importance. He looks defeated, a father helpless in the face of his own child's suffering.

He composes himself. 'What exactly do you need to know?'

40

BEN

I don't feel like returning to Pimlico after the interview ends. I leave Chester Square and walk to Harley Street instead. I mull over everything Richard Ogilvy told me. I think about fathers and daughters and see Kitty's final look over her shoulder as she left the flat last weekend.

I enter through the back entrance of the Abbey. Time stops inside. During the worst stages of my marriage, I would hibernate within these walls and pretend the emotional storm at home didn't exist. I remember the weekend I found those texts on Clara's phone. The number was saved in her contacts as 'HOSPITAL'. I tortured myself for months wondering who the guy was. I imagined a brain surgeon or a neurologist, someone contemptuous of sleep psychology. The sense of anger and betrayal has never really left me.

I retreat to my office for half an hour. I write up the report on my interview with Richard.

I summarise the main points:

- Richard confirmed that he wasn't aware of Anna's sleep-walking until Emily told him about it during the school expulsion incident.

- Richard claims to be the one who thought seeking treatment would create a political scandal. He regarded time as the best healer for Anna's parasomnia.
- Richard had doubts about Anna starting *Elementary* magazine after Oxford but claimed to have admired her entrepreneurial spirit.
- Richard admitted that he struggled at times to connect with his daughter. But they bonded over Manchester United football matches, a tradition since childhood.
- Richard claimed that Anna visited Broadmoor several times for research purposes.
- Richard said Anna used his credit card to buy a clean laptop, supposedly to communicate with a source regarding the Broadmoor story. Neither the laptop, nor the source, emerged after that fateful night in 2019.
- Richard confirmed ES's testimony that Anna's new investigation had something to do with the Stockwell Monster and she was obsessed with reading the play *Medea*.
- Richard knew no reason why the incidents in the Forest that night should have triggered an episode of parasomnia.

I save the summary and encrypt it. Then I unlock my desk drawer and take out Anna's copy of *Medea and Other Plays*. I flick through the pages again. I pause over a passage near the end.

What can be strange or terrible after this?
O bed of women, full of passion and pain,
What wickedness, what sorrow you have caused
on the earth!

I dwell on the words while I brew another mug of coffee.

A caretaker nurse is here on the night shift. But I think of Harriet's freckled smile and watching her with Anna. There is a peculiar intimacy to a world focused on sleep. I am so tired of being alone with my thoughts. I have a sudden urge to confess and confide in another human being.

Harriet is the one who keeps Anna going. She changes the sheets, dresses and washes the patient, does the unglamorous work. She has lived and breathed the walls of high-security psychiatric hospitals and can translate Bloom's file into layman's terms, give it colour and context. Solve the riddle.

I hear my office landline ring. I reluctantly pick up the receiver. 'Hello?'

I pour milk and stir.

'Dr Prince, it's the VIP room on floor two. You're needed urgently.'

41

BEN

There is stillness, the Abbey and all its bustle halted. It is impossible and yet it is possible.

The call from the caretaker nurse.

Dr Prince to the VIP room.

I see myself looking down on events, like an out-of-body experience.

The run down the stairs, the hasty anti-bacterial cleansing, the entrance. The caretaker nurse standing by the bed. The treatment room feels chilly, somehow, and I regret being in shirtsleeves. Maybe it's the ice-cold water in the taps as I scrub away possible infections. Or something else, almost ethereal. But there is a stillness to the room like nothing I've felt before.

'When did it happen?'

The nurse is jumpy, nervous. She coughs and says, 'I just had to take a personal call. I was checking some test results when I came back in and saw it on the monitors.'

'And you're sure? There's no way you could have been mistaken?'

The nurse doesn't hesitate. Her voice is strong, clear. 'No.'

'How long did it last for?'

'Again, it's impossible—'

I wave away the caveats. 'Your best estimate will do.'

'A few minutes. By the time I called you, it seemed to have stopped.'

'"Seemed" doesn't sound very sure.'

'It definitely stopped.'

'It didn't happen again from the time you called me until I arrived?'

'No.'

'Were you doing anything different to normal?' I ask. 'I'm interested in the small details. Music, movement, speech, touch. Anything Anna could have reacted to?'

'I'm not sure.'

'Think. There must have been a trigger.'

The nurse retreats into herself. I want to nudge her in the right direction. But prompts could be fatal here. I need to understand exactly what went on in the minutes leading up to the event. The minutes before she called me.

Finally, the nurse remembers something. 'I put the TV on. Just to check on the score.'

My role is to stay clinical and detached. I try not to betray emotion. Personal call, watching TV at work. I will deal with that later. 'Which match?'

The nurse looks embarrassed. 'It's silly, really.'

'Trust me. Nothing is silly. Just be honest.'

The nurse sighs. 'Chelsea versus Man United. I put a bit of money on United to win. I just wanted to check if I was quids in.'

I remember Richard watching Manchester United games with Anna. Before she became aware of her father's infidelities, her parents' frailties. Those matches signal childhood, excitement, late bedtimes, the mysteries of a world beyond her own. I curse myself for missing it.

'It was playing continuously?'

'Yes. I turned it off after it happened.'

I want my theory to be right. I have tried books, music, films,

200

flowers, perfume, feathers, speech. The beautiful game is a logical extension of that therapeutic approach. It is my vindication. Prince's Cure.

I need her; she needs me. That unique connection binds us. The only two people in the world.

And yet still those other worries too: if by waking her I am also locking the cell door. Betraying my oath to cure and not condemn. Helping the state to imprison someone for a crime she wasn't aware of committing. On the wrong side of history.

I stand near the bed and look down at Anna and hear that call from the nurse again.

Those words that change everything.

The patient has just opened her eyes.

ANNA'S NOTEBOOK

2019

April 1

Brasserie Zédel, Piccadilly Circus. Indira's birthday! We sit in the red booths. It screams wartime Paris. I think of all those tales about women joining the Special Operations Executive in Baker Street and being parachuted into Vichy France and wonder how I would cope behind enemy lines.

A band plays. Loved-up couples ogle each other. There will be the compulsory celebration in the flat with bad music and worse friends. But tonight it's just us.

We drink and Indira unwraps my present. I still hope she'll confess about the secret meetings with GVM. About why my two best friends are secretly plotting behind my back to sell the company I started. She will say it was Doug's idea to shut me out and I will pretend to be shocked then sympathetic. It will be the two of us against the world. I will tell her about my sleepwalking episode and my fear of it happening again. She will shrink my fear. We will laugh together. Order will be restored.

But she says nothing. Instead, we drink too much. I talk about the Stockwell Monster story. She remembers the Sally Turner case too. That instinctive sense of outrage about a woman breaking society's greatest taboo. A stepmum killing two kids. Against the laws of nature.

Afterwards we drunkenly patrol the sodium-lit city by ourselves. I am not the only fluent liar. She has no tells. No blinks, shuffles or missteps. I keep waiting even as we return to the flat. But we simply stumble inside. We hug and sigh and go our separate ways. There is no epic showdown or pistols at dawn.

I realise for the first time that I don't trust her anymore. Or even like her, come to that. This is how flatmates become enemies. We are too timid to openly confront one another, but too scheming to avoid those little coups and landgrabs.

Yes, it could be the drink. But for a moment, as we hug, I actually hate her. The lies, the pretence. Indira with her classical beauty and sculpted body thinks she can flatten me. That I will do nothing. She thinks I'm too naïve to know.

Back in my room I search out that wonkish academic article again from *Neuroethics* magazine and read the paragraph that haunts me. It is an example from Aristotle's *Ethics*. It concerns who is responsible for criminal actions.

Aristotle uses the example of a drunkard:

> . . . even though a drunken individual does not act voluntarily or with full capacity while he is intoxicated, he acts voluntarily and with mental capacity when choosing to become intoxicated and should therefore be held accountable for doing so. An individual whose parasomnia episodes are triggered by excessive alcohol consumption or other factors within their control mirrors this example.

Ancient to modern. I think of the Sally Turner case. Alcohol fuelled her parasomnia. She drank heavily in the days before the murders. She precipitated her own madness.

I have broken my vow and drunk more than I should tonight.

I close my laptop. I lie on the bed. Alcohol triggers sleepwalking. So does insomnia. This demon won't let me live. I am caught between sleep and sanity – damned if I do, damned if I don't.

Damned from tip to toe.

April 8

The flat again today. I'm still digging.

Back to my true crime piece. The ghost of Sally Turner.

I look through the newspaper clippings of the Stockwell Monster case from twenty years ago. NEW POLL: 74% SAY HANG THE 'STOCKWELL MONSTER' (*Sun*); 'KIDDIE KILLER' IN THE DOCK (*Daily Express*); 'MONSTER MUM' FACES JUSTICE (*Daily Mail*); TURNER USES SLEEPWALKING DEFENCE FOR DOUBLE MURDER (*The Times*).

I file more Freedom of Information requests to the Home Office, Ministry of Justice, Metropolitan Police, West London NHS Trust and the Department for Health. I issue callouts on Twitter through my @AnnaO handle to crowd-source any further leads. Not mentioning specifics but looking for any sources inside Broadmoor.

Cranks, of course, fill my DMs. But there is one message that intrigues me. I see their handle and smile.

It's catchy if hardly original.

I click open the first message.

@PatientX.

42

LOLA

It intrigues her more than anything. She has listened to all his lectures online, even downloaded some of his podcast appearances. As the self-appointed curator of the Anna O legacy, Lola gives her begrudging approval.

After so many false starts, Dr Benedict Prince might just be the man for the job.

She knows him now or thinks she does. She can see the pinched look on his face when stressed, or the quiver in his cheekbones when tired. Monitoring him up close and in the flesh is even more interesting.

Lola watches him carefully now at the back entrance of the Abbey, still deep in conversation with another figure. Stalking is such an ugly word for what this is. Lola much prefers investigation. That's what police officers and private eyes do all the time. It's what the entire art of surveillance is for. Dr Prince is more awkwardly handsome than his photo suggests. The smudge of blond-brown hair, a conservatively fashionable dress sense, a tie-less shirt and inoffensive chinos, some scuffed Chelsea boots on dress-down Fridays. Always that rakishly perfect smile.

Yes, some might say this – like all of her work, by night and day – is obsession writ large, a failure to properly come to terms with the trauma of that one night. But, in reality, she needs to be sure. The entire Anna O investigation has been botched from the start. The media pumped out sensationalist nonsense until Anna became a myth rather than a human being. She needs to be sure that Dr Prince isn't more of the same.

That's why she follows him. That's why she has got so close to this investigation.

Lola sees Ben finishing his conversation with the other figure – a woman, also a member of the Abbey staff. It looks like one of the late-duty porters. A supporting artist in this drama, among the other cleaners, receptionists, IT fixers and delivery drivers. Not starry enough to make the boards. But Dr Prince does like to seduce the auxiliary staff. Both figures head their separate ways. Without Nurse Roberts beside him, the doctor cuts an isolated, slightly tragic figure. The nurse is the making of him. Not that a lowly nurse ever gets much credit.

Lola has listened carefully. She knows enough to make sense of tonight. Something is clearly afoot, a breakthrough of sorts with Anna that is being monitored around the clock. The night-duty porter promising to be extra-vigilant. Dr Prince heading back inside. The lights still aglow on the top floor.

Lola takes out her own phone. She makes sure no one else is looking and quietly snaps a photo of Dr Prince for her collection.

The truth about what really happened that night still needs to be told. She won't allow them to erase her role from history.

The guilty parties need to pay for their sins.

It's time for another post.

43

BEN

I have dreamed of this moment.

Yet still the scene looks stubbornly familiar. Anna's eyes are shut. Her body is frozen on the bed. The tangle of tubes and wires protrude from her body like redundant limbs.

I move towards the bed, taking up my usual position on the stool. The tests for patients emerging from a minimally conscious state are simple.

First: can the patient follow a simple command?

'Anna, it's Dr Prince. Benedict. I want you to flex your left hand for me. Move it in any way. Can you do that for me, Anna?'

I sound patronising. But that's because I have an audience. The intimacy of my solo sessions with Anna will sound unprofessional here. I am back to being a doctor again. A therapist, a professional. Not a card-carrying member of Team Anna.

'Ben . . .'

Harriet's voice startles me. Her shift ended hours ago. I texted her with an update after I got the call from the duty nurse. But I didn't expect her this quickly. She is still wet from scrubbing her hands and arms.

'I left my wallet here,' she says. 'I was coming back for it when I got your message.'

'Perfect timing.'

I glance back to the bed now. I see the faintest twitch of movement in Anna's left hand. I wait, begging the others to remain still.

Then, finally, there is another distinct twitch. Anna's left hand is moving. I see a small flicker around her eyelids.

Now I try the second question. The standard MCS formula.

'Anna, I know you can hear me. Just a few more things I need to ask you. Can you tilt your head to the right for me?'

It is the easiest gesture to ask for. The rest of her limbs are atrophied from so long in bed. She can move her head onto the pillow. I feel Harriet's presence beside me. The outside world has become quiet.

'Anna, just tilt your head if you can hear me. You can do this, Anna.'

I sound like a motivational coach or a school netball teacher. But studies have shown that identification is everything. Constant repetition of her name, encouraging words, replicating the rhythms and assurances of childhood – a time when the patient felt safe – can be helpful.

'Look . . .'

Harriet has become my scout and lieutenant, able to spot small changes in battle formations and reporting them back to high command. I focus on Anna again. I try not to get distracted by my own thoughts. I look closely and see Anna's head tilt fractionally to the right. Almost invisible. But, yes, there is something.

'Good, Anna. That's so good. You're safe here at the Abbey Sleep Clinic.'

There are further tests to undertake. The next stage is seeing if Anna can reach for an object or demonstrate any kind of self-directed action. It is important to confirm that the link between mind and body is normalising. That the thought can be translated into movement. All of it is building up to the point where Anna can open her eyes again – once, twice, on command. I must keep communicating.

'Anna, you're doing really well. We're almost there. I just have a few more questions . . .'

I go through the rest of it now. I've imagined this so many times that the questions are automatic. I ask Anna to touch her face. I wait, ask again, then watch spellbound as her right hand fumbles for the outline of her upper body. Her eyes are still shut. She shows no outward signs of wakefulness. But her brain is still working. She is in there somewhere.

Next, I tell Harriet to prepare Anna to be moved to the third floor where the MRI machine is located. A functional MRI is used to test residual brain function. I can compare Anna's results with the documented cases of other MCS patients and those suffering from resignation syndrome.

I wait while Harriet and the caretaker nurse prepare Anna. I keep lacing my voice with that Radio 4 softness. I must ensure Anna isn't scared by what's occurring. The minute her mind goes into fight-or-flight mode then the chance of waking her up will be gone again.

'Anna, it's Dr Prince. You've done so well. We're moving you to a room on the third floor where we have our equipment for a functional MRI. That will allow me to measure your brain activity and get a better handle on how the treatment is progressing. I'll be asking a few more questions and it will be over very soon. You're doing fantastically, Anna. We're so nearly there. Stay with me, Anna.'

I wonder if I should call Emily or Richard Ogilvy personally. But I decide that a false dawn is more painful than silence. For now, I should wait.

We reach the next floor. Harriet, the caretaker nurse and a technician get the MRI equipment ready. I take my place in front of the monitors. Anna is gently positioned within the machine. Strictly speaking, MRI tests are a job for neurologists. I am trespassing here, exceeding my brief.

But I refuse to let my case be stolen. Protocol be damned.

I keep my voice soft, reassuring. I lean towards the microphone.

209

'Anna, these questions are slightly different. For this round, I'm going to ask you to imagine various things. Just let your mind work. If you can't imagine anything, or no thoughts emerge, then don't worry. You're doing amazingly well, Anna.' I cover the microphone. I take a sip of water. 'Okay . . . I want you to imagine playing your favourite sport. When you were young, practising in the garden before you were called in for tea.'

Two minutes. I wait. I watch. I make notes.

'Next, Anna, I want you to imagine walking through your childhood home. The house in Hampstead. All those rooms: the kitchen, the living room, your bedroom, the bathroom, the cupboards. Run your hand along the surfaces, hear the voices and noises.'

The same procedure: waiting, watching, noting the results.

'Now, Anna, imagine something else for me. Imagine what it feels like to write. Think of using that special skill of yours. The words slowly crafted on the page. The limitless potential of your own imagination. What does writing feel like to you? What sort of high do you get from it?'

I don't need Harriet's prompts this time. I can see the results on the monitors. These results, like those movements earlier, will be landmarks in the treatment of resignation syndrome. My book will need a sequel. Documentaries, Reith Lectures. I will dine out on this story until kingdom come.

'Finally, Anna, imagine saying the name of your mum and dad and brother. Their first names. Their nicknames. What you call them when you're all together. The four of you. Let those names float around your brain. Savour those names until they have a physical taste on your tongue.'

I hear the neurologists and 'real' doctors laughing again. I don't care. They are stuck with their materialist, flesh-and-blood view of medicine, Victorian butchers with better sideburns and a flirtier bedside manner. They dismiss functional disease as witchdoctor stuff, the realm of quacks and priests.

I glance at Harriet. I have what I need. Even a layman can

see that Anna's levels of brain activation increased significantly as I asked the questions. She is stirring back to life.

Harriet looks towards the MRI machine. 'Ready to move her back?'

'Gently does it.'

'Are we moving to the amber protocol?'

I don't answer immediately. The amber protocol is shorthand for the awakening. It triggers everything else: next of kin, the MoJ, press announcement, the lot.

It is a seismic call to make.

I take a breath. There are two case studies I teach to my class at Birkbeck. A woman called Munira Abdulla spends twenty-seven years in a coma following a car accident. She falls into a minimally conscious state trying to protect her four-year-old son from harm. Almost three decades later she wakes up in a specialist clinic in Bavaria. The reason is disarmingly simple: there is a fracas in her hospital room and she senses that her son is in danger again. Her first word is 'Omar', her son's name. She has last seen him as a four-year-old. He is now thirty-two. That fierce maternal instinct breaks through almost three decades of the deepest sleep imaginable. It brings her back to life.

The second case study involves an American patient from Arkansas named Terry Wallis. His truck goes off a bridge in 1984 and he spends nineteen years in a minimally conscious state before waking up in 2003. On waking he thinks he is still a teenager. He asks for his mum and a can of Pepsi. A team from Cornell University publish a pioneering paper on the case in the *Journal of Clinical Investigation*. Mr Wallis's short-term memory is badly impaired. Despite the nineteen-year time gap, he remains convinced it is still 1984.

From that moment on, he is effectively stuck in time.

I feel the sudden urge for pen and paper, to record these events before the finer details escape me. My theory has worked. The unexplained incident at Rampton has been repeated. The hypothesis I sketched out in that journal article has just produced its first, and most spectacular, case study. I have used the ephemera of the past to bring a patient back to the present.

Harriet finishes doing her checks. 'So,' she says. 'Have you decided?'

The duty nurse steps outside. The doors hiss shut, maintaining the sterile environment. It is still cold. I look at Anna, now transferred from the MRI machine and back on the trolley. Her brain wrestling with wakefulness.

'Ben . . . are we moving to the amber protocol?'

I don't want to articulate the next thought in my head. It risks jinxing things. Instead, I just stand there. I fix on Anna and the movement around her eyes and the very slow and painful way in which the lids on both sides begin to roll and the whites of her eyes emerge with a keen, almost blistering brightness.

A voiceless sensation fills the room, as if the medical miracle in front of us has a spiritual dimension too, a life-force it never had before.

I am at the foot of the bed now, making sure my body is aligned with hers, when I find myself looking directly into the open eyes of Anna Ogilvy.

ANNA'S NOTEBOOK
2019

April 15

London Library. Journalism is about sources. And I've snared one here.

Patient X.

Yes, it might be a blind alley. The 'patient' prefix is freighted with issues. But we've corresponded enough that I know they are semi-credible. This, though, is the moment it could all fall apart. Broadmoor is a big institution. Hundreds of patients, nearly a thousand staff.

But I have no other choice. I must reveal my hand.

I review my latest draft:

I'm researching an article on the Sally Turner case in 1999. She was found not guilty by reason of insane automatism at the Old Bailey in June 1999 and detained indefinitely at Broadmoor. She was later found dead in her cell in August 1999. Given the security protocols around her, I want to know how she got hold of a plastic knife to cut her wrists. Did Sally Turner commit suicide, or was she killed with the help or neglect of the staff at Broadmoor? How was she viewed inside Broadmoor? Why did that case in particular grab the media spotlight as opposed to many others? Any inside detail or 'colour' for the piece would be v useful.

I read the message one last time. It is slightly gauche, slightly desperate, but I need something chewy now. Getting sources inside secure hospitals is like getting blood from a stone. I need a lead.

I take a breath.

I press send.

April 22

This is new. It's like I'm editing a story that already exists. I brush away the cobwebs, clean the surface. I think of that quote from Michelangelo:

Every block of stone has a statue inside it.

The sculptor's job is one of discovery not creation.

I have checked the website. I've read the profile page for Professor V. Bloom. I have one source. I need more.

The Abbey Sleep Clinic is ahead of me. Harley Street either side. I need to cross the road, ring the buzzer and wait in reception. I will tell them my history as a sleep-walker. The fantasies I entertain. Then I'll pounce with my questions about Sally Turner:

Who treated Turner all those years ago?

Why did Professor Bloom appear for the defence at the Old Bailey?

What really happened on the Cranfield Ward at Broadmoor twenty years ago?

How did Sally Turner get a knife into her room despite all the precautions and safety measures?

It starts to rain. Patients and staff trickle in and out of the newly painted door ahead. Traffic snorts past. I wonder if I can be reported for confessing to violent thoughts. I debate if I have enough to doorstep Professor Bloom or if I'm just getting desperate.

I stay there for minutes, even hours. The rain stops. I am saved by a new message. It is a reply from @PatientX. They are fluent and convincing. I believe what they are telling me. Or, rather, I want to believe. Which is more dangerous.

I read their reply:

Hey, I wasn't on Cranfield. But I was at Broadmoor during '99 and the Sally Turner case. Cranfield only had eleven beds. It was the smallest ward. But I heard rumours that a special section was reserved for Turner, given how much publicity the case got. People said they built some kind of special cage on the instructions of the therapy team. No one ever had details. But some of the nurses said they'd heard that Turner was the subject of a psych 'trial' being conducted at Broadmoor. I never knew whether that was true. All I heard was the name they called it. I didn't understand the reference at the time. I only looked it up when I got out. It was called 'MEDEA'.

April 29

I open my eyes now. But not in the living room. I am in the hallway.

I adjust to the dawn light.

There is a doorway ahead. Doug is sleeping, spit leaking pathetically on the pillow. I can taste the sulphuric fumes of alcohol and weed. It takes me a moment to understand. To blink fully awake. Surface from sleep. And feel the item gripped in my right hand.

I see Doug still sleeping. I process what must have happened.

I imagine myself getting up and unlocking the bedroom

door. Taking the item from the kitchen and tiptoeing down the hall.

Waiting for the right moment. Debating what to do.

This can't be real. But I am no longer dreaming.

This isn't a night terror. It's another episode.

Even worse than before.

In my right hand is a knife.

44

EMILY

It is like an answer to prayer. That is the ironic thing. Mobiles are not strictly allowed in the morning prayer meetings. But she has never switched hers off. There is always the chance for news. To switch off her phone would be to concede defeat.

The ringtone gets a dirty look from the twenty-something curate. Emily knows she should silence the phone and continue but she sees the caller ID and the contact she saved before that first interview.

DR PRINCE (THE ABBEY).

'Excuse me,' she says, breaking off mid-prayer, much to the flamboyant confusion of the curate and the others. Her words break the spell. She disappears through the church office door. She hears the rector hastily cover with a prayer of his own.

Time is a strange beast. She remembers swiping her thumb across the screen. She remembers the freshness of the carpet outside the church office. Then, after that, events fuzz and crackle. Afterwards she can never recall how long she waited for a cab or how quick the journey from St Margaret's to the Abbey was. She remembers looking at the name 'RICHARD' in her phone contacts and knowing she must call him but without knowing how. All she hears is the melodic sound of Benedict Prince on repeat.

I think you should get to the Abbey as quickly as possible. It's Anna . . .

There is a cab. Central London washes by in a blur of land-marks and tourists and traffic. She fiddles with her contactless payment and stumbles onto Harley Street and feels blood-sugar weak, strength drained from each limb. There is more, of course: Dr Prince waiting for her on the ground floor; rushing up to the third floor, rather than the usual second floor; explanations about the functional MRI test and a superstitious reluctance to move Anna in case her eyes close again.

Emily hears very little of it. Instead, there are just nerves. She is a different person to the last time Anna saw her. The Emily Ogilvy of 2019 was in her pomp. She was a member of the Shadow Cabinet, a heavyweight figure within the Opposition, poised on the threshold of major government office. She had staff, an entourage, fellow travellers, hangers-on, supporters, even fans. Her old self had a husband, two peachily perfect children. Today she is rebuked by a man twenty years her junior during a morning prayer meeting. She is single. Her son has fled halfway across the world. She isn't the person Anna once knew.

There is that other worry too. The unspoken one. Not Anna asleep. But Anna awake. All the things she might remember.

And then, like that, Anna is there. Or the person masquerading as Anna. The Ill Anna, she must think of her daughter now. The strength-starved limbs, the matted hair, the skeleton thinness and air of decay. The Ill Anna who has aged decades, growing old while still being young. But that doesn't matter somehow. The worries, the media, the questions, the guilt – all is temporarily stilled. Emily sees her child lying in bed with her eyes open for the first time in four years. And the memories come: the bedtime stories, the holiday snuggles, the school bugs, the Christmas mornings, the birthday surprises, the brow-stroking, the endless cycle of interactions, each one humdrum and blissful.

Emily sees her tears drip onto Anna's face. She wipes them

dry. She leaves her hand there, caressing her daughter's cheeks, the eyes reacting.

Anna's personality slowly overtakes everything, her face suddenly injected with soul again, the miracle of life enacted before them both.

'Hello, my darling,' says Emily. 'Welcome back.'

45

EMILY

Emily holds Anna's hand.

This is the moment she's waited so long for. The mother-daughter reunion. She looks up and sees Dr Prince and Harriet, the nurse, enter the treatment room and, before she's formulated the right words, says, 'I'm not sure what to say.'

Dr Prince smiles. 'There's no need to say anything.'

'I owe you an apology. I really didn't think your method would work.'

'Truthfully, I wasn't entirely sure either,' he says. 'But it's still the early stages of recovery. The ultimate goal is for Anna to regain full consciousness and stay awake. We'll have to keep monitoring her progress on that front.'

It is the question Emily doesn't want to ask. But she can't help it. 'What happens now? With the trial, I mean.'

Dr Prince glances at the nurse. Both seem uncomfortable. 'That's entirely out of our hands, I'm afraid,' he says. 'Our job is to look after the wellbeing of our patient. But I can assure you that nothing will happen until all the medical elements have been resolved.'

'I see.' She is too stunned to think of anything more to say. But she knows how political imperatives bully and defeat all others. The Ministry of Justice wants Anna in the dock. They will have their way.

Harriet speaks now, spotting Emily's despondency. 'We'll let you have some quiet time with Anna,' she says. 'Let us know if you need anything.'

Emily looks up, remembers where she is. 'Thank you,' she says, meaning it for once, no longer just mere politeness. 'Thank you for everything.'

Dr Prince and Harriet leave the treatment room. She hears the door lock but her eyes are stuck firmly on her daughter. She remembers one of those odd facts she learned before Anna was born: the human eyeball remains largely unchanged from birth while everything else grows around it. It's one of the most peculiar, but beautiful, truths. Babies have saucer eyes that slowly become proportionate. She remembers the moment her eyes first met Anna's in the delivery room at the hospital. The magic of that simple interaction. She stays lost in her daughter until Anna's eyes grow tired. Her lids are weighted after so long asleep. Emily watches Anna blink, wrestling with the effort of staying awake.

The sleepiness is almost contagious now. Emily looks around the sterile treatment room but only sees the darkness of that night swallow them both. She prays this isn't a one-off and Anna hasn't fallen asleep again for good. She was always a moderate optimist before, but now she fears each new moment and what fresh cruelties life will bring. Seeing Anna wake and regress would be worse than her not waking at all.

She sits back. The initial euphoria wears off.

Instead, the past intrudes again. Sleep seems so dangerous yet inviting. Emily feels herself being caught between now and dreamland.

Those memories she has tried to bury.

She can no longer keep her eyes open. She has spent so much energy wishing for this moment that the emotion is almost too much.

She is tumbling, somehow. Pitched back to the very beginning.

The Farm. Yes, of course.

Spiralling into the past.

The Farm was her idea. That's the tragic irony. So was the Forest.

She wants them to be a family. Here in the country mud. Laughing, being silly, a brief sabbatical from adult life and the chance for childish joy again.

The reality of the Forest is duller. It is not quite *Swallows and Amazons* or *Stig of the Dump*, two bedtime favourites she used to read to Theo and Anna. The division into teams is also slightly unfortunate. Emily longs for Anna to be part of the family group. But the Survivors complete their head start. The gusty country air seems to work. Richard is his old self for the first time in months, no longer addicted to a phone or iPad, liberated from monitoring every tremor of the markets.

The rest of the Forest is smudged by time. She remembers that other glimpse of Richard and a second person, and the thoughts that used to haunt her. An old obsession, made redundant by the divorce and the reinvention. But, yes, she remembers that. Otherwise the reel jumps to later and the waspy vibration of her phone and the new WhatsApp message. Two vibrations, technically, on two phones. Emily is the lighter sleeper. She wakes, gropes, reads. Those words which made so little sense at that time in the morning. Small letters on a screen, so innocuous by themselves but deadly together.

I'm sorry. I think I've killed them.

Emily sees the rest quite clearly. First the wounding anxiety. The mother-protector inheritance. It is impossible to describe, even now. But it remains the most asphyxiating sensation, a chokehold that starts in the throat and extends to the head and legs. The same panic when Anna or Theo went walkabout in the supermarket. Or fidgeted free and into the road.

Nothing – marriage, prayer – rivals it. The surface of life goes. Instead, there is the sense of life unvarnished. The knowledge that everything can be snatched away. Like the doctor's appointment about a recent scan or a call from the police regarding next of kin, the sense of the universe laughing at human pretensions, the illusion of control.

She wakes Richard. He groans, turns onto his side. She shows him the phone. He puts on his glasses. They read the message together. Their instincts collide. They get up and find yesterday's clothes and jackets and stumble out of the Orange Cabin into the darkness. No words pass, or not that she remembers. They've been married too long, seen too much. They are across the boggy turf. Theo's cabin – green, she thinks, or yellow or something – is on the left. Anna's cabin is straight ahead neighbouring the Red Cabin for Indira and Douglas.

Still, though, that other obsession. Emily remembers now. Those last seconds of innocence. She looks at Richard. He is so different, stripped of his armour. No Armani suits or catalogue-perfect loungewear. No ornamentation or chauffeurs or confetti from his glittering life as a fund manager; that dandified person he's become.

This is the man she married. The cocky, slightly dishevelled economist with an opinion on everything and an Eeyore vulnerability in his eyes. The student who blushed around pretty women and kissed without finesse. She was the more romantically experienced. She never saw her future as the betrayed wife, the cuckolded bride. The old Richard – her Richard – was never the type. Success changed that.

As they near the Blue Cabin, those were her last thoughts: those small, mediocre jealousies.

Richard only speaks when they reach the Blue Cabin door. He knocks firmly, then shouts, 'Anna! It's Dad. Anna, please open the door.'

Nothing.

'Anna! Mum and I got your message. Not funny, Anna. Open the door and show us you're all right. We won't be angry. We just need to know you're safe.'

Nothing.

Richard sizes up the door. Emily nods. It's the only way now. Anna could be inside drugged up to her eyeballs, choking on her own vomit; or, worse, sleepwalking her way to another disaster. Like the dog or school or the holiday.

'Anna, I'm coming in.'

Richard tries the handle and shoves it open. It gives more easily, the excess force almost tipping him headlong into the small cabin. Emily is prepared to find Anna on the bed or the floor. But the Blue Cabin is empty. There is a small chair with clothes draped carelessly. No one is here.

Empty.

Richard searches nonetheless. Emily gets her phone. She tries ringing Anna. There is a sound, but the volume is wrong. Richard hears it, Emily tries to place it. They search some more and Emily keeps ringing but the sound isn't coming from inside this cabin. And then the warbled ringtone and the exact words from the WhatsApp message make sense.

Neither say it. The thought – the real thought, not the hazy, protected parental version – is too cold and awful.

I'm sorry. I think I've killed them.

Instead, they run. They run like their old lives are leaving. Like luck is ahead and must be caught before it escapes.

By the time they reach the Red Cabin there is no need for warnings or shouts. Richard hesitates for only a second before fumbling at the handle. And they know as surely as they've known anything that their old lives are over. They weren't quick enough. All that came before – meeting, marriage, children, the giddy highs and terrible lows – is mere prequel. This is all their time on earth will be remembered for. This is what they will be judged on.

The bodies are the first things she sees. People mention blood, but that came later. It is dark still, the scene lit only by moonlight. But the cabin is small enough that three motionless bodies dominate the scene. For a moment, Emily thinks they are sleeping. Indira and Douglas are still in their respective beds. Both are face-down, the humps of their backsides visible. Douglas is naked from the waist up. Indira wears pyjamas. Anna is lying on the floor between them both. It reminds Emily of those childhood sleepovers when Anna's friends were put in the guest bedroom. Anna would sneak in with a midnight feast. Emily would find them all tangled together the next morning with half-empty Twix wrappers, sleeping bags and pillows hopelessly muddled during the night.

'Ems.'

Richard's voice. Emily's delusion breaks. She knows that tone. She looks up and sees Richard standing by the beds and the whimper of terror as he understands what is before them. The odd, streaky nature of the scene – fragments, really – matures into something coherent. Those streaks aren't accidental. Sleep and death are so hard to tell apart. Emily's O level Greek class comes back to her: Hypnos is the God of sleep; his twin brother is Thanatos, the God of death. Both reside in the sun-starved underworld.

Those streaks are blood.

'Anna! Anna!'

This must be the underworld. What else can hell look like? Emily sees Richard bending down, straining to feel their daughter's pulse, hear signs of breathing.

'She's alive! Ems, she's alive!'

He says it with hope. And yet, for Emily, the despair deepens. She gets there sooner than Richard. She sees the bodies and the knife in Anna's hand and the blood-splashed cabin and she traces every part of it back to that night in the holiday home in Cornwall. Her daughter needing help. Emily hushing it up.

Another jump cut. It is later. The Farm is abuzz with police cars, strobing blue lights. She and Richard have removed their clothes and are sitting in police-issue grey being checked over by medics. A woman arrives. She looks youthfully middle-aged, her figure still fuller from childbirth, eyes sore from sleepless nights. She holds up her warrant card and introduces herself as

DI Clara Fennel from Thames Valley Police and asks Emily to describe what happened.

They have their stories straight by then. Or just about. Yes, they received a WhatsApp message from Anna. They found her asleep in the Blue Cabin, a knife by her side. It looked like she'd been attacked. They tried to help her, hence the blood and fibre on their clothes. Anna was clearly alive but she wouldn't wake up. That's when they called for an ambulance.

And what about the other cabin? says DI Fennel. When did you first realise what had happened there?

Later, says Emily. Much later.

That's when we called the police.

46

EMILY

Afterwards, she is never sure how long she sat there. Half-asleep and lost in the past.

She surfaces now. Yawns. Remembers. No words are big enough for the moment.

There is the pain, too. All those wasted moments. The petty anxieties and pop-up arguments, the scratchy friction that existed between them, too similar and too different. If someone had told her what was to come, she would rather have died. But, somehow, she is still going. Anna is still here. Emily is still fighting. Fate can't break their family entirely.

Time loses all sense. It is minutes, or perhaps hours, later when Dr Prince puts a hand on her shoulder and says something about talking outside. Harriet, the nurse, has a tray with tea and biscuits and tissues. And they sit there, still only metres from Anna in the treatment room, the silence echoing.

At last, Dr Prince says, 'There are some basic housekeeping issues we should probably go through.'

Emily flinches at his tone. The words sound dry and desiccated. It's so at odds with how she feels. This is a miracle, an occasion fit for divine insights, for life-changing euphoria. She sips her tea.

She nibbles a chocolate digestive. She tries to bring herself down to earth again.

'Of course,' she says. Everything feels like an out-of-body experience. She will wake up, blinking into another featureless night.

Dr Prince continues, 'As you know, the Abbey has a duty to liaise with the Ministry of Justice. The timing is within our discretion up to a point. But Anna is technically still in the custody of His Majesty's Government. We can't delay too long before informing them.'

Emily nods again. There is a compassion to Dr Prince. She sees that now. He is on her side. On Anna's side. He will do this humanely. 'Yes.'

'We can't be sure how long Anna's awakening will last or if she will sink back into a minimally conscious state again. If she does stay awake, then I will have to inform the MoJ and it will be up to them how things proceed from here.'

Sometimes Emily almost forgets she was once a politician, playing God with other people's lives. She sees tie-less bureaucrats in overheated offices deciding her daughter's fate with the tap of a mouse and the whoosh of an email. She thinks of the cases she decided on as minister, the ordinary people waiting mutely for her decision. She feels shame at her former indifference.

Emily takes another sip of tea. 'What's the prognosis?' she says. 'How likely is it that Anna might slide back into a minimally conscious state?'

Dr Prince wriggles uncomfortably in his chair. 'The data is still patchy,' he says. 'There aren't enough studies of resignation syndrome to get a big enough sample size about this type of FND. But with careful monitoring, and ongoing therapy, I believe Anna can stay awake.'

There is something in his tone. She knows when people are hedging. 'You're not certain?'

'Wonderful though the stories of resurrection are, the medical reality is often quite different. The Lazarus-style reawakening is more science-fiction than fact. Anna has been asleep for over four years. The consequences of that are likely to be profound, both for her physical health and her mental health.'

Emily has read all the books and blogs, listened to the podcasts. She knows every case study. 'Like what exactly?'

'How much do you know about post-traumatic amnesia?'

She sighs. The three dreaded words. 'A bit.'

'In almost every documented case of a patient waking up after so long asleep they suffer from a form of PTA. For some patients it goes quickly. For others it lasts weeks, months, even years. In a few cases the damage to the short-term memory is so profound that PTA is effectively permanent.'

'Like that American truck driver in the eighties.'

'Terry Wallis, yes. He had no memory of the crash and still believed he was living in 1984. Despite the fact he woke up in 2003.'

'So you think Anna will have no idea she's been asleep for so long?'

'Anna's case is a functional neurological disease rather than a traumatic brain injury. In cases of non-organic diseases, it's more difficult to know or predict. But I think it's something you should prepare yourself for. And your ex-husband. The awakening might, in some very real ways, be almost more traumatic than falling asleep.'

Emily's mouth feels scratchy. 'Prepare ourselves for what exactly?'

Dr Prince looks at her kindly. 'There's a strong possibility that in Anna's mind the last four years never happened. For her it could still be 2019.'

Emily waits for it, a thought too gruesome to contemplate.

'She may well think that Indira and Douglas are still alive.'

47

BEN

The next twelve hours will decide everything. My hopes of career advancement, financial redemption, earning the respect of KitKat and Clara, having my theories about resignation syndrome enshrined in the textbooks – all rest on Anna's eyes remaining open. I see it hovering before me, a better life than I have now. Perhaps, just perhaps, those old ambitions can come true after all.

I watch the monitors. I pace my office. I debate when to alert the Ministry of Justice. Eyes open, eyes shut. But for how long.

Everything depends on that simple calculus.

Now, though, the other fears hit me. Anna is still a killer. Someone who slaughtered her two best friends in cold blood. I've become emotionally attached to a murderer, someone responsible for taking two lives. I have proclaimed myself a member of Team Anna. That was one thing when she was asleep, a medical puzzle to solve. Now she is a legal bomb sitting next to us all. I remember seeing the whites of her eyes at the moment of awakening, the spell finally broken. I must be careful.

At the twelve-hour mark Harriet confirms Anna's eyes are still open. Further tests before now were too risky. I leave my office, scrub up and enter the treatment room. I walk in and see that Anna's eyes are shut. I feel that jitterbug of panic in my chest.

'She goes in and out,' says Harriet. 'You just have to try saying her name.'

I take a breath. 'Anna,' I say, approaching the bed. 'It's Dr Prince from the Abbey Sleep Clinic, Anna. How are you feeling now?'

And, slowly, I see the whites of the eyes and those emerald-green circles and the jet-black pupils expand. Her skin is papery, mottled. There is no voice yet, the throat too sore and dry from disuse. Her eyes blink instead until they find me. There is a small, jerky facial movement, a caterpillar crawl between the bottom of her nose and the chapped upper lip, like an itch that needs scratching.

'You've done so well, Anna. I have a few more questions and then we're done for the day. How does that sound?'

The most famous test for newly awakening patients is the Glasgow Coma Scale. The GCS looks at three separate functions: eye opening, verbal response and voluntary movement. Each result is assigned a number. A low number means no result; a high number means substantial progress. Harriet stands next to me playing scorer. The first function has already been tested.

'Your eye opening was really good, Anna,' I say. 'You opened them spontaneously. That's a GCS score of four.'

Harriet makes a note. I move to the second test: verbal response to a command.

'Okay, Anna, this is going to be difficult. I want to see if you can use your voice again. After I've counted to three, try saying "Anna" for me.'

The tension feels almost unbearable. Anna hasn't used her vocal cords in over four years. The media coverage has featured her writing or photographic stills. There are few videos or audio recordings. Everyone knows her face. Almost no one knows what she sounds like.

'One, two, three . . .'

Harriet has a cup of water. She waits, seeing if Anna needs it.

I can't risk pushing Anna back inside her protective shell. I debate whether to ask again or resume later on.

Then she moves. Anna's lips slowly part. I see the tip of her tongue and the watery greyness of her mouth. I lean closer, trying to pick up any sound while being careful not to scare her.

I hear something.

There is a faint, gravelly rasp, a single phut of air emitted from her lungs and mouth. I think I recognise an 'A', like a nursery exercise before the adult pronunciations take over.

I tell Harriet to mark it as a three – midway between one (no response) and five (alert and replying). Comatose patients usually score eight or fewer. Anna is on seven. One more mark and I can tell the Ministry of Justice that, according to the Glasgow Coma Scale, Anna is no longer minimally conscious.

For the third function test, I try a more elaborate version of the previous exercise. I ask Anna to lift her right arm. Her eyes flutter shut again. I say her name. I repeat the command. I wait to see any kind of voluntary movement. Finally, I watch her right arm lift from the covers on the bed before tumbling back.

'Also a four,' I tell Harriet. For the movement function, six means a command is fully obeyed; one indicates no response.

Harriet adds up the total. 'Total score is eleven.'

Scoring eleven on the GCS means I have no further excuses. I am duty-bound to inform the Ministry of Justice that Anna Ogilvy, currently in the custody of HMG, is conscious. I think back to my conversation with Emily. I look at Harriet and the glass of water she's still holding. I remember my first conversation with Stephen Donnelly and wonder again if I've cured Anna only to condemn her.

'All done?' asks Harriet tersely. She, too, is feeling the strain.

'Not yet. Try administering the water. We need her vocal cords to be lubricated.'

'You're sure?'

'Yes.'

I wait while Harriet props Anna up in bed and administers the water. I pick up my notes and reach the section regarding tests for post-traumatic amnesia. I read the list of basic questions that must be asked for an initial diagnosis. They are grouped around time, place and person.

What is your name?

What day of the week is it?

What year is it?

After that come more personal questions.

What was your last memory before the accident?

What happened to bring you here?

A patient suffering from post-traumatic amnesia won't be able to answer. If the PTA wears off, then the patient's answers will slowly become more accurate. If the PTA persists long-term, then the memories are lost forever.

A patient scoring well on the GCS may nearly be fit to stand trial. But someone suffering from acute PTA is not.

That is my get-out clause, I decide, my temporary salvation. I don't have to hand Anna over and surrender her to a life behind bars. Or, at least, not yet.

I wait until Harriet finishes with the water. Then I resume my position by the bed.

'It's Dr Prince again, Anna. One more question.' I pause, clear my throat, then begin. 'Can you tell me your full name?'

48

BEN

It's the next morning when I phone Stephen Donnelly at the Ministry of Justice. I haven't slept. I stumble sleepily into the shower and let the water pound my body. Afterwards, I see the dark bruising under my eyes in the bathroom mirror. I am eating less. My skin is dry. I need coffee, sugar, anything to get me through the day.

Dark obsessions loom: I was sure I could feel eyes on me during the commute home last night. A stalker, or one of those media obsessives. I took a different route from the Tube back to the flat in Pimlico. I kept hearing other steps syncopated with my own. I take paracetamol to calm the pain.

I imagine Bloom's last hours before she died and wonder if this is how it started. Eyes on the Tube. Steps trailing. Then the front door unlocking, the wink of the knife. I feel sick at the idea.

Everything changed when Anna opened her eyes. The dead came back to life. A ghost became flesh again. The stakes feel even higher now. The puzzle harder to solve.

The past is now present.

I wait in the John Lewis café and Stephen Donnelly arrives with his usual routine: a government car, the noiseless entrance, everything hushed and fidgety. He looks even narrower than last time. His raincoat drowns him; his umbrella overwhelms his head. He declines tea or coffee. The biscuit plate is left untouched this time.

'Tell me everything,' he says.

I spare no detail, though fudge the chronology slightly.

'Has any family member visited?'

'Yes. Emily Ogilvy was informed as next of kin.'

Donnelly swallows his irritation. He looks pained. 'You should have let us know first. Failure to do so is a breach of security protocol. You probably have no idea of the risks you've already taken.'

It is the question I've been dreading. But it can't be ignored. The same question Emily asked at her daughter's bedside. 'So what happens now?'

'Exactly what I promised when I offered you this case. You do the medical side. We do the justice side. A trial date will be set and the courts will get their say before the Amnesty debacle frees her forever.'

'Except for one thing.' This is my moment. It is the one way I can keep Anna at the Abbey, stop her being fast-tracked into a stone cell for all eternity. Fulfil my oath as a healer. I am winging it, improvising. But there's just a chance it could work. 'You can't put someone on trial who's suffering from post-traumatic amnesia.'

Donnelly looks stung. 'Who says she suffers from PTA?'

'I do. After so many years asleep, it's to be expected.'

'Are you qualified to make such a diagnosis?'

'I'd say I'm over-qualified.'

This is the most difficult bit. Post-traumatic amnesia is notoriously hard to define. It can range from short-term memory loss to long-term blanks. Anna has just woken up from four years of sleep. That change alone is enough to fuddle the brain. But I can't just stand back and let her be swallowed by the prison system. The PTA card is the only one left to play. It might buy me some more time. After that, who knows.

235

'How long will it take for her to recover?'

'That's an impossible question to answer. It depends.'

'I see.' Donnelly looks at me sternly, leaning forward in his chair. 'Well, the risk is on you and your family, I suppose.'

The mention of my family jolts me, as intended. 'How so?'

'The longer you spend with Anna, especially now she's awake, the more danger you're in. I thought that much would be blindingly obvious. My team monitors the online chatter about the case. Anna O doesn't have fans. She has obsessives. Nutjobs. Psychos. Fringe elements. But dangerous. Very dangerous. Conspiracy theorists who think Anna is being drugged and held against her will here at the Abbey. So far they've just commented. Soon they might act.'

I think of the steps following me from the Tube last night. The sense of being watched. Donnelly is trying to intimidate me, that much is clear. But his warnings bristle with truth. 'Do you think the Abbey could be a target?'

Donnelly sniffs. 'Bloom's already been killed. We think it was probably someone close to her. A face she already knew. We also know some people want to kill Anna too and others want to kill the people holding Anna. There was a reason I told you to contact the MoJ as soon as Anna woke up. By failing to do so you have put more than your own life at risk. Once she's back in the criminal justice system we have barbed wire and armed guards. The longer she's with you the more vulnerable you are.'

'And my family?'

Donnelly stares at me. 'There's a killer still out there, Dr Prince. None of us are safe. That includes you and your family.'

ANNA'S NOTEBOOK

2019

May 6

Ogilvy Towers. Hampstead. It has been a week since The Incident.

The sleepwalking. The knife in my hand. Approaching Doug's bedroom. The terrifying logic of my actions. The near-miss of it all, life-altering and unsavable.

Was I going to kill him as he slept?

Am I really capable of an act like that?

Unconscious desires becoming real.

The Incident. Yes, that's what I'm now calling it. Mum is away on a shadow ministerial trip. Dad has done one of his mea culpa routines and moved back into the family house. He idles in his study. I still wonder who the Other Woman is this time. Whether it's the same Other Woman as last time or someone new. My brain is filled with roomfuls of Other Women.

I retreat to my old childhood bedroom and lock the door.

Two chairs. A trail of sharp objects on the floor. I am less of a danger here.

Doug keeps WhatsApping me. Indira phones and leaves concerned voice notes. The summer edition of *Elementary* has adverts but no content. Deadlines are urgent. Contents tables, page layout – all depend on my long-form piece. And I haven't yet written a word.

Blank screen. White page. The cursor blinking.

I download sleep apps, instead. Sleep Expert. White Noise Sound Machine. Siberian Breath. Make It Rain. I find another app called The Walking Sleep. It promises 'an alarm and phone vibration' with 'your steps and location tracked to wake you up' which ensures 'the safety of yourself and those around'.

I pause over those fateful words: 'your steps and location tracked'. I delete the app. I drink coffee. I feel like Scheherazade in *The Arabian Nights* spinning an endless web of stories to delay her death in the morning.

I go back to the NHS webpage and read all the things that trigger sleepwalking. Stress, anxiety, alcohol, sedatives. Sleepwalking 'can start at any age but is more common in children. One in five children will sleepwalk at least once. Most grow out of it by the time they reach puberty, but it can sometimes persist into adulthood.' I am that child again. The girl with her air of bewildered confusion and sweaty pyjamas.

I ignore my problems. I return to Sally Turner in solitary confinement in the Cranfield Ward at Broadmoor twenty years ago. And that whispered codeword: MEDEA. The Greek goddess who murders her own sons.

I am back on Wikipedia again, my trusty guide:

Euripides's 5th century BCE tragedy *Medea* depicts the ending of the union with Jason, when, after ten years of marriage, Jason abandons her to wed King Creon's daughter Creusa. Medea and her sons by Jason are to be banished from Corinth. In revenge, Medea murders Creusa with poisoned gifts and then murders her own sons by Jason before fleeing for Athens.

Two women, two crimes. Jason abandoned Medea for another woman and banished her family. Tom Cornwell used Sally Turner and let his sons terrorise her.

Both women had that Freudian *precipitating cause*. An inciting incident for their condition. An emotional trigger. The limbic system in overdrive.

Fight or flight. Fear as the engine of sleepwalking.

I wonder if I am the same. If I am capable of such deeds too.

The question is simple.

What do I most fear?

May 16

A knock on the bedroom door.

I am writing. Monk mode. Headphones on, door closed, world excluded.

I have done more research on Broadmoor. No matter how many showers I take, I still don't feel clean. The stories stick to me. I am entering a world outside morality or convention.

Another knock. Mum opens the door.

We have time-travelled to 2009.

She is checking on my homework. Maternal mode rather than shadow ministerial, casually dressed in a shirt and jeans. Her cheering-up face.

She sits on the end of my bed.

You haven't been looking well, darling.

Yes, it's one of those chats.

I pretend to listen to the rest. Mum has won some kind of holiday competition. A prized invitation to an outward-bound weekend away place for all the family.

A chance for us to spend some quality time together, as we used to, without work calls or deadlines or stress. August, most likely, end of summer.

Fresh air, the great outdoors.

There is no website, apparently, just a brochure.

She leaves it on my bed. She even pecks me on the forehead and says there's some shepherd's pie in the oven if I'm staying.

No maternal cliché, it seems, can be left untouched today.

Then she goes, gently closing the door just like she used to.

I pick up the brochure.

There are no photos, just a black background with white text. Minimalist, faintly avant garde.

It lists activities. The marketing screams exclusivity. Just like the mysterious invitation itself.

I look at the front flap again and the plainness of the name.

Welcome to The Farm . . .

49

BEN

I am never quite sure who first suggests we visit the Farm. But it lurks so large in the story of Anna Ogilvy and what happened that night. It is impossible to ignore.

Harriet has never been and nor have I. To understand Anna's condition, and move her to the next stage of treatment, the trip must be made. I can claim that the visit is part of Anna's treatment and that my interest is purely professional. But I know that is a half-truth.

There is a deeper, more personal ache. I am so close to Anna. I need to understand the events of that night. Moreover, I want to even though I am not a police officer or crime scene investigator. Technically I am still a civilian consultant. But I'm a detective of the mind. I believe that mental clues can be found in material landscapes, traces scattered in space and time.

This is part of my terrain.

Solve the riddle. Untangle the mystery.

I want to taste and feel and walk the crime scene, see what final clues I can pick up from immersing myself in the physical location. I won't rest until then.

Since the separation I've existed on Tubes and buses and rental cars. Clara still has custody of the mothy Ford Mondeo. Harriet, meanwhile, claims a nurse's salary doesn't stretch to petrol prices. She too only uses rail, Tube, bus or shoe leather.

We rent a car from Hertz and gather at an unspeakable hour the next Saturday, fuelled by Costa coffee and plastic breakfast food. The roads are ghostly, almost peaceful. Once free of West London we chug towards the Cotswolds, leaving the blackened city for the dips and inclines of seed-yellowed fields, arthritic trees and loose leaves bullied by strong winds.

The Abbey confers intimacy. Outside its walls we're almost strangers again. It takes half an hour for Harriet and me to warm up and become fluent. We talk of life outside the Abbey. No Anna, at least for now. I repeat anecdotes about KitKat. Harriet confesses to binge-watching Netflix reality shows, the cheesier the better. At the third time of asking, she teases the outline of a crime novel based on her experiences in secure hospitals. She looks embarrassed. I am intrigued. She pivots and asks about Clara and why we're no longer together and I recount the story with only minor edits.

Finally, the satnav directs us off the main roads and down bosky tracks and tells us we have nearly arrived.

Already I can see why the media were so intrigued. I have seen countless photos, of course. But reproductions don't capture the gothic gloom. The Farm is located down a long, narrow, earthy track of ground, too rough to be called a proper road.

The rental car bucks, stuttering and retreating at the unfamiliar terrain. We should have hired an off-road vehicle. Harriet agrees. I can already imagine wheels spinning furiously in the gluey mud. I nudge the rental car to the side and turn off the engine. We must peel back the centuries. Engines and rubber are useless. Thick coats and wellies are the only solution now. We are totally reliant on our feet.

'It's wilder than I imagined,' says Harriet. 'Less scenic, too. More Middle Earth than Brideshead.'

I finish sliding a damp, socked foot into a welly and then zip my coat. I stand and look down the muddy track and the derelict site beyond. 'Apparently the Fox family had to abandon it after the murder,' I say. 'It's become a sort of mecca for true crime junkies.'

Everything is mulchy, a pure blast of mud and compost and countryside.

'Not a very well-tended mecca.'

'No.'

'Shall we?'

We are silent for the rest of the walk. Our feet, instead, provide squelches and slurps, like KitKat inhaling her milkshake through a plastic straw. I take out my phone. The signal is poor, but enough to display a PDF map from the police files showing the layout of the Farm on the morning of August 30th, 2019.

I look to the right, tallying the map with the desolate reality. 'The trees at the back mark where the Forest starts,' I say. 'To the left there is the Ruins, or what was called the Ruins four years ago, where visitors had meals. Then straight ahead here, just before the Forest, are the cabins. The Blue Cabin where Anna slept. The Red Cabin for Indira and Douglas. The Green Cabin for Theo Ogilvy. And the Orange Cabin for Emily and Richard Ogilvy.'

Stretches of sad-looking tape girdle the main entrance from the path. It is not quite police tape, but not amateur either. It is symbolic of the whole thing. Four years is long enough for somewhere to decay without going fully extinct. The layout is still clear. The stony Ruins, once part of a great Augustan country house, stand much as they did on the night of the murder. The shell-like cabins are similarly intact, squatting on the threadbare grass. There are large, ugly gaps on the outside where the cheap roofing has dislodged and blown away. The insides are uninhabitable. The Forest, meanwhile, remains like a relic.

I feel ant-sized suddenly. The trees guarding the Forest entrance are ancient, swaying loftily. They go right back into England's deep past. I wonder at all the things the trees have seen. The Wikipedia page talks of the perils of the Fox family during the civil war; the family member in the early eighteenth century who saved the estate with mercantile cunning and built a house full of Palladian bling; the dissolute Victorian Fox who gambled away that fortune; then the drabber, besuited Foxes, slowly tipping back into the middle class, lumbered with this land and a history of fleeting triumph and terminal decline.

Harriet and I stand there looking at it all. We are the only people in the world at this moment. Nothing else exists. This is where the story began. This patch of earth changed everything. I feel emotional just being here. I curse this land and yet can't take my eyes off it.

'Where shall we start?' she asks.

I check the light and take in the grounds.

'Follow me,' I say.

50

BEN

It is the only place we can start. Psychological detectives, like archaeological ones, must diagnose the cause and not just the symptoms. The Red Cabin and Blue Cabin are symptoms. The dark world of the Forest might be too. But we must start here and work our way forwards.

It is a vast and lonely space. The trees are so thick they elbow each other. The branches form a roof of sorts. The ancient oak trunks bend and snarl until they take on semi-human form. The ground underfoot is a mix of mud, gravel and leaves. I almost feel like crossing myself or saying a silent prayer before entering. I look back and see the rental car still stuck on the mud track. I check my pockets. But there will be no signal inside the Forest anyway. I imagine us walking inside and never coming out again, swallowed by the darkness, like Jonah in the belly of the whale. I take a breath, close my eyes, then put one foot in front of another.

'People actually paid to do this?'

Harriet catches up now. Her wellies keep sellotaping to the mud. She has fallen once already, brownish gloop hardening around her knees and up her jeans. She too eyes the Forest with terror. This is outside her comfort zone. I can tell by the reluctant look in her eyes that this landscape brings back memories she'd rather forget: school cross-country, bad family camping trips, regrettable music festivals with too much mud and too few toilets. Youth only glows from a distance.

She stops, slightly breathless, and tries to adjust to the darkness. 'I can think of better ways to pour a few hundred quid down the drain.'

I smile. 'More like a few thousand.'

'So this is the infamous Forest.'

'Yes.'

'It feels haunted somehow. Like going back in time.'

'Fight or flight. Mankind as predator. Stone Age brains in a space age world.'

I feel that old paranoia squeeze at my chest. I hear the low crackle of twigs and shoe leather in the wilderness. I want to glance behind me, just to be sure, but I resist. Fear starts in the head and infects the body. So many disorders of the mind can be traced back to the primordial forest. It is why it is such a unique symbol in fairy tales and myths. Leaving home and entering the Forest is a metaphor for shedding the comforts and traumas of childhood and entering the wilderness of adulthood.

Without the right tools or preparation, crossing that threshold results in psychic fracture and disintegration. The mind either fails to recognise enough danger or fails to stop recognising danger. It is in places like this that our species learned how to survive. Anxiety, the besetting vice of modern industrial societies, emerges in that crossover between survival mode and the stresses of life in the twenty-first century. We feel hunted.

'It still doesn't make sense,' I say.

'Which bit?'

We continue walking further into the Forest. The darkness tightens. Light bleeds through the trees. Sounds taunt us. 'The theory of the armchair detectives,' I say. 'That something must have happened in the Forest that caused Anna to carry out the double murder only a short time later. That without the Forest none of it would have happened.'

'You don't agree?'

'It's chronologically possible. I just question whether it's psychologically possible.'

'Something terrible happens. It causes Anna to flip. I've seen patients in secure hospitals with similar stories.'

'How many of them had previously diagnosed mental illness?'

Harriet playfully mocks my naivety. 'The fact they were in secure hospitals is a teensy bit of a giveaway.'

'Yes. Except for Anna. She had no diagnosed mental illness. That's what doesn't make sense. Ordinary people don't turn into monsters overnight. Or within a matter of hours. Even with an untreated history of sleepwalking.'

'That's assuming Anna Ogilvy was always normal. Sounding ordinary doesn't mean your mind works in an ordinary way. Look at Shipman.'

It's the one British serial killer everyone always falls back on. The solid, dull country doctor with a devoted patient list who was also Britain's worst-ever serial killer. The full list of his crimes was never confirmed. A seemingly ordinary person with an extraordinary brain.

'Paralogism,' I say. 'Aristotle talked about it a lot. A false conclusion reached through faulty reasoning. A happens before B so A must have caused B. The Hunters versus Survivors game preceded the double murder. Therefore something in the Forest must have caused the double murder. It sounds convincing but, logically, it's nonsense.'

Harriet isn't impressed by cod philosophy. She sounds weary of my mansplaining. 'Go on, genius, what's your alternative theory?'

I smile. It's a side of her I've never seen before. More cutting, faintly sarcastic, no longer playing a nursing role and forced into platitudes about patient care. 'I didn't say I had one.'

'If Anna didn't flip suddenly because of the Forest, then she must have planned it. Which means she consciously intended to commit the crime.'

I stop again. I imagine them all here in the Forest: Emily, Richard, Theo, Anna, Indira, Douglas. I see them juggling paintball weaponry and squinting in the darkness. According to the rules of the game, the Survivors have a head start. Each of the Hunters must hit each of the Survivors to win. The odds favour the Survivors. Everything depends on the Hunters and their tactics. Do they stick together or pursue their quarry separately? Does teamwork win the day or individual self-reliance? At what point do the benefits of a team outweigh the cumbersome nature of a social group?

I look at the trees. I wish they would reveal such secrets. Once the Anna O legend is dusty and forgotten, they will still be here. So much history is contained in those trunks.

There is just breeze and rustling and shapeless sounds with no start and no end. For the first time since childhood, I feel cold terror seize me.

I turn, eager now to get out of this place. To run from such a scene of desolation.

'Bailing already?' says Harriet, smiling. That tone, again, almost sisterly. I imagine family mealtimes and barbed jokes and fighting over the last slice of cheesecake.

I take another deep breath. I try to see where the path leads ahead. 'Ten more minutes,' I say. 'Then it's time to move on.'

51

BEN

The Red Cabin.

So much is invested in a name. The Anna O story lucked out on that front. I always think of 'The Red Cabin' as a short story by Edgar Allan Poe, or a late work by Henry James alongside other curios like *The Turn of the Screw*. Three simple words conjure such mystery. It is haunted and inviting.

The reality is predictably neither. We finish in the Forest, unsettled by its gnarly beauty. It takes some time to find our way out, then we are back in the main part of the Farm. It is a short walk to the cabins. I look at my phone and confirm there's no signal. I have been to crime scenes before. Death always stains a place, marking it as forbidden. There is a strong odour of mortality and an underlying sense of evil.

I don't want to stay a moment longer than necessary.

The cabins are all derelict wooden structures now gap-toothed and deserted, sinking slowly into the surrounding mud. Graffiti covers all sides. There are traces of the true crime tourists with #JusticeforAnna on the right and #LockHerUp on the other side. Some debris from the original police investigation has survived, including bedraggled police tape and a scatter of plastic forensic coverings.

Harriet and I study the PDF map on my phone to determine which cabin is Red, Blue, Green or Orange. The last part of our pilgrimage here is recreating the exact events of the morning of August 30th.

'Which one of us is playing Anna?' says Harriet. She sounds both disgusted and half-comical, darkly amused. She is less squeamish than I expected. Then I remember she's a nurse. She has seen more of humanity than I ever will. Humour is a way to survive. This feels like one of those Jack the Ripper walking tours, except the killer and the victims are so much more vividly real.

I want to get inside Anna's head. I want to tread in her footsteps. In both a literal and psychological sense. 'I'll be Anna,' I say. 'You'll be a composite for her parents.'

Harriet raises her eyebrows. 'Someone's cooking the books on the age front. What about the two victims?'

'Forgotten in life as they were in death, I'm afraid. Ready?'

We take our places. I walk to the Blue Cabin and inspect the insides. It is slightly more intact than the Red Cabin but similarly defaced by graffiti and creepy messages. Some tourists have written their names above Anna's. Others call for Anna to burn in hell, face the lethal injection, roast for her crimes – a litany of misogyny and abuse, like an analogue version of social media.

I wait until the hour strikes. I go full method and shoulder-barge the wooden door of the Blue Cabin closed. I want to inhabit Anna's final waking moments as much as possible. I remember the rumoured screen projects on Anna's story and imagine Hollywood actors here in the name of research.

I thumb open a photo on my phone from the police files. It shows the Blue Cabin from the morning Anna was found. She was asleep on the bed. There were traces of ink on her right hand. But no notebook or pen was ever found. The bed is gone, as is the other furniture, kept in some exhibit locker ahead of the trial. Some of the decorative touches remain though, like tapestries drained of original colour, doomed to exist in phantom form.

I see my watch hit the hour mark. Then I begin. I must use my imagination. It is pitch-black in the dying seconds of August 29th. Anna, and the others, return from their ordeal in the Forest and eat supper together in the Ruins. Then everyone retreats to their respective cabins. The exact timing of the murders has never been established. All we have are estimates. I squeeze through the swollen wooden door of the Blue Cabin. I am Anna now. The mud and turf squelches with each step. The Forest murmurs. Four years ago, the Farm is speckled with light from the Ruins and candles from other cabins.

I see the Red Cabin ahead of me. What is Anna feeling at this very moment?

And then it strikes me. I fix on the Red Cabin. I place one squelchy foot in front of another, sticking and unsticking. I shiver. My lungs tickle with effort. Because that's what this is: an effort. A conscious effort. The Red Cabin is further away than it appears from a first glance. The ground is elastic and alive, snarling every toe and refusing to release my feet. I am closer now. But there is still distance. My heart rate accelerates.

I push. I will myself forward.

My watch ticks.

Finally, I approach the Red Cabin. It is supposed to be dark now, that's what I must remember. The pale, dusty light should be black. The cabin door will be shut too, which makes opening it more perilous, louder, the split-second chance of being heard. I grip the door and muscle it open and stand in the doorway for a moment. I picture where the two beds were that night. I sense how close the doorway is to the rest of the room.

Could they really have slept through this? Were neither of them disturbed by the door squeak? Did Anna slip them something over dinner to mask her entrance?

I check the time. I glance behind me and see Harriet waiting patiently in the Orange Cabin. We are two people in the middle of a rambling field playacting a horrific murder. This is bad taste, B-list comedy. But now, looming in that doorway, it feels more like one of those twisted slasher movies. The sort that begins cheaply then darkens into something altogether uncomfortable, fleeing the mainstream into cultish terrain.

That feeling pokes at me again. The same one from the Forest. This is wrong. There is some diseased karmic energy here, a heaviness to every second I spend trying to recreate the bloody murder of two young people on the cusp of the rest of their lives. This case has become a parlour game. Endless coverage mutes the real effect. But standing at the very spot, the excuses vanish. I step further in, coil my right hand round an imaginary knife, imagine the logistics of the first blow, then the next, a symphonic build until twenty blows are struck. The deed is done.

What now? That is the most unexpected question. Murder is meant to be planned or instinctive, telling a killer what to do next. But I freeze. The imaginary knife is still in my palm. The bodies are fresh and liquid behind me. I look down at my clothes and imagine blood spatter echoing down the crisp white shirt, splattered into the jacket lining, spotting my cheeks like stick-on acne. One wipe and it's gone.

I turn. I stagger. It is chillier outside. The Blue Cabin seems even further away now the act has been committed. Now two fully grown humans have been slain in cold blood. It is silly, I know, but guilt makes my steps heavier. The knockout effect of breaking that unbreakable taboo for the first time. I have read enough about killers to know that the first time is immeasurably worse than any other. The act of killing is one thing. Becoming a killer, an outcast, a pariah, is another. That only happens once. The soul-scarring.

I remember to look at my watch. I misjudge the next step and almost dip face-first into the gloop. The effort isn't conscious, now, but existential. I wonder how anyone fails to wake at this moment. Or, alternatively, sleep anaesthetises trauma. Yes, perhaps.

I feel for the door to the Blue Cabin and step inside. The staging has become so real to me that I experience a terrible psychic disturbance at this return, leaving fully human and coming back with the devil inside me. Anna may have glided through all this. And yet, deep down, the mind must be working on some level. It must leave a residue.

I breathe. I recover. This is play-acting. I have not committed a crime. Not today, anyway. I imagine the bed in front of me and Anna collapsing onto it. Except there's one final act. The bit everyone forgets. The text message sent via WhatsApp to her family with those fateful words: *I'm sorry. I think I've killed them.*

I take out my phone. I tap on the WhatsApp chat with Harriet. I type out the words and feel queasy when I press send. Those assumptions tremble now. Could Anna really have sent a message like that while still being asleep? The mechanics are possible. Case studies show patients driving cars while asleep and following complex navigation. But there is conscious intent within those words. The apology, the recognition. Guilt implies sentience. If she was awake then, perhaps she was awake earlier. Perhaps she knew exactly what she was doing.

I see the two ticks. I pocket the phone. I move to where the bed was. Then I wait and hear the squelchy approach of Harriet. The same approach made by Emily and Richard Ogilvy that night after they received that cryptic message. The delay seems longer than I imagined. I see those two parents now. Hair askew, eyes gummy. So many false alarms over the last twenty-five years: the accidents, the near misses, the drugs, the alcohol, the dead-ends and cul-de-sacs of growing up. The way in which disaster so often fizzles into anecdote. Something laughed away.

Apart from the last two words. Not: *I'm sorry, I think I've overdosed.* Or: *I'm sorry, I think I wrote off the car.* Or: *I'm sorry, I think I'm pregnant.*

All those are survivable. Nightmares, possibly. But survivable. Not this. Never, ever this.

Everyone always asks: was she guilty? And now, here, I realise the answer is clearly, emphatically yes. Whether she is legally culpable or not is a different matter. But she is guilty in the most basic sense of that term. She wielded the dagger. Her actions killed two fellow human beings. She will always have to live with that. Guilt will be a permanent part of her. I have woken Anna to a different world than the one she left behind.

'Under ten minutes.' Harriet's voice startles me. Her cheeks are red from the walk. She looks untroubled. The diffidence and social awkwardness from the Abbey is gone now. Out here, in the wilderness, she no longer has to pay respects to the doctors and psychiatrists and neurologists. I like this Harriet even better. The out-of-office version rather than the uniformed one. 'Under one minute, technically, from Orange to Blue. Assuming the ground wasn't as boggy. And factoring in a faster walking speed.'

I close my eyes. I stop the thoughts. They are packaged up, firmly shut in the attic of my mind. Back to reality.

The present. Here. Now.

'So?' says Harriet. 'Time to spill the beans. Any bolts of lightning? Are those little grey cells whirring?'

I've spent too long here. I feel that terror again, like I've tried to raise the dead or disturbed the spirit world. This was a mistake. The light is failing outside. A sense of profound evil lurks within these walls, that Forest, polluted by the terrible events on this ground.

'You look like you've seen a ghost,' says Harriet. She sounds concerned now, that more familiar note of compassion returning, the nurse taking over from the ghoulish tourist and sightseer.

I smile. It takes all my strength. I check the time again.

'Yes,' I say. 'Maybe I have.'

52

BEN

The church is full. The songs have been sung. The coffin consumes attention, perched there like an omen. It seems too small for her somehow. I expect Bloom to suddenly awake, one final practical joke at our expense. But the lid remains firmly closed. The post-mortem is complete and the coroner has agreed to release the body.

Virginia Bloom can finally be put to rest.

I focus again on the notes. The lectern is cold and rough to the touch. I clear my throat, hear the sound echo around the ancient stone walls.

'Professor Bloom wasn't your typical Christian,' I say, reaching the final section of the eulogy and relaxing slightly now. 'But she had a real faith in people. Above all, she believed in redemption, that no one was beyond saving. Many of you here today are familiar with Virginia's professional accomplishments: the pioneering work on the psychology of sleep, the life-changing work she conducted at the Abbey with people whose lives had been ruined by the inability to shut their eyes or the inability to open them again.'

I pause and look out at the staff from the Abbey decked out in their Sunday best. Clara is here, so is KitKat. I compose myself.

Bloom was an only child and had no children herself. She collected friends, colleagues and acquaintances, instead. 'But if sleep is our second life, then Virginia also had a second existence. The church warden, the volunteer, the pillar of the local community, however unconventionally dressed. Hers was a subtle but profound faith. She let her actions do all the talking. As she so memorably put it, why did God create fun unless we were all meant to enjoy it?'

There is a soft chuckle from the congregation. The church fills with it.

'Most of all, she never gave up on people. She believed her solemn duty was to make better what is fallen, to heal what is sick and to redeem what is broken, both as a professional and as a friend. That was her creed. For so many of us, it was also our daily inspiration.'

I glance around the church again. Yes, I see the appeal now. It is the opposite of the Farm's godlessness, a place without hope or mercy. The silence lingers, like a guest outstaying its welcome. I collect my notes and creak my way down from the pulpit, each collision of shoe leather and wood louder than the one before.

I return to the front pew and sit alongside the other senior staff at the Abbey. It is the vicar's turn now to hymn the praises of a woman who – against type, perhaps – always had a spiritual dimension alongside her five o'clock martini. Bloom was quixotic like that. She hated categories and putting others into boxes. She adored contradiction.

I barely listen to the vicar's whispery tones. Rather I see Bloom lying there in her house and hear the frantic words on the phone call about the file. I think about her description of Patient X and the connecting threads to the Anna O case. I am still thinking of it when the service is over and the ensemble of family, work colleagues and friends decant to the village hall for lukewarm squash and sandwiches on saggy paper plates. I mutter instructions to the organiser and ensure no gatecrashers are admitted.

This is an entirely private affair. Bloggers and journalists are not welcome.

It is later, after the funeral service is over, that Clara and KitKat and I go to the local park. We are never just the three of us anymore. But now it seems right. KitKat plays on the climbing frame. Clara and I sit watching her on a bench with two takeaway coffees. I tell Clara about the recent trip. The ground zero for everything since.

'I hear the Farm is abandoned these days.'

'It was scary enough in the daylight,' I say, taking a sip. 'I can hardly imagine what it must have been like in the dark.'

'Any lightbulb revelations?'

'I tried to play Anna's part and time myself between the two cabins. First, I don't think she walked back to the Blue Cabin, or certainly not without help.'

'How can you be so sure?'

'I can't. It's a hunch, an educated guess. Getting back to the Blue Cabin from the Red Cabin having carried out an act like that requires real effort.'

'Which suggests she could have been conscious when doing it.'

'Or other people were involved in moving her.'

Just at that moment KitKat surprises us both. It is her newest party trick. She likes to sneak up on us and then emerge when we least suspect it.

'Moving who, Daddy?'

I see Clara's frown of disapproval. We have been talking too openly. 'No one, sweetheart.'

'Are you talking about the sleeping lady?'

It's my turn to look at Clara. We agreed not to mention it. 'The sleeping lady?'

KitKat looks distracted, eyeing up the swings. 'The sleeping lady is bad.'

'Is that all?'

KitKat seems conflicted now, tugging at her jumper as she

always does when things don't quite make sense. 'Mummy says you will make the bad lady better.'

She loses interest in the swings and runs off to the sandpit instead. I try to understand what I've just heard.

'Why is she talking about Anna Ogilvy?'

Clara stares at me like she always does when truly angry. 'Wake up, Ben,' she says. 'People can go online. They saw that conspiracy blog naming you. Even kids talk. This comes with a cost. For you and her.'

I look over at KitKat playing in the sandpit. I think of Bloom's funeral service and my growing obsession with Anna. I imagine those online threats becoming gruesomely real. The smell of the Farm still hasn't left me. All this has achieved the exact opposite of what I wanted. Clara is further away from me than ever.

I wonder what I'm doing to myself and my family.

And why I find it impossible to stop.

ANNA'S NOTEBOOK
2019

June 3

The Camden flat. There is a further week of messages from
@PatientX. The timing suggests GMT. The grammar
suggests educated, rehabilitated, released into the world to
start a new life. They are cryptic.

I reread the latest exchange:

@PatientX: Take some friendly advice. You won't find
anything in the public domain. Stop wasting your time
on FOIs.

@ElementaryMag: How do you know about my FOI
requests? Do you work in government?

@PatientX: I told you where to focus. The Cranfield Ward.
Look at the approved visitors list.

@ElementaryMag: How do I get that?

@PatientX: Try harder, Anna. Think of a way.

I have the intro of the piece. I have some concluding paragraphs. What I need is the sandwich filling. The meat.

I consider my options. I still need a face-to-face meeting with @PatientX. I don't care for their patronising, mansplaining tone. Or the idea of my FOI requests being snooped on. But, for now, I need them. I think of Broadmoor, Mum, Sally Turner, Dr Bloom. I think of Dad and his mysterious Other Woman.

Try harder. Think.

I read the final line from @PatientX again.

@PatientX: Someone is behind all of this, Anna. Wake up. Sally Turner has a child. Find the suspect, find the story. It's hunting time.

June 10

Broadmoor Hospital, Berkshire.

Forty miles out of London. I have read the history. It is a story of gargoyles stumbling into the light: founded in 1863 as a lunatic asylum for the criminally insane; run by the Home Office until 1949; then officially renamed the Broadmoor Institution; taken over by the Ministry of Health in 1960 and christened Broadmoor Hospital; now run by the tedious-sounding West London NHS Trust. From spine-chilling terror to yawn-inducing bureaucracy in 156 years.

Broadmoor Hospital is a vast campus of Victorian red brick that looks even bigger and more loathsome than the photos suggest. I reach the NHS-coloured signs and see large high-rise walling and security measures on each side. I've heard so much about this place. The most notorious criminal asylum in the world. Home to the worst serial killers ever known. Immortalised in true crime history for its pioneering work on the psychology of society's most deviant minds.

The suspect. I am allergic to most conspiracy theories. Criminal investigations can rarely be tied together with a neat bow. But I haven't been able to stop thinking about that last line from @PatientX.

Sally Turner has a child. One jigsaw piece that completes the puzzle of her death. Logically, does that mean Sally Turner's own child killed her? Or helped smuggle in the plastic knife that Sally used to end her own life?

Find the suspect. Find the story.

It could mean so much.

I have been hunting among all the names connected with this story and have one suspect I can't ignore. A candidate for Sally Turner's biological child. Their birth name was changed, of course, all links to Sally erased from the earth. Passport, driving licence, National Insurance number. But already I imagine what it must have been like for this teenager to visit Sally Turner on the inside. I wonder if the suspect – my suspect, let's call them – still has nightmares about Broadmoor and its demons even now. How my suspect copes with having a mother as infamous as the Stockwell Monster.

I've done my research. I know that Broadmoor, like most Department of Health outposts, was a late adopter of digital record-keeping. The bulky patient files from the late nineties are stored in an archive centre run by Berkshire Record Office. Visitors to the archive, including historians, criminology specialists and psychologists, register at the main entrance. Visitors must be recognised by an institution of higher education or have authorisation from a former staff member directly concerned with the archive.

I scan the laminated rules of admission as I wait:

Clinical and non-clinical records of Broadmoor Hospital (formerly Broadmoor Clinical Lunatic Asylum) are to be preserved for research by the BRO, in accordance with the Public Records Act 1958. Access will be provided on the basis of the Freedom of Information Act 2000 (FOIA) and the Department of Health's *Guidance for Access to Health Records Requests* (2010).

I am the last in the queue. The bored-looking staffer asks my name and which research institution I'm attached to.

'I'm here on behalf of Baroness Ogilvy,' I say, handing over a letter of permission.

It is typed on Mum's House of Lords headed paper. I have faked her signature at the end. It explains that she was a Minister of State at the Department for Health between 1997–2005. Her portfolio included mental health services and supervision of Broadmoor, Rampton and Ashworth Secure Hospitals. She wishes to consult the official record for her forthcoming memoir. I am her researcher and am to be granted permission to consult the archive on her behalf. It is yet another lie. But one of my better ones.

The staffer reads the note slowly. Several minutes later, he lowers his glasses and pouts slightly with mock, la-di-da gravitas. He waves me through. I join four other researchers. We are led through a large courtyard and across to the west side of the Broadmoor campus. Only then do I remember to breathe.

The BRO Archive Centre is cavernous and overheated. It reminds me of a grand nineteenth-century library with men flaunting mutton-chop whiskers and measuring the size of patient skulls. There is a creepy, fetid aura. One of the guards stands watch as we begin. There is a small room-map on the right which I consult. I narrow my search by period, then location. I am looking for information regarding the Cranfield Ward during the late 1990s.

I sift through endless cardboard folders in a fruitless search for a mention of 'MEDEA'. Nothing. I try 'BLOOM' and find a hodgepodge of documentary material and correspondence regarding Dr V. Bloom's work as a consultant clinical psychologist at Broadmoor, mentioning hundreds of patients. Finally, I try 'TURNER'. That leads me to box 27. Tucked on a single sheet of paper in a soggy corner of the box, I reach the information I'm looking for. There is a typed-out memo from Dr V. Bloom, Consultant Clinical Psychologist, to the Director for Specialist and Forensic Services. It reads:

FROM: BLOOM, DR. V
TO: DSFS (SHU)
SUBJECT: PATIENT 8637892CRAN
DATE: 02.06.99

Regarding the proposed heightened security requirements outlined at the last departmental board meeting, I hereby request a 5% budget uplift for the special project discussed. Given the extraordinary level of public and press interest in this patient, it would be advisable for the special project to be delivered discreetly and the distribution list to be kept to a minimum internally (if the case proceeds). I require only a small team of two nursing assistants. I request that only the DSFS and the CD are briefed on the project. I will follow up this note in person. VB

June 2, 1999. The memo was sent while Sally Turner was still on trial at the Old Bailey. 'DSFS' stands for Director for Specialist and Forensic Services. 'CD' for Clinical Director. The 'special project' must be MEDEA, even if it isn't yet given that name. I search through other documents to find the name for the Clinical Director. But there is only the name for the Director of Forensic Services at the end of another

263

dull letter about budgets. The letter is signed by a man named 'Stephen Donnelly'.

No documents are allowed out of the archive room. I memorise the document. I look through further files. Each has a slip inside with the words: 'Section 41 exemption'.

When our time slot elapses, we're escorted from the building and led back towards the entrance desk. I collect my mobile and quickly type out as much as I can remember in the Notes app of my iPhone. I google Section 41 exemptions of the Freedom of Information Act 2000 and read:

> **Section 41 exemption:** information withheld from Freedom of Information requests if the disclosure of the information was provided in confidence (such as medical or clinical information) and would constitute an actionable breach of confidence.

I close the tab. I have a new message. It's from @PatientX again – my golden source, my Deep Throat – replying to one of my earlier suggestions.

The message is even shorter than usual. It simply says:

17th. 10AM.

My request has become reality.
A face-to-face meeting is on.

53

BEN

The Abbey, Harley Street.

After the funeral, life goes on. My fear and paranoia are still there. But diluted, somehow, lost under the demands of everyday life.

It takes several sessions for the breakthrough to happen. Anna's memory loss, whether full-on PTA or a short-term readjustment to life after so long asleep, means that older memories will take time to surface. Her dream world, however, will be much more accessible and vivid. It is the world she has inhabited for the last four years. She has existed in a mental dreamscape ever since that night at the Farm. Dreams can be a gateway to memory.

That's where I'm going to start.

Her recovery is gradual: her vocal cords are rusty, her energy levels depleted, her diet increased and modified daily. She stays awake for minutes, then a whole hour. She manages fragments, then more complex sentences. Her vocabulary slowly builds.

I watch her recover and still feel torn. My professional duty is to get Anna fit to stand trial. But my moral duty is to keep Anna here at the Abbey for as long as I can. Donnelly tried to scare me with the threats against me and my family. But, in some ways, the opposite is true. As long as Anna is at the Abbey we are encircled by the promise of police protection. The MoJ won't let anything happen to its most high-profile murder suspect. Once she is shunted into the prison system to await trial, however, the authorities will wash their hands of the Abbey and me forever.

Donnelly can try and get a different diagnosis. But I know too much. The PTA diagnosis won't keep Anna here forever. I'm not naïve. But it gives me time to try and connect the dots. Find out what Bloom discovered before her death.

A few more weeks gives me hope. And hope, as we've discovered, is a potent thing indeed.

It is several weeks before I enter the treatment room for our first proper analysis session. Harriet props Anna up on the pillows then leaves. She still looks ghostly. She badly needs sunlight. We look at each other now and I try and read her expression. But there is something oddly mysterious about it. Anna's face is still, almost disturbingly so. She is like an actor displaying heroic levels of self-control. Or a sitter in a painter's studio. Except the eyes. They look too self-aware, as if the stillness is calculated, even rehearsed.

I wait for the door to click shut. Something has changed since Bloom's funeral. I am in charge here now. My obsession with Anna's case has free rein. She is both killer and medical mystery. That type of deviance is why I do this job.

I run through the usual introductions: my name, the Abbey, the daily health check. This is the trickiest patient session I've ever prepared for. Tell her the whole truth and her mind will hibernate again. Emily and any other visitors have been under strict instructions to refer only to an unspecified accident in the past.

I frame it gently too. I am a member of staff at the Abbey Sleep Clinic in Harley Street. You have been a patient with us for a long period of time, Anna, following an incident in Oxfordshire. Since then, you have been stuck in a deep sleep.

Our job is to help you recover. This session is part of that. You'll have lots of questions. But let's take this slowly to begin with.

I have a wallchart in my office which lists the most popular dreams in the world: teeth falling out, being chased by someone, being helpless and unable to find a toilet, appearing naked in public, being unprepared for an exam, flying somewhere, falling with no safety net, getting stuck in an out-of-control vehicle, stumbling across an empty, unused room and being late for something.

Dreams are a highway to our darkest secrets. Possibly even our darkest memories too. Anna's dreams could unlock everything.

I've been playing it patiently. Four years of sleep demands no less. But today, as her voice returns stronger, I risk it and say, 'Tell me about your dream life, Anna. What do you dream?'

Anna's voice is still hoarse and awkward, like a toddler learning to enunciate. 'It starts in a forest.'

'How do you know it's a forest?'

'It's dark. There are trees everywhere.'

'Is it always the same forest in the dream?'

'Yes.'

The forest in the dream. The Forest at the Farm on the night of the double murder. I watch her closely again. 'What are you wearing?'

'Outdoor clothes. Red, I think. And blue.'

'How do you feel?'

'As if the devil is breathing through me.'

'What happens in this forest?'

Anna closes her eyes now. 'I am carrying something.'

I pause, breathe, wait.

'A knife.'

I try to keep my voice even. Not to betray even a tremor of anticipation. 'What happens then?'

Anna continues. 'I see my hands are covered in blood. But I can't see a wound. I run to the edge of the forest.'

'Do you know what lies beyond the forest?'

'Yes, a town called Marathon.'

'What happens after that?'

'I see the light at the edge of the forest. Then the dream stops.'

I make another note. I pause, allow Anna to surface again. She opens her eyes now, blinking at the room light.

'Does the dream follow the same pattern every time?' I ask. 'Yes.'

The Forest. The knife. The blood. Running to freedom.

'I want to try some free association now,' I say. 'I'll say a word and you reply with the first things that come to you.'

Anna nods tiredly.

I look down at my notes. Each symbol is itemised by a bullet point. 'The forest. What automatically comes into your head when I say that word?'

Anna sighs. 'Danger.'

'Knife?'

'Blood.'

'Marathon?'

'Truth.'

I imagine others reading a transcript of this session and asking what possible relevance dreams have to a double murder. But I must work with the grain of her mind. The symbolic truth is the gatekeeper to the literal truth.

Anna yawns. Her eyes become sleepy. Then she says quietly, 'You look familiar.'

I smile. 'Most MCS patients experience acute post-traumatic amnesia and paranoia. It's very common. I've been treating you for the last few months. But we've never met outside this clinic before. I'm a senior partner here at the Abbey.'

That is enough for today. I motion through the glass. Seconds later, Harriet arrives having monitored events on a live feed outside. I wonder how much she heard. And how dangerous this might get.

Harriet calms down Anna with a sedative. I wait until the monitors show that Anna is stabilised. Then I leave the room and head back to my office.

Anna's dream still playing in my mind.

54

CLARA

It is not a message she expects. Or at least not like this. Stephen Donnelly is Deputy Legal Director for the Ministry of Justice. His diary is planned months, sometimes years, in advance. He doesn't message Assistant Commissioners, let alone DCIs. But the email is clearly from his address. It includes a time and location and a request that she doesn't inform anyone about the meeting until they've spoken.

Clara does all the usual checks and is satisfied the message is genuine.

She arrives at the eastbound entrance for the Ministry of Justice headquarters at 102 Petty France and is greeted by a junior official. Her phone is taken and docked. She is given a visitor's lanyard and led to one of the secure rooms on the fourth floor.

Donnelly is already seated inside. There are no handshakes, no sign of coffee. The Anna O case is still only ever referred to as 'Project Downton' within Whitehall, a play on the Abbey. Clara debates what the meeting could be about. Someone has breached the Abbey's security and tried to attack Anna? A journalist has news of the awakening? Or the scenario that sickens every part of her. A sentence about Kitty, the school, an incident.

270

'I'm sorry for the subterfuge,' Donnelly begins. 'But I'm afraid there's been a development. Quite a serious one. Please, take a seat.'

Donnelly removes some pages from a manila file on the table. He hands one to Clara.

'How much do you know about your ex-husband's work on dream analysis?' he asks.

Clara wonders if she's misheard. She sees that Donnelly is serious. 'He wrote a book about it once, I think,' she says. 'It's also one of the subjects he teaches at Birkbeck.'

'I see.'

'Why?'

'We've been monitoring his analysis sessions with Anna. The prisoner claims to have a recurrent dream in which she feels "the devil breathing through me". Normally, of course, we'd take no notice.' Donnelly takes out another piece of paper from a file. 'But, sadly, this case is by no means normal.'

Clara looks at the second piece of paper. She sees the official header and crest of the Ministry of Defence. Beneath it is the logo of the Defence Science and Technology Laboratory at Porton Down.

'Ever since the Salisbury poisonings,' says Donnelly, 'Porton Down has been monitoring the street drug scopolamine.'

'Date rape?'

'That's one use. Scopolamine disables the victim's short-term memory, blocking the nerve cells in the brain. The worst part is that scopolamine disappears from the bloodstream within hours. Making it very difficult to pick up.'

'What are the other uses?'

'Scopolamine is a plant-based psychoactive alkaloid. It comes from the seeds of the borrachero tree. Appearance-wise, it's white powder and looks like cocaine. Completely odourless and tasteless too. It's particularly vicious when combined with alcohol. Very small amounts are used for common conditions like Parkinson's, Alzheimer's, motion sickness and post-surgical

271

nausea. But a gram of the stuff could kill a whole group. It puts victims into a hypnotic state: zombified behaviour, no free will, very suggestible, and often leads to paralysis, hallucinations and heart seizures. It's used as a mind control drug in robbery and kidnappings. Victims suffer total memory loss after the event.'

'You think Anna Ogilvy might have been spiked with scopolamine?'

'The keyword trigger was alerted because of the words "devil" and "breathing". Scopolamine, as you may know, has a more common street name.'

Clara sees it now. 'Devil's Breath.'

'Yes.' Donnelly takes another sheet of paper from his file. He hands it over. 'This is the latest forensic report from the crime scene at Virginia Bloom's house. Small traces of scopolamine were found in the safe in her study. Forensics also have a match on a small hair found by the safe in Bloom's study belonging to Dr Prince.'

Clara doesn't like where this is going. 'Ben was the one who found the body. That isn't altogether surprising.'

Donnelly consults his file again. 'In his statement, Dr Prince is asked repeatedly whether he went anywhere else in the house other than the hallway and the living room. He denies doing so on three separate occasions. We also have Dr Prince's admission that he picked up the knife.'

'You can't seriously think Ben had anything to do with Bloom's murder?'

'My job – my only job – is to preserve the integrity of a future trial. Any suggestion that Anna has been drugged or your ex-husband lied to the police would jeopardise everything.'

'Why are you telling me?'

'Because, right now,' says Donnelly, 'I think you're the only person in this whole thing I can trust. We've also found further cyber-ops evidence linking the blog which first revealed your husband's involvement in the case with another person working in the Abbey. The user goes under the handle @Suspect8.'

'Who is it?'

'We've matched the server hosting the @Suspect8 blog with a crypto trail. That crypto trail is linked to the bogus health and safety consultancy hired by Melanie Fox at the Farm on the night of the murders. We believe the person calling themselves "Lola Ridgeway" and @Suspect8 are the same person. To post the information, she must also be one of the five people who knew the prisoner was being transferred to the Abbey.'

Clara listens but doesn't fully take in the words. 'Who knew?'

Donnelly counts them off on his right hand. 'The two of us. Emily Ogilvy, now Emily Shepherd, as next of kin.' He pauses. 'Your ex-husband. And the one person who's been with Anna from the very beginning.'

Clara feels the name form on her lips.

The angelic helper there without being seen.

Harriet.

ANNA'S NOTEBOOK

2019

June 17

The Diana Memorial Fountain. Hyde Park.

I arrive early. It is a weekday. The sky is scattered with rain. Hyde Park is busy rather than seething. I've spent the last week reading about investigative journalists going undercover and operations behind enemy lines. I wonder if @PatientX has chosen a location close to the water to avoid being recorded, like spies in old movies who turn on taps to avoid eavesdropping.

The Contact is sitting on a bench near the fountain with a copy of today's *Times*. That is the signal we've agreed on. He looks younger than I expect. All investigations follow the same basic rules: never use your real name; subtle alterations to basic appearance (blonde hair darkened with a woolly hat, add in some thick-framed glasses, heels to alter height); mobile with the battery out, only ever use burners. It is standard stuff taught on every journalism MA in London. But still.

I sit down on the bench. The Contact asks if I am recording the meet. This is a make-or-break moment. For the article, the magazine, the takeover hopes, my future finances and career prospects – I decide to lie. That's when the first odd thing happens. The Contact takes out another burner mobile and hands it to me. He's not the real contact, he explains, but the cut-out. I am to stay where I am and await further instructions. After that, the man gets up and leaves.

I am unsettled for a moment. This doesn't feel right. I am about to leave too when the burner mobile buzzes. There is one new message on a pre-loaded secure messaging app. I read the message:

PATIENTX: You've been careless, Anna.

That mansplaining tone again. Half of me wonders if this is a set-up. I feel a dreadful, clammy fear around my neck. My palms sweat as I reply:

ME: I thought we were meeting in person.

PATIENTX: I still don't know I can trust you.

ME: Why not?

PATIENTX: Because you have a tail. Male, six one, 90-ish kg, pushing a buggy. Nice blue coat, by the way.

I whip round and stare at the other tourists nearby. I have done everything the online articles tell you: check the reflection of shop windows, stop and tie your shoelaces, take circuitous routes, double back. But I'm out of my depth. There's a chance I missed someone. Sure enough, there is a man standing behind me who is six foot one, around fourteen stone, with a buggy in front of him containing a small baby. He is sipping coffee and scrolling through his phone. There is no sign of a partner or wife.

Nice blue coat . . .

So Patient X can see me. Which means they are nearby. Or perhaps they just saw me leaving the flat. Either way. This could be a sick joke by a sick person which I've been stupid enough to fall for. But I am in this now. My plan to defeat Doug and Indy and stop the GVM takeover of the magazine – *my* magazine – rests on publishing this article and asserting editorial control.

I decide to hold my ground. Play hardball.

ME: You're bluffing. I checked my tail. I'm clean. You promised me face-to-face and more info. You haven't delivered. Give me something in the next ten seconds or this ends here.

I wait. If the source walks, then I am left with dud FOI requests and an old memo from a rotting file. I count to five in my head. Then I see the 'typing' signal at the top of the app.

PATIENTX: Did you find what we discussed in the archive?

ME: No visitor records. But I found a memo from Bloom to the director of Specialist and Forensic Services. The date fits. It mentions a special project being run at Broadmoor. Is that MEDEA?

PATIENTX: Yes.

ME: Why did Bloom request a 5% budget uplift?

PATIENTX: The MEDEA experiment was expensive to run. She needed her own budget. Separate from normal government financing. Something deniable.

ME: Why?

276

PATIENTX: Why do you think?

ME: What did the MEDEA experiment consist of?

PATIENTX: Have you read Bloom's academic work?

ME: Some of it. As much as I can understand.

PATIENTX: Find an article titled 'The Medea Method: Personality and Parasomnia'. It was one of her earliest pieces. It was never digitised.

ME: How do you know so much about this? Who are you?

PATIENTX: Take out the SIM and ditch the phone on the walk home. I'll know if you don't. Don't bring company next time. Goodbye, Anna.

The chat stops. I have the visceral sense of being watched. Somewhere in this bustle a pair of eyes are locked on me. I debate whether to go all out and share what else I've uncovered. But I hold back. Fear nicks my skin again.

I buy a coffee, drain it, then put the mobile into the empty cup. On the walk home, I ditch the coffee cup in a bin. I keep checking my surroundings. I think of those malevolent Victorian buildings at Broadmoor, the arid words typed in the memo, the knowledge the source had about my FOI requests.

For the first time, I'm on the edge of something I don't fully understand, far beyond my normal boundaries. A world where madness and evil reign. Where danger bedevils each encounter.

I don't go back to the flat. I get the Tube to Hampstead. I need safety tonight. Home comforts. I see Mum at the kitchen table. I want to hug her tightly, like a child running for safety. I feel sorry for her. She deserves more than Dad, the Other Woman, the whole humiliating charade.

She smiles at me. 'Well, this is a nice surprise.'

I stay there with her in the kitchen, just to be close, willing the day not to end.

I mustn't be alone tonight.

I can hear the demons calling.

55

BEN

I am with Anna when they come for me.

It is fitting, I suppose. In my end is my beginning.

I'm alone in the treatment room. She is asleep, rather than awake. I don't talk anymore, but just sit and watch. This is my silent vigil.

I have always imagined myself as the saner type of Hitchcock hero, if such a thing exists. I am Cary Grant in *Notorious* or *North by Northwest* or romancing Grace Kelly in *To Catch a Thief*. Now, in my dark nights of the soul, I wonder if I have it all wrong.

I am not the Rat-Pack, tuxedoed, impeccably dressed hero who always gets the girl. No, I am James Stewart in *Vertigo*. I am Scottie, the scarred and damaged former detective, medicating his wounds with twisted schemes to make Kim Novak turn into a fantasy. I look at Anna lying there and feel like my entire self is scattering on the carpet around me.

I am cracking up. There is no rational explanation for my growing obsession with this case. For this unethical blurring of boundaries. But sitting here with Anna stops me thinking just of Bloom's body, the knife in my hands, the blood and the trauma of those few hours. What I really did that night. The steps I had to take. Playing the innocent.

Harriet is not on shift this morning, a rare absence. I sit with a cup of milky English breakfast tea and hear the vague thrum of traffic outside on Harley Street. I imagine KitKat at school today and puzzle over Clara's lack of reply to my latest WhatsApp about my next weekend.

That's when I hear it.

It starts as a jostling noise. The grunt of tyres and brakes halting directly outside the building. More than one vehicle. A taxi, then. Or some A-lister's entourage, ignoring instructions about approaching via the back entrance and keeping all hangers-on to a minimum. I hear car doors slam loudly outside. Footsteps like an approaching army. The rat-tat-tat.

I venture towards the windows. I play curtain-twitcher now, careful not to let the light wake Anna. I look down at the entrance to the Abbey and see two police vehicles parked outside. A third unmarked car is just behind. Lids and tech, as the jargon goes. Uniforms and CID. The cavalry and the sharpshooters.

The panic starts here. It is instinctive, animalistic.

I know they are coming for me as surely as I've known anything.

I am a rat gnawing through rope, unwilling to be taken.

I haven't been seen. I slept here last night, meaning there's no record of me signing out or in. I know the floorplans and emergency fire exits in this building. But the police will too. There will be more uniforms, I'm sure, ready to catch me if I run.

Panic prompts useless thoughts. I can find somewhere to hide in the Abbey and escape overnight and go underground in London. I am a forensic psychologist who can use my expertise to dupe the police and play on the faults and weaknesses of the human mind. I imagine smuggling into air vents, dangling over lift shafts, all the absurdities I've seen repeated on the screen as a child.

But the Anna O case is too well known. My escape will be futile. It will damage Clara and KitKat. Escape means I'm guilty.

More footsteps. Raised voices.

Fate is slowly closing in on me.

There is no gentlemanly knock on the door. Just the wait. Time for one last look at Anna, observing the scene of my own ruin. Then the door opens and all treatment room protocol is violated. I see the crumpled suits and the egg-stained ties. The grimy plastic warrant cards. The dull, coffee-breathed boredom as a plainclothes detective recites the familiar lines arresting me on suspicion of the murder of Virginia Bloom, conspiracy to pervert the course of justice and suspicion of breaking the Official Secrets Act.

I am led downstairs. Staff part like waves. There are quizzical frowns, shamed glances. I am something to be pitied or ignored. My status has changed. I have been temporarily cast out of the tribe, turned on by my own people.

We reach the ground floor and the reception area. Some staff behind the front desk watch with glassy-eyed disbelief. I think of Clara not replying to my WhatsApp messages and KitKat hearing about this at school.

Until now, I have just been Dad. Fun, huggable, late for pick-up, with a side hustle in overcooked pasta and beans on toast. Now I will be someone different for her. An adult male full of holes and flaws, no longer dependable. I have lost my claim to parental infallibility.

I want to wake up now, to push this nightmare into the recesses of my brain.

But as we walk outside to the waiting police car I catch the first flash of a waiting camera-phone. The scrum of journalists already tipped off about the arrest. Curious tourists pausing at the scene before them. The circus show with me as the headline act.

My life as I know it is over.

56

BEN

It is the photo that graces every front page. The one that I can't escape. The brutal finale.

My face is around the world in seconds, borne aloft by the magic of social media. Harriet is also arrested at home on suspicion of the murder of Virginia Bloom and conspiring to pervert the course of justice. Both of us are seized in a co-ordinated strike and suffer a similar fate. The headlines go viral on social media. Broadsheets, tabloids, YouTubers, social media stars, the mob-like roar.

Later, I go back over the feverish coverage of those days. I see the timeline of our mutual destruction: within half an hour the first profiles are up on *MailOnline*; the *News at Ten* includes the arrest in its summary of the day's headlines; the next morning's papers carry the photo; the internet explodes with armchair criminologists.

We are the new Bonnie and Clyde. Lovers, conspirators, a devilish pairing clouded and dirtied by suspicion.

Anna Ogilvy.

Benedict Prince.

Harriet Roberts.

Three names branded into online history.

The interview room at Putney Station is a grey shoebox that smells of instant coffee and intermittent showers. The last few hours still haven't become real. This is the age of suspicion, cancellation and erasure. Accusations never die. They live on, fossilised by the internet, waiting to be discovered by each new generation. My sins may not be proved. But guilt is the default setting. Innocence is too twentieth century.

There are two interviewing DCs. The first is the talker, flashing a mouldy grin. He is a showman. Each revelation crash-lands, a burst of rhetorical fire. The other sits silently, scribbling and watch-checking, a silent hangman. I have a duty solicitor beside me with a schoolboy suit and nicotine cuffs.

The first DC says, 'How long have you been working with Harriet Roberts?'

There is only one thing I can do now. The answer I've seen repeated from the other side of the two-way mirror. 'No comment.'

'Did you help Harriet Roberts run the @Suspect8 blog?'

'No comment.'

'Did you help her leak your involvement in the case to gain publicity?'

'No comment.'

'Did you help Harriet Roberts gain the contract as the health and safety consultant hired by Melanie Fox on August 29th, 2019, under the name "Lola Ridgeway"?'

'No comment.'

'Did you help Harriet Roberts gain employment at Rampton Secure Hospital when Anna Ogilvy was admitted in 2019?'

'No comment.'

'Did you meet Harriet Roberts during your time as an orderly working in various secure hospitals at the start of your career? And when she worked as a trainee nurse at Broadmoor in 1999?'

Harriet at Broadmoor. 1999. Sally Turner. I digest that news. 'No comment.'

'Why did Anna Ogilvy claim to have met you before?'

I pause. This is bad. No, this is even worse than bad. They have filleted the transcripts. They have enough facts to make me look guilty. I think of Bloom's instructions, my lies about the file, the study, my movements.

'Dr Prince?'

There is so much I want to say. That Anna Ogilvy claims to have met me before thanks to the phenomenon known as 'transference'. The patient's emotion gets transferred to the psychologist. Anger at their family, friends, lovers, all of it is temporarily dumped on the analyst. She is conflating her dream with my presence in the room.

Instead, I simply say, 'No comment.'

I see the DC smirking. I look at the blue-grey walls of the interview room.

'During your time as a behavioural investigative adviser, did you come across the drug scopolamine?'

I know where they are going with this. That line from Anna during the dream analysis about the devil breathing through her. The street name for scopolamine is Devil's Breath. They must have bugged the session. I have walked into a trap. 'No comment.'

'Did you use scopolamine to drug Virginia Bloom before killing her?'

'No comment.'

'Is that why traces of scopolamine were found near the safe in her study alongside a clump of fibres containing your DNA?'

I see myself crouching, opening the safe, taking out the file. Obeying Bloom's instructions. I was careful. 'No comment.'

I've been set up. That is the one, inescapable conclusion. The noose and the drop wait for me. I am locked in my own nightmare. Someone has arranged the fragments of the last few months to damn me for eternity.

'Did you use scopolamine to persuade Anna Ogilvy to carry out the attack on August 30th at the Farm in Burford, Oxfordshire?'

'No comment.'

'Did you and Harriet Roberts conspire to pervert the course of justice by giving yourselves starring roles in the treatment of Anna Ogilvy?'

'No comment.'

'Did you send emails recommending Harriet Roberts for the job at Rampton Secure Hospital and transference to the Abbey?'

Emails. I think of someone planting them on my computer. They must exist. This is even more calculating than I imagined.

'No comment.'

Then comes the final flourish. It is the climax of the nightmare. The moment of maximum threat.

'Why was evidence found at your flat linking you to an anonymous social media account using the handle @PatientX?'

Broadmoor. Medea. Patient X. Everything I read in Bloom's file.

Yes, it is all there.

'No comment.'

I'm in the middle of a web. I am Theseus groping my way out of the labyrinth.

'Why did you send messages to Anna Ogilvy using the @PatientX handle agreeing to meet in person at the Farm on the night of the murders?'

I think of standing in the doorway of the Red Cabin and imagining the bodies lying there. The words sound so feeble. But they are all I have. I hear them without being conscious of speaking.

'No comment.'

ANNA'S NOTEBOOK

2019

June 21

Ogilvy Towers Part II. Mum is back. Dad is away. I remain barricaded inside my childhood bedroom. The elaborate security measures continue. The bedroom door is locked when I sleep. Two chairs block the exit with excellent toe-stubbing potential. I position other items – books, shoes, whatever I can find – in the path between bed and door. Getting out of this room will require pain. Which is good.

Pain will wake me. Pain will be cathartic, saving me from sin. It's all very Catholic. The Opus Dei of sleepwalkers. Mum is concerned. She has finally noticed there is something wrong. Theo drops by and laughs at my hermit-like behaviour. I snoop remotely on Indira and Doug's encrypted emails and texts and know the GVM deal is inching closer. My absence is working in their favour. I feel my irritation building. My hatred for them both.

I sit in my bedroom with the curtains closed. I still haven't written a word of the article. I am too scared of what I might do. I think of Lady Macbeth washing her hands of blood as she sleepwalks:

DOCTOR: You see her eyes are open.

GENTLEWOMAN: Ay, but their sense is shut . . .

DOCTOR: A great perturbation in nature, to receive at once the benefit of sleep and do the effects of watching! . . .

LADY MACBETH: To bed, to bed; there's knocking at the gate. Come, come, come, come, give me your hand. What's done cannot be undone.

More FOIs. Home Office, MoJ, Department of Health, NHS England, Her Majesty's Prison Service. There are no matches for the keyword 'MEDEA'. That means no official documents exist, or the keyword is too sensitive to be included under Freedom of Information rules.

I consider some old-school journalism and more vigils outside the Abbey. I should doorstep Bloom and put the questions to her directly. Stop being cowardly. I have tried to find out more about others who worked on the Cranfield Ward at Broadmoor in the late nineties. But few people publicly admit to having worked there. The odour of the place is too great.

Instead, I read Bloom's old academic papers, trying to get inside her head. I must understand what types of psychological experiments – or 'interventions' as they are technically known – might have been carried out on a patient as infamous as Sally Turner, aka the Stockwell Monster. What @PatientX could be referring to by the special project.

I also keep returning to my suspect for Sally Turner's biological child. The one we know she had but was never named. The person @PatientX claims is behind all this. That, after all, is the crux of the matter. Everything, I feel, hinges on the identity of that person. If I figure that out, all the rest will follow.

The name is too sensitive, or libellous, to be said out

loud. My methods of narrowing the suspect list are not entirely legal. But a recent yearbook spurred a chain of thought. I have followed it ever since. I may be totally wrong. Or not. It is a hunch in search of evidence.

For now, until I have further proof, I will simply refer to them by a codename of my own devising, a classical flourish that is both literal and disguised: MARATHON.

I read for another two hours. Then when everything is in place – chairs, shoes, etc. – I lie on the bed and allow my eyes to close. I try and summon happy thoughts. No blood, no bodies. No knives. No Medea or Lady Macbeth. I am a child again, poised between ignorance and knowledge. I am watching a United game with Dad. Or listening to Mum play the piano. I am happy, unthinking, free.

I will turn back the clock. I will cure myself of this.

What's done cannot be undone.

June 24

The Camden flat. I feel better. Facing the demons of this place helps too. I see the kitchen knife back in place. The flat has been cleaned. Indira and Doug sit at the kitchen table with laptops crunching data on the summer issue of *Elementary*. Our recent subscription drive has produced results. Ad revenue is up. Newsstand sales are marginally higher. Cancellations have dropped to under 4 per cent. Reader satisfaction is peaking. This despite the Creative Director and Chief Content Officer – yours truly – displaying key signs of anxiety and agoraphobia.

They ask me about my flu. I lie well. I remind myself that neither Doug nor Indy knows about The Incident. Only I do. How close I came to plunging the twenty-centimetre kitchen knife into someone else's skin. A belated revenge for their secret plotting. A blood-splattered detail in a murder case.

I unpack my things. I play happy flatmates again. Indira is regal and serene. Doug is busy on calls. Clients, dealers. I wonder whether to confront them now over the takeover. But I do not. I eat. I laugh. I drink. I wonder if they are together. If Indira, the numerate Roman goddess, has fallen for Doug, the pretty-boy marketeer.

Part of me hopes that life might be normal again. My friends are still my friends. The Incident is just a wake-up call (no pun intended). Sleep can once again be dull and comforting not dangerous.

But I feel the madness gather. I hear the witches' cry:

Fair is foul, and foul is fair:
Hover through the fog and filthy air.

June 27

The London Library. I have started writing. The printing schedule for the summer issue has been pushed back. Indira and Douglas are predictably furious. Doug does drunken, drugged-up verbals. Indy is far sneakier. She radiates disapproval through looks and gestures. Nothing is ever said. I feel her fury through a thousand micro-aggressions. It stings.

They fear cancelled subscriptions. Really, they worry GV Media will take fright and drop the acquisition of Elementary Media Ltd. Boo-hoo. Content is king. I am the *Elementary* brand. Without me, they have nothing. That was their mistake. They are courtiers, not the monarch. They are plotting a coup. My fingers are still on the throne.

I bring up the Word document. I select all, change the font – Times New Roman to Garamond – and read my opening again:

The true crime cases that grab the headlines tend to involve two things: an angelic girl and a monstrous man. Think of Soham, Milly Dowler, Madeleine McCann. The list goes on. But this issue of *Elementary* delves into a true crime story that came before all of those. It was the original tabloid crime, caught between the shock of the Bulger case and the unfathomable evil of the Shipman conviction. There have been no Netflix documentaries or BBC Storyville films. But that may be about to change. It was a case that book-ended the twentieth century. The bloodiest century in human history. It encapsulated so much of that transition moment: the last hurrah of print newspapers, five channels and flip phones. It was an analogue world where one story could hold an entire nation's attention. This piece is about the trial of Sally Turner, known in true crime history as the Stockwell Monster. Arrested, convicted, sectioned and dead all within the year 1999.

But this long-read for the summer issue explores more than blood and gore. It looks at the long-tail that violent crime leaves behind. After all, the facts leading up to the Turner murders are well known: Sally Turner's new relationship, the cuckooing ploy, drug-running, two stepsons raised in violence and bullying their stand-in mother figure, Sally's tragic wish for a 'perfect family', the bloody finale, her sleepwalking defence and the 'insane automatism' verdict at the Old Bailey.

Less well known are the months after the verdict when Sally was held indefinitely at Broadmoor Hospital. She was detained on Broadmoor's most sensitive ward – Cranfield. She was held in solitary and used as a subject for a psychological intervention codenamed MEDEA which was carried out under the clinical supervision of Dr Virginia Bloom, a consultant clinical psychologist who specialised in parasomnia and who testified at Turner's Old Bailey trial. Months after the experiment started, Sally

Turner was found dead in her room.

But did she really kill herself, or is there a more sinister explanation? Turn to page five of this issue to read our full piece and find out the answer to that tantalising question and so much more . . .

I mutter the words to myself. I reread that penultimate line. I wonder if that's what drew me to this story all along. I am using Sally Turner as an avatar. If I can understand Sally Turner's actions, monstrous as they are, maybe I can understand my own.

I think about my suspect MARATHON – Sally Turner's biological child, potentially her killer too – and the life they've led. Publishing a name like that without enough evidence could bankrupt the magazine. The defamation case that ruins me. MARATHON is my secret for now. I don't want Doug or Indy snooping on these journals and stealing my scoop. The real name is only in my head. It will stay there until I have enough proof. I can't lose everything on a hunch.

I save the Word document. I see another secure message arrive. After a week of silence, my contact is back.

I am inching closer to the truth.

I open the latest message from @PatientX.

57

BEN

The police interview pauses.

The tape is stopped and I'm led back to the custody suite. The cell door shuts. My hands are still shaking.

I see Bloom's body on the floor again and the oddness of it makes sense to me now. There was no sign of a struggle. Everything was immaculate, pristine.

I return to the present. I itemise the evidence listed by the police: traces of scopolamine found near Bloom's safe; emails recommending Harriet Roberts for a job at Rampton Secure Hospital; a digital trail linking me to a social media account using the handle @PatientX.

Enough for the police. Enough for the CPS. Enough for a jury to convict me on the three separate counts: the murder of Virginia Bloom; conspiracy to pervert the course of justice; and breaking the Official Secrets Act. The first is life. The first combined with the second and third is life without parole.

So many thoughts. I think of Harriet again. She has been at the heart of all this, the one constant throughout Anna's treatment and the ever-present angel by the bedside. Her arrest means the police have something solid. I feel the entire case stretch and invert until I can no longer grasp it.

Harriet, what have you done?

I think of Devil's Breath too. There have been numerous stories in criminology journals about scopolamine. It is a particularly vicious mind-control drug. Many of the most lurid tales are also the most horrifying. Mothers giving up their own babies to strangers when under the influence of the drug. People having their internal organs taken out. Hundreds of US tourists in Mexico being drugged and subject to rape and robbery. Perhaps the closest parallel to Bloom is the ancient myth of South American tribes using scopolamine to control the minds of widows, persuading them to be buried alive with their dead husbands, a joint pilgrimage into the afterlife.

Scopolamine is capable of almost anything.

I can imagine the profiles, ranging from the studious to the sensational. They will mine every possible source, from my YouTube lectures at Birkbeck to my published works. Gory details of the scene, aided by off-the-record police sources. My prints found on the murder weapon. Inserting myself into the investigation by tricking the Ministry of Justice into transferring Anna to the Abbey. A voyeur and a killer.

More will follow. The Justice Select Committee launching a full inquiry into the Ministry of Justice and Anna's transfer. The Home Office ordering the Met to review every case I consulted on as a behavioural investigative adviser. Former students, total strangers, middling acquaintances – all quoted as the red-tops, grey-tops and broadsheets tar and feather me in the rush to boost circulation.

I can't stay seated. I walk the cell like a circuit. I tug at my collar and feel grease and sweat on my skin. I want water and food. My stomach roils, lurches, tightens. I want to get out of here. Today won't end.

It contains all my greatest fears: my marriage, my role as a father, dreams for a future, the hope of joint residency destroyed with that photo outside the Abbey.

No matter what happens, I am one of the accused now.

After what seems like a lifetime I am granted my single call. One of the custody guards leads me out to the landline in the hallway. There is only one person I want to speak to. The person who, despite everything, is still there for me as I would be for her.

'Ben?'

I feel the tears threaten just at the sound of her voice. The emotion of the last few days has been so overwhelming. I want to stand there and sob like a small boy at prep school, banished from familial warmth into hellish brutality.

'Yes,' I say. 'Yes, it's me. Thank you for taking the call.'

'How are you bearing up?'

I know Clara must have been briefed before the arrest. That's why she didn't reply to my WhatsApp message. I wonder if she has seen the evidence against me. Whether she really believes I could have killed Bloom, flawless in every aspect apart from the stray smudge of scopolamine. The one mistake.

'Fine, fine,' I say, lying now. 'The custody suite's not too bad. Remand will be the big worry. Let's hope they see sense before that.'

'I'm sure they will.'

I parse that reply. She is in reassurance mode. It doesn't sound like she's just trying to comfort me. 'You know it's all nonsense,' I say. 'They've put two and two together and got five.'

'I know. Ben, of course I know.'

Those tears again. I wish Clara was here with me now. I wish we had never broken up. I long for the counter-factual where she didn't attend the Farm that night and Anna Ogilvy and her benighted family never entered our lives.

'Is KitKat there?'

A pause. Then, 'Yes, she is. Ben—'

I don't wait for the objections. 'Can you put her on. Just quickly. I promise. I want to hear her voice.'

'I'm not sure—'

There is a scuffling sound, then a distant voice picked up by the receiver on the other line. 'Daddy!'

It is useless now. The tears come. I let the hot, salty taste of them drip onto my lips. I feel like my hold on life is slipping. I am falling apart. A teary, confused, middle-aged mess. I used to understand the world. Now it makes no sense anymore. Every bit of me has fallen apart, cracked along the edges.

I close my eyes, breathe. 'Hello sweetheart.'

Clara has clearly given in and handed the receiver to KitKat. Her voice is louder and clearer now. 'When are you coming back, Daddy?'

I try and imagine what story Clara might have concocted to explain my absence. 'Soon, sweetheart. Very soon. Daddy is missing you a lot.'

'I miss you too, Daddy.'

'How's school going, darling?'

'I—'

There is a high, joyful syllable of KitKat's voice and then the line cuts dead. The custody guard taps on the side of the phone booth to signal time. It is an act of such mundane, heartless violence that I almost lose it. I want to beat the guard until all traces of personality are removed. I have never felt so angry, so hopeless.

I realise this is how things will be from now. My dignity was left behind at the Abbey when they arrested me. My human rights temporarily misplaced.

In the eyes of the world, I'm already a guilty man.

58

LOLA

So this is it.

Already she feels the pain dull over. The worst has happened. Soon she won't feel anything. Her right hand goes loose. She hears the clipper hit the floor.

Somehow, she thought it might go on forever. It was thrilling to play all those parts.

Harriet the angelic nurse by day.

Lola the armchair sleuth by night.

@Suspect8 to the online world.

It gave meaning to life. Added flavour to weeks. After all, why should Anna Ogilvy be the only one to reap the celebrity of the case?

It wasn't fair. But, then again, life's not fair. She can still hear all those teachers at school or her parents or her mocking, catty classmates.

Some people were born haloed with beauty and stardust. Anna Ogilvy seemed to have glided through life with barely a care. The nepo baby with her fancy politician mother and tieless financier father. The liberal, artsy, Bedales-style boarding school. The hallowed quads of Oxford. Then enough start-up capital to bootstrap a small magazine and pose as a media entrepreneur.

Lola – or Harriet as, just occasionally, she still thinks of herself – doesn't regret it. None of it. She would do it again in a heartbeat.

She sits down on the hard, stone-like bed. She has seen custody suites on TV documentaries and read about them in newspapers. But the reality is even scuzzier. The walls, the floor, the air itself – all is stained, begrimed. It's like returning to a state of nature. This is a concrete wildness. A jungle of stone. The rules of civilsation don't operate here. This is lawless.

For a moment, she imagines the coverage of her arrest. She replays her interview with the police. Not that it matters now. Nothing matters.

The rest has all been in place ever since the start.

She can recite her final message verbatim. Pre-loaded, ready to drop right around now. That first line, soon to be immortalised in true crime history:

My name is Harriet Lola Roberts. This is my full confession . . .

Yes, her name will always be there. No one can take that away from her. She was the nurse at Broadmoor all those years ago. The health and safety consultant on the Farm that night. The selfless healthcare professional tending the patient no one else would treat, even following the infamous Anna O from Rampton Secure Hospital to the Abbey.

The world underestimated her.

Everyone always has.

Apart from one person. The person all this has really been for.

Lola glances round the cell for one final time. She already feels fainter now. She sits back, forces her feet up onto the bed, and then lies there staring up at the ceiling. Blood drips onto the mattress surface. It joins the other stains.

She imagines Sally Turner in her room at Broadmoor.

Indira and Douglas dead with sleep in the Red Cabin.

Her eyes shut. The note will be published online any second now.

She has done it. Just like they agreed. The pain is almost gone. The hurt of living.

Sleep beckons.

ANNA'S NOTEBOOK
2019

August 24

Brasserie Zédel, Piccadilly. It's been weeks since I last wrote in this diary.

Today we are back to the wartime, jazzy ambience with its basement chic and sense of impending aerial bombardment. Three rather than two this time. Doug suggests it, Indy seconds the motion. And I know that this is it. The great announcement.

I am still snooping on their emails. I know GVM have tabled a formal offer for Elementary Media Ltd. That jean-wearing IP lawyers with offices in Greek Street have been hired. WeWork-surfers posing as accountants are on the case. Which just leaves me. The founder. The Creative Director. Chief Content Dogsbody. The person who drags their sorry behind to the laptop every day while Indy and Dougie swan round Shoreditch singing for their supper to ad clients.

Champagne is ordered. Doug and Indira sit together on the couch side. I am marooned on the hard chair opposite. The band strikes up. I feel as if I'm about to receive a proposal I'm supposed to know nothing about. I need a pretend-surprised face.

Indira starts. The diplomat of the group. The holier-than-thou tone. We've received an offer for the *Elementary* brand, she says. The magazine, the trademark, all our proprietary subscriber data. GVM are a new media company based in Seattle. They've aced the social, digital marketing and podcasting game, but want to add something different to their portfolio. The offer is decent. We can finally move out of start-up mode and join them in a proper office in Soho. Get out of the flat. Stop doing this thing on a shoestring. No more lifestyle hustle. But a proper media company.

Douglas plays bad cop now. If Indira is the poised ambassador, Doug is the salesman, the PR man, the boozer and brawler, the moisturised master of the hard sell. Didn't want to bother you with it. So much on your plate. We are as surprised as anyone. A firm offer. Cash deal. Keep the independence of the brand but share all back-office functions. The two of them will join GVM as 'Directors'. I can retain the Creative Director title and work exclusively on the content side. Win–win. Hooray.

And then I wait. The champagne arrives. Doug and Indira raise a glass. We started the magazine as flatmates. Indira and Doug established the limited vehicle with Companies House when we reached the VAT threshold. They did all the boring finance side. I was too busy stressing about content to bother with becoming a Director or filling in mountains of paperwork.

I wait some more. The minutes tick by, and still I wait . . .

And now I realise the full, crushing, funny-if-it-wasn't-true extent of my mistake. The late adolescent slip-up that crucifies you in adult life. I relied on friendship rather than formality. I assumed. I hoped. I believed. I bought into the chats over Deliveroo about how everything was shared equally and that we would sort out the details of the 'next stage' if we could keep the whole thing afloat.

They are not asking me, I realise. It's a done deal.

I am not legally entitled to a third of the purchase price. They have taken my idea. They have stolen my business. Now they have sold it and banked the rewards exclusively for themselves. They have cut me out. Left me with nothing.

I've been stupid and young and naïve and distracted.

I feared betrayal.

But this is so, so much worse.

59

BEN

I resort to counting sheep. Still I lie awake.

With nothing to read or watch, I conjure another memory instead. The one Clara always jokes about. I can picture it now, see the email address in my inbox and the subject title and those words that promised another life, a glimpse of a road not taken:

Dear Dr Prince,

I recently finished your book on mystery illnesses and your academic paper on dream analysis. I am the Pro Vice-Chancellor for Social Sciences at UCCI, the University College of the Cayman Islands. I am looking to establish a sleep psychology seminar at UCCI and wanted to get in touch about our Visiting Fellowship programme which serves as a paid sabbatical year to pursue book projects or general research. We would be delighted to explore this exciting opportunity with you. If you would be interested in talking further about becoming a Visiting Fellow here at Grand Cayman, do let me know.

Yours sincerely,
Emmanuel

Professor Emmanuel Ferguson
Pro Vice-Chancellor (Social Sciences)
University College of the Cayman Islands (UCCI)

I inhale the stink of chemical toilets and damp walls and I make a vow. If I ever get out of this cell, I will take up the offer. I will escape to the Cayman Islands and slowly rebuild my sanity. I will lie in the sun and swim in the sea until reason and logic are restored. Until I understand the world and how it works. Until this madness is over.

I need to start again.

I try to focus on something external, a puzzle to discipline myself. Emotional excavation is simply too painful. I won't survive much more.

Instead, I turn to questions about the case. I try to be methodical and itemise each one. This is how I will survive this. I curse Harriet for all that she has done.

She is @Suspect8.

She is Lola Ridgeway.

She was there on the Farm on the night of the murders.

Is she also Patient X? The final pseudonym.

Did she kill Douglas and Indira and frame Anna? Was that why she infiltrated Rampton and the Abbey to keep control of Anna and the case?

Or did she somehow persuade Anna to do the deed herself? And, if so, how exactly?

I curse myself for ever being persuaded by that artless, freckled smile. I am only here because of her. I see Harriet walking round the Farm with me, the cabins, through the Forest. She played me every step of the way, relying on the fact that I would never suspect a nurse. That my antenna was off as I saw her treating Anna so kindly, so compassionately, sainthood hiding sin.

Harriet Roberts has made fools of us all.

Then I stop myself. Go back to first principles. The answer

to the mystery lies with the Sally Turner case. Of that I am sure. The symmetry of the dates is unavoidable. It always has been. Sally Turner is found dead in her room at Broadmoor on August 30th, 1999. Anna Ogilvy is found in the Blue Cabin at the Farm on August 30th, 2019.

The exact anniversary.

Harriet worked at Broadmoor as a nurse in 1999. Broadmoor wouldn't employ the daughter of a patient. Bloom is also clear in the file that Patient X is a minor. Harriet is over eighteen in 1999. That makes it unlikely that Harriet is Patient X.

What if Harriet was working with Patient X, first at Broadmoor and then afterwards? What if that's the right way round to see this?

More questions now, gushing out of me.

Why would Harriet target Anna Ogilvy? If Harriet was helping Patient X, then the answer seems clear. Anna is investigating the Sally Turner case for *Elementary* magazine. She can unmask the true identity of Sally Turner's biological child and Harriet's collusion with Patient X for reasons as yet unknown. But why not just kill Professor Bloom instead? Because she is still useful somehow. That's why they keep her alive. The mention of Sally Turner and Medea triggers a moment of revelation in Bloom's office. Perhaps Bloom finally recognises Harriet from all those years ago. Perhaps she makes the connection with Patient X. So, only then, Bloom needs to be eliminated.

Why try and frame me? I am close to Bloom. I am a credible suspect. Harriet can easily gain access to my office and plant material about Rampton Secure Hospital, the @PatientX account and the @Suspect8 blog.

Did Harriet and Patient X plan for Anna's resignation syndrome? No, impossible. The resignation syndrome complicates everything. That's why Harriet has to get the job at Rampton Secure Hospital to monitor Anna. The original plan is for Anna to be caught red-handed and convicted. The rest is improvised.

And then the final question. Why kill Douglas and Indira but not Anna? I still have no answer for that one. The riddle of it continues to baffle me.

By the time the cell door opens, I have no concept of hours. Light or dark. Sleep or consciousness. Dead or alive. There is just the small cell with dirt-smeared walls and unwashed flooring and a blood-speckled mattress and no sense of time.

The cell opening sounds like a ship leaving harbour, a medley of metallic groans and whines. One of the custody guards nods at me to follow. The twenty-four hours are up. Final judgement awaits.

I see it all now: the solemn procession to the front desk, the custody sergeant reading out the formal charge, the moment when a citizen becomes a suspect, one step closer to being a prisoner, liberty stolen by increments.

I wait to see one of the interviewing DCs or their superiors in the corridor. I imagine a small crowd by the custody desk. But the hallway is empty. I reach the desk and a custody guard has my clothes and phone in a plastic bag and she hands them to me. I hear scripted words about follow-ups, passports, not leaving the country. But no charge. No further questioning. It sounds like an admin error, an office mix-up.

I don't understand.

The grey custody pyjamas are big and clownish. I sign for my proper clothes, phone and laptop. The custody guard escorts me to the back exit of the police station and the car park and morning light. I almost ask permission to step outside. Then I comprehend.

I am a free man.

I wonder if the media have been tipped off again. I half-expect to see a pool of reporters. But the car park is deserted. It is a foul, sleety day. The air prickles with rain. I am thirsty and tired.

I am about to use my mobile to call a cab when I see a figure up ahead. She has her hands in her pockets, assessing me in the way only she ever can.

All the others have disowned me.

But, somehow, one person still cares.

Clara.

60

BEN

I follow Clara to her car. We exchange formalities of the are-
you-hungry variety as I buckle up and she drives away and I
am returned to semi-normal life again. After ten minutes or so,
we reach a Costa drive-through. I recite our order from memory.
Clara finds a spot on the side of the road. The world is oblivious
to us here. I see my watch, wallet and phone on the back seat.
I look at Clara. I sip coffee and chew a cold bacon roll.

'What happened?' I say, my voice still unsteady. Though that's
not what I mean. I know what happened. I want to understand
how.

Clara doesn't reply. She just looks at me. Despite the divorce,
I still know every bit of her. Her eyes, her body language, her
breathing – all of it is rich with meaning.

'Harriet?' I say, at last.

Clara reaches into her jacket pocket and takes out her phone.
She swipes up, waits for facial recognition and thumbs through
to her photos.

I look at the screen. It is a photo of the Lola Ridgeway/
@Suspect8 blog. Everything has been deleted apart from one
message. It looks like a statement. Or, more ghoulishly, a suicide
note. It is signed 'Harriet Roberts', yesterday, 23:29.

I brace myself to read:

> My name is Harriet Lola Roberts. This is my full confession: I am the nurse to Anna Ogilvy at Rampton Secure Hospital and the Abbey Sleep Clinic and the user known as @Suspect8. Under the name of Lola Ridgeway, I was at the Farm on August 30th, 2019. I've been by Anna's side ever since. I worked on the Cranfield Ward at Broadmoor Hospital in 1999 when Sally Turner, aka the Stockwell Monster, was found dead in her room following a psychological experiment codenamed MEDEA run by Dr Virginia Bloom. I make no apology for my actions. My only quest was for justice. Professor Bloom has paid the necessary price. If you are reading this, then I have achieved all my aims, or the system has silenced me. Either way, it's time for others to carry the torch of justice now.

I finish reading.

'Suicide?'

Clara nods. 'They think Harriet smuggled in a small nail clipper and used the serrated edge to cut her wrists. She bled out on the cell floor. They rushed her to the Chelsea and Westminster Hospital. But they couldn't save her. She was pronounced dead a few hours ago.'

Harriet is dead. So many answers go with her. And there are still so many questions that remain. Harriet's note is mysterious and cryptic, falling far short of the promised full confession. It tantalises, teases even, as if the full truth is still too secret to ever be completely known. It clouds rather than enlightens.

Who was Harriet trying to avenge? Sally Turner? Patient X?

Is she admitting here to murdering Professor Bloom?

How does the Sally Turner death at Broadmoor relate to the Anna O double murders? Why mark the anniversary of Sally's death like that?

And, perhaps most importantly, who is Patient X? Are they

still the key to unlocking this entire mystery? Is Harriet Patient X or merely X's accomplice?

I feel sick as I think about Harriet and Bloom. Even more confused, too. Just when the answer seems within reach the mysteries spread further, like a living organism multiplying. I can't stop toying with each hypothetical, how things could have gone differently, teasing out the endless what-ifs.

Eventually, Clara says, 'They think she must have automated the message ready to send before she was arrested. Cyber forensics only picked it up a few hours ago. She had this whole thing planned for a very long time. @Suspect8's final statement to the world.'

I think of Anna Ogilvy at the Abbey. Of Harriet training at Broadmoor in 1999. Of Bloom in her own front room. Of the twisted horrors of the human mind.

Clara continues, 'The police searched her flat and found a treasure trove of things she used for her blog about the Anna O case. She was completely obsessed with it. Wallcharts, suspect boards, like she was running the case herself. She compromised it all from the very beginning.'

'Did the police question you?'

'Donnelly briefed me.'

'What happens now about a trial for Anna?'

'The million-dollar question. It looks like Harriet has contaminated the entire evidence chain for Anna's case. She was at the Farm when the murders took place and there at the bedside throughout Anna's time at Rampton and the Abbey. Anna's defence team could claim that Harriet interfered with the evidence or planted it, and the prosecution won't be able to prove that she didn't. That makes it almost impossible for Anna to receive a fair trial, not to mention the oodles of prejudicial media coverage of the case. The CPS uses public money. The DPP will only decide to prosecute if there's a realistic chance of conviction. That's already a pipe dream. Harriet's suicide changes everything.'

'What about me?'

'Harriet has practically confessed to murdering Bloom in her note. Plus, we're back to the contamination issue. Harriet has compromised all the evidence that might be used to prosecute you on all the charges as well. She was by Anna's side at the Abbey more than you were. With you a lot, too. Your lawyers will be able to claim she orchestrated all of it. Or tried to frame you. The law doesn't decide if you're guilty or innocent but whether your guilt is beyond reasonable doubt. Harriet's presence throughout all your dealings with Anna and at the Farm on the night of the murders means that threshold can't realistically be reached. There is too much doubt now. Therefore the same logic applies.'

'I see.'

I am struck again by the scale of what Harriet has done. She always seemed to be on the margins of things. That was her greatest trick. She was right there in front of me all that time hiding in plain sight. A fair trial may be impossible, but nothing can ever go back to what it was. And the real gem – the true identity of Patient X – is no closer to being found. Harriet has ensured that the story will never really be over. Harriet Roberts, or Lola Ridgeway, is still manipulating us all.

Clara says, 'The Director of Public Prosecutions has to judge whether years of legal wrangling, with no realistic prospect of a fair trial for either you or Anna, is really in the public interest. He's getting pressure from Downing Street. It's far easier to let Harriet take the cop for everything, especially now she's dead and can't defend herself, and save spending millions on a hopeless cause. That means letting you and Anna go.'

I think of Anna's dream again. I wonder how much of it was real: the forest, the knife, the blood. Or whether she was taunting me knowing others might be listening. That is the problem with it all now. Harriet was always there. No fact survives intact.

Sally Turner. The Stockwell Monster. Anna Ogilvy. Indira Sharma. Douglas Bute. Professor Bloom. Broadmoor.

1999. 2019.

Two key events, twenty years apart.

It all fits together, I know it must, but how?

Why would Harriet Roberts help Patient X?

Why would they target Anna Ogilvy?

What is the end goal of their plan?

Did Harriet somehow force Anna to commit those two murders that night? Or did Harriet kill both victims and then frame Anna? Or is it the other way round: did Anna use Harriet to get away with murder?

So many questions. So many possible answers.

I reread the final @Suspect8 post again now. Playing the long game, duping so many people over such a long period of time. I have rarely encountered a criminal with such know-how or actorly persuasion.

The drumbeat of facts in my head.

Harriet Roberts is dead.

She has confessed to murdering Professor Bloom.

I have been released.

The Crown Prosecution Service may decide that pursuing charges against me is not in the public interest. Which means I am, and will remain, a free man.

Anna Ogilvy will be too.

Harriet has taken the fall, a sponge soaking up every sin imaginable. Anna wins, Harriet loses, I am caught in between.

I think of Anna now. I imagine her leaving the Abbey and stepping into the rest of her life. I am a curio here. She is the main event.

She always has been.

Like so many others, I have spent so long beguiled by Anna's brain, her beauty, the elegance of her. Society doesn't want to believe that beauty can be evil; that sophistication can be savage. And so we deceive ourselves. We fall for the lie about sleep-walking or resignation syndrome to process uncomfortable events rather than confront our own misconceptions.

I have always been firmly on Team Anna. Now, though, I've

changed my mind. I think of her lying beyond the glass divide, the killer in the room next door. I chart the whole history of this case and that warning from Emily about Anna's determination to secure her fifteen minutes of fame. And I wonder if I have been duped from the very beginning.

I made the mistake of believing her. The latest in a long line of fools. Mistaking beauty for morality, youth for innocence, brains for wisdom.

I make one vow now: never again.

'So Harriet Roberts takes all the blame,' I say. 'Harriet dies. Anna walks free.'

'Yes,' says Clara, finishing her coffee and starting the car. 'That's how the fairy tale ends. Sleeping Beauty wakes up and lives happily ever after.'

ANNA'S NOTEBOOK

2019

August 25

The Camden flat. I lock my bedroom door. I don't use any other measures. I feel the walls close round me like a prison. These people aren't my friends. They never were. It's Indy's betrayal that hurts me the most. She is the Judas. All those chats and midnight walks and sofa surfing – sleight-of-hand while they signed the paperwork.

The GVM bid is not retirement money. Not even close. But it is enough to pay off student debts, put down flat deposits, plan for the future. Make the last few years of bootstrapping worth it. I've made the mistake of all founders and let someone else deal with the money. They've played me for a fool.

I think of the humiliation as I tell my parents. The way Theo will turn this into a joke. Anna the artsy creative with her delusional belief in other people. Dad will call it a learning experience. Mum will barely notice. I was the one who invited the others to join me. To add some commercial nous to my student idea for a late millennial and Gen Z-focused print title that surfed the vintage wave for all things hard copy and retro. The little mag that could. A new way to connect with the demographic brands found so hard to reach.

The traitors have one other request. I must finally file my story for the summer issue. Jeopardise this and the deal could still fall through. I smile and lie as fluently as ever and apologise for being so tardy. Now I see their crocodile smiles.

But that is not the worst of it.

I am still snooping on Indy and Doug's phones. And I've found something else. I think of that early message I stumbled on: *Best on private email. I've set up joint account to discuss RO etc.* It is the puzzle running through all this: how did Indy get GVM's interest in the first place? How did she bag the contacts and interest of a big media firm with deep pockets? We are just a small, independent print magazine operating out of a cruddy rented flat.

No, realistically, there was always someone else involved. Another part of this whole story. Now I know who. Each little incident means something different. All the pieces in my life have come together. That latest message I saw recently on Indy's phone shines new light on everything.

This isn't the first betrayal. It's the last of many. I have been so stupid.

I've set up joint account to discuss RO etc.

RO doesn't stand for 'rollover'. Or responsible officer. It isn't a financial acronym. It's a name.

I want to hurt them, to shock them, get back in any way I can.

I want revenge.

I know who helped Indy betray me. Who fell for her charms. The mystery man with his Other Woman.

RO.

Richard Ogilvy.

PART FOUR

61

BEN

Grand Cayman

'The average human spends thirty-three years of their life asleep.'

She leans closer, enough for me to catch a gust of expensive perfume. This is usually the moment when I know. 'And that's what you do?'

'Yes.'

'A sleep doctor?'

'I study people who commit crimes when they sleep.' I still have 'Dr' before my name on business cards. Dr Benedict Prince, The Abbey, Harley Street. I am an expert in sleep. Nowhere do I claim to be a medical doctor.

She sees that I'm serious. 'How's that even possible?'

'Don't you ever wonder what you might have done when you were asleep?'

Most people get uncomfortable right around here. The majority of crimes have a distancing factor. We revel in stories about people just like us; but who are also not like us. But sleep doesn't allow that qualification.

Sleep is the one universal, the night as constant as the day.

'What kind of crimes?'

She hasn't changed the topic. I still have her attention. 'All the worst ones.'

'Surely people would wake up?'

'Not if they're sleepwalking. I've known patients who lock their doors and drive their cars while still asleep. Some people even kill.'

'Surely you'd remember?'

'From the lines around your eyes, I'm guessing you slept five and a half hours last night.'

She frowns. 'It's that obvious?'

'Do you have any memory of what happened during those five and a half hours?'

She pauses, cupping her chin in her right hand. 'I dreamt something.'

'Like what?'

'I can't remember.'

'My point is proved.'

Her eyes suddenly change now. She looks at me differently. Her voice is louder, the body language animated. 'Wait, there was that case. What was it called—'

This is the final point. Few dates ever reach this far. I bore them with my job description. I scare them away with stories about crimes committed during sleep. If that doesn't work, then this last thing always gets me.

No one stays once they realise.

No one.

'Anna O,' I say. I take a final sip of my wine – an expensive Merlot, more's the pity – and then reach for my jacket.

'You're the guy. In the photo. The psychologist.'

I smile dimly. I check my watch. 'Yes,' I say. 'I was.'

It was the photo on the front of every major daily newspaper after it happened – my arrest, my disgrace. Tragedy seems to cling to that day.

I am a different person. I am the same person.

I wait for the question because it is the question I am always asked. It is the one mystery that, despite everything – Harriet's death, the awakening, the evidence in the flat – still lingers. It divides families, spouses, even friends. It is the one question no one seems able to let go of. The lust for a puppet-master, a deity silently pulling the strings.

Patient X. Anna Ogilvy.

'Was she guilty?' my date asks, or the woman who was formerly my date. 'When she stabbed those two people. Did she really get away with murder?'

62

BEN

I am back from my date. Like a reflex, I reach for my mobile and speed-dial the number.

It is the same call I make every week, juggling time zones. It is formal, now. But necessary. I am still the father maintaining a vigil outside his daughter's bedroom door. Some see my exile as cowardice, deserting my family. The opposite is true. While I was there, they were part of the Anna O story.

They had to come first. My exile gives them freedom. It is a price worth paying.

Or that's what I tell myself.

We do the usual introductions, the hellos and how-are-yous, before I ask the dreaded question. 'Has there been any more trouble?'

Clara is dogged, competent. 'Just one last week. Journalist from a European news magazine was hanging round Kitty's school. The police had a word.'

'What about the other children at school?'

'You know what kids are like.'

Yes, I do. 'How's she bearing up?'

'She's hanging in there. If the bloody paps would just leave us alone.'

'I know.'

'What about the flat?'

She sighs. 'Some of the neighbours are still complaining that tourists try and visit. Apparently the address got leaked again last month on another of those conspiracy websites.'

'You got it taken down?'

'We're working on it.'

'If there's anything—'

'Look, Kitty's calling me, Ben. I've got to go.'

And, like that, she's gone.

I feel guilty, as I should. They contend with the lingering media presence while I escape attention in secluded isolation. But we both agreed it was for the best. I am the one the papers want. My presence at home would only add to the misery. They endure occasional media skirmishes. If I was still in the UK it would be all-out war.

I picture KitKat emerging from school with her gym bag and violin case and some stranger hovering on the road trying to get a shot. Rage consumes me. And sorrow too. The deepest, gut-aching sorrow I've ever felt. I want to smash the walls and scream into the wind and weep until my tear ducts are empty. I can't protect my daughter. I am impotent, useless, a failure as a father. I spend every evening worrying about her, haunted by the very worst scenarios. The newspapers send female paps now to avoid suspicion. Posing as mums at the school gate. All for some sidebar news item about the family of the 'disgraced forensic psychologist, Dr Benedict Prince'.

Bastards. Evil, heartless bastards.

I load up WhatsApp and type out a new message, another part of my daily routine: Hi sweetheart, it's Daddy. Hope you have a great day at school. Sending lots of hugs. Love you loads, Daddy.

I see the WhatsApp message has reached KitKat's phone. The two ticks turn blue.

There's no reply. There never is now.

It's a school day, after all. And she is under Clara's orders.

It breaks me every single time.

63

BEN

The last act of the Anna O case clogged up the headlines for months.

The news stories focused, inevitably, on the gorier details: Harriet's suicide, her background as Lola, the access at both Rampton Hospital and the Abbey, the way in which she managed to fool everyone, the @Suspect8 blog.

An entire media cycle is born from those few months in London. The Abbey doesn't survive the scandal. The #AnnaO hashtag trends for five months straight. The public appetite for death, blood, tragedy and trauma shows no sign of abating.

There are rumours of a feature film in development and whispers about eye-popping advances for Anna to write her memoirs. A treasure trove of evidence is uncovered in Harriet's flat. There is a copy of Professor Bloom's article 'The Medea Method: Personality and Parasomnia' in *Psychiatry Today* magazine from 1991 with copious highlights and underlining. There is also a stash of the drug scopolamine, better known by its street name Devil's Breath, used as a date rape or mind control drug and slipped into alcohol to disable the victim's short-term memory by blocking nerve cells in the brain.

The theories continue to swirl: police suspect scopolamine is how Harriet got Anna to physically carry out the attacks at the Farm, and also how Harriet subdued Bloom before stabbing her; others claim Harriet committed the Farm murders herself, merely framing Anna; yet more people allege that Anna is the real mastermind behind all of it and may have faked the deep sleep with Harriet's assistance to get away with murdering Indira and Douglas. The Anna O versus Sleeping Beauty warfare continues.

The identity of the real Patient X, meanwhile, remains unknown.

As Clara predicted, Harriet's proximity to Anna and her presence at the Farm on the night of the murders mean the CPS formally drops the charges against Anna and decides not to prosecute me. The Ministry of Justice agrees to release Anna from custody. She claims to suffer from post-traumatic amnesia since the awakening, unable to remember anything about the Farm or her crimes. Some believe her; some do not.

I was once a believer. But I've crossed the divide from Team Anna to Sleeping Beauty. There are too many questions left unanswered by Harriet's suicide. I once worried I was on the wrong side of things, helping to wake Anna only to condemn her. Now I wonder if Stephen Donnelly was right all along.

Anna continues her recovery outside the UK. My role in her treatment ends. My part-time teaching post at Birkbeck is discontinued. Photographers continue to squat outside my flat. KitKat is harassed at school. No clinic or university in Britain will hire me. I am tainted by association.

The turning point comes two months later. A reporter smuggles a note inside KitKat's schoolbag to try and get an interview. That is when Clara tells me to go. That night I reply to the offer from UCCI in Grand Cayman for a Visiting Fellowship in their graduate studies programme and fly out here.

Then, as it does, life moves on. According to media rumours, Anna changes her appearance and goes into self-imposed exile. Clara quits the Met and re-joins Thames Valley Police. She and

KitKat flee the publicity and move back to Oxfordshire. Bloom's house in Islington is sold. I hire expensive lawyers and social media teams to try and wipe my online presence.

And yet there is an itch I continue to scratch.

Those questions that still need answers.

I've started assembling an archive of the case. Old newspapers, magazine articles, handwritten notes. It's part of my personal therapy, trying to rationalise what happened.

Anna Ogilvy is free. Yet I am condemned to exile. My family is permanently misshapen. Harriet is the scapegoat, yet the most important mysteries remain unresolved.

Closure isn't enough. Not by a long way.

I must find the truth.

Or die trying.

64

BEN

Theories, theories.

I am back to my old theories. This is my new ritual.

I have my own boards on the wall.

The first board starts with Harriet Roberts. No definitive evidence has emerged to verify that she was Sally Turner's daughter. Nor has any evidence emerged to suggest she wasn't. Patient X is still a ghost, an absence. The past ultimately unknowable.

I still favour the argument against. The dates don't add up. Nor does the logic. Broadmoor wouldn't have employed the child of a patient as a nurse.

Harriet was the sidekick, not the leading part. I think back to those hints from Bloom's case notes. The riddle of Patient X's mythical friend:

VB: Have you seen your friend recently?
PX: Yes.
VB: Does your friend have a name?
PX: Yes.

And then Bloom's observations, dismissing the 'friend' as a psychic illusion:

> I still think the friend is more likely made up than real. A devil on X's shoulder. It is a psychological cushion, a familiar symptom among children with psychological damage.

What if Bloom was wrong and the friend was real? What if Harriet isn't X, but the friend of X? The confidant mentioned in the case notes. I imagine visits, a sympathy developing. A young male (Patient X) seducing a young woman (Harriet). Is that the hold that Patient X had over Harriet? Love across the nurse–visitor divide. And how does Anna's role fit into that theory? How can any one theory of the case encompass all the moving parts?

I turn to the other boards now. Notes in Harriet's flat cast new light on everything, including the existence of the so-called Medea experiment at Broadmoor in the late nineties, run by one Professor V. Bloom.

According to Harriet's notes, Sally Turner was kept in solitary (like all Cranfield patients). But her room was different. Given the notoriety of the case, the high suicide risk, the threat to and from other patients and for the ease of the Medea experiment, Sally Turner was housed in a bespoke glass cell known by staff as 'the cage'. It allowed her to be monitored 24/7. Her meals were delivered through a slot. A six-person unlock was required for Turner's daily hour of exercise. Sally Turner's cell had precedent: it was based on the custom-built room for the serial killer – and former Broadmoor resident – Robert Maudsley at HMP Wakefield in Yorkshire. His glass cell, also known as 'the cage', resembled Hannibal Lecter's room in *The Silence of the Lambs*.

The exact details of the Medea experiment remain speculative. But Bloom's old article is ransacked by the press. The methods listed in that piece for the November issue of *Psychiatry Today* are taken as gospel: sleep deprivation, enhanced restraint methods, sensory overload. Psychic disintegration.

I move away from the boards. I open my laptop again now and bring up the email that came in last night:

TO: benedictprince9@outlook.com
FROM: socialservices@lambeth.gov.uk
SUBJECT: Query #7HYU8902

Dear Dr Prince,

 We regret to inform you that Lambeth Borough Council is unable to release any archived records regarding the work of our Social Services Team connected to the period January–December 1999 or the keywords 'Sally Turner'. If you wish to lodge a complaint regarding this decision, please contact the Data Ombudsman.

 Yours sincerely,
 Social Services Admin Team
 Lambeth Borough Council

Another cul-de-sac.

I drag it into the folder titled 'Patient X'. There are more polite blanks from the Home Office, Department of Health, Ministry of Justice and Cabinet Office. Contemporary reports at the time of Sally Turner's arrest confirm she had one teenage child. The teenager was clearly below eighteen. They were never named. This was the era before widespread Facebook and Instagram use. There were no family group photos to help. Even if there were, the child in question would have been put under the protection of social services and – according to hints from Bloom's case file – witness protection, now part of the NCA's UK Protected Persons Service.

The real identity of Patient X always slips away. I should delete my files. Burn the scrapbooks. Forget about Bloom, Harriet, Broadmoor, Cranfield Ward, Medea. But it's a compulsion. One I still can't shake. It sustains me through the other parts of my life.

I spend two days a week now teaching at the UCCI campus in Olympic Way, with a specialist evening course in the psychology of sleep. For the rest of the week, I treat patients in my own private clinic. I have a small, but stable, client list looking for cognitive behavioural therapy, help with anxiety disorders, even occasional sleeping difficulties. I don't consult on police cases.

I live a quiet, semi-invisible life. But I know it can't last forever. The dates are ill-advised, but I long for contact and conversation. Sooner or later my sins will catch up with me. A bag is packed in the flat ready to make a quick getaway. One of my dates will alert someone, gossip will travel, my emails and calls will be hacked, the media will swarm. I live expecting a knock on the door or a car outside my office.

My life is spent reading British newspapers, grappling with the implications of the Anna O case in relation to resignation syndrome and my stimulus theory, or patrolling the boards and debating theories. Most of my dates end with Anna. Some end with stories of the family I've left behind.

I have time to lose myself in the mysteries and riddles and contradictions of this case. I can chart the ways in which I was duped and betrayed. I carry on the quest, refusing to let it be relegated to gossip or trivia, still fighting and waiting.

I have to uncover the answer. I must solve the mystery. The alternative is too painful to think about.

Finding Patient X is the only meaningful thing I have left.

ANNA'S NOTEBOOK
2019

August 26

The flat. I am all smiles today. I get up early, go for a run. I return as Doug and Indira surface. We sit around the circular glass table. Indira is on granola. Doug on Coco Pops. I eat a banana slowly and drain a smoothie. I see them look at each other, as if judging my reaction from last night, and feel my determination rise again.

I place down the brochure. I give them the pitch. Mum has won a private invite to a weekend away. It came through the post, one of those marketing gimmicks. No phones. No distractions. It's a place called the Farm. Yes, *that* one. This is my gift to them for us to celebrate the start of the new adventure!

They fake-smile and agree. I head out to St James's Square and the London Library. Lying is a muscle that needs regular exercise.

I check my phone. There is another message from @PatientX. I reply with the details of the Farm, our arrival times, the hours I'll be free. It is the perfect place for our first proper meet. I can put a face to the name. I can finally publish my piece.

I feel hope again.

August 27

Ogilvy Towers, Hampstead. A family conference to plan for the weekend trip.

Mum is CEO. Dad is CFO. I am COO. Theo is Chief of Morale.

The itinerary is as follows: we arrive at the Farm on the 29th. The 'Family Package' consists of six guests, including all equipment, accommodation and food. The Family Package allows guests, which is where Indira and Doug come in.

From 4 p.m. to 12 a.m. we embark on the centrepiece of the visit known only as 'The Forest'. Two teams. Hunters and Survivors. I imagine those outward-bound reality shows that pepper Channels 4 and 5.

I put on my game face with Mum today. I don't look at Dad. I lie to them all and play happy families. I avoid destroying my own father for his betrayal. That will come later.

I say nothing about the GVM takeover. I wonder how much Dad knows and how much Indy has scammed him into. But I am ready. If I can't join the buyout, I can make sure it never happens. I look at the brochure for the Farm again and think about meeting @PatientX.

The Forest. A media storm. No more GVM.

I win. I always win.

It's an Ogilvy family rule.

65

BEN

The end, when it arrives, is sudden. My exile in Grand Cayman is broken without warning. One day I am in semi-hiding, the next I've been found. The moment of reckoning makes me realise something even more profound. Exile implies the promise of return. Banishment does not. What if I have mistaken one for the other? What if I am never to leave this island again?

The day begins as usual. It is just after ten thirty when I arrive at the office. The weather forecast predicts a thunderstorm this week. My part-time secretary, Sofia, is busy on a phone call. I brew a cup of English breakfast tea, think of another line for my journal article, then open today's appointment calendar and familiarise myself with the names.

Sofia joins me in the office after her call. She brings in a plate of biscuits. She takes one for herself and sets the rest down.

'Bit of a paddling day, I'm afraid,' she says. She is an expat, like me, with a diplomat husband who works at the Governor's Office and a small son who sometimes likes to use my office as a racing circuit. 'Mix of regulars and newbies.'

'Did Angus enjoy my birthday present?'

Sofia smiles. 'An introduction to psychology might be slightly advanced reading for a six-year-old.'

'Nonsense. I started on Freud when I was not much older.'

'Now you tell me.'

I keep flicking through the details of my first patient. 'Elizabeth Cartwright. That name doesn't ring a bell.'

Sofia busies herself tidying my office. She stacks papers neatly on the shelves with a sprinter's speed. 'Bolt from the blue yesterday. She asked for the next available slot.'

'Did she say what it was about?'

'She hung up before I could ask. And it's not as if we can really afford to turn down paying customers.'

'True.' I finish reading the scant details for E. Cartwright and sit back in my chair. 'Though, technically, I think they prefer to be called patients rather than customers. Did she pay in advance or will this be another door-locking exercise?'

Sometimes I still dream of Harley Street and the Abbey. The sophisticated clientele, the air of luxury. One of the perils of running such a small operation is the patients who promise to settle their invoice later and mysteriously never do. Now I insist on payments before they leave. Sometimes that means Sofia keeping the front door locked until the money has gone through.

'All upfront,' says Sofia.

'No medical history provided?'

'None.'

'What about reasons for visiting me?'

'Nothing on that front either.'

'Did this Ms Cartwright provide any context at all?'

Sofia finishes tucking one of the stray books back into place. She runs her forefinger across the surface of the shelf. 'She did seem very keen to know that it was you she was going to see and not some other member of staff.'

'How many staff does she imagine we have?'

'I can always give her a test-drive first if you're too busy.'

I smile, a rare event these days. Sofia has one of those no-nonsense and slightly schoolgirlish voices that have largely died out in England. I imagine her busily revising for A level Latin. Expats seem to exaggerate themselves, parodies of their home-land. I have a horrible feeling that today will be a bad one.

I check the time. I have another fifteen minutes to spare. 'Buzz her in when she arrives. I'll try and find out if she's linked to any tabloid or gossip site.'

I search for any sign of 'Elizabeth Cartwright' online. There are hundreds of people matching that name. But I narrow the field through various other factors, not least the bank details on the money transfer. Nothing emerges. I try to shake off the lingering unease.

At eleven, the entrance buzzer sounds. Seconds later Sofia is greeting the new arrival. She does the usual mile-a-minute ques-tions about tea or coffee, another form to fill in, just wait there until the call comes through, surreptitiously checking for any signs of alarm or things hidden inside rucksacks and pockets.

I think back to Harriet. I wonder if this new patient could be one of her @Suspect8 followers, a true believer, convinced that I am the devil incarnate and should have died instead of her. Or, worse, a Team Anna follower who claims I falsely imprisoned their beloved Anna at the Abbey to brainwash her and is here to enact revenge.

There is the trademark rap on the door – a knuckle-roll, almost – and then it creaks open. Sofia sticks her head through. 'Ms Cartwright is here.'

'Thank you,' I say, putting on my deepest and sharpest client-facing voice. 'Please send her in.'

I am still a professional. It is the one part of my old identity that has remained intact. I pride myself on offering a good patient service and bedside manner.

I hear Sofia say, 'You can go through now.'

I am on my feet. Sofia moves out of view. I am halfway towards my new patient when I glance up. She is medium height, with slender shoulders and darkish hair trimmed to chin-length. The upper half of her face is hidden under a wide-brimmed hat to ward off the heat. She removes her sunglasses now. She smiles at me.

It is a smile I recognise, despite the alterations. It is a smile that seems to see through me, staring deep into the soul.

A storm finding me in paradise and blotting out the sun.

Only then do I understand.

Suddenly, painfully, as clear as day.

I will not escape this. No matter how far I run.

Anna.

ANNA'S NOTEBOOK
2019

August 28

The London Library, St James's Square. I bury myself in work. Revenge is all I have now. Revenge on Indira, Douglas, Dad. A plague on all of them. I wish they were dead.

No, work is my salvation. This research into the past – Bloom, Medea, Sally Turner, the Stockwell Monster – is keeping me sane. I've spent weeks trying to find it, ever since @PatientX mentioned the title. But, finally, an assistant discovers a copy in the depths of their overflow facility. There is one remaining physical copy of the November issue of *Psychiatry Today* from 1991. I look at the contents page. I feel a catch of excitement as I see the article on page 22: 'The Medea Method: Personality and Parasomnia' by Dr Virginia Bloom.

The bio at the top says: 'Dr Bloom is Consultant Clinical Psychologist at Broadmoor Hospital and specialises in sleep disorders and sleep-related crimes. She is currently re-searching her first book'. The article is five pages of dense text. I take a seat, prepare myself, then start reading.

It is written for a technical audience. Much of it is beyond me as a layperson. But there are certain paragraphs that I pick up. This is the moment. One browning, forgotten article in an extinct psychology journal from the early nineties could unlock the entire mystery.

I read the final section for a second time:

Conclusion: Formulating the Medea Method

The Medea Method is a proposal for a new form of psychological intervention to address the most extreme cases and, indeed, the most extreme crimes seen within the secure hospital environment. An adult killing a child. A parent killing their son or daughter. An adult killing their parents or grandparents. Like Medea in Euripides's play, these crimes break the greatest taboos of Western society. They go beyond normal moral boundaries or conventional ethics. They are the sort of aberrant and unsocialised thoughts that Freud popularised with his idea of the 'id'. Indeed, Euripides encapsulates the general public reaction to these crimes in the words of Jason as he discovers what Medea has done: 'After such murder do you outface both Sun and Earth— / Guilty of gross pollution? May the gods blast your life!'

Such extreme crimes can, this paper argues, only be treated with similarly extreme remedies. When the patient's mind is manifestly failing, it cannot be repaired by tweaks or amendments or pharmacological solutions alone. Instead, it must be fundamentally broken down and reformed. The Medea Method, though still in abstract, proposes several means of doing so within a specialist and forensic setting: long-term isolation, 24/7 surveillance, sleep deprivation, enhanced restraint methods and sensory overload. Only then can the current damaged thought processes be removed and a healthier psyche rebuilt in its place. A surgeon doesn't treat a tumour by keeping it in the body. Excision is the first step to healing. Modern psychology has finally stepped out of the psychoanalytic shadow. We no longer believe treatment is open-ended, a talking cure that never stops talking. We need results. We need metrics. This is one way to achieve that.

The obvious objections to the Medea proposal come from an ethical standpoint. Do these proposals amount to torture as defined by the Geneva Convention of 'cruel and unusual punishments'? Do they breach the ECHR?

My answer is clear: no. It is, in fact, a far greater cruelty in the long-term to condemn these patients to indefinite detention while accommodating their madness rather than trying to cure it. The days of sectioning patients to a cradle-to-grave sentence within a lunatic asylum must be over. It costs six figures a year to keep a single patient within a secure medical facility. We need to reduce the average length of stay at facilities like Broadmoor. That means taking tough action to cure rather than simply contain.

Fieldwork will be necessary to provide proper data for this hypothesis. By the nature of the subject matter, running a full trial will be logistically difficult. It is nevertheless my contention that such an intervention should be staged within a controlled environment as a means of patient rehabilitation. There is an old phrase: 'to be cruel to be kind'. I firmly believe that any potential cruelty of the Medea Method is far outweighed by the long-term kindness in giving the most extreme patients the chance of recovery.

I hope this abstract proposal for a new type of psychological intervention can be considered in due course and that a controlled experiment will be set up within the near future.

I google the Medea Method, but nothing comes up. I try researching other famous psychological experiments. Lots come up: from the infamous (the Stanford Prison

Experiment) to the comical (the Philip Experiment in para-psychology) and the deadly serious (the MIDAS Trial for schizophrenia).

I read on late into the night and the early morning. Stanford, Philip, MIDAS, Rosenhan, Diogenes, Milgram, Good Friday – but no MEDEA.

I think about my suspect MARATHON again. This case brims with the letter M. I wonder if my suspicions are misplaced, whether my suspect really is Sally Turner's child. Perhaps there will never be a way to know for sure. The photo, the yearbook, the connective spark – lost in the jumble of the past.

It is just gone 2 a.m. when I have an idea. It has itched in the corner of my mind, lurked throughout everything. The unspoken fear.

I go back to Wikipedia and type in 'UK Minister of State for Health' and look at the items listed under 'Responsibilities', scrolling back through the decades until I reach the late 1990s.

I read the line once, then again. I wish I hadn't been so curious. But already I know. I feel the ache of it throughout my body.

My suspicion – my dread – is confirmed here in black and white.

I can feel the full weight of the past crush me. Justice is coming.

I think of Mum and Dad and the tangled, horrifying mess that is my family and everything that has happened so far.

And I realise one thing.

We've been damned from the start.

66

BEN

I've feared this moment for so long. Imagined it too. But never quite this way. My exile here seems so distinct from the life I used to lead.

Despite my search for Patient X, I hoped the past could be sealed off and allowed to become history. I have tried to establish other people's guilt and forget my own. Now, suddenly, that former existence is back again. Secrets which refuse to die. Old sins which must be paid for.

The silence lingers. Neither of us are bold enough to break it. Or not immediately. We are content to circle each other. I think of those Greek myths about the furies pursuing their prey and taking vengeance. Anna's arrival is a sign. I can fight and struggle, but this is bigger than me. Tragic heroes can't outrun their fate. I feel a cold, sudden premonition of my own mortality.

Anna has restyled herself. All the tropes associated with Anna O – that fabled butterscotch-blonde hair, those chunky, post-grad glasses, the slouchy style paraded lasciviously across countless website banners, TV screens and newspaper supplements – have been replaced. She is someone else entirely, a reinvention that only pays minimal homage to the original. The hair is no longer lush or pixyish. It's scissored into tidy symmetry. For the first time I see the echo of Richard in the face and the way in which the sensible hair frames the cheeks and jawline, scrubbed clean of youth. Time has won. The various masks have been put aside.

She is no longer haunted by a lost adolescence. The body is set in stone; time is charted through the face. Skin crinkles, hair ages, but everything else remains the same. Anna's clothes are sharper, more crisply fashionable. Instead of store-bought glasses there are contact lenses. The naked skin with its lingering teenage blotches is now baby-bottom smooth and aided by subtle dabs of colour. There is a sense that every other version was a prototype and this, finally, is the real thing.

I take a moment to gather myself. I must look like a complete stranger too. My face is leathery and scorched thanks to the Grand Cayman sun. My arms look like they've been made in a tannery and my hair is bleached lighter, giving a slightly Nordic aspect. The Benedict Prince who answered that fatal call and rushed to Harley Street was a typical Englishman of his generation – pale, wobbly, breathless from too many microwaved meals. No longer.

I am slimmer now. My muscles plastered into skin, the scales firmly towards the lower end of ninety kilos. My hair is barbered to a sleek shave at the sides, plucked around the top to complement the beard. I look styled for the first time. I stand in my rundown bathroom with a shaver and gladly destroy those reminders of the old me. I exercise now. Despite the injustice of ageing, I'm in the best shape of my life.

Death no longer scares me.

Which is just as well. Because I'm standing opposite a killer.

'Please, have a seat,' I say. My brain is on autopilot. It's all I can think of. I want to know what she knows, why she's here, how much danger I'm in.

Whether I still have time to find the small bag in my flat with enough supplies to sustain me for a month or two. Flee into another exile.

But I know it's too late for that. Somehow, I've always known.

Anna nods. She sits. I remain silent and motionless. There is a faint clatter from outside, the bark of raised voices.

I feel the dull ache in my knees again. The heat of the room – thick, like soup – tastes sour. I debate whether to call through for water. All my instinct vanishes. Her arrival has undone me.

There is further pin-drop silence. Anna finally reacts with a smile. I have heard her voice during our sessions, of course. But the new depth of it still surprises me. The Anna O legend was always about image rather than sound. Everyone projected their own reality onto the eternal youth of Sleeping Beauty. She was mythic and monstrous, both predator and victim, frozen in photographs and stills. Objectified in a hundred different ways. Now she is three-dimensional again.

Anna looks around my shabby office and says, 'Tell me. Is this a long-lost dream or an early mid-life crisis?'

There is a jesting tone that I can't quite place. She is no longer my patient. She flirts and damns, like a fencer lunging. I can't imagine having the nerves to be so composed in a situation like this. She already has the upper hand. My tormentor, my pursuer.

'A bit of both,' I say. I know how hollow it sounds. 'A dream fulfilled maybe.'

'I see,' she says. 'We both know how dangerous dreams can be.'

67

BEN

We have never met as equals. That is the first paradox. I was arrested soon after the awakening. She disappeared after Harriet's suicide and my release. She has haunted me, instead, like a spectre. We are names to each other. I imagine the Duke of Wellington pacing Apsley House with a painting of Napoleon on the wall, or Churchill looking at video reels of Hitler at Chartwell.

Strangers and intimates, foes and friends. Hero and Nemesis.

I look back at the questionnaire. 'Is this a work visit or pleasure?'

Anna thinks or pretends to. She teases me with her answers, enjoying my discomfort. Eventually, she says, 'Which would you put your money on?'

There is that tone again. I get the feeling she won't stop until she wins. That this is the first salvo of many. I am sure in a way I can't describe. Her arrival heralds something. Death hovers around me. Life's only certainty is its ending.

'I'm not sure,' I say. 'That's why I'm asking.'

'You knew I'd track you down. You hid rather than disappeared. Was that intentional?'

'Funny,' I say. 'None of the other journalists have managed. I must have done something right.'

'I've offended you. Clearly.'

'I rather think that was your intention.'

'Though I'm intrigued you still think of me as a journalist.'

I'm being lulled into a rhythm here. This is how she'll skewer me. Get inside my head and then use my own brain against me. I need to withdraw. Keep focused. 'I called you a journalist because I thought that was the polite thing to do. There are always other options. Celebrity victim. Global media sensation. True crime's poster girl. Or, if the original is still the best, then one of the golden oldies. Sleeping Beauty, perhaps.'

'You sound bitter.'

I pause, swallow, inhale. 'Last time I checked, I lost my marriage, my daughter and my career because of taking on your case. I helped you wake up and then found myself in the middle of a feeding frenzy. I took your side and thought you were an innocent woman who'd been badly wronged. Now I'm not at all sure. If you've come to apologise to me, then it's rather too late.'

The last bit hits the spot. 'Dr Prince plays the victim,' she says. 'It's certainly an original angle, if not quite your best work.'

'No?'

Anna looks at the bookshelves now. The office is a far cry from the decadence of the Abbey with its piped scent and womb-like interiors. Sometimes I sit here and laugh at the fact that the Abbey used to have a lift. It seems so outrageous and unnecessary.

Even Harley Street itself could be something plucked from my dreams. I often imagine travelling back in time and observing curious figures in frock coats getting out of hansom cabs with their sticks and snuff boxes. I see them hurrying up the stairs to the same buildings I used to enter, pilgrims in search of a remedy.

I miss it. I ache for it sometimes. Yet, still, I wouldn't go back.

'Why are you really here?' I ask. 'Why come all the way to the Caribbean?'

Anna looks at me, as if she can read my thoughts. The firmness of her stare discomforts me. 'The past is the only way to cure the present.'

'One of the better lines from my books.'

'Yes,' she says. 'But what if you were right?'

68

BEN

The heat is overwhelming. The sky is heavier than it was, the promise of violence ahead. I think of the weather forecast and the thunderstorm due any day now. There is a fresh edge to everything. The air is jagged with suspicion.

I suggest taking a walk outside. There is a small café located five minutes from the office. I buy two cold drinks – sparkling water for her, Diet Coke for me. We remove our shoes and walk across an emptyish stretch of the Seven Mile Beach. I look at the ocean and the waves with their white moustaches and the cymbal crash as they hit the shoreline. It is peaceful. The golden surface hiding the corrupt reality, a metaphor for so much.

I often imagine bringing KitKat here and feeling the stickiness of her hand in mine. I picture the two of us in the sea together. She practises her swimming and rehearses the tale of the mythical tropical paradise for when she gets back to rainy Oxford. But it's daydreaming. Anna is the only English visitor I've had since arriving.

We continue walking up to the shore and dip our toes in the cold sea water. Then we find a place to sit. Our watery toes turn the sand into paste. I remember building sandcastles with

KitKat when she was two. I fear happiness is like youth, squandered by those who have it, torturing those who don't.

I feel that premonition again. But, for now, I must maintain my cover. Be polite, play along. 'Where are you staying?' I ask.

Anna sniffs the breeze, captivated by the view. Out here she looks smaller and more human. The breeze fumbles her hair. Salt-spray pings her face. 'The Ritz-Carlton,' she says. 'I had some money left over from the government payout once they dropped the charges. There's nothing I love more than people watching.'

'The victim becomes the voyeur.'

'Something like that.'

I wonder for a second what her life would have been like without the case. I imagine her striking out on her own again after *Elementary*. The House of Commons, perhaps, political panel shows, a rent-a-quote act on social media. Like mother, like daughter.

I sip my drink and take in the scene. Yes, the weather has changed. The heat is prelude to the storm. The golden days are gone. Anna's arrival has changed it all.

Already, I know the mistakes I've made: failing to check for hidden microphones; a camera concealed in her bag; a lingering police or private security presence. But I am tired of running. There is so much I still want to ask her: about Harriet, Devil's Breath, the Farm, the Forest, Patient X. And, beneath it all, that simple question: did she intend to kill Indira and Douglas that night? Was she conscious? Did she fake the resignation syndrome and play on her history of sleepwalking to get away with two murders? Did she dupe me into being part of her grand scheme?

'If the past is the only way to cure the present,' I ask, 'what's your plan?'

Anna clutches her knees, like an echo of childhood. She takes one last look at the panoramic view – sun, sea, sand, all leaking into each other, a riot of yellowish-blues and creamy-whites – then turns to me and smiles sadly.

'The Ritz-Carlton tonight at eight p.m.,' she says, getting up. Her hand brushes against the ridge of my shoulder. 'Don't be late, Doctor. And try to look vaguely respectable.'

69

BEN

That last instruction plays on a loop. It's the sort of line I associate with Clara in those days when divorce felt as impossible as death or old age. I may be fitter physically, but in other respects I've let myself go. It is the melancholy that our ancestors wrote about.

Still the heat grows. The storm beckons outside. Each cloud taunts me, threatening to spill its load. The suspense is the worst part. It will come without warning, I know, the flash of rain that wipes out all before it, like a biblical cleansing.

I return home and the flat looks different to me now. Empty bottles by the bins. Food-stained plates. There is a loveless odour. I wonder if most versions of hell masquerade as a version of paradise. I stand in front of the small hallway mirror and quickly turn away.

I shower, dress in my one good shirt and pair of trousers. I trim my beard, comb my hair. I haven't made an effort like this for months. It feels almost like another date. I see Anna's smile at the clinic and Harriet and that hint of mutual attraction.

I walk along the beachfront until I reach the speckled lights of the Ritz-Carlton Hotel, one of the biggest hotels on the island. I imagine other diners leaping out with cameras and microphones and packaging this up for a shock-and-awe documentary. Or Interpol and the Met cornering me as I walk through the lobby. Even now, after all this time, I see eyes everywhere.

I reach the hotel entrance and try to remain calm. I splash my face with cold water in the bathroom. I have one promise to myself.

No running. Not anymore.

I look ahead and see that Anna is already seated. I feel that hiccup of fear again. I want to believe she is innocent. But I know, deep down, she is not. She is capable of taking someone else's life. She can sit here in polite society knowing there is literal and metaphorical blood on her hands. If Harriet was the scapegoat, then Anna wasn't drugged when she committed the murders. Which means she meant to do it. The sleepwalking and resignation syndrome were cover. Harriet helped her fake the resignation syndrome with those hip flask sips disguised as Jack Daniel's. Anna Ogilvy got away with murdering two people in cold blood and pushed Harriet towards suicide.

Three deaths. Three bodies.

I am about to break bread with a killer.

ANNA'S NOTEBOOK

2019

August 29 – Morning

The motorway flashes past. The clutch is feather light. The Clio is a last-minute impulse rental. I drive. Doug is in the back, Indira in the front passenger seat. The satnav is wonky. Indy tries to find the location on her phone. Mum, Dad and Theo are in a separate vehicle and will arrive ahead of us.

Doug is under forbearance, I can see. Indira tries to keep the show on the road. The summer issue still isn't put to bed. The GVM deal hasn't been signed. They don't have the money. After this weekend, they never will.

A car horn beeps. I try to keep my eyes on the road. Everything depends on meeting the person behind the @PatientX handle tonight. Verifying their bona fides. Only then can I confirm whether my MARATHON suspect really is Sally Turner's biological child. After that, I could have my first proper splash. Far beyond the reach of the magazine itself. National pick-up. Broadsheets, tabloids. *Newsnight*. Documentaries and dramas. I will find a good lawyer and sue Doug and Indy. I will publicly humiliate my philandering father. I will take my talents and form a company of my own. This time I'll do the paperwork myself.

I think of Bloom's justification in her article: *to be cruel to be kind*. I think of those other 'methods' and 'hypotheses' carried out on mental patients. I have read about psychiatrists who staged epileptic seizures, surgically removed teeth, eviscerated spleens, cervixes and colons, deliberately infected patients with malaria, created artificial insulin-induced comas, injected horse serum to induce meningitis and, most infamously, severed brain tissue by operating on the frontal lobes – otherwise known as transorbital lobotomies.

All those experiments were carried out by respected clinicians trying to find a cure for illnesses they didn't fully understand. Almost all the worst psychiatric treatments were tried on women. I think of that tiny, innocuous-looking line on Wikipedia last night. I imagine Sally Turner and the horrors of the Medea experiment at the Cranfield Ward, Broadmoor, in the summer of 1999. And I wonder until I feel sick all over.

The Farm itself, as the name suggests, is tucked down twisty Cotswold single lanes. The tarmac becomes stubby and potholed. Eventually it turns into unpaved road, the rental car hobbling over puddles and sloping mud tracks.

Finally, the destination appears. I see a sign and the dirt-splattered rear of the family car with Dad and Theo unloading things from the boot. The sky is bruised and prune-grey. We park just as the rain begins.

The mud gathers at our ankles. Doug's trainers disappear in the brownish glue. The area around us is immense. Wind howls through the forestry to the right, trees whistle to the left. We are shown to the cabins by Owen Lane, a bearded, macho groundskeeper with a barrel chest and rolling Highland brogue. Indy and Doug are in the Red Cabin. I get a smaller cabin of my own – the Blue Cabin. There is a site map on the wall. I familiarise myself with the geography of this place: the Forest, the Cabins, the Ruins. I am glad to be away from London. I feel free for the first time

351

in months. I take out my phone and message @PatientX again with my location.

After the Forest. After midnight. Then we can meet. Only then.

Rain hisses on the windows. The Blue Cabin shakes with water. A bell sounds from somewhere. We troop out for the promised meal. The Ruins are a sight to behold, like the aftermath of some grand castle left to rot for centuries, still misty with secrets and gold. There is makeshift cover here. We sit on two long wooden benches. We drink from squat wooden tankards. Doug looks bored. Indy hates roughing it. Dad seems more pathetic to me than ever, a collection of weaknesses. Their discomfort pleases me.

The food is posh-pub stuff, served on platters and boards with that trying-not-to-try aesthetic. Mum is no longer the stressed shadow ministerial persona. She is back to the old version I knew. Dad reverts too, away from his phone. He becomes slightly grand, like Gandalf without the beard and glasses. Doug hoovers food. Indira picks unenthusiastically at a plate of wild boar. Theo tucks into a tankard of ale. I follow him and feel heady.

The rain eases slightly. The director of the Farm, Melanie Fox, emerges now. She is flanked by Owen, the grounds-keeper, a male intern and then a late-thirties woman with a wasp waist who is introduced as Lola, the on-site health and safety adviser. Lola recites some basics. Wristbands are distributed. Black denotes Hunters. White signals Survivors. The six of us are divided into two groups: Dad, Mum and Theo on one side; me, Indira and Douglas on the other. We are the Hunters. The rest are Survivors. We are told to meet at the Forest entrance at 4 p.m. Until then, we head back to our cabins and prepare.

I watch Indy and Doug disappear into the Red Cabin. I see Dad and Mum separate now, two islands divided. I head back to the Blue Cabin, rain-soaked. I sit here and look at my watch: twenty-three minutes until the ordeal in the Forest begins. I think about the rest. The takeover, the flat, the magazine, the looks between Indira and Douglas, the betrayal, Dad's affair. It sounds petty, and perhaps it is. But then kingdoms have been fought over for less.

I imagine how I'll do it. Picture Douglas and Indira drowning in legal and accountancy bills as the magazine stops printing and the company is wound up. The smug looks wiped from both their faces as they realise. Dad's humiliation as his true character is revealed, a father so duped by a younger woman's charms that he helps swindle his own daughter. None of them will see it coming.

They won't survive this. I will have my revenge on them all.

Anna the ditzy dreamer. The werewolf. The sleepwalker. Fraulein Anna O. No more episodes or chairs propped against locked bedroom doors.

A new year that feels curiously unlike the one before.

Sleep doesn't have to be a weakness; it's a superpower.

Carpe diem.

70

BEN

Anna's outfit has changed from earlier. The dress is smarter, but deliberately modest rather than head-spinning. I have judged the mood correctly. I am ready to do battle.

She has a glass of house red. I stick to water. I marvel again at how calm she seems. There is something almost pathological about such strength.

We order food. She asks about the island. I do my Grand Cayman greatest hits. I tell her about some of the bad dates and my need for human company. I fail to mention the worsening weather and the thunderstorm breaking at any moment. But it is all around us like a promise and a threat. The careless mood of the last few weeks has turned. Other guests fidget and flinch at the throat-clearing sounds outside. Something bad is coming.

As the main courses arrive, Anna asks about the clinic and my success rate and whether curing patients puts me out of business.

I bat the idea away. 'There is no such thing as an ex-patient in my book. There is a patient who is well again. As such, they cease to be my patient any longer. They become just another healthy person.'

I watch her reaction closely.

354

Anna sips at her wine. 'Have you ever had a relationship with a former patient?'

'That entirely depends on the exact meaning of the word relationship.'

'Surely every therapist has been tempted. You know more about your patients than even their spouses or families.'

She is goading me. The visit, the invitation. Distracting me. I wonder if this is how she softens up all her victims. All the ways I'm being played.

'Romantic relationships are strictly forbidden,' I say. 'No matter which field you're practising in.'

'Ah, but you just said that former patients – those who you'd so expertly cured – weren't really patients at all. They were just people again. Surely a therapist is allowed to romance a normal member of the public.'

'If enough time has passed, and there's no ongoing clinical relationship, perhaps.'

'How long is enough time, in your book? Strictly hypothetically, of course.'

'Of course.' We are playing a game, dancing round each other. She doesn't break the spell. Her eyes lock on mine. 'A year would be the usual definition. It sounds like a scenario you've given some thought to.'

She doesn't demur. Instead, Anna finishes her main course and sits back, dabbing her lips with a napkin. 'It goes back to my new project. It involves going over the case again. At first, I just wanted to escape. But that was naïve. The post-traumatic amnesia hasn't fully gone away. I have almost no memory of what led up to the attacks. Those months and weeks. No memory of how I got here. All I remember is being told about them for the first time.'

Yes, she is a good actor. Flawless, in fact.

'Who told you what happened?'

Anna stops, revisiting the painful memory. 'My mum,' she says.

'You really remembered nothing at all?'

'Fragments. But nothing that makes any sense. Mum kept trying but couldn't quite spell it out. She knew as I got more mobile that I'd read about it. So, one night, she told me. About the case, the PTA, about it all.'

'Did you believe her?'

Anna glances at me. 'Not at first. It seemed impossible, too horrific to contemplate. Then, slowly, it began to sink in. Mum tried to stop me, but as soon as I got a device with an internet connection I started searching my name. Tried to comprehend that all this stuff was somehow connected to me. That I'd become public property without consenting.'

I am sympathy incarnate now, swallowing my scepticism and anger. If she can act the innocent, so can I. 'It must have felt like a violation?'

'In a way. I knew there was no going back to normal. I was a freak, an outcast, one of the shamed. It was only later I realised that if I was going to carry on with life I had to somehow reclaim my own story. Live my own truth. If I'm always going to be "Anna O", then I need to understand how and why that name came to exist. Properly, honestly. I need to recover the memories that the PTA erased. As a journalist rather than a patient.'

'The truth will set you free.'

'Yes.'

The tale is prettified, gagging for a publisher. I've read all those diary items in the *Daily Mail* about editors desperate to sign the memoirs of Sleeping Beauty. There is such precision to her words, as if every part of this has been rehearsed and is being acted for my benefit. She is dangerous, using her power to trap me.

I look outside at those clouds, grey and puffy and pregnant with rain. The storm waiting. For the island, for me. For us all.

I am certain now. It is the same sensation I had at Bloom's

house. Mortality feels so heavy, so real. She doesn't want my help in reclaiming her story. She wants to write a better ending. For Anna to have a happy ending, I must be the villain. Her or me. A zero-sum game. It always has been.

'You're going back to writing. The papers suggest you could earn retirement money by putting pen to paper again.'

She finishes dabbing her lips, folds the napkin neatly by her plate. 'That's the problem with being asleep for four years. The world moves on without you. I'm yesterday's news now.'

'Not from what I've read.'

'Well, you can't believe everything you see in the media.'

'Your articles showed a serious literary style. I thought the publishing world was begging for the autobiography of the century.'

'Well that's where you're wrong.'

'What about the movie deals?'

'They don't want my autobiography. They want *her* auto-biography.'

I watch her as she says it. The person opposite me now is quite distinct from that figure I once treated. The voice, the eyes, the personality, the soul even. One is flesh-and-blood reality. The other is a figment of the public imagination, an archetype re-cycled down the centuries, the eternal feminine and the fallen woman, reimagined by every culture. Both Eve before and after the apple. I wonder how much of my sense of betrayal is believing one over the other. Whether I'm as trapped by that archetype as she is.

'And by her, you mean . . .' It feels almost transgressive saying the name out loud. It's like Macbeth, bewitching and cursed.

Anna follows my gaze. 'Yes. That other person. The myth that doesn't exist.' Exhaustion riddles her face. For once, I think I see the mask slipping. 'They don't want me. They never did,' she says. 'The world wants Anna O.'

71

BEN

She is tired after a long journey. We pay the bill. Before too long we are back in the hotel lobby saying our goodbyes. I wait for any last-minute invitations – coffee, cognac, cigars.

But none arrive.

I am safe. At least until morning.

I trudge back outside into the darkness until I am on the beach. The cold sea water bleeds into my skin. I look at the view ahead. I feel that shiver of unease again. I replay each moment of our dinner. The memoir is just cover, I'm sure of it. I am the last loose end that needs tidying up.

I walk on for ten more minutes until I turn briefly. It's then that I spot someone behind me, veiled by a moonish half-light. The silhouette is slight, female. The right height, too. I rub my eyes. Try to order my thoughts. The dinner has rattled me. The heat too, possibly. I am seeing things.

But I look again. The shadow is still there.

I keep walking, quicker now.

I turn every minute or so and still see the figure behind me. My steps grow quicker, until I am almost running. The heat and the clouds and stormy premonitions. I was a fool to hide somewhere so remote. I need crowds and distraction, the noise and chaos of a city.

I run and run and keep running until the sand tears my skin. Eventually, I reach artificial light again. I see other people and the entrance to my shack.

I stop and pant. I suck in air. I look around. A group of teenagers huddle by a fire to my left. Music blasts from one of their phones. The air is alive with laughter. Bottles clank, a joint circulates. I try to remember experiencing joy like that. It seems so long ago.

I reach my front door. I double-lock it behind me. I slide down against the back of the door and feel my heart rate punch uncontrollably. The aftermath of tears in my eyes. I think of Clara and KitKat and everything I will leave behind.

Was it her? Did I imagine it?

Is this what Bloom felt in her final moments?

Sleep is impossible. I change my shirt, drink some water. I wonder now, in the sterile silence of the shack, if I'm being paranoid.

I can no longer entirely tell what is real and what is not. Anna was asleep when Bloom was killed. Or, at least, we all thought she was. Anna, Patient X, Harriet. How can it all compute? The confetti of facts join together into a single answer.

Inside the flat, I return to the boards on the wall. I swore off this case once. But Anna's arrival has brought it all back. She has hunted me down for a reason. Somewhere on these boards lies the answers that are still just beyond reach. The missing links and golden nuggets that solve the mystery. This is the only way I will make sense of it, put the ducks in a row. There must be an answer. There is always an answer.

I stand there contemplating the boards, groping in the dark. I am hunting shadows, chasing phantoms. But I know one thing.

Anna Ogilvy isn't here to help me.

She is here to bury me.

72

BEN

I still have an old coaster on my desk with the logo of the Freud Museum in Hampstead. I remember seeing his study preserved in aspic. Freud believed that psychology was detective work, digging through layers of history. I feel a strange kinship now.

I think of that shadowy figure following me on the beach. The lisp of the shoreline and the fear of being lost in the waves. Truth is my only way to find closure. I must strip away the alias, see the connection Bloom saw on the night of her death, unmask the person hiding behind a single letter.

X.

If it wasn't Harriet, who is Patient X?

I return, as always, to the other suspects. The stragglers. The left-behinds. The squad players. Each has a board of their own. I look round them again now.

Melanie Fox. The owner of the Farm, the entrepreneur behind it all.

Owen Lane. The groundskeeper at the Farm, responsible for maintaining the course and responding to any emergencies.

Danny Hudson. The intern there that night, a local paid under the counter with the occasional tip to be gopher to Lane and Fox.

The results are taped to the walls of the room.

The first board contains a short printout of an article in *The Times* regarding one Lance Corporal Daniel Gordon Hudson. He is found dead on the Brecon Beacons during Special Forces selection in 2022. His cause of death is given as heatstroke suffered during a timed march in a heatwave.

Suspect 1 – deceased.

The second board concerns Melanie Fox. There are numerous newspaper gossip items chronicling her battle with alcohol and substance addiction following the Anna O incident. The Farm collapsing as a viable business concern, Fox losing all her money.

By piecing together various fragments from social media and acres of material on the blogosphere – some of it public, others requiring layers of encryption – I finally discover the death notice in an Australian newspaper which reads: 'FOX, MELANIE K. Died by her own hand. No next of kin'.

Suspect 2 – suicide.

To the third board. Owen Lane is easier to find. He was already in his late sixties at the time of the Anna O incident, the veteran of the group. The intervening years haven't been kind to him either. A Facebook page contains a birthday photo of Lane and his two daughters and a sign for a care home on the outskirts of Burford in Oxfordshire. Another page posts a link for the Stroke Association and the webpage for donations.

Suspect 3 – incapacitated.

There ends the canonical suspects (excluding Ogilvy family members). Now I move to non-canonical suspects. The final board includes all extra-canonical material, the apocrypha of the Anna O case. The outlandish theories, the heretical suspects and crazy conspiracies.

The first few items concern DCI Fennel. I have the choice headlines from the tabloids pinned at the top:

TOP COP AND SLEEPING BEAUTY: OXFORD'S SHAMEFUL SECRET

(*Daily Mail*)

THE DETECTIVE AND THE WRITER: A HIDDEN LINK?

(*Sun*)

Even now online information about Oxford University includes an obligatory reference in the 'Alumni' section. Among the scholars, diplomats, philosophers and minor royalty there is a reference to Anna Ogilvy (BA English Literature) and Clara Fennel (MSt Applied Criminology) and a link in the references section to those two tabloid stories as authoritative sources. The fact they did different courses and never actually met doesn't seem to register. One truth produces a hundred lies. And lies are stickier than facts.

I move to the next non-canonical suspect. Dr Benedict Prince. Since Harriet's suicide, I have been accused of everything: being a sociopath, a psychopath, a predatory psychologist, having faked my academic credentials, not knowing the difference between truth and fiction, having a second family, plagiarising the work of others for my books, even committing the sleep-related crimes I then helped the police to solve. After the arrest, the secondary literature has grown further. A large section of Anna O devotees still believe there is no smoke without fire and that I, inevitably, must be guilty of something.

Finally, there is the section devoted to Anna herself. This goes up another level. Anna is Sleeping Beauty and the Antichrist rolled into one. She stops being a human and becomes a target board instead, a place for others to hang their own prejudices. Every theory possible is suggested by someone: she is the mastermind, she is Patient X, she faked the whole thing. Articles, tweets, posts, messages and blogs are found across every continent and time zone. She is a member of the Illuminati. Part of a secret

362

masonic sisterhood. Leader of an underground cult. And, my personal favourite, a figment of the mainstream media's imagination. The genuine concerns lost among the conspiracies.

Dawn breaks before I finally fall asleep in the main room. I wake to find the boards looming over me. My hair is greasy. My eyes feel crusty, mouth superglued inside, bones sore and unoiled. I brew coffee. I check the newspapers on my iPad. I skim my work emails and see a new message from a Gmail address under the name 'Elizabeth Cartwright' which arrived overnight. It contains a single subject line:

Hollow Creek 3pm?

Hollow Creek is an old smuggling route about ten minutes from my flat. It sits on the Seven Mile Beach like a gnarly curiosity, a meeting place for island locals and the nerdier type of tourist.

I don't answer immediately. I shower, instead, and pick through a bowl of soggy cornflakes while finishing the digital edition of *The Times*. I open Anna's email again and type out a reply agreeing to the meeting at Hollow Creek. I contact Sofia and tell her to cancel my afternoon appointments. I check my phone and see there is still no reply from KitKat to any of my voice notes or messages.

Outside the clouds gather. The storm is nearly upon us.

So many victims and casualties in the story of Anna O.

Will I be the last of them?

ANNA'S NOTEBOOK

2019

August 29 – Evening

It is nearly the end when I see it.

The one thing I can't unsee. The spectre that haunts my dreams. Freud called it condensation. The process where multiple dream elements melt into one coherent story.

I must get this down. Before now I believed it in theory. Now I have seen it for real.

We are in the Forest. Splashes of blue-black sky. Spits of rain. The wilderness envelops us. It is all-consuming. There is the complete lack of natural light. There is a medieval darkness to it. I imagine all those generations without electric light. They creep and skulk with candles, the darkness of night-time more like a demonic thing. Because that is what it feels like here. There are demons in this Forest. This is no longer strictly a game. It is something more than that. It is a purgatory, an in-between place, immune from the rules of ordinary life.

Hunters versus Survivors.

Fighting to the death.

Though that is not strictly true. We do have torches. That is our one concession to the age of battery-power and electricity. We also have our guns. They are loaded with paint rather than bullets, but even paint can be lethal at point-blank range.

The two teams have a poetic justice to them. Indira, Douglas and I are on one team. The three amigos. The musketeers. The holy trinity. We are the Hunters. Mum, Dad and Brother are on the other team. They are the Survivors. Our marching orders are deliciously clear. The Survivors must hide in the Forest and live off the land for the next eight hours. The Hunters must, as the name suggests, hunt their quarry. Each of us have different-coloured bullets. We win if each Survivor is marked with each colour. It is total annihilation or total failure.

In the darkness I feel poised between wake and sleep. I am in one of my states again. The night terrors close round me. Only the weight of the gun in my hand and across my shoulder tells me I am still awake. Doug and Indy are nearby. With a gash of torchlight, I see them whispering. There is a hot sensation in my chest.

It is squally, gusty. The Survivors have half an hour to spread across the Forest, to hide themselves. Apparently, it is based on a game used in SAS selection. Potential recruits hunted across the Brecon Beacons. Outrunning armed guards and sniffer dogs and surviving a night undetected. If caught, they fail selection and are RTU'd.

The game is silly. It is juvenile, beneath us, a throwback to I-spy and hide and seek and other childhood diversions. But I want to win. I must show my spirit isn't broken. I will not be left behind, straggling behind Indy and Doug as they go full Rambo and spray-paint the other members of my family. I will also not concede defeat to Dad. He must be marked. And I must be the one to do it.

Doug is convinced we should stay together. Indy, sensibly, insists we split up. We must use the element of surprise. Three of us on each approach will be impossible to disguise.

We should each take responsibility for our own kills. Indy has the gall to claim we trust each other. If we each do our jobs well, the team wins. Mutual self-interest. The butcher, the baker, the candlestick-maker. I want to kill her now. Dad is a fool. Doug, too. But Indira is far worse. She has deliberately destroyed everything I hold onto. I invited her into the nest, shared my secrets. She has stolen my professional life and shattered my personal one. She is the traitor who deserves the gravest punishment.

Doug snarls his disagreement. I cast the deciding vote. One goes to the left. The other to the right. I head down through the middle of the Forest. Three targets. Three bullseyes. An entire night of Stygian gloom. No one tells you how much waiting is involved in operations like this. I imagine true-to-life action films. I see Arnie and the Rock and Stallone kicking their heels for two hours before a tepid firefight breaks out in the closing thirty seconds of the movie, ruined by fading light.

The Forest is small enough to give the Hunters a chance, yet big enough to be survivable. That is the genius of the space. I lose all sense of time. I have no watch. I feel like an insomniac wishing away hours and finding only minutes have gone. Despair encircles me. I wander through the godforsaken land, half-asleep and half-awake, and find no signs of life. There is just darkness, the rustle of the woods and no other human beings in sight. I have wandered for hours without a kill. I will fail the Forest. Return to base camp.

The traitors will win. Indy will crush me.

Then, at last, I hear a twig crackle up ahead. I wonder if I can identify the target just by their tread. It's like being a child again with the light on too late and guessing whether it's Mum or Dad coming up the stairs. There is another leaf crunch, a second twiggy crackle. I hear a sigh, the sound of laboured breathing. I know those sounds.

I keep low. I am hidden behind a tree. I glance around

and see Dad up ahead. He is in a half-crouch, as if coiled and ready to spring. I bring my paint-gun up, just as instructed, and ready it soundlessly. One shot of red paint to the back and I will have my first kill. The Arch Deceiver. One down, two to go. All of us are issued with body armour to lessen the whiplash. The humiliation will be worse than any spinal agony.

My finger brushes the trigger. Dad hasn't moved, oblivious to me. I count down from five in my head. I see how addictive this must be. The first kill means more kills. There is such power in this action, such authority. This Traitor-in-Chief. I still have time to find the other two. To redeem my record.

Three. Two. One . . .

That's when I see it. At first the figure is all shadow and reflection. I see them move to Dad. Careless, surely, two Survivors grouping together. Sitting ducks. Poor tradecraft. The second figure's right hand brushes Dad's chest. Their left hand is obscured by something. I see the outline of another paint-gun. They are whispering now. Dad leans closer. Their lips brush. They smile. There is no fear in them. They are hidden by the Forest, cowled by the trees, disguised by the night's sounds. It is the moment I have both feared and anticipated.

They are intimate together. It is the intimacy of months, not hours. They are synced. They kiss again. The figure points. Dad makes a joke, pats the figure on the bottom. The figure turns. For the first time, I see more than just their back.

I know that hair, the priestly smugness of the expression.

I think back to that first message I discovered about the secure email account. I think back to Dad being thrown in the doghouse after evidence of another liaison. The Other Woman, the happy families routine in the Peers' Dining Room.

I realise I have been wrong again. They are equal-opportunity traitors. Indira hasn't used Dad. Both are guilty. Dad had a choice and chose Indira over me. Not once, but time and time again. Lust over love.

I watch the figure creep away. I see that final parting kiss again. I check my phone, hidden in the one place no male groundskeeper would dare to look. I check the photo and see the framing is perfect. I have all the proof I need. The visual evidence to damn them both.

My father. My friend.

Richard and his Other Woman.

From this point on, both their lives will be ruined.

Tonight will change everything.

73

BEN

Hollow Creek still maintains a slightly piratical look with its gargoyle caves and mists of sea spray. The romantic in me imagines sticky-haired ruffians stowing away barrels of hard liquor inside these caves. The truth, I'm sure, was far less enticing. But the legends have been carefully crafted. Rumours suggest Hollow Creek is still used to import cocaine for the wealthier island visitors. Somehow the world never really changes.

Anna is already here. She sits on a ridge near one of the cave entrances. She stares out to sea and doesn't look up as I arrive. The hotel mystique is gone. She wears a simple polka-dot dress with a straw-coloured hat and open-toed sandals that are overrun with sand. She sips from a small plastic water bottle. A handbag – the no-frills holiday kind that I remember Clara carrying – loops around her right shoulder. She looks so ordinary.

And yet that is where the danger hides. She captivates the unsuspecting. I remember KitKat and the paparazzi and all the indignities my family has faced. Anger and sadness burn through me. I must not forget who she really is. A killer yet to face justice. The monster sleeping behind the glass divide.

I take a seat on the ridge. She doesn't respond but keeps staring at the sea. I wonder whether she slept last night and why she chose here for the meeting. Rogue dabs of sun cream pimple her back. A hot, airless wind gusts round us both.

Eventually, I say, 'I'm a good psychologist, but not worth crossing continents for. Please tell me you came here for the views instead.'

She breaks her vigil now and glances at me. She wears no make-up today. Her face is bare. 'Think of it as a research trip for my new project. All tax deductible too, apparently. The perks of a writer's life. Or perhaps a cure for post-traumatic amnesia. The views certainly help.'

'I thought you said that the world only wanted Anna O?'

'I did.' She pauses, takes a breath.

Another wave crashes on the beachfront. I can almost taste the spray. I feel that sense of childhood isolation again. Her presence is beguiling. It tantalises me, our hands centimetres away across the rock. It's been so long since I've been this close to another human being. I feel infectious, almost, like a leper. One of the damned.

'Which is why I'm giving them what they want,' she says. 'A true history of Anna O. My first book. Not a tell-all memoir, but something even better.'

A distant memory stirs. I think back to those interviews a year ago. Anna's writing ambitions. The great work. The literary legacy. 'Your very own *In Cold Blood*.'

'The most iconic true crime book ever written,' she says. 'It reads like a novel but every incident is true. It's what Shakespeare did in his history plays. It's what the gospel writers did in the Bible. The greatest drama has always taken fact and presented it using fictional techniques. Why not me?'

'Writing as personal therapy?'

'If you like.'

'You come to terms with those who wronged you by getting inside their heads, understanding things from their perspective.' There is a quote from a writing guide I once consulted for my pop-psychology book, the one referenced by the Ministry of

Justice during that first meeting. Every villain thinks of themselves as the hero of their own story. I wonder if it's true.

Anna toys with her water bottle, then cradles her chin. 'It's time to reclaim the narrative. It's my story, after all. History will be kind to me because I intend to write it.'

'Winston Churchill.'

'Correct.'

The mood turns now. I feel a hot sense of discomfort. I look up at the sky and see the grey clouds again. The thunderstorm has still not come. It lingers, instead, menacing us all like an omen. I think of the boards in the flat. She is teasing the solution but making me wait for it, a writer to the end.

How can I ever prove her guilt? How can anyone prove whether or not she meant to kill her two best friends? What is the line between unconscious desires and conscious, culpable intent?

The dream, the answers, now this.

Anna Ogilvy is still playing me.

I remember sitting in the car with Clara after I walked out of the custody suite all those months ago. The vow I made. The one I will stick to.

Anna might have fooled me once.

But she won't fool me again.

74

BEN

'Let me guess,' I say. 'I'm the first name on your interview list. I'm witness number one in the quest to fill in the memory blanks.'

'You flatter yourself.'

'The story can be told so many ways,' I say. 'I suppose it all depends on which angle you choose.'

'You think so?'

'All stories can.' I think back to my old Hitchcock obsession and the danger hiding behind domesticity, the terrors of the everyday. I still play my favourites at night: *Notorious*, *Strangers on a Train*, *The Man Who Knew Too Much* (the original black-and-white version, not the glossier remake), *North by Northwest*, *I Confess*, *The Lodger*.

'What are my options?' she says.

'First, the ordinary psychologist plunged into extraordinary circumstances. I become your main character. You approach the case through my eyes. You elevate the mystery of it, holding things back for the reader, torture them in God-like fashion by spreading clues like breadcrumbs.'

'There's a certain classical elegance to that, I suppose. What else?'

'Alternatively, you could go for full shock and awe and use dramatic irony. The secret is revealed at the very beginning and the reader becomes complicit. The murderer confesses right at the start of the book. You make Harriet the anti-hero and see if she gets away with it. An open mystery rather than a closed one. The narrator isn't God, but the Devil, corrupting the reader. The audience hopes the murderer gets away with it.'

'Is that all?'

'Or, of course, you could blend the two.'

'Yes.' There is a moment of hostility. Anna smiles again. One moment I am being watched with suspicious detachment; the next I'm welcomed back into the fold. I refuse to be beaten. I am cornered, but not eliminated.

'Do you have a publisher?' I ask.

'Not yet. I want to start with the facts. Present the case to the reader so they understand the psychology of it rather than just the chronology.'

'You make it sound almost easy.'

'Psychology is the one thing true crime rarely does well. Everyone focuses on the who and the how rather than the why. A dry history of the case misses the essence of it. Only drama, art – fiction, if you like – gets to the emotional truth of things.'

'Perhaps I should try it with some of my patients. Forget the Freudian couch, antidepressants or cognitive behavioural therapy. Just give them an A4 pad and a rollerball and get them to write the great English novel.'

'You're mocking me.'

'No. I'm not.'

I see other wanderers on the beach now. We are no longer entirely alone. My stomach rumbles. I look at my watch and realise it's already late afternoon. She has been here long enough now. Anna didn't come to Grand Cayman for beachside chats. She isn't waiting like the islanders for the storm and the rain. She is a hunter and I am the prey.

'I was the one who missed her,' I say. 'If anything, you should be mocking me. I was so consumed with my own theories that I didn't spot Harriet standing right there.'

Anna doesn't contradict me. 'She was convincing and vulnerable. Those two qualities don't often go together. No one else spotted her either.'

'Except for one person,' I say, thinking back to that fateful conversation about Sally Turner and Medea. 'Bloom knew. That's why Harriet did what she did. Bloom saw something wasn't right and was about to expose the whole thing. In the end she saw more than any of us. Perhaps she even saw that Harriet wasn't working alone. That she was just one part of a bigger mystery. A link in the chain to the child she once treated. Patient X.'

Anna is silent for a second, as if caught by a stray thought. She doesn't challenge my theory. She says, 'There might be one way to honour Professor Bloom's memory. To atone.'

Finally. After so much foreplay we are getting there. Slowly, dangerously.

I glance round the beachfront. Stillness all around. The furies knocking. The dementors ready. Sins can't be outrun forever.

I glance at the sky and long for the storm to come and quench my thirst and wash me clean.

I breathe deeply. 'How?'

75

BEN

The Anna Sessions, as I soon come to dub them, are a new experience for me. Usually, I ask the questions. Now I am the witness. Anna claims her book research proposal is simple: a true history of the case as told by those involved. She says it will restore what the PTA took away.

I sip beer in my shack and consider what Anna has proposed. I feel safer being able to watch her rather than checking over my shoulder like that night on the beachfront. Those are the most dangerous moments. In this cat and mouse game we are playing, turning your back is the only fatal error.

I try to distract myself with other things. I visit the small local bookshop near the centre of George Town and the assistant finds a tatty edition of *In Cold Blood* by Truman Capote. I glance at the silvery spine and turn to the title page and read the sub-title: *A True Account of a Multiple Murder and Its Consequences*. I glance at the back cover and read the pull quote:

> Dick became convinced that Perry was that rarity, a 'natural killer' – absolutely sane, but conscienceless, and capable of dealing, with or without motive, the coldest-blooded deathblows.

It's so exact. The parallels eerie. Sane, but conscienceless. Anna Ogilvy not as the damsel in distress or the sleeping princess who needs saving but the natural killer. Every killer has a signature and Anna favours the grand gesture: knives, blood, spectacle, whispering Harriet into suicide. I can't prove that last accusation, perhaps I never will. But I believe it now. Anna is a sensationalist in the art of murder. I feel it in my soul.

I google the book and read that *In Cold Blood* 'is the second bestselling true crime book in history'. I click on the link at the top of the page and read on:

> The non-fiction novel is a literary genre which depicts real historical figures and actual events woven together with fictitious conversations and uses the storytelling techniques of fiction. The genre is sometimes referred to using the slang term "faction", a portmanteau of the words *fact* and *fiction*.

I think back to interviewing Emily Ogilvy and our walk along Victoria Street and her concern about Anna's obsession with true crime. I hear that warning again, echoing across the Atlantic:

Anna was always the sort of person who would kill for her fifteen minutes of fame. She needed to see her name in lights . . . my daughter didn't want to be a good writer. She wanted to be a great one.

I see Harriet, or Lola, ministering to the figure in the bed. I think of everything that's happened and know the Anna Sessions are the coda, the final chapter.

We agree to record the sessions in the shed outside my cabin by the seafront with its golden stretches of beach and ocean. It is rickety, but secure. The rules of the Anna Sessions are clear. I am one of many. I pretend to believe her. Clara, Emily, Richard and others from the original case will endure the same treatment. My answers will be used for dramatic reconstructions, the bare facts filtered through narrative and buffed into prose.

This is the Anna O story.

Or, to put it another way, the true account of a multiple murder and its consequences.

Only, this time, it's written by the murderer herself.

The sessions themselves are refreshingly low-tech. Anna takes charge of drinks and coffee. She has a miracle hangover cure which consists of espresso, cream and other magic ingredients. There are no cameras but a slightly battered Sony MP3 voice recorder. Anna lets the voice recorder roll while scribbling notes on a yellow legal pad.

I can still sense the darkness in this. My head tells me to get up, walk away, find the next plane out of here and a new hiding spot. But my heart tells me it would be futile. That we are stuck, the two of us, in this loop. We are compelled by the mystery of each other. I have made my choice. This only ends when one of us is left standing.

The early part of the case fills the first day. I drink but forget to eat. I watch Anna's reaction as I discuss Bloom, the call, Stephen Donnelly, Harriet and the stimulus theory. We are like war survivors, witness to events that few others can comprehend. Anna reacts as if hearing the detail for the first time. I wait for the slip or flaw, but there is none. It's another impeccable show.

At night, once the day's session is done, we walk along the beachfront again. The sand is softer than usual. The sun fades but it is too hot to sleep. My throat is parched. I slake my insides with beer then whisky. I feel like a farmer on my knees imploring the rain god to take pity and bless the land.

We sit on the beach. Darkness finally falls. It isn't the day that terrifies me, but the night. I am tired, sleepy, just as she wants me. Anna moves closer, even rests her head against my shoulder. This is all part of it. I've been denied human company for so long. The softness of someone else's skin is irresistible.

My eyes struggle to stay open. Sleep pushes at me. I wait for the sound of movement, the sudden presence of her reaching for something, blood dressing the scene like spilled wine.

But, so far, there is nothing. I am still alive.
If only I can stay awake.
Sleep is danger.
Sleep is death.
Whatever happens, I must not close my eyes.

ANNA'S NOTEBOOK
2019

August 30

The midnight meal is over.

It's a new day. But the world has changed forever.

I keep thinking about what happened with the Hunters and Survivors. I see Indira's treacherous face. I watch my father's oily kiss. I hear my last, vestigial faith in humanity turn to ash.

I don't eat. I merely drink. I watch my glass being refilled and keep on drinking until my liver protests. I feel different than usual.

I am waiting. The meet, the rendezvous. Yes, I am like those SOE women behind enemy lines. Waiting for my confidential source. The person who can save me.

The only reason I ever agreed to come to this godforsaken place.

The cabin door opens now. A knock, an entrance. I see the figure. The same person at the meal, hovering by my glass. I recognise her from the briefing. The health and safety person. The wasp waist. I wonder if I am seeing things.

She doesn't shut the door. Her hands are gloved. She is

saying something. My marching orders. I wonder if she is @PatientX.

There is someone behind her too. I recognise this person. It is the same face as the photos I have saved on my laptop.

It is the face of my MARATHON suspect.

And I realise, suddenly, how wrong I have it. How badly I've miscalculated.

Coming here to the Farm was a terrible error. A catastrophic mistake.

Run, run, run, Anna. Run as fast as your legs will carry you.

Too late. My vision blurring slightly. The world curved at an angle.

I think of those drinks at the Ruins after the Forest was over. The way in which they could have slipped something inside the tankard. That the meeting with @PatientX was the perfect pretext.

Stupid, stupid, stupid.

The strange feeling builds. Viral, almost, taking over every floor. The change is fuzzed but concrete. Something terrible is happening to me. The smash, bang, wallop of it. I have never felt like this before. It's as if my body and brain have been hijacked by someone else. I am thinking thoughts that are not my own. Thinking other people's thoughts.

Thoughts from the unconscious. Free from inhibitions. There is a knife beside me. It is there like a symbol from my dreams, imploring me to use it. I am Lady Macbeth. The demon woman.

Infirm of purpose!
Give me the daggers. The sleeping and the dead
Are but as pictures; 'tis the eye of childhood
That fears a painted devil.

Now the thoughts become unstoppable.

The two of them are beside me. They have done this to me. I drank my own demise earlier. I no longer have control over my own mind. I am their puppet, tugged by them, tormented.

I will catch them. I will expose the traitors. The voices are on my shoulder, inside my head. These two intruders are spurring me to action.

The sleeping and the dead.

I can't let what happened in the Forest stand.

Indira has stolen my company, my family and my life.

Yes, it is so clear now. It always has been.

The bitch must die.

76

BEN

I jolt awake.

My dreams are filled with blood and monsters.

I open my eyes and taste the first drop of rain. It takes me seconds to adjust.

I look up at the sky and the storm clouds and know that today they will break. That I have passed through some initiation, appeased the rain god. Sleep claimed me but I am still here. I check my body, take more breaths.

I am alive.

Heart beating. Breath inhaling. Yes, somehow I survived the night. No stab wounds or blood. No spectacle or sirens.

I look around but Anna is nowhere to be seen. I feel almost grateful at the temporary reprieve. I wonder again if paranoia and isolation are planting these disturbing thoughts in my head. That madness is taking hold. Perhaps I need help, rest, to stop peering into the abyss of the criminal mind. To slowly become normal and sane again.

My head hurts. I drank too much last night. There is a clock-tower chime in my ears. Relief turns into confusion. I peer at the sky and those silty-grey clouds. I must have imagined the raindrop, the last echo of a dream.

I get up and go in search of water and Anna. I reach the cabin and hear the shower being used. Eventually, Anna emerges dripping wet with a towel draped across her body. She makes another batch of her miracle hangover cure and washes her own mug out by hand before placing it back in the cupboard. As promised, the hangover cure works miraculously. My mind clears. Order is temporarily restored. I shower, prepare. Then we begin all over again. More tapes, more interviews. The Anna Sessions. Day 2.

It is only later, after we've been going for hours, that we take a detour from the strict chronology of the case. Like all good interrogators, she cares about some parts more than others. I continue playing along with her questions. Still wondering if I have this wrong. If perhaps I will survive this. Step off this island. Find sanity again.

'Why you though?' she says.

She is more direct than before. I take a sip of whisky. The question snags. 'I'm sorry?'

'Why were you and no one else the one to pursue this type of treatment?' Anna says. 'Was there something in your own past that influenced the stimulus theory? Why did you believe hope could be so transformative for a mental disorder like resignation syndrome?'

I clear my throat. The debate in the psychological literature still rages over whether Anna woke because of my methods or whether Harriet engineered the deep sleep, using her little vial to slip scopolamine into Anna's system while knowing it wouldn't show up on test results. And whether Harriet masterminded things or simply acted on Anna's original orders, a way to fake deep sleep and get off a double murder charge.

For now, I must stick to my old beliefs. Prince's Cure. Keep up the pretence.

'The modern world sees science against art, mind versus the body, the spiritual versus the material,' I say. 'But the scientists of the Royal Society were also theologians and alchemists. Isaac Newton was as active in biblical studies as he was in physics.

Aristotle wrote about drama and poetry as well as biology and politics. That's why the issue of functional neurological disorders interested me so much.'

'That doesn't sound like a medical answer.'

'It isn't. Or not exclusively. FNDs change the nature of traditional medical understanding. Is it possible for no organic disease to be found in the brain, and yet for the illness to be perfectly real and completely devastating? Can the mythic become fully material? If we answer that, we begin to answer the mysteries of life itself.'

In the past, this is the point where Clara would escape to the kitchen while KitKat yawns and plays with her latest toy. The staff at the Abbey, particularly those on the top floor, would crack bitter jokes. I miss their mockery now. Life is such a strange, mercurial thing.

'Why though?'

Her insistence surprises me again. Anna the writer, as opposed to Anna the patient.

'Who knows why?' I say, finally. 'Why is the impossible question to answer.'

'Except if you're a psychologist and your job is to study the mind.'

'Now you're flattering me.'

'I still want to know. What made you realise that hope could be as powerful as heroin? What made you think happiness is as much a stimulant as any other type of high?'

I take a deep breath. 'The facts of history.'

'Such as?'

'The mind is peculiarly human. No other animal has a brain with such capacity. But that gift is also a curse. It's what Milton meant when he wrote his famous line. The same line your mother recited to me when we first met at St Margaret's Church. "The mind is its own place, and in itself can make a heaven of hell, a hell of heaven." Poets knew that long before psychologists or psychiatrists.'

384

'So it wasn't something more personal?' she says. 'Something in your own past? An arc of redemption you've experienced yourself?'

At last. So here we are. The questioning more personal, more barbed. There is a sudden change in the dynamic between us. Anna spots the unease on my face. I can hear a background rumble of thunder outside. The air newly fresh and expectant.

The furies are coming for me, just like before.

'What are you talking about?'

'This book is about the truth, Ben,' Anna says, with terrifying calmness. 'That was the deal. The whole truth and nothing but the truth.'

I wait.

'I think it's time you honoured that bargain, don't you?'

77

BEN

No more games now. We are finally being honest. All pretence dropped.

Anna is impossibly still. That is the first thing. Her voice is strong, almost uncanny. The voice recorder runs. The red eye accuses me. Danger is clammy on my skin.

I am sitting opposite a killer. I never wanted to do cognitive behavioural therapy or sit in a consulting room talking to sad rich people. Danger is the air I breathe. Criminals are my patients. And Anna is the most interesting patient and criminal of them all.

'Why won't you tell me the truth, Ben?'

She says it so forensically. She wants battle. The early sparring is now being replaced by trench warfare – mud-soaked, red-in-tooth-and-claw stuff.

The light of the audio equipment blinks. There is the sound of waves lapping the shoreline outside. I hear shouts in the water. Music blasts from portable speakers nearby, competing with the sounds of nature itself, until the whole thing – sea, screams, speakers, thunder – combines in a sonic splodge, each part indistinguishable from the rest.

I am sweating more than usual. I'm sick, shaky even.

The storm. The rains. If only they would break.

'I never lied,' I say. 'My job at the Abbey was to find the truth. That's all I've ever been concerned with. Just like you.'

Anna is barely sweating. 'You're still lying,' she says. 'Everything you've done, everything you've written, has been a lie. Perhaps you've even convinced yourself at times. What do you psychologists call it? False memory syndrome. Dissociative identity disorder. Psychogenic amnesia. Repressed memories. Take your pick. The ability to compartmentalise to such a degree that one part of your mind doesn't even acknowledge the other. It allows you to live two lives. The past isn't a foreign country. It's a different galaxy. Your self-reinvention is all that exists.'

False memory syndrome. Dissociative identity disorder. Psychogenic amnesia. Repressed memories.

Yes, I see it now. I see it all. That is the angle she's chosen. I should have seen it before. Predicted such behaviour. This is how she will trap me. Doomed by my own theories.

A thick, greasy rope of sweat slithers down my forehead. It drops fatly on my trousers. I cough violently and reach for more whisky. My vision feels off. I force myself to stay with it, not to admit to such weakness. 'This sounds less and less like an interview and more and more like an interrogation.'

'Interrogations are only for guilty people. Are you guilty, Ben?'

I look at the tape recording again. I see myself lying on that beach with Anna resting nearby and the primal sense of closeness. All this – the flirtation, the dinner, the deliberate intimacy of these days alone in the cabin – has been rehearsed and planned. I am lonely, vulnerable, pining for all that I have lost. All talented murderers know how to play their victims, find the weak spots.

Anna sees my whisky glass is empty. She watches me sweat. She hears the hacking cough and doesn't stir. Instead, she says, 'Did Professor Bloom know you were guilty?'

I hear my last conversation with Bloom on the night she died, her instructions about retrieving the file from the safe. No one else heard the call that night. I hid the file well. It is still a secret between Bloom and me.

Memory blindspots. Forgotten actions. Of course. She wants me to admit it. That's why I'm still here. Anna wants her diagnosis to be correct.

'For someone with post-traumatic amnesia,' I say, 'your memory seems remarkably clear to me.'

'That's what this entire case comes down to, isn't it? It's been like an illusion, diverting the audience while the real sleight-of-hand is performed. That's what I've pieced together from all my interviews. You're the last witness, not the first. I've done what journalists do and carefully examined all the facts of my own downfall.'

'A journalist solving their own crime.'

'Yes. This was never truly about Bloom or Harriet or me. It was about someone else. The person Professor Bloom once referred to as Patient X.'

I've spent so long searching for it while also trying to forget. My obsession, my downfall. The other half of me.

There is still no knife. My back isn't turned. Night has yet to fall. And yet I know, deep down, that this is it. There can be no other ending now.

She is watching me. I need water. 'I don't know who the child was. Or, at least, I can't prove it. No one can.'

'The world believes it was Harriet.'

'Yes.'

'But you don't agree?'

'Not unless the information in Bloom's file is wrong. Bloom's case notes clearly state that in 1999 Patient X was under eighteen and treated at Broadmoor. The hospital wouldn't simultaneously employ a patient as a nurse or employ someone under eighteen. Of course, if either of those two facts are wrong, or Bloom's file has somehow been altered, then all bets are off.'

'I agree. It wasn't Harriet.' Anna pauses again now. 'Finding

Patient X means finding the truth about what happened at the Farm. The why, not the how. Everyone has always believed that the murders that night were really about the victims. But what if the two victims were just collateral damage? What if the murders were never about Douglas or Indira but about the act of murder itself? What if everyone has been looking in the wrong direction all this time?'

'I'm not sure I follow.'

'What if it was a carefully orchestrated act? The number of stab wounds, the blood around the Red Cabin, the way the bodies were laid out. All of it was designed to conjure up the maximum amount of horror. To be a media event and to trigger what is now termed resignation syndrome.'

Now I understand. Or think I do. 'Harriet was a trained nurse. She had some medical understanding. Whoever worked with her knew that. Used that, maybe.'

Anna smiles. 'Yes. But a plan like that doesn't require some medical understanding. It needs a pioneering appreciation of the psychology of sleep. Of exactly what triggers a patient. Someone who spends their days treating patients. Who understands the criminal justice system and forensic psychology.'

I collect my thoughts. I see the trap laid and try to think of a way out. 'That would mean Lola Ridgeway, or Harriet, was always a scapegoat. That the real culprit used her for their own ends. She was just the decoy.'

'Yes,' says Anna, 'it would.'

'That, in turn, would require another suspect? Someone who fit the profile of Patient X?'

'We know the child known as X was intelligent, highly manipulative, a consummate actor. Most likely a person capable of pulling all the strings. Of manipulating Harriet and masterminding the whole thing.'

I wait for it. I know what's coming. On some level, I've always known. I've known it ever since she turned up at the clinic, finding me in exile. Her or me. It always has been. From the moment she arrived I've been a dead man walking. 'Do you have a candidate in mind?'

'Yes,' Anna says, holding my gaze. 'I do.'

ANNA'S NOTEBOOK

2019

August 30

And so I have done it. Though I still can't be sure exactly what 'it' is.

All I can see is the blood.

It sticks to my clothes and skin.

Blood spits round my neck, blobs wetly on my chin.

Even now, as I write this, the page cloys with it.

I am dreaming. Yet, still, this dream feels too real. But all dreams seem real, don't they? That is the point.

Those anxiety dreams of escape. Those red dreams of murderous revenge. Those school-exam dreams where the texture of the paper and the scratch of the biro and the firmness of the school collar are real enough to be touched, tasted even.

So must this be.

All I can see is the two of them lying there. Indira and Douglas. My flatmates. My best friends. My betrayers. The two people who have shared my incipient adulthood, that purgatorial journey towards real life.

Except this feels like the end. My head has gone. Someone

has done this to me. Earlier, I think, after what happened in the Forest. Nothing has been the same since.

Hunters versus Survivors.

I must run from here. And yet, more than anything, sleep seems to be capturing me. I feel more fatigued than ever before.

I can see myself standing in the doorway of the Red Cabin. Both Indira and Douglas are stoned and sleeping deadly in their beds.

My step is muffled, my movements crabbed and self-aware and leerily drunken at the same time.

There is a voice beside me, echoing in my head. It is a woman's voice. But not my own. The voice is repeating the mantra like a chant. The words chime musically. The sound is inside and outside my body. But it propels me forward.

I stand in the doorway and see the two figures and clasp the handle of the knife coldly in the flesh of my palm and hear those words intoned almost prayerfully until I'm right above the two of them on the bed and must make the fateful choice. Like Eve, like Medea, like all the rest of them.

Then it happens. Once, twice, again, four, five, six, seven, eight, nine, a frenzy now. Douglas stirs blearily, blood flicking his nose and lips. But I don't give him time to react. The voice is clear. They both must die. And so I turn and start again. Once, twice, three, four, again, six . . .

Sleep closes in now. Soon they will come for me. But still the words won't leave. My marching orders. That is how I'll do it. The words are written, typed out by instruction: *I'm sorry. I think I've killed them.*

As a child my eyes were never shut. From now on my eyes will never be open.

This is how the nightmare ends; and the dream begins.

I retreat from the bed.

This is how I get away with murder.

78

BEN

Patient X.

It is too hot. The ocean outside is too loud. My skin itches. I need air, yet there is none. I look at the voice recorder and that annoying, blinking, blood-red eye. My suspicion was correct. But my timing was out.

'Why would I want to kill two twenty-somethings and frame you?'

Anna doesn't look fazed. She sounds as quietly authoritative as before. 'Because that's what it's all been for, Ben. Becoming a forensic psychologist. Working under Bloom's mentorship at the Abbey. The lifelong fascination with sleep conditions. You've spent over twenty years planning this. Two decades since you were that child called X. This was never a silencing operation. It just looked that way. That's what you wanted us all to believe. This was always a revenge mission.'

There is the dull ache at the back of my head. I feel something breaking loose now, the rawness of it consuming me. Gaps in time which I can't fill. Nightmares that are no longer nightmares but real events repressed in memory. Shadows haunting my dreams. 'Against whom?'

'The people who carried out the Medea experiment. Bloom

was the obvious one. That's what stopped me seeing it for so long. Why wasn't she killed first? She conducted the Medea trial. She was the one leading the project at Broadmoor. The chronology blinded me. Until it didn't.'

I wait. I don't answer but just watch instead.

'The plan was to strike on the twentieth anniversary of Sally Turner's death,' says Anna. '2019. Then my investigation for the magazine changed the calculation entirely. If I kept digging, there was a chance I'd uncover the real identity of Sally Turner's biological child. Patient X. That changed all your plans. That meant I had to be taken out first.'

'So why didn't I just do that? If I'm Patient X, why would I make it so elaborate?'

'I told you. Your plan wasn't about silence. It was about revenge for the Medea experiment. Killing me alone like that would be too easy. Too painless.'

'Nonsense.'

'Sally Turner. The Stockwell Monster. For a very brief moment at the end of the last millennium, she was the most reviled person on earth. She was the woman who killed two children in cold blood. She was tabloid fodder. Evil personified. Even the name Sally fell out of use because of her. She was a pariah among murderers. An exile from the human race. That's why Bloom was allowed to try out the methods outlined in that Medea research paper. Sally Turner's actions somehow made her less than human. As far as the public were concerned, she deserved everything she got.'

'How does that relate to your case?'

Anna opens her bag and takes out a book. She holds it up: the Penguin Classics edition of *Medea* by Euripides. 'It's a story as ancient as the hills. Silencing me wasn't the ultimate goal. No, *shaming* me was. This was a revenge tragedy from the very start.'

I stay silent.

'You wanted to turn me into a tabloid villain. A first-name

criminal. A myth, an archetype. Sally Turner was the evil step-mother. So I became the spoiled little princess. I had to suffer like she suffered. Murder was just a means to that end.'

Those other thoughts again now. The ones-that-can't-be-named. 'But why?' I say, doing my best to sound convincing. 'Why would I do that?'

'I couldn't figure it out. Or not at first. But there was one connection I didn't see. One fact that was obvious from the start. It wasn't me you wanted revenge on. It was another member of my family,' she says. 'That's when it all started making sense. That's what it's been about from the very beginning.'

79

BEN

I look down at the glass in my hand.

I think of Anna washing her own glass out by hand this morning. Not that there will be any traces. It will look natural.

She doesn't need a knife. Not this time. My body will do the rest for her. My death requires no spectacle. I am just a pawn that needs elimination. A final piece of the puzzle.

We lock eyes. Anna watching me. Me watching her. The two of us caught in this singular, deadly moment.

I can read everything in her expression: the vindication, the calculation, the predatory coolness of someone who has done this before and got away with it.

She has imagined this moment, the glory and the triumph.

This is how she removes the final obstacle. One drink.

After everything, this is how it ends.

I die on this island as the villain. She leaves the hero.

Happy ever after.

Anna continues, 'I was only five years old in 1999. I couldn't even remember the Sally Turner case. It made no sense for me to be the target. Unless, of course, I wasn't the target. It just *seemed* like I was.'

Already my strength is going. My words slurring. Every bit of me malfunctioning. 'You've lost me.'

'I don't think so.'

'Who then? Who was the real target?'

'There is one type of pain even worse than death. Only one. A living death. A family member watching it happen to someone they love and being powerless to stop it. That is an agony beyond bearing. It destroys all chance of contentment or resolution. Suffering like that is the worst pain that any human being can suffer.'

The words hurt. But I force them out. 'Your family then?'

'In 1999, my mum was Minister of State at the Department of Health. Her portfolio included direct authority over the UK's three secure psychiatric facilities: Ashworth Hospital near Liverpool, Rampton Secure Hospital in Nottinghamshire and Broadmoor Hospital in Berkshire. I was never the target for your revenge. *She* was.'

I am struggling to keep any composure. The words form slowly, loosely. I spit out each syllable. Everything seems impossible and eternal. 'You're still not making sense.'

'Twenty-five years ago, Professor Bloom was just a clinical psychologist. A consultant, yes, but nowhere near the level to authorise pilot interventions on the wards of Broadmoor. No, something like the Medea experiment – something which, if it got out, could cause all sorts of sensational headlines – was far above her paygrade. It needed direct approval. More than merely medical. This had to go to the very top.'

'Ministerial?'

'Specifically, the Minister of State for Mental Health. Baroness Emily Ogilvy of Kensington. She was the minister who gave legal backing for Bloom to try the treatment methods outlined in her Medea article. Without my mother, it would never have happened. Sally Turner would still be alive. More importantly, you as her biological child wouldn't have been forced to stand by and watch your own mother suffer like that.'

There is a neat, almost mathematical elegance to it. 'Targeting Emily directly wouldn't have been enough,' I say, following the logic, leading me to places I desperately don't want to go. 'The only thing that could cause her more pain than her own suffering was standing by and watching a member of her own family suffer. Just like Child X did.'

'Like you did, yes. Admit it, Ben. Say the words. An eye for an eye. A tooth for a tooth. The ultimate revenge. Two decades in the making.'

'Do you have any proof?'

'Bloom treated you like the son she never had. She met you in 1999. I think she rehabilitated you. I think she saw your interest in the mind and tried to steer it in a good direction. Bloom believed in redemption. That no soul was beyond saving. Child X could have a full, rewarding life. Not as the son of Sally Turner. But as the newly minted Benedict Prince.'

I shake my head. But the thoughts won't leave me. The gaps, the elisions, those shadows in my head. 'This is absurd.'

'No, Ben. The best way to escape suspicion is to invite it. That's why you were clumsy at the crime scene. Once your guilt was raised then discounted, you were free. Everything could be dumped on Harriet. You hounded her into an early grave. She was the special friend you mentioned in your sessions with Bloom. You met her when she was a trainee on the Cranfield Ward. She was with you until she outlived her usefulness. You didn't even try to hide it. You admitted to being an orderly at secure psychiatric hospitals on the jacket of your first book. You knew that world better than anyone.'

I am struggling. Both mechanically and mentally. My lungs won't work. The simple act of breathing is difficult. Thoughts stick and stutter in my head. My chest punches, elbows, punches again. False memory syndrome. Dissociative identity disorder. Psychogenic amnesia. Repressed memories. Can that really be true?

And yet I know it can. A patient not even aware of the gap

between fiction and reality. Convinced that the false memories are real. The mind splitting in two, protecting its darkest innermost secrets. Memories and actions failing to match. Gaps, absences.

I am about to reply when, finally, I hear it. The elemental roar outside. It happens so quickly that I can hardly imagine what it was like before. Water in a desert. The storm clouds breaking. The violent rain. Days of rainwater gushing towards the ground. The stampede beating at the shed walls. Throat, lips, neck, chest, stomach, gut – all of it is failing me. Raindrops mimic applause, as if this is my final curtain call, banged out of the world. My last encore.

I am desperate for water. Dying to end my thirst with the rain.

'No,' I stammer. It is all I can say. Every little mistake, every wrong turning, flashes before me now. My entire life in reverse. I thought she would strike last night. My psychology training predicted spectacle, Anna's signature. But she anticipated that and did the opposite. She is smarter than me. Always one step ahead. I have been outdone by the limits of my own mind. 'No, you've put two and two together and got five.'

'Not this time.'

I stare at my whisky glass. My heart rattles. 'The whole idea is madness. You have no proof. No evidence.'

'We know Sally Turner had a child of her own. We know Bloom assessed that child at the same time as carrying out her Medea experiment. Most likely, that child was taken into care following Sally Turner's death and given a new name. All traces of their link with Sally Turner were wiped from the records. After the leaks around the Bulger case, new legislation was brought in to ensure a media frenzy like that could never happen again to a minor. The old name died. The new name was all that existed. Only Bloom would have known they were the same person.'

'You still can't prove that person was me.'

Patient X.

Anna reaches over to the voice recorder and stops it. The red eye goes blank. The room somehow becomes more dangerous still. The tremors working down into my hands. The top of my stomach contracting. A stabbing sensation moving directly at my ribcage. My entire body disintegrating. Senses obliterated.

The thunderstorm continues drowning us with rain. I am forced to shout against it, 'You don't understand.'

Anna remains silent, still, just like before. 'Help me, Ben. Help me understand.'

I see the rest now. I will be found in days, possibly weeks. There will be no whisky glass, no bottles. I am a middle-aged man who drinks too much. There are statistics like me in all corners of the globe. I am falling now. The phut of sound as my body hits the ground. Knees, back, head.

'You're wrong,' I force out. 'Please, you have to believe me. You've got it all wrong. There's only one person who could have got to Harriet in her cell. Only one person who could have done all this . . .'

I look up, the shed empty. I will bellow into nothingness. There will be just me and the walls and the dusty flooring. The sounds crashing into each other, a symphony of noise. Waiting for the thunderstorm to pass, like an invader pillaging the town, leaving destruction in its wake.

Once normality returns, Anna will be gone. All mark of her rubbed out. Leaving just the sea slapping against the shoreline, fragments of half-remembered voices, sun burning like liquid fire into my eyes, and the ghosts of our old house in Oxford and life as it should be and the truth that dare not speak its name.

I hear the recollection of Anna's dream again. Running through a dark forest to find the answer in a town called Marathon.

I crawl as best I can towards the door. The rain leaks under the flimsy sides. Thunder buffets the air itself. My fingernails scratch for an opening, a last chance for air, the final bid for

400

freedom. I will lie on my back and stare up at the wooden ceiling of the shed and think of KitKat in bed asking me if next time she can be the one to play dead.

She is the last face I remember. The years I won't get to see. The triumphs and disasters, the boyfriends and partners, the children of her own, an entire span of human life. The rest means nothing. Only love like that survives us.

I wish I could hug KitKat for one last time. Say that my love for her is wider than the sky, deeper than the oceans. More than she can ever comprehend.

'How is a story like this supposed to end?' I ask.

'Like all stories end,' says Anna now. 'The righteous survive. The unrighteous do not. Evil is vanquished and order restored. Goodbye, Doctor.'

And in that moment Sleeping Beauty leaves her Prince and travels to a far-off kingdom.

She is never seen again.

AO

London, New York City, Port Maria

PART FIVE

One year later

80

CLARA

The book is waiting for her at the airport.

She collects her bags and walks through duty-free. The loud cover is sprayed across WHSmith's window, the tipsy pile of hardbacks lounging on front tables, an unmissable sight for returning travellers. The book has been trailed across social media for weeks now. Adverts in newspapers. Celebrity endorsements. The true crime memoir of the century.

Prince Harry and Michelle Obama are one thing.

But Anna Ogilvy is Sleeping Beauty herself.

Clara buys a copy of *Anna O: A True Story* and stows it in her bag for later.

She searches the airport car park until she finds her small Citroën waiting. There is the faint promise of late afternoon sun and a new, foamy lightness to everything, as if the mundane side of life can intrude again. She goes through a mental checklist as she clips in her seatbelt: picking Kitty up from the sleepover, restocking the fridge, washing the school uniform, signing a school trip permission form, then back to the stresses of work.

She pulls out of the car park and turns on Radio 4. She checks her wing-mirrors, waiting for a vehicle to match her exit. But, so far, the road is empty.

There is a discussion programme on Radio 4 and Clara listens to the earnest back-and-forth about Anna Ogilvy's memoir. The reactions, the controversy, the lure of murder and mystery. Oedipus Rex, Cain and Abel, Hamlet, Agatha Christie. It amuses her to think of all those podcasters, bloggers and tweeters earnestly hailing the book as a pivotal moment. They use all those buzzwords: lived experience, reclaiming narratives, the objectification of the male gaze, liberation from the mainstream media, 'her' truth.

But it is far more ancient than that. Murder is a story as old as time.

Humans are primed for stories. People will believe anything if you package it correctly. As in the story of Anna O, and the decline of Benedict Prince. Even now, people will swear that Anna Ogilvy killed her best friends out of revenge and then faked resignation syndrome with the help of her troubled accomplice. Since the book's publication, others have lauded the bravery of Anna in hunting down her pursuer and forcing the truth out of him. Anna or Ben. Her or Him.

Two perfect endings for two perfect stories.

Sometimes Clara wonders if truth as a singular entity can survive any longer. There used to be fact and fiction with a clear, immutable divide. Now there are only truths, plural, each one as righteously indignant as the other.

She remembers standing by the Blue Cabin at the Farm that night and witnessing the bluish haze of reinforcements emerge out of the coal-black sky and knowing that, from this point on, nothing would be like it was before. The SIO plunged into her first case. Miraculously on hand. Every aspect of her life about to change.

She arrives at the pick-up spot before she quite wants to. Snaps out of the daydream. She turns the radio off and takes a second.

Kitty eventually emerges from the house. Clara gets out and switches into mum mode and goes through the usual slobbery ritual. Looking enthusiastic is 90 per cent of life. She hugs and kisses and strokes as well as any mum. They reach the car again and Kitty relates a garbled version of the sleepover.

Finally, once Kitty has settled down and giggled her way through the first anecdote, she looks at Clara and, almost as an afterthought, says, 'How was the trip?'

'Good,' she replies. 'Do you know the best part?'

'What?'

Clara smiles. She leans over and kisses her daughter on the forehead.

'I'm looking right at it.'

81

CLARA

It is a regular pilgrimage now to the park. The bench is an odd thing to have. Clara associates benches and trees with older people. They are for wise souls who chaired the parish council or led the local choir. Benches aren't for ex-husbands with decades of life ahead of them. Sometimes she regrets commissioning it. But the act must be maintained. The faithful ex-wife who steadfastly believes in her husband's innocence.

Originally, the bench was for Kitty too, a way to remember her father. Ben was cremated rather than buried. This provides a lasting physical presence without a gravestone. They reach the usual spot now and Clara is almost grateful to find it unoccupied if not untouched. Ever since the story broke, and particularly since excerpts from *Anna O: A True Story* were featured in the press, the bench has been targeted. The occasional visits have become acts of cleaning rather than commemoration.

She stares at the wording again, so familiar and still so odd.

Dr Benedict Prince – psychologist and father. The mind is its own place.

She feels Kitty's hand squash moistly against hers. The grip is tighter, more ferocious with each step. Clara can tell, even from here, that underneath the furry coat and layering her daughter's heartbeat is pounding against her body.

Kitty goes loose, running up to the bench and thumping down on it. She strokes the silver plaque, as she always does, and then dangles her legs over the side. They are longer now, almost touching the ground. She is more confident, boisterous even. That is another thing Ben will never see. Soon this bench will be old and gnarly and their little daughter will be all grown up.

Clara sits down beside Kitty. She unzips the bag and takes out the picnic they always have. They are both quiet. Kitty has exhausted every question. Clara has worn out every answer. There is nothing more to say about that collection of days when their world turned upside down.

Ben's body was discovered in the shed of his rented place in Grand Cayman. Forensics found titanic quantities of booze. There was no note or confession. No trace of third-party involvement either, despite the later revelation about Anna's visit there.

The initial conclusion was straightforward: Dr Benedict Prince drank himself to death. A lonely, divorced exile. Pure and simple. Then the police searched his flat and found more troubling material. Items of interest linking back to Sally Turner, Medea and the past.

As soon as the news broke, Clara found herself in the same interview rooms where Ben had once been, listening to questions launched like weapons by former colleagues. Did Ben ever talk about his personal history? Did he talk about his childhood and how he first knew Professor Virginia Bloom? Was he violent with her? Did she ever impede the process of an active police investigation? Did he ever mention anything about Sally Turner or his time at Broadmoor?

She stayed silent mostly. Only occasionally did she break, forced to confront the truth and analyse the man she once loved. He was clever, she says. Yes, looking back, there *were* moments. But that was the point with the sociopathic types. They didn't present like that. The control and manipulation were carefully obscured by vivid imitations of normal, everyday behaviour. No, he never mentioned much about his childhood. His family life sounded perfect, though both his parents were dead when she met him. Or that's what he told her. That's what she always believed.

Eventually, they let her go. There is no definitive evidence that Ben was Patient X or suffering from false memory syndrome. But there never will be. Just like there wasn't with Harriet. Both are dead. The case files are closed. There is only rumour, theories, innuendo, gossip. Clara lasts another six months on the force then quits. She finds a job in the private sector under her maiden name. Kitty's name is changed too. They are Princes no longer.

They finish the picnic in silence then walk back home slowly. Only later that night, once supper has been cooked and Kitty tucked into bed, does Clara settle on the sofa with a second glass of wine and turn off her phone. The copy of *Anna O* is on the coffee table, still face-down. She strokes it, feeling the expensive texture of the jacket.

She gently creaks open the thick covers and inhales that unbeatable new-book smell. She looks at the front flap and reads the breathless publisher blurb about 'the non-fiction book of the decade' and 'an *In Cold Blood* for the 2020s'. There is a potted history of the case. Arguably the first time, she thinks, that the case has been framed in the past tense rather than the present.

Clara turns to the author bio on the back flap:

ANNA OGILVY studied English at Oxford University before founding the cultural magazine *Elementary*, once described as 'the authentic voice of a generation'. As creative director, she pioneered a print revival and published numerous ground-breaking features on the social issues facing twenty-somethings today. In 2019, Anna suffered from a functional neurological disorder known as resignation syndrome. The incident was reported across the world

as the 'Anna O' case, spawning books, films, documentaries and countless op-eds. On being released, Anna returned
to her first love: journalism and writing. This is her first
book.

When she can resist no longer, Clara turns to the title page.
More than anything, she feels a profound sense of relief.
The ribbons have been tied. The mystery solved.
The threat is surely now over.
Clara starts reading.

82

CLARA

It is dawn when she reaches the final page. The real world is subsumed by another. Except this novel is true. Anna has used all the material from the interviews. She has described Clara's thoughts exactly as Clara described them to her.

The curtains are still open. Kitty will need to be woken in a few hours. Despite everything, it feels like a new chapter. The beginning of something.

Clara turns on her phone and sees the overnight emails. The book's publication in the US has caused another wave of interest in the story. Her new firm's comms team has a rundown: the *New York Post* wants a piece for tomorrow's edition. The big networks are after interviews. Every tabloid, broadsheet and glossy magazine is hunting for an exclusive.

After a brief hiatus, Sleeping Beauty and her prince are back in the headlines.

Clara instructs the comms team to decline all offers. Then she heads to the kitchen and makes breakfast. She wakes Kitty. They eat and walk to school in the sunshine, hand in hand. There is a curious beauty to everything now. Despite the book, despite the case, it's behind them.

They can, at last, move on.

She waves Kitty goodbye at the school gates. She stops at the local newsagent on the way home and buys all the newspapers and international magazines, flicking through the stories and the profiles. There is nothing quite like this feeling. Total and complete victory never pales. She sees all of them now: Douglas Bute, Indira Sharma, Anna Ogilvy, Virginia Bloom, Ben. Their theories, their egos.

She returns home and shuts the door. She makes another hot drink and heads upstairs. Clara takes out the ladder and turns on the light in the attic. The box is tucked in the very far corner. She drags it towards her and opens the secure lock and sees the diary and the document hidden at the bottom.

The diary was the easy bit. It was sitting right there in the Blue Cabin after it happened. Not that Anna remembered she even kept a diary when she woke up four years later. Or the half-glimpsed face of Harriet at the Farm on the night of the murders. The PTA had seen to that. Harriet had the diary first, of course. Then Clara took it just before Harriet's flat was raided by the police. The contents are now Clara's secret alone.

She flicks through the pages and sees the last entry dated August 30th. The ink is similar, and Harriet tried so hard to mimic the style, but it is the one false entry, added in later. By the end poor Harriet stopped being able to tell fact from fiction. She wrote the last entry just to complete the story. From the evidence on the page, she even tried multiple versions. She wanted to play the lead, for once, not just the understudy. To be at the centre of things, even if vicariously.

She turns to the next item. The document came through a police order during the original investigation. Those tingly, adrenaline-fuelled days as SIO. Monitoring evidence, being present at the search of Anna's flat in Camden, ensuring parts of Anna's digital history were never found. She misses those days. Being a detective had its benefits.

Clara wipes dust from the document. She straightens it out and reads the words again in that distinctive late-nineties font:

OFFICIAL: SECRET / RESTRICTED
Department of Health / April 2, 1999
Ministerial Authorisation #A7890WE

Under the emergency powers invested in this office by the Mental Health Act 1983, I hereby directly and explicitly authorise the use of 'heightened' treatment capabilities in the case of Ms Sally Turner (Patient BSH28904) as part of the MEDEA pilot intervention being carried out at Broadmoor Hospital under the leadership of Dr V. Bloom. This direct ministerial authorisation includes various capabilities on the Section 37 restricted list, including: sleep deprivation, isolation, 24/7 supervision, Class A anti-psychotic medication and enhanced restraint procedures. According to Section 41 of the Mental Health Act 1983, this authorisation takes precedence in the Courts of England and Wales above Article 3 and Article 15(2) of the European Convention on Human Rights (ECHR).

Signed,
Emily Ogilvy

Rt Hon Emily Ogilvy (Minister of State for Mental Health)
Department of Health
Richmond House, 79 Whitehall, SW1

There in writing.

Article 3 of the European Convention on Human Rights. The legal text that prohibits 'inhuman or degrading treatment or punishment'. Or, more simply, the 'prohibition of torture'.

It was the final confirmation.

She thinks of those lines from Ben again. Recorded by Anna, used as part of the dramatic reconstruction in the book.

You've got it all wrong. There's only one person who could have got to Harriet in her cell. Only one person who could have done all this.

Clara thinks back to that freak moment a few years ago when Kitty found those photos of the bodies in her bag, the little mementoes she always keeps with her. Or when Ben saw the texts between her and Harriet, the number she carelessly saved as 'HOSPITAL', and thought she was having an affair with a male surgeon or consultant.

Those were the most dangerous points. Kitty was still small, uncontrollable, liable to talk out of turn and raise doubts. Ben saw everything through his own prism, a blabbermouth who never let questions go unanswered.

Clara rescued things, but they were perilous moments.

She was far more careful after that.

She had to be.

She still has nightmares sometimes about Anna's diary and that codename: 'MARATHON'. It was clever. Too clever, thankfully. Just the sort of aggrandising thing an Oxford-educated journalist in their mid-twenties would use, a peacock displaying its feathers.

Ever since, Clara has wondered if Anna told others about the codename. But it's been long enough now. The post-traumatic amnesia ensured Anna didn't recall anything later. It lay buried, instead, in her unconscious, spilling out during the dream analysis, becoming the name of the town that promised answers and the truth.

One search on Wikipedia would have given the game away. Clara can still recite the wording, the illicit thrill of disaster averted:

The Greek name for fennel is marathon (μάραθον) or marathos (μάραθος), and the place of the famous battle of Marathon literally means a plain with fennel.

415

Clara Fennel. Marathon.

A journalist protecting her scoop. A twenty-five-year-old giddy with her own brilliance. The memory and the notebook both lost to history. The yearbook Anna mentions in her diaries was a photo from Clara's Oxford matriculation for the Masters in Applied Criminology showing a facial resemblance to Sally. The hunch in search of hard evidence that spawned the entire theory.

Clara almost feels sorry for Ben now. She always planned to mark the twentieth anniversary of Sally's death with a statement. Getting wind of *Elementary*'s investigation simply added fuel to the fire. Indira and Douglas were collateral damage. Anna was never the target. Or not exclusively. No, the entire Ogilvy family needed to suffer.

Anna was right on some of it though. The scopolamine, for instance. Clara first heard about the miracle mind control drug called 'Devil's Breath' as a street rumour from the Met narcotics squad. It was being imported into London, marketed as the new cocaine, but a hundred times deadlier. Perfect for kidnappers and robbers, and for her uses too. She bought it on the dark web, got Harriet to slip it into Anna's drink at the Farm with a smaller dose for Indira and Douglas. Tasteless, odourless. Untraceable.

Clara still remembers watching the hypnotic effect take hold. Short-term memory jamming. An extreme version of non-REM parasomnia. Clara could get Anna to do anything that night. It was always more efficient to get Anna to commit the murders herself. That provided further insulation. Emily and Richard got the WhatsApp confession and succumbed to panic, just as she hoped, and moved Anna from the Red Cabin back to the Blue Cabin, tampering with a crime scene and lying about it to the police and therefore compromising themselves in the process.

But no crime goes entirely to plan. Anna was mistaken on some points. The resignation syndrome, for instance, was the only bump. Clara had to improvise after that, getting Harriet placed at Rampton.

Anna, though, was right on the motive: it wasn't about silence but shame. This was never a whodunnit, or not strictly, but a revenge tragedy. Clara needed Emily Ogilvy to suffer like she had once suffered. Emily was the one who signed the order to torture Sally. She was the one responsible for Sally's death. Clara needed Emily to know what it felt like, watching her own flesh and blood being mauled by the world. She needed Emily to feel the bottomless fury of being singled out by fellow tribe members, to become an exile in her own land. Emily had to lose everything and become a pariah.

The public, after all, want a story above the truth. People never stopped to consider that Indira Sharma and Douglas Bute were merely sacrifices for a higher cause. Just like no one noticed that powerless teenage girl in her bedroom so many years ago stuck with a drug dealer for a stepdad and two awful step-brothers. She was keen to run away, spread her wings, get out of that dingy council flat in Stockwell with its stink of failure and low-level criminality. She was too good for the Cornwell family, her drunk mother and this cuckooing ploy. It was the only logical decision. It was her bid for freedom.

The plan was beautifully prepared. She would take a knife from the kitchen and carry out the attack. She was older than the stepbrothers, stronger too. She would phone Tom Cornwell and say something terrible had happened, pretend that Sally had tried to attack her. Then she would get Sally up and walk her into the bedroom and place the knife in her hands. When the scene was set and Tom was nearly home, she would wake Sally and watch her masterplan take hold.

It was all mapped out: Sally would be sectioned, Tom would flee, Clara would get a better, shinier future in a proper home. Everything almost worked perfectly until it didn't. Clara was taken by social services and given assessment sessions with Virginia Bloom, known temporarily as 'X'. Soon after that she had a new name, new identity documents, new foster parents, her old life as Sally Turner's daughter scrubbed from history entirely.

She became Clara Fennel.

But not before things went badly awry. Sally was meant to be safe in the hospital. The place where murderers worked on the allotment and got music in their rooms and which Clara had read about in books. Sally, though, wasn't sectioned and forgotten. Experiments were never part of the plan. The glass cage, the media storm, the accusations against Sally as Britain's Most Evil Woman – none of that was meant to happen. Dr Bloom and her enablers ruined the whole thing. That meant they needed to pay too. Not today, perhaps. But one day.

Harriet was the only good thing that emerged from Broadmoor. The eighteen-year-old nurse and the sixteen-year-old child, the bond forged so unexpectedly. Clara could be different with Harriet. She was the only one who still knew her as she once was. For Ben and Kitty and the rest of the world, she was this new being, acting out the role of Clara and compartmentalising her old self. Harriet was a drug she couldn't kick. And love – stupid, lustful first love – makes people do crazy things. Harriet worshipped her. She was a willing participant. It suited them both: Harriet wanted love; Clara needed an accomplice. Clara pushed Harriet, showed her a life outside the rules. Harriet never moved on, even when Clara married Ben. That early love was everlasting. They would still do anything for each other.

On balance, though, Bloom was useful alive. That's why she survived so long. Bloom became a mentor, sympathy born of guilt. Bloom had been all too willing to believe that Clara was a child innocent, schooled in violence but – with the right therapy, the right cure – ready to choose the path of virtue instead. If Sally was Bloom's greatest failure, Clara was her greatest success.

No, another target was needed. The person above Bloom. Someone who had authorised the Medea experiment in the first place. The real culprit of all this. The figure who let them build that glass cage; or allowed those methods to be tried; who failed to protect Sally from the medical people and the mob outside the hospital gates.

The rest followed neatly after that. The preparation took years of careful planning: identifying Emily Ogilvy as the Minister responsible for signing the authorisation memo; posing as the @PatientX whistleblower and infiltrating Anna's life; getting Harriet to pose as a cut-price health and safety consultant during the Ogilvy visit to the Farm and helping massage the police reports to discount Harriet from suspicion; then using her law enforcement connections to get Harriet the job at Rampton. When she heard the MoJ were considering transferring Anna to the Abbey, well, the opportunity to control the case even more closely was simply too good to miss.

Admittedly, the timing of Bloom's death was unfortunate. But Clara always vowed to wait until Bloom became a liability. She bugged Ben's mobile and heard the call between Ben and Bloom and knew she had to act. The copycat style was deliberate. A risk, of course, but an artistically necessary one. The symmetry was delicious. And the risks made the final rewards even sweeter.

She didn't want to move against Ben, or not specifically, but he was still pushing for joint residency. Clara's own mother was taken from her. She would never allow that to happen to Kitty. Ben dug his own grave. She knew the way his mind worked, too. By inviting her to the scene after finding Bloom's body, any trace evidence on her part could be discounted. She could plant those other digital clues on his laptop and ensure he was arrested with Harriet, taking him out of the picture.

Looking back, perhaps she should have taken her file from Bloom's safe. But that was part of the game. Just like the detour story near the Farm that night, giving her an excuse to be first at the crime scene. It was a risk, but a necessary one. She needed to take control of the scene immediately, stake her claim to be SIO. Otherwise one of the DCIs would have snatched the case, putting the entire plan in jeopardy.

Anna's pursuit of Ben was useful too. Though, even there, Clara deserves some of the credit. Clara steered Anna towards the idea during their interviews for the book, letting the idea of

419

scopolamine enter the conversation. The perfect drug to be slipped into a magic hangover cure. And the rest as well: false memory syndrome, dissociative identity disorder, psychogenic amnesia, repressed memories. The method of revelation is also genius. The book is part novel, part memoir. Faction. No prosecutor will get a conviction by citing a non-fiction novel. Anna has confessed without confessing. Reclaimed her story while putting herself beyond the law's reach. One step ahead right until the very end.

As for the @Suspect8 confession and the smuggled nail clipper – yes, that is the one act that still hurts. A lover's last sacrifice. But that was the oath she and Harriet swore right at the start. They wouldn't let each other be sent to prison. They would offer each other the humane way out. Fate is funny that way.

Why wait twenty years? First, they wouldn't have gotten away with it before. Killing Emily Ogilvy would have been revenge, but also reckless. Clara and Harriet would have been arrested, sentenced. Also Emily wasn't the right person to become mythic and monstrous either. Only Anna could be that. Second, Clara wasn't a mother before. Ben always said she changed when Kitty was born. It wasn't postnatal depression but something even more elemental: a return to her old – no, her real – self. The rages, the withdrawal, the frightening thoughts about harming Kitty – those were all part of the old pre-Clara personality, the self she'd repressed for so long.

Having a daughter of her own brought back all the anger. The fury at seeing Sally brutalised by the media, tortured by those meant to help her. Becoming a mother to a daughter changed everything. She could no longer hide from the past. For Kitty's sake, for her own wellbeing, she could avenge it. That was the only way she could carry on, keep breathing. That's how she put one foot in front of the other.

But enough of all that now. It is ancient history. The present is all that matters. Clara has the day off. She spends most of the afternoon tidying Kitty's room and putting in an endless cycle of washing. As usual, pick-up time arrives too soon. Today being Friday, they have their sacred after-school tradition, the one unbreakable commitment. Clara drives Kitty to their favourite café in the centre of Oxford and they order one banana milkshake to share between them.

As they sit on the high stools facing each other, both holding a straw, Clara feels that sense of relief again. She knows now that it was all worth it.

'Mummy?'

'Yes, sweetheart.'

Kitty wipes a milky moustache away with her hand. 'Why are you smiling?'

'Because I'm with you,' she says. 'You're all I've ever wanted.'

'I love you, Mummy.'

'I love you too, darling.'

There have been so many lies along the way.

But that, finally, is the truth.

ACKNOWLEDGEMENTS

This book wouldn't exist without many people. I would like to particularly thank the following:

To Maddy – thank you for being the greatest, most dynamic and most entrepreneurial agent on the planet. You changed my life with two Friday phone calls that I will never forget. The global publishing frenzy that erupted in June 2022 was the most magical and surreal two weeks possible. There is no greater champion an author could wish for and you have my eternal gratitude. I can't wait to work with you for many years to come.

To everyone at the MM Literary Agency both past and present – Giles, Liane, Rachel, Valentina, Hannah, Georgina, Emma, Amanda, Georgia, Saskia, Esme. Thank you for selling *Anna O* across the world with such passion, enthusiasm and success!

To Josie at CAA – for making my year by being the first to invoke the Thomas Harris comparison and helping me navigate Hollywood.

To Conrad at Blake Friedmann – for all your continued support on the screenwriting side, advice when it was most needed and for always being a wise and friendly ear.

To Rhian – for such immaculate copy-editing and the finest of editorial toothcombs.

To Charlie, Kim, Charlotte and everyone else at HarperCollins UK – for backing the book, selling the vision and delivering the best-looking proofs in publishing history!

To Sara and Iris at Harper US and Harper Canada – for believing in the story and getting the book to readers across North America!

To all my publishers around the world – for such enthusiasm and passion in taking *Anna O* to all corners of the globe and making it a truly global publishing event.

To Suzanne O'Sullivan, Guy Leschziner, Andrew Scull, Jonathan Levi, Emma French and many, many more – your work introduced me to the world of sleep crime, resignation syndrome and the history of psychiatry and psychology. Huge thanks to Helen Pepper for all forensic advice.

To Ilaria – you were there before all this happened, by my side when the news came through and have been there at every stage of the journey. Thank you for making me realise there was something far more important than achieving lifelong professional dreams.

To John, Peter, Sarah and Mary – thank you for all your support and the innumerable things you do every single day.

Finally, to Ruth – you are the only person alive who's read everything I've ever written. You've seen the perilous lows and the triumphant highs. You were the one I turned to when I was writing the very first pages of *Anna O*. All of this is down to your love, guidance, kindness, expertise and attention. Two words are inadequate for a lifetime of devotion, love and care, but they are all I have – thank you!

DON'T MISS THE TWISTY NEW THRILLER
FROM MATTHEW BLAKE

A
MURDER
IN
PARIS

AVAILABLE FROM SUMMER 2025